TWO DARING NOVELS OF THE IMAGINATION

from the World Fantasy…

UNKNOWN REGIONS

ROBERT HOLDSTOCK

A ROC BOOK

ROC
Published by the Penguin Group
Penguin Books U.S.A Inc., 375 Hudson Street,
New York, New York 10014, U.S.A.
Penguin Books Ltd, 27 Wrights Lane,
London W8 5TZ, England
Penguin Books Australia Ltd, Ringwood,
Victoria, Australia
Penguin Books Canada Ltd, 10 Alcorn Avenue,
Toronto, Ontario, Canada M4V 3B2
Penguin Books (N.Z.) Ltd, 182–190 Wairau Road,
Auckland 10, New Zealand

Penguin Books Ltd, Registered Offices:
Harmondsworth, Middlesex, England

Published by Roc, an imprint of Dutton Signet,
a division of Penguin Books U.S.A Inc.
Originally published in Great Britain by Orbit Books
under the title *The Fetch*.

First Printing, December, 1996
10 9 8 7 6 5 4 3 2 1

 REGISTERED TRADEMARK—MARCA REGISTRADA

Printed in the United States of America

For Peter Lavery
and John Jarrold

Prologue

In the early evening, with the light going, the boy moved away from the white wall of the chalk quarry, slipping slowly into the green shadows of the scrub wood that filled the center of this ancient pit. Above him, the rim of the quarry was a dark, broken line of trees, stark against the deepening sky. He could hear a voice up there, his mother coming toward that edge to find him. He knew he had to hide.

He slipped deeper into the bushes, crawling between tall, tangling blackthorn and crowding gorse, merging with the green, his chalk-covered body swallowed by the leaves and bark, so that he was lost within the undergrowth, creeping along the twisting tracks he had marked out over the years.

His name was called again. His mother was very close to the deep quarry. She sounded agitated, her voice distant but clear in the calm evening air.

He froze and watched the spiky line of the pit-edge wood against the sky. Then he moved on, touching the heart-shaped fossils he had carefully laid down on the trails. He picked up a chalk block and used it to whiten his body further, rubbing hard against his skin, his face, then crumbling the skin of the chalk and smearing it through his hair.

His name . . . the voice quite anxious now.

The breeze from the silent farmland beyond the quarry curled in through the "gate" to this place, his castle, the open end where men had once approached to work the chalk. It stirred the gnarled branches of the alders and thorns, whipped the bright gorse, eddied in the pit.

A new shadow appeared above him, against the sky, a figure that peered down and crouched low.

He froze and closed his eyes, knowing that the gleam of light would reveal him.

He sensed the shadow move. Earth and chalk rattled from the edge, tumbling down, to crash and spread within the quarry.

"Michael?"

It's coming back. I saw it again. Leave me alone. It's coming back . . .

He turned his head, denying the name. The figure prowled above him, searching the greenery below, scanning the white chalk of the pit.

"Come on, Michael. It's time for supper. Come *on* . . ."

He tried to draw more deeply into the white shells that covered him, into the ancient sea, into the dry dust of the creatures that had formed this place; *hide me, hide me. It's so close again. I saw it. Hide me.*

He imagined the sounds of earth movements, the dull, deep echoes that would have passed through the heaving chalk waters. The feeling soothed him. The shadow called again:

"It's time for supper, Michael. Come on. Come home, now."

The sea in his mind caught him. The trees in the pit shifted in the current. He floated through the chalk sea, grasped the branches of the gorse and thorn that waved in the gentle evening light.

It was coming closer. He couldn't go home now. He had to wait. The shadow on the rim of the pit would have to wait. It was coming back. And that was what she wanted, wasn't it?

And from above, his mother's voice, harsh and angry:

"Can you hear me, Michael? Michael! It's time to go home!"

The words struck him like a hand.

Old memory surfaced to hurt him. He stood up from his hiding place and listened to the sudden shout of outrage, the woman's voice, shocked by his appearance:

"What have you *done* to yourself?"

With a sad glance backward, Michael began to walk out of the pit . . .

PART ONE

Resurrection

One

She reached for the silent infant, gathered him up, bent to enfold him as she whispered to him.

"Can you hear me, Michael?" She smoothed a hand gently across the baby's sparse, ginger hair, loving the touch. "Michael? It's time to go home . . ."

She blinked back tears of delight, tears of relief. The man next to her shuffled slightly and flipped a page of his clipboard. It was enough to break the moment and she looked up at him. He smiled warmly.

"May I be the first to wish you a happy and not too boisterous life with this fine young man."

"Thank you, doctor. Thank you for everything."

He looked uncomfortable, peering down at his clipboard through half-frame spectacles. He was an indulgent-looking man, smooth, pink-faced and plump, packaged in a double-breasted suit from Savile Row and smelling sweetly of eau-de-Cologne. His hands shook a great deal when he talked business.

"There are a few formalities, Susan. Some paperwork . . ."

You mean you want your check . . .

She passed the infant back to the nurse, hating the feeling of letting Michael go. The child began to murmur, becoming restless.

Dr. Wilson led her to a chair in the waiting room of the clinic. "Again, Susan, I'm sorry about the unfortunate delay. But the child's health *did* give some cause for concern . . ."

"I know. I understand. We don't have to talk about it."

He looked at her carefully, watching her eyes, then her lips. He said, "I'd like to repeat . . . Susan . . . I sincerely believe that it was the only way to save his life."

"I do accept that."

"And I would like to ask again . . ."

She waited for him to finish, irritated with him, aware that he was hoping she would take the initiative. When she said nothing, he prompted her:

"About your discretion?"

She controlled the feeling of insult and smiled, nodding. "I gave you my word, Dr. Wilson. I'll keep my word. As I said, I *do* understand that there were difficulties."

"Thank you."

He passed papers to her for her signature. She scrawled her name gladly, if distractedly. Michael had started to cry and she wanted it to be *her*, now, who soothed him, who rocked him. She watched the nurse through the clear window of the small nursery. A tap on her arm signaled that there was still another form to witness.

"And when did you say your husband would be here?"

"In about an hour . . ."

"I need his signature too."

"Yes, I know. I called him three hours ago. He's driving down from York."

Alone for a while, as Michael was prepared for the journey to his new parents' home, Susan Whitlock paced the corridors of the clinic as she waited for Richard.

From an upstairs window she peered down on to the London street below. What she saw there made her swear loudly, unable to keep the concern and distress from her voice and her face.

She stared down for a long time at the pale, red-haired woman who stood across the road, watching the building. Only when she felt that their eyes had met, fleetingly across the distance, did Susan move away, angry and disturbed that the woman was still there, and that the clinic had done nothing about it!

Michael had been born two weeks early, an event which had taken Susan by surprise. But a complication during the birth itself had meant a period of several weeks in intensive care, and the Whitlocks' plans had been frustrated completely. For reasons not given to the parents, the clinic did not allow them to see the infant.

Even on the day of Michael's "liberation," a slight infection caused concern at the clinic, and Susan was required to spend a night in London. Only when she was sure that Michael would be released to her did she call her husband in York.

When the call came through that he was about to become a father, Richard Whitlock was ankle-deep in mud, splashed, soaked and miserable, photographing the timbers of a Viking harbor as they emerged from an excavation site near the Coopergate. He struggled out of the pit to take the call, not really expecting the news that he was about to receive.

Susan was at the clinic already, and her voice sounded strangely subdued as she described what was needed, and how much she needed *him*, and *soon*. She had gone up to Harley Street yesterday, by train from Maidstone, and she wanted to get home *now*.

"How does he look?"

"He's beautiful. He's very quiet. He's *wrinkled*. He has a tiny birthmark on the back of his neck. And he has a gorgeous spray of fine, downy, ginger hair."

"What? All over?"

"*No,* you fool."

"Ginger! Ginger?" Richard ran a hand through his black hair and thought of Susan's own dark brown curls. "Oh well ... A bit of a giveaway, but ..."

"What the hell does it matter?" she said sharply, and Richard frowned. He would have expected her to sound fraught, but she sounded angry, which was out of character.

Gently, he said, "That's just what I was about to say."

"Can you get away?" she asked. "I really need you."

"Within half an hour. I'll be with you by four."

"Hurry! But drive carefully. But *hurry* ..."

He arranged for one of the students to complete the photographic record on his behalf, and earned a spontaneous and warm round of applause when he announced the reason for his abrupt departure from the excavation. The motorway to the south was almost empty and he crossed London's North Circular Road at three in the afternoon, but then crawled in traffic for an hour to Harley Street. He couldn't park legally and so resigned himself to getting a ticket.

Inside the clinic, Susan was waiting for him with the infant. After a few minutes' fuss and hugging, he signed the appropriate papers for the consultant, who wished all three of them a long and happy life together.

Susan had taken care of the financial arrangement.

Again, a crawl out of London, this time to the east, into Kent (the car had not been booked for parking on a double yellow line, which Richard took as a good omen). When at last they picked up the motorway they made excellent time to the village of Ruckinghurst, where they had their house, Eastwell, on the hills that dropped sharply to the wide expanse of the Romney Marsh.

For much of the journey Susan was very subdued, although she responded positively to Richard's conversation and questions. But she didn't want to talk about Michael's natural mother, and Richard imagined well enough why that should be.

When he asked, "Was everything all right? No difficulties?" Susan was silent for a long while. He prompted her. She sat in the back, Michael asleep in her arms, and stared blankly at the Kent countryside.

Eventually she said, "There *was* a problem."

"With the boy?"

"With the mother."

"She wasn't there! Surely ... !"

"She was there earlier. The look in her eyes . . . when she looked at me . . . that look. It . . ." She shuddered and stared through the window. "It frightened me."

"Had she changed her mind?"

"I don't know. No. Of course not. She would have kept the child if she had. But there was something horrible about her look."

"Try not to let it upset you . . ."

It was pointless thing to say. He winced as the words were articulated. Susan glared at him in the mirror.

"I'm working on it, Rick. I'm working on it."

He smiled, feeling grim. Susan had swept her hair back into a loose ponytail, and she wore no make-up; her eyes looked hollow. But she sang quietly and rocked the infant, and after an hour or so the gloom in her mood had passed considerably.

The rain of earlier had passed over the Channel, and the evening sun was warm and glowing. The woods between their house and the chalk escarpment glistened with green and orange color. A fresh breeze brought the smells of late summer into the house when they opened the French windows.

Michael was restless and Susan fed him as she had been shown. Richard tried to familiarize himself with the sterilizing tank, the bottles, the nappies, the instructions, everything taught to Susan in the local ante-natal clinic, everything he had managed to avoid learning himself.

It was such an odd feeling: to be a father, but not to have been through nine months of supporting: through morning sickness, helping a hugely pregnant spouse up out of chairs, preparing odd concoctions for meals—everything he imagined was the labor of gestation. One hour he had been wading around in mud and Viking timbers, while Susan was teaching art at Maidstone College; four hours later they had a *child*. And he was theirs until death did them part. They were parents. Suddenly. Incredibly. (And expensively!)

His head started to spin as he opened the champagne. He had eaten very little since breakfast, nothing

more than a sandwich and a chocolate bar. So when he
raised the glass, and clinked Susan's, and drank to Michael's health, the wine went quickly to his head.
"Let's welcome him properly . . ."

Susan sighed, knowing what was coming. "All right.
Just so long as you don't get embarrassing."

He lifted Michael from her arms and carried him
outside. They walked down the long garden, past the
ramshackle greenhouses.

"My grandfather built those," he said, turning to
show the staring infant the whitewashed glasshouses,
where tomatoes and spaghetti squash were about the
only growing things. "Forty years ago . . ."

They moved on through the hedges that separated
flower from vegetable patches. These made a crude but
effective maze system, which his nephews and nieces
loved, and the trio walked solemnly through the winding path and down to the fence. The gate here opened
on to farmland, a cornfield, now harvested and part-
blackened from the burning of the stubble. A few yards
away a rough, grassy hump marked the site of a
Bronze Age barrow, a flattened tumulus, its identity
marked by a rusting iron notice leaning aslant from its
summit. The barrow had a catalog number and was one
of several that scattered this high ground, looking out
over the marsh to the distant sea. There were three further tumuli in the thin woods across the field, one of
them partially cut away by the disused chalk quarry.

Nothing was buried in the mound, now (or indeed,
in any of them). The bones of the single burial were in
Dover Museum, the bronze implements and horse trappings that had been excavated were on display in the
British Museum in London. Locally, the mound was
known as "the scar," although in the Whitlock family
they called it "the tump."

They stood on the mound and Richard said, "Make
a wish."

"You make yours first," Susan said. "I'll make mine
later."

She seemed edgy, but the wine had blunted Rich-

ard's perception, so that although he noticed her un-
ease, he did not respond to it.

He looked down at Michael. The child watched the
sky through eyes so translucent Richard felt he could
dip a finger and feel the cool water of the infant's soul.
Michael was so calm. There was something almost
knowing in his gaze. Sometimes he stared heaven-
wards, sometimes at his parents, and at times he turned
slightly away, as if he could see something from the
corner of his water-blue eyes.

And all of this, of course, was just the new father, in
romantic mood, looking for signs of awareness in the
guileless features of the newly born.

"When I was two weeks old, young Michael, my father carried me out to this bruised and battered old tumulus and stood with me and wished me something that
I've never regretted, and which I wish you now . . ."

"Oh, dear God," Susan groaned, but Richard ignored her.

". . . May you have a love for the past and a respect for
everything that reflects it, especially the land itself . . ."

"An ageing hippie," Susan muttered, shaking her
head. "I married an ageing hippie."

He looked at her with mock sharpness.

"I'm an archaeologist. These things are important to
me. And less of the 'ageing,' if you don't mind."

"Get on with it. You're traumatizing him."

The teasing exchange was interrupted by a sudden
gust of wind. A spray of fine dirt blew in their eyes
and spattered the restless child. They shook their
heads, blinking to soothe the stinging. Susan brushed
the dust from Michael's swaddling, but the child was
quiet again, and alert.

"Your turn," Richard said. "Make your wish."

"As I said: later."

"But this is the place to do it. This mound is
propitious."

"Later . . ."

Magpies screeched in the far woods. Three of the
birds came swooping and soaring toward the tumulus,
but settled suddenly in the burned stubble field.

"One for sorrow," Richard remembered, "two for joy . . ."

He glanced at Susan. "Three for a girl?"

He tugged at Michael's nappy, peered down through the vapors of talcum powder and early-human soil.

"It's still there. Thank God for that."

Susan laughed. "Superstitious idiot."

"A joke. It was a joke . . ."

It was after two in the morning before Susan finally, quietly, made her own wish.

Richard was sleeping soundly. Michael had woken from his own restless slumber, and had been fed, and for a while Susan had cradled him, and stroked the skin of his face. She had thought that Richard would wake too, but the day had been long, the drive from the clinic exhausting, and their private ceremonies had ended with food and wine. His body—older than Susan's—could not take the pace.

"We were so lucky to get you."

Michael spluttered bottled milk, a sequence of bubbles that formed a stream down his chin.

A gentle chime from the hall: two o'clock. Richard stirred but didn't wake.

Susan reached to her bedside cabinet, and from among the packs of pills, the tissues and the books, drew out a small, red-clay figurine. She had fashioned it in minutes out of the modelling clay she used for teaching. It was a very simple shape, a head, legs, arms, sex unspecified. It was unfired, dry and fractile.

She eased herself out of bed and walked quietly down to the sitting room, where she switched on a corner light. From behind the sofa she fetched the crude wooden cradle she had made that evening, a simple weave of the ivy stem and dry twigs they used for kindling. The cradle was decked with brightly colored flowers of the field in a way that she vaguely remembered from her childhood, when her aunt Ruth had shown her how to banish shadows.

She laid Michael in the cradle; the dry twigs cracked beneath his tiny weight. But the child remained quiet,

and his pale eyes watched his new mother in the dim
light from the lamp. Susan smiled at him, then raised
the small, crude figurine. She whispered, "There was
bad in your mother. You don't know it. Your father
doesn't know it. But I know it. I saw it in her eyes. If
there was bad in your mother, then perhaps there is a
shadow of that in you." She moved the doll through
the air. "All the bad from your mother, come into this
doll. Come on. Come on. Into the doll."

She lifted Michael from the cradle and opened his
woolen jacket. Then she rubbed the crumbling clay figure against the infant's mouth, against his cheeks and
eyes, over his head, down his breast, across his back
and down his legs. She left him smeared with a fine
layer of red clay.

"All the bad has been swallowed," she said, and
thought briefly of those dusk evenings when the aunts,
in their claustrophobic living room, had passed similar
figurines from hand to hand and spoken soft words that
Susan, watching from a corner, could only partly
understand.

Now she placed Michael on the floor and put the
cradle in the clean grate of the fireplace, crushing the
twigs to make a small pyre. She crumbled the doll over
the pyre, let the pieces fall through her fingers, scattered on the wood. Then she set light to the fire and
watched it burn, listening to the sharp, dry snaps as the
kindling flared and was consumed in seconds.

Michael's eyes blazed in the brief firelight and he
turned his head to watch the burning. Susan rested a
hand lightly on his chest and drew the glitter of his
pale gaze back to her.

"You belong to us," she whispered. "You are ours,
now. We couldn't have our own child, but we will love
you no less. We love you. The shadow stuff from your
mother is gone."

She leaned down to kiss her son.

"What the hell's going on?"

Susan was startled by the sudden, angry voice from
the doorway. Richard stood there, naked and disheveled, his eyes telling clearly of his suspicion.

"What are you doing down here?"

"I didn't know I'd woken you. Sorry."

"You didn't wake me. The smell of burning woke me. I thought there was a fire." He walked over to the grate and crouched before the dying embers; he was puzzled, curious, but perhaps too sleepy to frame his thoughts clearly. "What were doing? Keeping warm?"

"Nothing. Nothing at all. Michael was restless. I've just fed him."

He reached into the grate and drew out the half-charred head of a dandelion. He met her gaze and she shrugged, looked quickly away. Then he noticed the red coloration on Michael's face.

"Christ! And you call *me* superstitious!"

He flung the shred of flower back into the embers, picked up Michael and rocked the silent child. His anger subsided. He looked at Susan and muttered, "I do *know* about the aunts. The old witches. You told me, remember? Which ritual was this? Bind his soul to the spirit world of your family? Link him with the ancestral spirits from ancient Hungary?"

She smiled, and told the partial lie with the greatest of ease: "I was linking him with the spirit of his parents. With us. That's all."

Richard sighed and she responded to his sudden, affectionate touch on her shoulder, kissing his fingers sadly. "We all do foolish things on whim. We do them for the best of reasons."

"Yes," he said tiredly. "I know. Like my ceremonial welcome on the tumulus."

"Kentish Bronze Age meets Hungarian Aunt Magic . . ."

That made him laugh. "Should develop into a well-mixed-up kid."

He stood up, red-skinned Michael nestling against his chest, secure in his father's large arms. "Are you going to clean him off, or shall I?"

"I'll do it. You do back to bed. Get some beauty sleep."

"I don't need it. Do I?"

They exchanged the infant and a hug. Susan watched

as Richard left the room, then rocked Michael in her arms and whispered to him as she brushed the dirt from the child's face.

Michael began to cry, but the sound was soft. Almost controlled.

Two

Susan had left the French windows open during the morning, glad of the sunshine and the freshness in the air after the days of miserable late-summer rain. With Michael soundly asleep in his carrycot, just inside the open doors, and a whole day to herself now that the health visitor had left, she set up for a few hours of her hobby: doll restoration.

She had found two dolls in a small shop in Bloomsbury, two months ago. They were Victorian bed-dolls, designed to be placed on the pillows in a child's room. She wasn't sure if they made an original pair, although they were "man" and "woman." They had been clumsily and crudely restored around the face and hair, and she had decided to unrestore them and return them as closely as possible to their original appearance.

The female doll wore a lacy dress, with linen underclothes. She was barefoot, but the letters A and Q had been drawn on the cotton covering that formed her socks. The male doll wore a tight black jacket and drainpipe trousers. The leather of his shoes was perfectly preserved, even to the tiny laces, one of which was tied in a double bow.

Susan had paid twenty pounds for the pair, but was convinced they would be worth much more. Meanwhile, the immediate pleasure was in the restoration. And she wouldn't be teaching again until the spring term.

Freedom.

She made herself a pot of coffee, peered down at

Michael, who was murmuring in his sleep, then began
the slow task of unpicking the clumsy stitchwork of
the dolls' previous owner. She wore reading glasses,
propped halfway down her nose. In recent years her
eyesight had begun to deteriorate rapidly, but she refused to wear contact lenses; they hurt, and they made
her eyes water. Richard thought she looked "sexy" in
the gold-rimmed spectacles. Susan herself was more
concerned with how increasingly difficult it was to focus for any extended period of time on anything, like
a book or a doll, which she held close to her vision.

After half an hour of the intense work her back began to twinge and she put down the doll, removed her
glasses and walked out into the garden. Despite the
rainy conditions of the previous day, everything
seemed so dry now, so hot. She could hear the neighbor's dog, barking among the fir trees that were a feature of next door's garden. She walked down to the
gate and swung on it, staring out across the cornfield,
over the "thump," at the drift of woodland above the
quarry, and the bare ridge of the land that marked the
drop down to the dykes and sedges of the saltmarsh itself. The wind was fresh. She could smell sea. From
the garden the Whitlocks couldn't see the English
Channel, but its scents and the feel of being close to
the edge of the land was sharp on these bright days
when the wind was on-shore.

Seagulls pestered the field.

Michael wailed suddenly, but the sound went away,
and as Susan returned through the fruit trees, mostly
alert for the child, passingly aware that the cherry trees
had rust-infection, she felt calm. At peace. Quite
content.

Stepping in through the French windows she was
aware of the phone ringing. She smelled fresh earth,
but dismissed the sensation, glancing at the carrycot,
aware of its stillness, vaguely aware of something
wrong . . .

The phone was an insistent call and she plucked the
receiver from its cradle.

It was Jenny, a close friend who taught at the same

college. She wanted to help with the christening party that Saturday, and had had an idea for contributing to the buffet meal.

"Thanks. But Richard wants to make roast lamb."

"For a christening party?"

"He sees it as a sort of challenge."

"Roast lamb for forty people?"

"He sees it as a challenge. He's a man. He can do it."

"But . . . roast lamb?"

"A challenge."

Jenny paused, then sighed. "So a tuna casserole would be superfluous."

"No room in the oven to swing a minnow."

"I'll make pudding, then. Fruit salad."

"Pudding has been organized by various 'mothers.' The real help we could do with is . . . well, to put it bluntly . . ."

"Baby-minding?"

"The woman is psychic. Yes. Baby-minding. Just for a few minutes here and there while I look after the aunts. Richard will be looking after the booze, of course. And his lamb."

"What am I going to do with all this tuna?"

"Throw them back. Let them have their freedom. And thanks for the thought, Jenny."

What was smelling so bad? What was that smell of freshly dug earth?

She went into the kitchen and set the percolator on for a second jug of coffee. She placed the leftovers of the previous evening's casserole into the oven and set the timer. Richard wouldn't be eating with her tonight, and she was hungry now, so the idea of supper at five in the afternoon seemed a good one.

But that smell!

Puzzled, she went back into the sitting room. It was an odor she associated with her father's garden; freshly tilled soil, the metallic smell of forks and other garden implements moist and slick with constant use. The scent of wet, of vegetation, of humus, of compost;

sharp, woody. So many feelings were evoked by the odor. So many memories . . .

She walked to the French windows. The smell was stronger here, and she became very disturbed, looking quickly round, beginning to feel panic.

When she saw the carrycot she nearly screamed as she ran for her child and plucked him into her arms.

"That damned dog. That bloody dog!"

Michael was covered with damp earth. The carrycot was filthy. His chubby hands were black where he had reached and grasped the dirt. There was a scattering of soil around the cot, on the carpet. It had been this darker stain on the dark fabric that had almost alerted her earlier.

"Damn! *Damn!*"

The creature was often to be seen in their garden, prowling and digging at the flower beds and in the vegetable patch. It must have come into the sitting room, filthy from its excavations, to stand right up on the cot, its muddy paws on her son.

Susan cradled the boy for a moment, then brushed him partly clean. She took him to the bathroom and washed the sticky earth from his fingers and face.

Michael was very quiet. Susan could hear the dog barking from across the fence. It had gone back home, then, after straying into Whitlock territory.

"You poor love. It's my fault. It's all my fault. I'm so silly. I should have thought about that bloody pet next door."

She finished cleaning the boy, then vacuumed the dirt from the carpet. She closed the windows and sat down with her dolls again. But she was angry now, so angry that she had risked her son's life. The dog could have been dangerous. It could have smothered him. She hadn't been attentive enough. A lesson learned!

So *angry*.

The dolls lay there, forgotten. Michael slept and whimpered. Slowly Susan relaxed, folding her arms across her chest, thinking about the boy, about the adoption, about the look in his birth-mother's eyes . . . and about Saturday. Such a big party! So much to do.

"It will all be fine," she told herself. "Just don't get upset. Don't get upset . . ."

Next door the dog howled. It had never entered the house before. Perhaps in its narrow, canine way, it knew that it had done wrong.

She walked out of the room and across the lawn to the fence, half inclined to call to her neighbor and say something about the dog's straying.

But when she looked over and into the next-door garden she felt shocked, then confused.

The dog—an Alsatian of dark and grim demeanor—was chained to a post in the middle of the lawn. Stretched at the end of its lead, it was watching Susan, and howling with frustration at being so cruelly tied . . .

Three

Richard stood in the corner of the room, camera and torch slung round his neck, ready for action, hands in his pockets. He was slumped and saddened, watching Susan through the puffy, reddening eyes of a man experiencing more distress and confusion than he had ever known. Susan sat before the empty grate of the fire, knees drawn up, head cradled in her hands.

The baby-speaker, connected to Michael's cot in their bedroom, dangled from the mantelpiece, a motionless piece of plastic, silent for the moment, but almost threatening. Susan watched the speaker through tired, dark-rimmed eyes. The strain of the last three days had begun to break her.

It had taken them both with such shocking surprise.

Her skin was a pallid, sickly yellow in the light from the corner lamp. Her shadow echoed her despair, cast in forlorn detail on the far wall. Her dressing-gown had parted around legs that looked thin and shaky. She hugged her knees, now, watching the microphone that would carry the sound from the room above.

She had been sick, earlier in the evening. There was something more on her mind, Richard was certain of it. He had known her too long. He knew the signs. But when he'd probed gently for the problem she wouldn't speak.

So now he watched from the corner, his own mind in a turmoil of fear and anticipation as he waited for the next attack on Michael.

He was half convinced himself that it was the mother! Michael's natural mother.

But if it was, how was she getting into the room? If it was his mother, how was she getting through the window? It made no sense!

And why would she torment them so?

"Do you want some tea?"

She shook her head. "No. Thanks."

"Coffee?"

"No . . ." (Irritably.)

"A brandy?"

"No! For *Christ's* sake, Richard!"

Her head slumped suddenly and she shuddered. The shadow on the far wall followed the exasperated motion. Richard felt his eyes sting and his mouth go dry. He wanted to go over to her, to touch her, to put his hand on her shoulder, but she would probably have screamed at him. There was moisture on her brow. When she glanced up at him the dark lines below her eyes were like make-up. Sweat had dampened the fringe of dark hair, and it stuck to her brow at odd angles. She was close to tears. "I'm sorry."

"Forget it."

And then the sound . . . *that* sound!

Susan almost screamed, startled and shocked by the noise. Richard ran to the middle of the room, listening hard to the dangling plastic speaker.

Yes. That *rustling*! The sound of the earth being thrown at the child. It was the same as before. Then the child's cry, a soft murmur, then a quick wail, then a more anguished, sustained sound, neither cry nor murmur, but a sort of pain.

"She's in the room. Go!" he shouted, but Susan was already on her feet and racing for the door to the hall. Flashlight on, camera ready, Richard went swiftly out through the French windows and into the garden, locking the doors behind him. He pounded round the garden to the lawn below their bedroom. He looked up, but when he saw that the window was closed he shouted his confusion, stunned and startled by what he could not see when he had so desperately hoped to *see* it! He flashed the torch around the garden. He ran to the trees, searched their branches, shone the light to right and left. The brilliant yellow beam picked out all the shadows and nooks of the small orchard, the wood-shed and tool sheds, and the high fence.

Turning back to the house he played the beam off the back wall, illuminating each window, each ledge, each length of drainpipe and gutter. There was nothing to be seen.

Susan appeared in the window of the room. The light picked her out, a ghostly figure standing there, holding the child, shaking her head, her face a mask of despair and fear. Tears gleamed on pale cheeks.

Richard went back into the house and up to the bed-room. He could smell the fresh earth even before he reached the stairs, the same heavy odor of newly exca-vated soil that had been haunting this house for five days now.

Susan watched him in silence as he entered the dark room. He turned on the light and Michael turned his face away, then began to cry. Richard stepped over the dirt-spattered floor. He photographed the room from every angle.

The main concentration of the loose earth was in the middle of the cot. The dirt was dry, this time, and quite light in color. It had small fragments of stone in it, and some dry leaf and twig.

There was no mark on the ceiling above the bed, and when Richard inspected the wire grille over the win-dow there was no sign or trace of earth that would sug-gest it had been thrown from the outside with the window open. Exasperated, aware that Susan was close to the edge of despair as she silently held the boy, Richard crouched down and started to scoop up the mess into a waste bin.

At a glance it seemed that someone had stood at the bottom of the cot and tipped or shaken a bucketful of dry dirt down on the baby's body. The soil had scat-tered in a circle around the bed.

And this was for the third night running!

There was a difference, though. Last night the earth

had been red-tinged and dry, like the soil in Devon.
And the night before it had been wet and foul-
smelling, alive with worms, odd, massive and green-
pink in color, some of them cut through as if a knife
had been taken to them.

"Every door is locked. Every window. If someone *was*
in this room, they're still in the house."

He searched upstairs first, looking under beds, in
cupboards, in clothes chests, and finally behind the
paneling on the bath. Downstairs, he double-checked
that all the doors were locked, then ran quickly from
room to room, even opening the chest freezer in the
cellar. The cellar was small and cramped, damp and
unpleasant, a junk room of old crates, bicycles, boxes
of moldering books and magazines, and fading furniture. He examined every inch of the place, finally
prodding an iron rod into the coal in the bunker. The
access doors to the cellar were both locked.

Returning to the bedroom he found Susan calmer.
She was tearful and very pale, but she seemed more in
control of herself. "What about the attic?" she whispered. "Could she have gone up there?"

Richard went out on the landing and looked up at
the small hatch to the roof-space. Surely nobody could
have scrambled through that small opening in the few
seconds before Susan had arrived upstairs after the
earthfall?

Even so, he pulled the stepladder from its storage
place and climbed to the hatch, opening it and turning
on the light.

It was cool up here, and dry; he moved a stoop
through the stacked boxes and under the supporting
beams of the heavily tiled roof. Water gurgled in one
of the large tanks. From below the eaves came the restless movement of birds, disturbed by the sudden light.

The attic was otherwise lifeless.

He climbed down to the landing and called for Susan. As he put the ladder away he called again and was
puzzled at the lack of response from her. She had gone
downstairs, he imagined, taking Michael with her.

The silence suddenly unnerved him. He followed down, glanced into the kitchen, then into the sitting room. Susan was standing by the fireplace, Michael cradled to her chest, her gaze on her husband. Her face was ashen, but she seemed more annoyed than shocked.

"What is it?"

"The doors," she said angrily. "The bloody doors!"

Richard walked over to the French doors and tried them. Unexpectedly, they swung in, revealing the cool night again.

"But I locked them. I *know* I locked them." He closed the doors and went over to the empty fire.

Susan's look changed from anger to frustration. In a tearful whisper she said, "It's how she got away. Oh God, Rick—she's so clever. She hides in the house and confuses us. Moves around behind us. Watches us. She might even have made herself a set of keys ... Oh Christ!"

Her own set of keys! It would have been easy enough for her to have copied Susan's keys during the first days after they had brought Michael home, when Susan had not been on her guard.

If she *had* been here, this evening, she had hidden outside, waiting for her opportunity. Seeing Michael's new parents alone, downstairs, she had slipped in through the back doors, thrown the dirt at the infant, then hidden somewhere upstairs until she could make her way—unseen—back to the sitting room, there to let herself out again.

Richard was certain he had locked the doors when he had come back in from the garden.

And yet ...

The thought did not escape him that in his haste he might have *thought* he had locked the doors. Or perhaps he had turned the key without first fully engaging it.

"I don't know. I just don't know ..."

"Well, I *do*," Susan said, and now her voice was like a snarling animal's. Her eyes were hard. Michael struggled in her suddenly over-protective grip. "She's been here. She's laughing at us. She's making a fool of us."

"But why? Why would she do this?"

"Because she's angry! Because she hates herself!"

Richard was confused. "*Why* is she angry? *Why* does she hate herself? I don't understand."

Susan shouted at him: "Because she's given up her child, you fool. And she can't live with the knowledge of that fact!"

"But she *agreed*. She was *happy* to give the child up."

"Was she? *Was* she?" Susan's face flushed red with rage. "How do you know? You didn't *see* her. You weren't there. I *saw* her, Richard. I *saw* the look in her eyes. I *know* what she was going through . . . Oh Jesus. Oh Jesus God. You *never* had your heart in this adoption. You let me do it *all*. Have you *ever* thought about anything other than your own selfish feelings? *Imagine* what it must have been like for that woman! Just *imagine*."

The raised voices, naturally enough, upset Michael and he started to cry. Susan rocked him in her arms. There was still some dry dirt on his face and she brushed it off, making soothing sounds and soothing actions.

Richard hugged them both, his arms stretching round mother and child. The tension eased slightly, and the anger passed away.

"I said some harsh things. I'm sorry."

Richard touched the tear-stained face of the infant. "No. You were right to say them. There are things that should have been said long ago. We'll have to talk them through. But not now. Now's not the time."

Susan's laugh was distinctly pointed, but then she shook her head. "I'm sorry. Sorry, Rick. I just can't stand it—this *limbo*—this *attack*. Not knowing what it means . . ."

"I know, I know." He tugged Michael's blanket to make it more secure around the child's tiny body. "What shall we do about the weekend? Cancel?"

Susan shook her head. "We can't. Too many people. It's too late in the day."

"It's only a party, for heaven's sake. I can get up early and ring around all morning."

She sighed and leaned against him, weary and ready to drop. "And waste all that lamb?"

He smiled, then laughed, and Susan looked up and smiled too.

"What an idiot you are. Roast lamb for a crowd that size. You'll be cooking all day."

He looked puzzled, then shook his head. "I'm not going to roast it. I'm going to barbecue it. That's why I dug the pit. For God's sake, can you imagine roasting seven legs of lamb in the oven?"

"Ah ..."

Susan nodded, smiling thinly. "I must admit, you had me worried."

Susan went to bed; Michael slept soundly in the cot next to her. Richard prowled restlessly around the house for an hour, finally sitting for a while in his study, a small, dark room, lined with books, his own photographs and racks of magazines. He turned the pages of an article he was writing for *Archaeological News*, but didn't register the words.

He was *certain* that he had locked the doors to the garden when he had come back in from searching outside. *And* he had locked them between leaving the house and returning. Why wouldn't he have done? That had been the whole point of tonight's exercise: to make sure that no one could get in or out at the time of the attack on Michael.

So perhaps Susan herself had opened them. But why? She had no reason to try to deceive her husband.

Someone had thrown raw earth at Michael on each of the last four nights, and perhaps during a day as well, when Susan had been alone with the boy. Someone in the house. Someone who could not be found. Not him, not Susan (they were each other's alibis). So: Michael's natural mother.

How had she done it? She had followed them here and cut herself a set of keys. Now she hid outside all day, but could enter the house and move about in absolute silence, leaving no trace of her feet in the wide scatter of dirt on the floor that she flung—abusively—at her natural offspring.

Richard gave that idea one out of a hundred when it came to likelihood. Susan had been obsessed with the mother since the day of the adoption, at the clinic. Her belief that the other woman was perpetrating these attacks was quite irrational—a transference of guilt or anxiety, perhaps.

Something else, then.

The house was a hundred years old. It had been in the family for two generations, and Richard had grown up here. There were family traditions, family stories, strong memories of bad winters, family tragedies and war-time damage, mostly from flying-bombs. But there were no stories of ghosts. To the best of his knowledge the house simply wasn't haunted.

He finally reached for a pencil and wrote the word "poltergeist" on the bottom of the last page of his article. He had only a vague idea of the concept behind the word. He knew that poltergeists were reputedly generated from disturbed minds, minds that were usually female and adolescent.

A poltergeist in the house?

But it was too late in the evening; he was too tired; there was too much to think about for the christening party tomorrow; he wasn't ready to start thinking seriously about psychic phenomena.

He underlined the word though, then closed the article, before creeping gently into bed beside Susan. She was breathing deeply and slowly, but he saw a glimmer of light reflected from her half-opened eyes.

Early in the morning Susan crept out of bed and went to the downstairs telephone. Shaking badly, she dialed Dr. Wilson's private number. He sounded tired and distinctly fraught when he answered, and was not pleased when Susan began to press him for the telephone number of Michael's birth-mother.

"I explained the situation. Total confidentiality. And she does *not* want contact with you."

"I think she's *making* contact with me. Did you give her our address?"

"Certainly not!"

"Dr. Wilson, please!" Susan's eyes stung and she blinked back the tears. She realized she was becoming anxious again, and took two or three very deep breaths. "Dr. Wilson ... All I want to do is talk to her. Just to ask her to leave us alone."

There was silence for a moment. Wilson was puzzled.

"I'm sure you're wrong, Susan. She can't know where you are. The arrangements we made were *quite* definite. And I don't need to remind you that we have stepped outside the law. Now *please*. Don't press me. Michael's mother does *not* want to be in touch with you. In fact, I happen to know that she's abroad at the moment ..."

Susan sat down heavily. Abroad? Or is that what she had told Wilson? A ruse?

She replaced the receiver and sat, silent and shaky, until Richard came down.

Four

The party was very successful, although it had been a tense and gloomy morning of preparation and a frantic dash to the church for the ceremony. Richard began to relax.

He was pleased to see Susan laughing as well. She spent most of her time in the sitting room with Michael and her friend Jenny, but trusted Jenny enough to leave Michael in her care while she took various children to her studio room and showed them her collection of odd and ancient dolls.

But in the way of these things, the party took over, an entity unto itself, and a form of chaos ruled the middle of the afternoon. At four o'clock Richard had lost touch with reality. It came as something of a relief. He had been fighting hard to keep a semblance of dignity and decorum in the festivities, but social entropy in the form of active children and equally active adults had finally taken its toll.

His own family were bad enough. But Susan's were something else . . .

And their mutual friends were the worst of all! It was a case of "any excuse to have a party," and party they had. With a vengeance.

Richard wandered through the orchard at the bottom of his garden. A girl of mature looks but dressed in doll-like clothes breezed across the lawn, arms outstretched, golden hair flowing, an Isadora Duncan of mischief, heading for the hidden places of the garden, where childish screams told Richard that the medieval stonework of the old church at Ruckinghurst had been found—a few pieces only, which he had acquired from an antique shop and which he intended to make into a garden feature. The stones were now objects of fantasy and fantasizing. He heard a cry of, "There might be bones in the stones, the bones of giants." He left the excavation, confident that any giants' bones in the sandstone would resist attempts to remove them.

In the kitchen the talk was of cricket, socialist politics and immunology. In the corner of the room a friend of Susan's sat slumped in a chair, talking loudly about the trouble he was having with his publishers, using his reeking cigarette to emphasize each point. He hadn't eaten and the champagne had gone to his head. His only audience was a child of about two who sat playing with bricks close by, watching the man with total bemusement.

The sink was full of bottles.

There was broken glass on the floor which Richard quickly swept up, despite being nearly bowled over by a gang of children playing a form of chase. The rule seemed to be: "If I catch you, you *shapechange* into something *evil,* but I won't know what it is unless I catch you again and *torture* you."

He sighed. In his own day they had called it "chains." Torture had never been mentioned.

"Can we dig the monster from the grave?"

Framed in the doorway from the garden were the Pre-Raphaelite girl and a three-foot-tall, freckled, red-haired, sullen little bruiser called Tony. He was a nephew of Susan's. His fingers were caked in earth, grass, and human blood (his own).

Richard shook his head firmly. "I don't want you to leave the garden, and I don't want you digging in that mound. Is that understood? It's a protected monument. You're not allowed by *law*."

Tony hid his hands behind his back.

"If you want to hear the story of what was once buried there you can come into the study and I'll show you some pictures and tell you about it."

The blankness of their faces told him that this was an unsatisfactory alternative to digging.

"Have you got pictures of the giant?" the girl asked.

"He wasn't a giant. He was a Bronze Age prince, buried with his horse, his weapons, and several huge joints of meat."

Tony stared darkly through his freckles (but what a fine and intense light glowed from the small figure's face), then growled huskily, "Want to see his bones."

"His bones aren't there anymore."

Ah, the disappointment! Richard almost laughed out loud.

Then the growl again. "Where's the bones now?"

A chance to draw order from the chaos: "If you want to see the bones you'll have to sit quietly on the lawn for an hour, then I'll show you some really *spooky* pictures. Can you do that? To see the bones?"

Even as he spoke the words, he realized mournfully that as a child psychologist he made a good train driver.

There was the briefest of pauses. Tony's brow furrowed and he stared at Richard steadily and contemptuously. Then he stuck two fingers up and fled from the doorway, the girl in hot pursuit.

Richard walked into the sitting room expecting to find Michael there, supervised by Jenny, but there were only several aunts sitting in armchairs talking together around the remains of the sherry. His heart racing, he went quickly upstairs to the bedroom, then the bathroom, but finally found the child asleep, in his study downstairs. Jenny was there, leafing through the pages of one of his archaeological photograph albums. Two pieces of the christening cake were on the desk, next to a cup of coffee that now had a skin of cold milk on its surface.

As Richard entered the room, she looked up from the album and smiled. "I hope you don't mind me looking at your work."

"Not at all. Which album is it?"

"The Roman farm at Hollingbourne. Nice photographs. Some of them are really eerie."

"Just special effects."

Michael, in his cradle, was sleeping noisily.

"Giving you a hard time, I see."

"He was getting restless. Too many 'Hungarian aunts.' Susan suggested we brought him through here for a snooze."

"Good God, he snores."

Jenny laughed. "I know. I like it. It helps me feel relaxed."

He leaned over the crib and watched the sleeping features of the boy. Michael's ginger hair was sticking out in damp spikes. His right hand was bunched and jammed against his chin. He had more wrinkles round his eyes than Richard himself.

"Is this or is this not a beautiful lad?"

"He's lovely." Jenny smiled again, watching Richard. "I'm happy things have worked out for you both."

Richard nodded wearily, then sat on the edge of the desk and flicked through the Hollingbourne photographs. "For a long time we didn't think they would. Work out, I mean. We tried for so many years, so much failure, so much hope so routinely dashed. It does something to your confidence after a while . . ."

"I can imagine."

"It makes you hard," he said, and immediately wished he could retract the personal indiscretion. Jenny just watched him, calm and reassuring. "And then: Michael. By pure luck: Michael. If Susan had been going to a different fertility clinic, someone else would have got the child. The clinic didn't expect Michael to be 'unwanted' by his natural mother. It was pure chance. Susan was in the right place at the right time for a simple, private transfer."

"And everything above board," Jenny said distractedly, looking at the snoring child. Richard felt cold for a moment and glanced at the woman sharply; but she had not been trying to score a point, merely making an idle statement that she assumed to be true. Jenny looked up again, slightly apprehensive.

"Susan's told me about the . . . well, what do I call it? The problem."

The room closed round him a little. He could hear the sound of children screaming, and a distant chant: "Dig the beast. Dig the beast."

"They're excavating the tumulus. There's nothing there now, but I don't suppose their parents will be happy about the filthy clothes."

Jenny stared at him without expression. Then she said, "Susan looks ill."

Sighing, Richard agreed with her. "She's certain it's Michael's natural mother."

"His mother?"

"Who's throwing the dirt . . . The *problem,* as you call it."

"But . . . his *birth*-mother?"

"Or perhaps one of her family. It's vicious. It's vindictive. And it's frightening the life out of us."

Jenny was solemn. "We haven't known you and Susan for long, but long enough to see the strain you're both under. You *must* ask Geoff and me for help. Any time."

Richard stood and prowled the study, nodding his thanks. "But what I can't understand is how she gets in here? How does she get into the house? It really doesn't make any sense. But we have no other answers . . ."

The door burst open and the "Isadora" child entered, breathless, her thin summer dress a mess of dirt and water. She said, "We've found a bone in the garden. It may belong to the giant."

"Good."

"Do you want to see it?"

"I wouldn't dare." Richard walked over to the door, dropping to a crouch before the girl. "This is a haunted house, you see. Has been for centuries. The people who lived here before us, and who found the giant's bones, all lost their hair within a week. It just fell out. All of it. They were utterly bald for the rest of their lives. I'd bury the bone again if I were you."

The girl hesitated, frowned, then looked alarmed and fled, her hair flowing. He noticed how she had started to gather it in, tying it into a tight knot, as she left the hall.

Jenny was shaking her head, an expression of amused puzzlement on her face. "You're so *good* to your guests, Richard. I've always liked that about you."

"Trying out my tactics on the opposition ready for Michael's childhood years. I think I've got a lot to learn."

"I think you probably have."

More seriously, Jenny went on, "What *I* don't understand is the simple 'why.' *Why* would the mother torment the child like this? She wouldn't have agreed to the adoption, would she? Unless she was sure? So why would she try and hurt the boy now?"

Richard raised his hands in exasperation. "I know. I know. As I say, it really doesn't make sense ..."

"Does it happen when you're *with* Michael? Does earth get thrown then?"

Shaking his head, Richard said, "We stayed downstairs last night, listening to the baby speaker. Earth was thrown. The night before, Susan had left him to go to the kitchen. A few minutes only. Earth was thrown. And I'm certain there was no one in the house ..."

"No one or no *thing* that you could see," Jenny murmured.

"You mean a poltergeist? I thought about that last night." He reached into his desk drawer and drew out the file copy of his article, turning to the back page where his spidery handwriting had scrawled the word several times, gouging the paper.

He was momentarily shocked. He hadn't realized he had been so brutal with his pencil. He hadn't been aware of the anger that the act of writing had been expressing.

Jenny stared at the page for a moment or two, then murmured, "Or perhaps the *mother's* spirit? Projected from her own tormented mind? She might not even be aware that she's doing it."

Richard sounded more dismissive than he'd intended. "I'm not quite ready to start thinking of astral projection. Not until I get to the edge of madness."

Undaunted, Jenny took him by the arm. She was

genuinely concerned for him, for Susan. "But if you've started to *think* about the possibility of a restless spirit in the house, why not from the mother herself? There's *something* going on, and it certainly isn't natural! What are you afraid of in accepting that?"

From the kitchen came the sound of a child's distressed sobbing. From the sitting room came the sound of laughter. Richard heard his name called. Upstairs, someone was trying to flush the toilet but without success. Feet thundered across the ceiling, and childish screams told of a game ending in tears.

"At the moment, Jenny, I'm terrified of my own shadow. So's Susan." He stared at the woman, at the thin but strong features of her face, her eyes so full of sympathy, but so certain, so sure. "Thanks for your help."

He left the study, closing the door on Michael and his minder, and went out into the garden again.

It was time to end the party.

Five

The last guest left at seven in the evening, taking the last child with him, leaving a sudden, wonderful peace. Cleaning and clearing took two hours, and that was only the kitchen and sitting room. The garden would have to wait until the next day.

Exhausted and shaking, Richard poured himself a Jack Daniels and flopped down across the armchair, wordless and dizzy. Susan was feeding Michael and the infant's tiny fists were clenched with ecstasy as he sucked at the bottle.

"Have you locked everywhere?"

"Everywhere," Richard murmured. "And I've searched the house from top to bottom. Just in case some brat with the bone of a giant is still in hiding." He smiled at the thought of "Isadora." "The brats, I am glad to report, are all tormenting adults elsewhere."

"It was a good day. I'm glad we went ahead with it."

"I agree. Hard work, but good. Brilliant barbecue, of course. And thank God for Jenny."

"She's a wonder."

"How do you feel now?" Richard asked after a moment.

Susan looked up, eyes red, moistening. "Terrified . . ." she said, and Richard felt a shiver pass through him.

"The house is empty. And we'll not leave Michael. And we'll sleep well, tonight. I'm quite determined."

"That's not the point, though. Is it? Nothing happens when we're with him." Her voice began to rise. "We can't *prove* anything by keeping him with us. She might be here and hiding and she won't come out if he's with us. We can't *prove* it, Rick, can we? If we're going to catch her—"

"Susan!" He rose and went over to her, sitting by her and watching the infant feed greedily. "Take it easy, love." He stroked her neck, pinching the stiff muscles, kneading them between thumb and forefinger.

"That's good."

They stayed up until one in the morning, then took the child quietly to his cot and went to bed themselves.

But Richard couldn't sleep. Every murmur and whimper from Michael startled him, sent a surge of shock through his system. After a while he sat up in bed and resigned himself to wakefulness.

He was thirsty. He had drunk too much wine, and too much Jack Daniel's. He walked downstairs quietly and drank a pint of water, then sat by lamplight in the study, leafing through one of his albums of photographs.

Past glories. Special effects . . .

After a while he became drowsy and put his head across his arms, leaning on the desk. His heart was pumping hard and he tried to will it to calm down, without success.

He jerked awake at the sound of movement in the kitchen. Alert in an instant he eased himself out of the office chair and tiptoed to the hall, drawing the cord of his dressing-gown tight around his waist. He glanced upstairs but there was silence. There was someone in the kitchen, though, moving about in the darkness.

When he switched on the light Susan's scream nearly gave him a heart attack. He lunged forward and caught the bottle of milk that had slipped from her fingers.

The relief was intense and he laughed, hugging his wife. "You gave me quite a fright."

"I thought you were sleeping," she murmured. She rubbed tiredness from her eyes, then took the bottle from him, raising it to her lips and gulping.

"I've been down for a little while. I was too restless."

"I didn't notice you'd gone. I must have been dreaming ..."

"Dreaming what?"

She leaned back against the table and closed her eyes. "That you were still there, next to me ... You were holding a large, silent, cuddly dog, which was nuzzling me ..."

"I *never* go to bed with dogs. Especially not cuddly ones."

"It felt so real ... you felt—the dog felt—so solid ..."

Something in her words ...

She opened her eyes and frowned. The words hung between them, meaningless in one way, yet sinister, suggestive.

"Rick?"

"Oh my God ..."

In the moment of silence that followed their eyes met in blank terror.

The image of a body in bed with Susan.

It felt so real ...

For the second time the milk bottle slipped from Susan's shaking fingers, though again Richard caught it.

"It was just a dream—"

She shuddered. "The dog. It was so huge—"

"Just a dream."

Susan started to cry. The kitchen was suddenly icy cold. Richard looked up at the ceiling. His heart threatened to burst.

It felt so real ...

And then, from upstairs, came the unmistakable sound of Michael wailing, a sudden, sharp sound, that was immediately followed by a crack of thunder.

The whole house shook.

Richard dropped the bottle, which shattered noisily. "Jesus Christ!"

Susan screamed and pushed past her husband. "Oh God! Oh God!"

They reached the bottom of the stairs together. Richard switched on the light to the landing. The stench of wet earth and vegetation was overpowering. It poured through the house, fetid, sharp. It was the smell of a dug grave, the smell of damp farmland.

The house still shuddered. There was no sound from the boy.

"Michael!"

Creaking . . . as of wood giving way. Creaking and screaming, wood being torn . . . slowly, giving way, beneath a weight . . .

"Michael!"

They slipped on the landing, skidding in the great slick spill of wet mud that poured from the bedroom. Susan crawled her way across the mound of rank sludge to the bedside light, scrabbling and kicking as the water-laden earth sucked and dragged at her. Richard followed her, his voice a shrill shriek of terror and despair. He started to chop at the mud, elbowing the earth away, cutting himself, feeling the sharpness of stones and fragments of wood, but digging down, digging down. He was only vaguely aware of Susan scratching and screaming at the black filth . . .

With a groan of breaking timber, the ceiling sagged then gave way.

They plunged in chaos into the sitting room. Richard found himself waist-deep in the soil. Susan's legs kicked as she struggled to surface, sobbing, spitting mud from her mouth.

Richard saw a limb, a small, clenched fist. "He's here!"

He carefully parted the earth around the arm, then reached strong fingers down and pulled Michael from the grave. The boy's eyes were open, his mouth gaping, but he wasn't breathing. Richard reached into the infant's mouth and extracted the bolus of clay. Then he blew breath down the child's throat, again and again, sobbing as he tried to restore his son's life.

Susan stood by him, a bedraggled mud-blackened shape, her hands spread wide over her son's face, but

frozen, immobile as life was pumped slowly back into
the corpse.

Michael suddenly shuddered and gulped breath,
then screwed up his eyes, flexed his arms and began
to wail.

"Oh thank God. Thank God."

"Get the doctor. Quickly . . . get him out here . . .
quickly . . ."

"You do it. Give me Michael."

She snatched at the boy, clutched at him, weeping
helplessly as she subsided back on to the slurry. The
double bed, which had been hanging precariously from
the ruins of the ceiling, slowly slid through the gap.
Richard caught its edge as it fell, and steered it away
from danger.

He felt oddly calm, serene, his head clear, his vision
sharp. He stopped and surveyed the scene in the room.
Half the ceiling was down, plaster dust still swirling
from the ragged edges. Worms flexed and struggled in
the mud. Several sharp, bright shapes glistened. The
stench of wet soil and fresh blood—had he cut
himself?—was almost overpowering.

When he reached the phone he couldn't use it.

What was he going to say? How would he explain
what had happened? The last thing he wanted, now,
was for anyone to see this mess. And if they took Michael to hospital and were asked how he came to have
dirt in his stomach . . .

Suddenly dizzy with confusion he replaced the receiver and stepped back into the mud-strewn living
room. Susan, cradling Michael, had calmed him. She
sat on the mound, her feet buried in earth up to the ankles. She was rocking slightly.

"Is he all right?"

She sang and nodded.

"I'll bring the doctor out if you think . . . if you
think it's necessary . . . ?"

She watched him for a long time, rocking and
singing. He felt cold and sick. Finally she shook
her head.

"He'll ask some awkward questions. I don't know what to do . . ."

Again, she nodded, smoothing Michael's hair, holding him tightly to her.

She went on singing.

Six

Richard returned to the phone and called Jenny. She was incoherent with tiredness when she answered, but rapidly woke up when she heard the tone in Richard's voice.

All he had said was, "We've got a real problem. Could you come and fetch Susan and Michael? I'll have a suitcase of clothes ready to take."

"Yes, of course . . . it'll take me half an hour . . ."

"Thanks."

Then he helped Susan out of the mud and up to the bathroom. He felt oddly calm, almost unreal. It was a form of shock, he knew, but he welcomed the fact that he felt no sense of panic. That would come later, he imagined. He had also expected Susan to want to leave the house immediately, but she too was in a strange, dulled state, and all she wanted was a bath.

Even a bath in *this* house.

She was mostly silent as they went upstairs. She undressed Michael, then herself, as Richard drew the water and tested it for temperature. She settled into the shallow bath and closed her eyes for a moment. She still held Michael, and together they cleaned the infant. The child was surprisingly quiet, apparently undisturbed by his near-fatal experience. When the mud was washed away, Richard ran a second bath to rinse them, then left Susan alone as he packed her clothes for her, and the bottles and sterilizing equipment, ready for Jenny's arrival.

He was trying to keep a clear head, trying not to let

the pure alienness of this event start to panic him. He
had an idea that he would stay in the house and clear
away the mess, shifting the massive earthfall into the
garden, maybe even as far as the quarry. Get the house
clean. Get the *ghost* out of the place.

*What had done this? What power could have done
this?*

"Keep calm!" he whispered to himself as he prowled
the rooms downstairs, waiting for Jenny. "Keep a firm
grip . . ."

Jenny was wearing jeans and a heavy jumper, and
without the touch of make-up that she normally used
her eyes looked pale and tired. Her hair was tousled,
her breath sweet with peppermint, and she shuddered
uncontrollably as she stood in the doorway of the sitting room and stared at the mud spill.

"Good God Almighty! You're lucky not to have
been crushed."

Richard looked up at the gaping ceiling. It had been
a fall of ten feet or more, and Michael had been under-
neath the slurry.

"Yes."

"I smell blood," Jenny said, and started to gag. "Oh
shit, I'm going to be sick."

She ran from the room, out through the back door,
and into the dawn. Richard blocked his ears against the
sound of her retching, feeling nauseous himself. And it
was as he stood there, the sharp odor of flesh strong in
his own nostrils, that he glimpsed the piece of gleaming white bone.

He used a muddy stick to prod at the shard, and had
to fight not to be sick as he unearthed the torn, still
bleeding fragment of a dog's skull. It had brown fur,
with a patch of white; a section of ear remained. There
was flesh and bone below the skin, a fragment of skull
and upper jaw, one canine still in place.

The blood was fresh, clotting but still textured. This
animal had been alive half an hour ago.

Jenny had gone upstairs to see Susan. Now she came
back to the sitting room just as Richard unearthed a
second piece of the dead animal, a paw attached to

four inches of leg. She stood there, hand over her mouth, but more controlled now.

"A dog?" she whispered hoarsely.

"What's left of it." He found a tuft of fur, some glistening white cartilage and two further pieces of red-raw bone.

"This will seem like a silly question," Jenny whispered, "but does this make any sort of sense at all?"

"No."

"No human being did this . . ."

"No. I know . . ."

There were other oddities in the earthfall, and he lifted them from the mound. "Look at this . . ."

Jenny came closer, hand still covering her mouth, and peered over Richard's shoulder.

"Wood?"

"It's wicker. A fragment of wicker." Now that he looked he could see several fragments of the wood and he reached for them, piling them up.

"There's chalk too . . ." Jenny said. "Christ, that smell!"

Richard picked up the chalk object, a ball, a block of chalk that looked as if it had been smoothed off. There were no marks on it that he could discern. He picked up two or three shards of flint and cast them aside. More bits of wood, and a second chalk ball . . .

Suddenly frightened, he stepped back from the earth and brushed his hands, as if to remove the taint of the haunting. He was shaking violently. Jenny was watching him through eyes that registered no emotion, only blankness. A sort of helplessness.

"Thanks for coming over," Richard said in a dull voice. "I didn't want to send for our neighbors . . . they'd make too much fuss . . ."

Jenny shrugged impatiently. Then she shook her head, despairing as she surveyed the chaos.

"I mean, what *did* this?"

He looked up through the open ceiling. "This has always been such a happy house. My family have lived here for two generations. Nothing sinister has occurred here. Not in our time."

"And before your time? How old is the place? A hundred and fifty years?"

He shook his head. "Not that old. Late Victorian."

She was thoughtful. "And what was here before the house?"

"A field, I imagine." He caught her drift and tried to smile wryly, but his face remained an impassive, shocked mask. "No, it's not built on the site of a Celtic burial ground. Or a Roman cemetery. Or a Druid's temple. I wish it was. Digging the garden would be more fun."

"What about the tump?"

"The tumulus? That's just a Bronze Age grassy knoll now. There's nothing left in it. Cleared out years ago. Spirits and all. And I've seen maps of this area before the house was built. There's nothing below the foundations."

She came up to him and took his arm, a determined look on her ashen features. "There's something in the house, Richard. Poltergeist, psychic power, call it what you like. There's *something* here and it's malicious. It's raw. If it's Michael's birth-mother, then she's powerful. And vicious. You have to find out if it's her. If it's the house, then something happened here and you can take steps to rid the house of the energy. You need help. You need expert help . . ."

"Exorcism, you mean. Bell, book and bullshit."

"Not necessarily exorcism. Not *even* that. Just some-one . . . someone who *knows* about these things."

"I can't think for the moment, Jenny. I've got to get Susan and Michael out of here. I've got to clean up this mess. Dump this dirt somewhere, the chalk pit . . . that's going to take hours . . . I can't think for the moment . . ."

But Jenny was insistent. "You've *got* to think. Both of you, Susan too. You're being attacked. *Psychically.* And Michael's life is in jeopardy. Perhaps yours too. You've got to get out of here, Richard. Work on the cause from the outside."

Even as she said the words the house seemed to shift, to flex inwards, crowding down upon him dizzyingly and with alarming consequences. He felt immediately panicky, stepping back from the earthfall, overwhelmed by its smell and the aliveness of it. There was furtive movement on its surface, and grains of drying soil slipped down the mound, disturbed by the worm-life below. The room seemed to be oppressing him, stifling him, and he labored for breath, feeling his heart pounding painfully, his skin breaking into an icy, unpleasant sweat.

Jenny tugged his sleeve, and he responded to her sudden concern with a hug.

"You're right," he whispered. "Get me out of here . . ."

Susan came downstairs, carrying Michael. Jenny went over to her and took her case. "Ready when you are."

"I'd better take my dolls," Susan murmured. "I think I'm going to need something to do."

She went into the workroom and reappeared with a carrier bag. Richard had packed a small case of his own things from the wardrobe and drawers in the spare room. He had intended to turn off the electricity in the house, but in his sudden haste to escape the place he forgot. He practically ran from the front door, returning only to lock it.

The sound of the car's engine, revving up, was welcome, and he almost flung himself into the front seat, closing his eyes as Jenny drove swiftly away from Eastwell.

He returned to the house a day later, shortly after dawn, entering by the front door and standing for a while in the heavy, oppressive stillness. When he entered the sitting room he began to shake again, feeling haunted by the silence, by the familiarity of the surroundings. It was as if the room was tainted, as if he was being watched. He knew this to be in his mind, but he couldn't help the unconscious response of fear that accompanied him as he stepped round the mound of earth.

The upstairs light was still on, its dim illumination spilling down on to the brooding mound. The earth, which had been so alive and vibrant, was dead now, the worms burrowed deep. When he touched it, it was cold; no colder, probably, than when it had fallen, but cold in a different way. It was drying out. It was settling. It was quite simply ... dead.

He rubbed dirt between his fingers, sniffed it, then brushed it away. Then he took up the two chalk balls and carried them from the room, opening the back door and stepping out into the gray light.

The land was swathed in a heavy ground mist and the air felt cold as well as damp. There was no sound in this new day, save for the distant, melancholy calling of a single rook, out in the gray fog that clung to the trees around the disused chalk quarry.

He walked over the field, now, and through the trees to the rusting wire fencing that protected animals and children from the pit. He was able to pull the fence down and tread out a path, through the dog's-mercury and fern, to the sheer edge of the chalk where it dropped away into the dense tangle of undergrowth and rubble below.

It would be hard work, getting the earthfall here, but he wanted it away from him, away from the house, as far away as possible.

Resigning himself to a long and aching day, he walked back to the garden and fetched the wheelbarrow and spade.

In the sitting room, he began to dig.

Seven

Eighteen months later ...

Michael sat in the corner of the kitchen, a sheet of white paper on the linoleum floor in front of him, bricks, wooden cars and crayons scattered in abundance. He was using the red crayon to fashion loops on the paper, winding one loop inside another, keeping a continuous form emerging as he listened to the excitement in the house.

The voices were high-pitched and happy. The movement around him was frantic, random, making breezes as it passed.

As he fashioned the spirals he kept his eyes on the white paper, glancing only at the feet that passed by in his peripheral vision: sometimes the green slippers of his mother; sometimes the muddy boots of his father; occasionally the shoes of people he knew only slightly.

The paper filled with his drawing.

As the buzz of voices and activity grew loud and near, so he drew more vigorously. When the storm passed deeper into the house, away from him, he slowed, letting the crayon idle in his fingers, the tip crawling like a snail over the paper.

He heard his name, and the word "picnic," which made him smile with anticipated pleasure. And sometimes the tone and the words he knew combined to give an impression of what was happening, so that as the shadows of the giants swept past him, looming briefly at the edge of vision, sweeping through, closing and opening doors, gathering food, gathering bottles, packing, preparing, throwing together boots and raincoats and all the familiar items of "picnics," so he began to understand that there was something special about today.

He filled in the gaps between the loops with other loops, then reached for the black crayon and drew in the shadows that walked these tunnels. He used the green crayon for his mother, and the brown crayon for his father, but placed their images *outside* the swirl of circles.

The fainter shadows in the house clustered and scurried about him, silent and curious. They mixed and mingled with the bulky vibrancy of the giants. They hovered and quivered, just out of sight. He sketched them all. Drew every one of them that he could imagine. They were nothing but blobs, with the extensions that were arms, and the extensions that were legs, and the slashes in their faces that were mouths. And all the time he drew on the paper he listened for his name, and for the mood, and for the *feel* of what was being said in the noise of the giants, the words that he *knew* were words, but could still only partly understand.

Around him, the strange and silent shadows faded suddenly against the bright sunlight that streamed in through the open door to the garden. On impulse he stood, then waddled to the door, to stand at the top of the step. He stared out into the brilliance of the day, across the lawn, the fence, to the blue of the sky above the distant sea.

He loved the sea. He loved its color. He loved the sound it made. He loved the stones on the beach, and the crisp sound that came from them when the breakers rushed and rolled across them. He loved that gray-green water. He dreamed of being down below it, waves surging above him. He dreamed great shadows in that water, dark masses moving through the gray-green . . .

Would they go to the beach for the picnic? Or to the woodland?

He started to step down, down across the concrete, down to the garden, his chubby legs quivering as they flexed into a position that his body was not yet ready to accommodate. He was aware only that his body was denying his need, and that his nappy was suddenly warm and sticky as a relief flooded from him. The smell touched his nostrils and he knew what would happen.

Strong hands whisked him up from the step. His name was spoken loudly, and there was laughter, and amused irritation from the man, his father, and he was on his back. Rough hands stripped him, and he was lifted by the feet as the stickiness was wiped from him.

Turning his head slightly he could see the white paper sheet in the corner of the room, and the great red loops, and the darting figures of the shadows he had drawn. There was such *comfort* in the feeling of the way those loops and lines led *inwards*. He knew it was the entrance to a tunnel. Sometimes he felt the tunnel reach out around him, swallowing him. At the end of the tunnel the sea shifted and surged. Massive shadows moved there and the sun was hot on red cliffs.

He smiled and chuckled and reached a hand toward the paper. But before he could make the shadows dance again he was once more in strong hands, held aloft, newly clad in fresh nappy, held before his father's face. The bearded man kissed him, shook him, and bawled words of excitement before passing him to the gentler of his parents . . .

They reached Hawkinge Woods just after eleven in the morning, parking close to a bridleway that led in and through the beechwoods. It was hot and still, an idyllic late July morning; surprisingly, there was little sign of other visitors to the parkland and forest.

Half an hour later they were below the trees, kicking through fern and bracken, bathed in the intense, green sunlight that played through the thin woodland canopy.

"This is magnificent!" Susan's father murmured. He carried the picnic hamper and trudged through last year's beech mast, his gaze dazzled by the shifting light.

The beeches were silent and formed strange animal shapes. Great bulked trunks, produced after ancient pollarding, gave the impression of four or five trees grown together, each pushing out faces or the smooth flanks of bodies drawn into the bark. Light coppicing made walking difficult in places, but the saplings were flexible.

Richard led the way down a slope through stands of holly and maythorn, to a muddy stream. Several trees had fallen across the wide, dirty water-course. They led to the far bank and the just-visible earthworks of the hidden fort.

"Iron Age?" Doug asked as they surveyed the rise of land.

He was right. The beechwoods had been cleared more than two thousand years ago, and a ring enclosure, defensive in purpose, built by the local clans. The fort had not known history, and there were no signs of any dramatic event having occurred here. It had been abandoned in late Roman times and the woods had re-established themselves.

Richard had discovered the place in his childhood, and had a romantic attachment to it. It was his old camp, and as a teenager he had often cycled here with his girlfriends, imagining the ring fort to be his secret and private place. On more than one occasion he had been disturbed during his "history" lesson.

They had to walk the tightrope, balancing on the fallen trunks to cross the water. Richard went first, Michael held carefully in his arms. The child was quite still and seemed very aware of the light through the branches. Doug, game for anything, made a performance out of the crossing, leaning forward then back, his ruddy face creased with a grin, then shock, causing Susan's mother, Gwen, to have five forms of fit. But he crossed all right, and Gwen herself, a plump woman clad in tight slacks and pristine white blouse, ran across the tree with an unexpected and applaudable daintiness.

Susan managed to slip, went up to her calf in water and mud. She was barefoot, though, and found the accident more amusing than irritating. She used handfuls of fresh fern to scrape the mud from her feet and from the hem of her summer skirt.

Inside the ring they found the signs of previous visitor, charred patches of ground, pits, and stones piled to make fire-shelters. A rope swing hung from one of the thicker branches of a beech; Doug tested it for strength, yanking the frayed rope hard, then took a courageous leap on to the horizontal wooden bar which formed the swing itself. A man of fifty, he yelled like a kid and swayed back and forward until his strength gave out and he fell, and stumbled down to the soft ground. His normally red face was now flushed and almost purple, and Gwen had short, sharp words to say to him. He ignored her, breathlessly proclaiming his continued youth.

Richard spread out the picnic mat while Susan unpacked the hamper. Michael waddled toward the inner rise of the earthwork, fell flat, eased himself up and continued his journey. Above him the massive beeches reached protective limbs across him. The earthwork ring was topped by thirty or forty of these vast trees, an odd palisade but one which gave the inner area a feeling of being isolated from the rest of the wood.

The conversation was light, in keeping with the lightness and the stillness of the day. Michael was complimented on being an advanced child for his eighteen months. The drawings he made were more in keeping with a three-year-old's, and Gwen was particularly struck by the infant's precocious talent in drawing rudimentary faces. (Richard doubted that they *were* faces, rather than just other swirls, but Gwen was insistent.) His alertness was commented on too. But this made Richard and Susan feel less comfortable, and they exchanged a glance.

Michael was sometimes *too* alert. They had halfheartedly joked about *The Omen,* about children who see the world with the eyes of mature evil. Sometimes Michael's silent staring and sudden quizzical expressions alarmed Susan so much that she felt unable to hold the boy. But he seemed happy enough, on the whole, and sat in his corners (a favored corner in every room) and covered sheets of drawing paper with circular lines and little black shapes that often had faces. He ate comfortably, cried little, slept well, and in the year or more that the family had lived away from Eastwell House, there had been no further incidents with earthfalling.

They had come up with a simple answer to the problem of the house. They had swapped with Jenny and Geoff. The arrangement was not intended as anything permanent, it was just to get away from the haunting for a while, to allow Michael to grow, to hope that whatever non-natural element had been attacking him would go away. In Jenny's house the Whitlocks had less space, and less garden, but they lived comfortably enough, sharing a study room. Richard's photographic work took him away for days at a time to remote and weather-battered locations; Susan used the crèche in the polytechnic at Maidstone; and the Hansons, in their suddenly larger domain, had filled it wonderfully with their two children, their two dogs, and their collections of books and model ships.

In all the time that the families had "swapped," there had been no phenomena that could be called "occult" or "supernatural." Jenny had been quite disappointed at first, since she had hoped to track down the source of the psychic attack. But all things had been quite silent.

Even when the Whitlocks had visited their old home, which they had done with increasing frequency, nothing untoward had occurred.

At the end of the summer the families were thinking of changing back. They had not become complacent about the gritty events at the time of Michael's homecoming, but Susan acknowledged that she felt a "sense of peace." Perhaps the mother *had* gone away; removed her spirit from the house; closed down her anger. Perhaps she had at last given Michael up to the Whitlocks.

There was another, more practical reason for thinking about returning to the bigger house, though.

With appetites satisfied, Richard opened the terracotta winecooler and produced a bottle of champagne. It was a cheap one, but the family never used champagne seriously, only for fun.

Gwen and Doug watched quietly, half aware of the news that would be announced. Susan glanced at Michael, who was standing below a root-mass from one of the trees that had begun to grow out of the earthen bank. He was staring down at the ground, quite motionless, quite safe, as if listening to something.

"If my own parents weren't on holiday, they'd be here too. But this is just . . ." Richard raised his glass, tapped it against Susan's, and waited for Susan to say:

"Here's to you two: about to be grandparents for the *second* time!"

Doug's reaction was typical of the man. "Well, I'll be buggered!" He drained his champagne glass, stood awkwardly, leaned to kiss Susan on the head, then ran to the rope swing, making childlike cries of delight. He leapt on it and swung four times in a shallow arc.

Susan laughed, then noticed her mother's frown.

"I thought . . ." Gwen started to say, and her frown deepened.

"You thought we couldn't have a natural child? So did we. Apparently this is very common. You adopt a child and something, some maternal change occurs, and the next thing you know . . ."

"You've got your *own* child . . ." Richard said lightly, and instantly turned away, furious with himself. "Damn!"

Susan was on her feet, blazing. "Don't *say* that! You stupid man! You *stupid* man!"

"I'm sorry, Sue . . ." He stood awkwardly and took her by the shoulders. His eyes had filled with tears. "I didn't mean it that way. I didn't mean that. You surely know I didn't . . ."

"*Michael's* your own child! Like it or not, Rick, you're *already* a real parent!"

"I didn't *mean* it . . ."

"You always mean it!" Susan bit off the words, folded her arms and looked down. She was shaking with anger.

Doug drifted gently on the rope swing, then let himself down and came over to the picnic party where tension hung silent and deadly in the air.

Michael was watching them. There was a light breeze, now, and his ginger locks were being blown about. The leaves around his feet were disturbed, as if being kicked by little feet.

"Take the words away from me," Richard said quietly, but his eyes suddenly shone with need. Susan watched him, her fury dissipating but her concern growing.

"It's OK, Rick. It's done. Forgotten."

"Take the words away . . ."

Now she looked suddenly frightened. "It's not necessary. It's over. Just . . . Just . . ." she punched him on the chest, her mouth grim. "Just bloody well be careful what you say. And if you ever *do* think like that, then for God's sake talk to me about it . . ."

But Richard was too angry, too mortified to be pacified. His face was ashen. Doug watched him in alarm, while Gwen kept an eye on Michael.

Richard said loudly, "Use the doll. Take the words away. Michael might have heard me . . ."

"Don't take family superstition too far," Gwen murmured as she realized what the man was asking. Irritably, Richard tried to reach into the pocket of Susan's skirt. "Use the doll," he said, his voice rising.

"Why do you think I've got a doll?"

"I know you have. You'll have brought one with you to make the link. Please, take the words away from me. Use the doll."

Again he reached into her pocket, grasped the small clay figurine, and struggled with Susan, forcing her grip from his wrist as he wrenched the object from her clothing.

"Give it back!"

"Use it!"

"No! I can't! I'm pregnant! I *can't* use it. Stop this, Rick. Stop it now!"

Richard swept his arm round, holding the crude figure toward Gwen. "You do it, then. You do it."

Gwen very calmly slapped the man's face, not hard, just very purposefully. Without a flicker of emotion on her face she said, grimly, "I didn't *make* the doll. Susan can't *use* it. And you don't *need* it. Why don't you listen to what she says? You're behaving like a damned fool."

There were tears in his eyes, and Susan reached out and touched his shoulder. He shook his head, then raised the doll to his lips and whispered, "Take those words from me. Take them from me. I love Michael. I love Michael. I love Michael . . ."

And then with a roar of anguish, he flung the object far into the distance. It vanished into the fern and leaf mold at the base of the earth wall.

In the sudden silence, all they could hear was a strange wind in the branches of the trees above and around them, and the sound of someone scrabbling through the bracken.

They turned toward Michael and all four of them started to run. The boy was halfway up the slope, crawling and dragging himself up and away from the enclosure as if being hauled by a rope. He ascended the earth bank in seconds, stood tottering at the top, his arms stretched to the sides as he faced into the distance, a moment only, a moment in which he was silhouetted against the green brightness of sun through leaves . . .

Then he was gone.

Richard reached the top of the earth wall first. Michael had rolled down the far slope and now was up and running again, through the crowded saplings, through the yellow and green light. He was clutching the back of his head with both hands, but making no sound.

"He's been stung. A bee sting!"

Richard slipped down the steeper bank, and raced the few yards to Michael's staggering shape. He reached toward the child, reached to sweep him up into secure arms.

The wood around him erupted, an explosion of wind that uprooted saplings, flung dirt, leaves and clumps of fern at him. The great trees swayed and bent, their branches waving frantically against the flickering brilliance of the sky.

Michael had fallen once more, but again was running. Richard staggered after him through the shadows and light, pistol-whipped by the lashing saplings, calling for the screaming infant who seemed to move with impossible speed through the dense leaf mold and waving ferns. Leaves, earth and chunks of wood swirled around the two of them like a tornado. The wind boomed and groaned, and the taller beeches cracked and screamed as their wood was torn and they bent against the hurricane.

Somewhere, Susan's voice was a cry of despair, but Richard was half-blind with the leaf matter that smacked at his face and clogged his mouth and eyes.

The boy was running *faster* than him!

He pursued. The gale swept around them, moving with them.

They crossed the damp stream. Spouts of muddy water streaked high above him, briefly taking on the shape of trees before shattering, spinning and swirling down to drench the man as he fell to his knees, scrambling to dry land.

As quickly as the storm had come, so it vanished. Michael was wailing, face down, half buried in leaves. Richard crawled toward him, vaguely aware that Susan was splashing through the stream behind him, and that his father-in-law was shouting encouragement from further back.

His head straining up above the leaf mold, his eyes closed, his mouth open, Michael shrieked his pain. When his father picked him up he kept crying but curled up into a ball, clinging to the man's chest.

His face was cut, nasty slash above the right eye, two inches long. A beech leaf had stuck to the flow of blood, and Richard pulled it away. He looked at the back of the child's neck, but saw no sign of a sting.

The others had followed through the line of devastation, shocked and frightened by the gale-force wind that had struck so suddenly in this summer wood. Susan's eyes were haunted as she reached for Michael, staring all the time at her husband.

"Dear God," she whispered. "Oh, Dear God .. she's back ..."

Richard said nothing for the moment, but shook his head. He reached to touch the cut on his son's face. What had done this?

And as if the thought drew his attention to the implement of attack, he saw the glitter of metal from the corner of his eye. He took two steps away from Susan and stooped to brush aside the leaves and broken ferns.

It was a fragment of bronze, once part of a broad spearhead. Michael's blood still glistened freshly on the sharp side that remained. It had been leaf-shaped, four inches long, and still had a part of the wooden haft attached. The metal seemed to have been *chopped*, cleanly cut from the whole as if by a guillotine.

Bronze.

Blooded.

The fragment of haft, of clean, smoothed alder, was not yet stained by time. It was bright wood, fresh wood, seasoned but newly carved to fit the blade.

Richard's hands shook as he stared at this weapon shard. He could visualize clearly two identical spearheads, both in the museums where he had recently worked, and where there were authentic replicas of the ancient weapons on display for the sort of "touch and feel" experience that schools were beginning to demand these days.

He was aware suddenly that Susan was beside him, staring at the sharp-edged piece of metal.

"Is that what cut him?"

Richard fingered the blood on the edge and nodded. "A replica, but a good one. The edge is razor-sharp."

Susan closed her eyes and stifled panic. "It's starting again," she whispered. "Oh God, she's starting on us again. I thought she'd gone away."

"It's not his mother. Sue, calm down. It's not his mother."

But Susan started to cry softly. Richard put his free arm around her.

"She's evil. She's terrifying ... Oh God, Rick. I can't stand this ..."

Richard kissed the top of her head, staring into the middle distance while Michael lay quiet in his arm. "It's not her, Sue. It's not his mother. It never was. Not her. Not the house. Not a poltergeist. Not any sort of ghost in the outside world."

She drew back and looked at him, her face white, her dark hair dishevelled and falling over tear-stained eyes. Her lips trembled.

"What then?"

"Michael himself. It's in Michael himself. It's the boy who's doing this."

There was a long silence. Gwen and Doug stood holding each other, a few yards distant, watching and waiting.

Then Susan said, "And if I asked you why you said that? How do you know?"

"I'd have to say I don't. I just feel it. I think I've known it from the day of his christening. He's doing it himself. He's haunted *inside* ..."

"And if that's right," Susan murmured, her body beginning to shake so badly that Richard reached out to steady her. "If that's right ... where do we go from here? What do we do? Who can help us?"

Richard said nothing. He led the way back to the car in silence, while Doug returned to the earthworks to gather up the scattered picnic.

Eight

He returned to Ruckinghurst the next day, shortly after dawn, driving past Eastwell House to an access road that led to the field and the disused quarry. Here he unloaded from the car the tools he would need for the excavation: sheets of polythene, a trowel and scraper, two sieves and several light, wooden boxes. He carried this simple equipment across the field and round into the L-shaped pit, to the pile of earth by the high, far wall that he had systematically tipped into the quarry a year and a half ago. He laid his bits and pieces out in an orderly and careful way, then returned to the car for a table, notebooks, pens, pencils, specimen bags and labels. And of course, his lunch box.

"Should have done this before," he muttered to himself as he began to trowel through the soil. "Should have damned well thought about this before!"

It was not exactly an excavation. There was no point in recording the position of objects, or their relation to each other, or in plotting levels. This was a sieve-through, and as such could progress fast. But like every sieve-through of the waste soil of excavations, the point was to find the *tiny* objects, not just the large.

Trowel by trowel, he searched the damp earth.

By midday he had processed half the soil, which now was piled on the several sheets of polythene. His back ached and his right arm was sore from the repetitive operation of scraping a kitchen spatula across the wire-mesh sieves.

As he stopped for a large, cold beer from his cool-box, he surveyed the results of the search so far. He had exhumed nearly a third of a large dog, with dry, coarse fur still clinging to some of the sharp, broken bones. He had collected forty fragments of thin wicker, found three more chalk balls, these the size of billiard balls. When he held the pieces of chalk against he light in different ways and looked for shadows, the tell-tale shadows that would show inscriptions or patterns on their surface, nothing was instantly revealed.

He had also sieved out nearly a hundred flint shards that had ben deliberately produced from a single core. He had fitted three of them together and the edges were sharp and clean, the match perfect.

He had not found the implement that had been fashioned from the core, of which these shards were the waste.

There were also several chunks of turf, the grass browned and rotten, but the texture still intact. Although at first he was inclined to dismiss these, he suddenly began to realize their significance.

In the late afternoon, running with sweat and uneasy in this silent, empty quarry, he unearthed the remains of a leather bag. It was split open and two fragments of flint chippings were embedded in it. It was old leather, but still strong, and a gut string had been used to draw it closed. The bag, on closer inspection, seemed to have been torn apart.

Searching in the same area he found two more pieces of hide, the leather of a slightly lighter tone, despite the earth staining, and with a patterning that suggested pigskin, not cowhide like the first. Two bags, then.

Fragments of a clay vessel came to light from the bottom of the mound. He rinsed them off and their slight red coloring showed clearly. There were fifteen fragments, four of which fitted neatly together to reveal part of a shallow dish. There was a trace of pale wax on one shard.

Five boxes, then:

One contained the remains of the dog, and he had already confirmed what he had suspected: the creature had been chopped to pieces by a thin, sharp blade, strong enough—and wielded with sufficient strength—to make a clean cut through the bone on each strike. A second case contained the flint shards, the leather and the chalk. A third contained the narrow wicker twigs; a fourth the larger fragments of wood and several chunks of compacted daub, a hardened mud used to fill the gaps between the wattle of the walls of primitive dwellings. In the fifth box were the decaying lumps of turf, the recognizable remains of rushes, and all the other stones, large seeds, and vegetable matter that had come through with the fall.

And it all added up to ... to what? Did it add up to anything at all?

He was sure it did. Or at least, the remains did. How they had got here ... what they had been doing in his bedroom at two in the morning eighteen months ago, was another question entirely.

But the remains of the dog, the newly killed dog ...

Whoever had killed it had done the deed only minutes before the dismembered creature had come into the Whitlocks' house. It had been chopped to pieces by an axe, a very heavy axe.

It was a dead dog and had been held in a cage made of wicker. The cage had been in a place which had wattle and daub walls supporting a turf roof: rushes on the floor had made walking easier.

Next to the dead dog in the cage had been placed leather bags containing flint chippings, and five chalk balls which someone had shaped perfectly smooth and round.

And there had been at least one crude clay dish with wax in it, and maybe a flame.

It was obvious to him that the fall of earth had concealed a shrine.

But a shrine to a dead, dismembered dog?

A shrine. Purpose unknown.

A large part of which had been suddenly dumped into his bedroom, out of nowhere, out of the blue, out of thin air.

* * *

Michael was sitting in the corner of the kitchen, head down, a sheet of paper on which he was drawing between his chubby legs. Spirals, of course, swirls, and blobs.

Richard stood in the doorway from the garden, watching the boy as he beavered away with his crayons. If Michael was aware that his father was watching him he didn't show it. Richard stooped and rolled one of the chalk balls toward the child. It came to a stop in front of the boy, and at last Michael looked up.

The plaster on his forehead made him look lopsided, and the tint of iodine at its edges gave him a bruised appearance.

"A little present for you," Richard said and rolled the second ball toward his son. Michael watched it strike the first ball and come to a stop by his foot. He reached out and picked up the chalk, then put it straight to his mouth, licking it.

"That's not quite what I had in mind," Richard said, and walked quickly over to stop the tasting.

Michael returned to his scribbling. When Richard tried to turn the paper round to see the marks, the boy became agitated.

"Circles and smudges. Circles and smudges."

Round and round the black crayon went, but Richard noticed that Michael was aware of the chalk balls, his gaze lifting from the paper to stare at the artefacts from the pit.

"If I clean the dirt and dog from the chalk so you can lick it, I might be tampering with archaeology."

Michael used a white crayon to smudge in two round objects in the middle of a swirl of black lines.

"What about a dog? You should put a dog in there. A large dog. Brown and gray."

The next smudge may have been an attempt at such an animal, but it was hard to be sure.

Susan moved about noisily upstairs, and water began to drain from the bath, rushing down the pipe at the side of the house. At once Michael stood and walked to the back door, peering round to see the water flood into the drain. It was one of his favorite things.

When he came back to his corner Richard picked him up and held the stiff, reluctant lad in his arms.

He said, "It's not your mother. It never was. It's you. Isn't it? It's you. There's something funny in that brain of yours. Something terrifying and strange. You're haunting yourself."

Michael became agitated again, struggling, and Richard placed him down, down into his corner, down to his dark circles. Like an automaton, the boy's hand reached for a crayon, and without pause or consideration the circles began to flow again. A machine, producing machine art.

"You're a living poltergeist. You throw stones at yourself, not at others. You drown yourself in earth, drawing it down on to yourself through that strange and frightening gray matter between your ears. There must be such a rage in you . . ."

Swirling, circling.

"But if that's true, where did it come from? That rage. I wish you could talk to me, Michael. I wish I could pick beyond that ginger hair, right down to the gray stuff. Where did it come from? Who *was* your mother?"

And he added as an afterthought, frowning slightly, "Or father. Who was your father, I wonder?"

Susan came down, dressed in a bathrobe, her hair soaking. She looked suspiciously at Richard as she entered the kitchen. "What's all the talking?"

"Talking to my son. Having a chat about dogs and temples."

"Dogs and temples?"

"Sue, I think you're right. It's time we both went to London and got some co-operation from your Dr. Wilson."

Unexpectedly, Susan was uncomfortable. She shook her head, toweling her hair quickly to start drying it. "No. No, I don't think so. I'll go alone. He won't want us both."

"We need to talk to Michael's mother. We need to

know something more about her. Maybe she was on drugs. Maybe she . . ."

"Maybe she what?"

He looked up, not happy with the thought. "Maybe she tampered with black magic. Maybe she did something to herself, something that damaged her during an experiment, something like that. A psychic experiment . . ."

Susan's uneasiness increased. Again she disagreed. "I'll talk to Wilson on my own. I'll call him. But he's still very discreet. He won't give me the address. I know he won't. He won't tell me a damn thing."

"But you can try."

"I'll try."

She left the kitchen. When Richard looked down he was startled to see Michael leaning back, his gaze fixed on his father. The boy's mouth worked, as if he was biting the skin on the inside. His hands hung limply beside his body. He seemed, suddenly, exhausted.

Richard had the uncanny feeling that the work of art was complete, that Michael's swirls and blobs had reached their final form.

And the artist was now empty and at peace with himself.

PART TWO

The Mocking
Cross

Nine

Michael ran across the field toward the house, but stopped at the gate, solemn-faced as he listened to the distant sound of his sister's laughter. He looked back over his shoulder, back to the woods, then down at the small object he was bringing home. The air was hot and he was still damp inside his loose shirt. The shock of what had happened a few minutes ago had brought him out in a feverish sweat.

From the house came the sound of his mother's voice, and Carol laughed again. They were playing the counting game; it was Carol's favorite. They played it all the time, while Michael drew pictures, or explored his camps in the garden.

He felt sad. At the same time he felt angry. Again, he looked back to the woods across the field, then brushed at his trousers and sleeves, knowing that he might be in trouble. He tried to pick the leaf litter from his ginger hair and smoothed the wild locks down with a smear of spit.

There was blood on his fingers, he noticed, and he wiped them carefully on the ground, then tore up some grass to use as a handkerchief, scrubbing at his face, at the stinging cut just below his cheek.

He pushed open the gate and stepped into the garden, darting up through the maze, peering cautiously over the top of the low hedge as he moved toward the house.

His mother's voice resolved, and he could hear her telling Carol a story. He ran from the maze to the apple tree and stood behind it, listening to the happiness in the house, holding the heavy little statue tightly. His body burned with anguish and his hands were wet. The cut on his face hurt him and he knew he should go in and have it washed.

His mother was in the sitting room, by the open doors. The back door was open too and he began to walk toward it, but heard his mother come into the kitchen and run water from the tap. So he changed direction.

Carol was sitting at the small desk she always used for her own writing and drawing. Michael stood in the doorway and watched her, then edged slowly over to her and peered down at what she was sketching.

It was a drawing of a house, their house. She showed smoke coming from the chimney. Three little stick figures, two large, one small, suggested their parents and Carol.

On impulse Michael snatched her pencil and drew the stick figure that was himself, complete with its shadow correctly orientated from the spiky sun she had drawn. The girl looked up at him sharply, but said nothing. He glared at her. She bit her lip, then looked down at the paper again and used her yellow crayon to sketch in Michael's hair. Michael felt suddenly pleased, but didn't show it.

"You look dirty," Carol said. "Mummy'll be angry. You've been in the quarry."

He said nothing. He held his hand behind his back and twisted slightly to look at the heavy, glinting object he'd found.

Carol kept drawing, and now she sang in her oddly tuneless singing voice. She was aware of Michael standing there, but determinedly ignored him. He knew she wanted him to go away, but he wasn't sure what to do. He wanted to show his mother what he'd found, but he knew he'd be in trouble as well.

He wanted Susan to tell him a story too. He loved stories, but he usually had to sit and listen to Carol's. Maybe if he washed his face and changed into another pair of jeans, his mother wouldn't be angry with him, and would tell him the story of the Fisher King. He loved that adventure especially. He'd got it in a book, and read it often, but he would like it to be read *to* him. The old king in his castle, living in a barren land, where famous and glorious knights rode on quests and the golden chalice of the Holy Grail glittered somewhere, hidden in a deep and frightening cave, guarded by terrible creatures.

Glittering.

He peered again at the gold gleam of the tiny figure from the pit.

His mother came into the room with two glasses of orange squash. She was wearing slacks and her hair was tied into a top-knot. She was humming to herself, but stopped, horrified, when she saw Michael.

He cringed.

"Where have you been? You're filthy!"

She put the glasses down and stormed over to him, her face a hard mask of irritation. "You're covered with chalk! And you're *bleeding*. What have you been doing?"

He backed away from her, but she grabbed him, turned him round and brushed at his clothes.

"Have you been playing in that quarry? Have you?"

He stared at her silently.

"How many times have I told you not to go there? You're not to play there. It's dangerous! There's all sorts of rubbish down there, and muddy pools. I *don't* want you playing there. Is that understood?"

She shook him by the shoulders, her face red, her eyes blazing. Carol had stopped drawing and was listening. Michael turned his head to look at his sister and as if she was aware of his eyes on her she started to draw fiercely.

"Go and wash!" his mother said sharply. She propelled him hard by the shoulder and he nearly stumbled as he took several paces across the sitting-room carpet. "Go and clean yourself . . ."

She had turned away from him. She glanced at Carol's drawing, smiled, then walked to the table where she had placed the orange squash. Catching him standing, looking at her, she pointed sharply to the door. "Go and *wash*, Michael. Go and do it now. I haven't got time to be chasing you. I've got a lesson to prepare."

He took his arm from behind his back and held out his hand. He opened his fingers and sunlight caught the tiny figure. Gold gleamed. The figure seemed to dance, but it was only because he was shaking with nerves.

"Pretty," he said. "Pretty."

"Stop talking in that *baby* way," Susan snapped. "How many times must you be told? You're seven years old, for heaven's sake."

He started to shake uncontrollably, but stood his ground. Then his mother saw what he was holding and came slowly over to him, her eyes wide, her face now puzzled rather than cold. Michael smiled, watching her apprehensively.

She reached for the figurine and he let her fingers take it from his trembling palm.

"Pretty," he said for the third time, but now there was a question in his voice.

Pretty?

"It's *very* pretty," his mother said slowly, softly. "It's made of gold. It's . . . yes, it's *very* pretty." She looked into his eyes, frowning. "Where did you find this, Michael . . . ? Where did you get it?"

"In my castle?" he said quietly.

"In your castle?"

He nodded, his teeth clenched together, his face grim. He wasn't supposed to talk about the castle. Chalk Boy wouldn't like it. He looked nervously at the French window, at the distant woods by the pit.

"Where's your castle? Michael? Tell me where your castle is."

"By the sea," he whispered. He hoped Chalk Boy couldn't hear him.

"But you've just been in the quarry. There's no sea in the quarry. Michael, *where* did you find this? You must tell me. It's very pretty. But it's not ours. It's very valuable. It might belong to someone."

Michael stood his ground, resolute in his silence now, not willing to betray his secret.

Susan stood up and stared again at the gold figurine of a girl with the head of a wolf. Then she touched Michael's shoulder.

"Go and wash," she whispered softly. "There's a good boy ..."

Richard was in the British Museum's bookshop, leafing through a newly published volume on Celtic archaeology, when Jack Goodman came looking for him, to give him the bad news. Goodman needn't have acted so awkward and concerned. Richard had known for over an hour that the job had been denied him.

He put the volume back on the shelf, turned and beamed at the younger man. Goodman wore a black leather jacket and sharp trousers. His spectacles were gold-rimmed, a round, designed look for the mid-eighties. He was one of the new breed of historians who worked their way ruthlessly through the system.

But he clearly felt embarrassed that Richard had fallen yet again at the hurdle called "a permanent position."

The reason Richard had known that his application had failed was because he could read the face of the main interviewer, Professor Edward Simpson, like a book. While the rest of the panel had talked about ideas, asked his thoughts on the set-up for photography at the BM, showed genuine interest, Simpson had remained silent, staring at the interviewee over his half-rims, a report sitting open at one page in front of him. In the hour of the interview that page was never turned.

It had become an intimidating, intrusive insult.

One page.

One fact.

One mistake.

Since that one fact, that one mistake, was all that interested Simpson, it meant he had no interest whatsoever in entertaining the idea of Dr. Richard Whitlock as candidate for a permanent post on the staff of the museum's documentation section.

"I'm sorry, Richard," Goodman said.

"What for? I knew I'd failed."

Goodman grinned half-heartedly. "How about lunch. We could go to The Plough, just down Museum Street. There are a couple of things we need to talk through . . ."

"Sounds good to me."

They walked stiffly and uncomfortably out of the building and into the sunshine. The steps were swarming with visitors and pigeons. Goodman put sunglasses on. He said, "I did my best. I want you to know that."

"Of course you did. But Doctor Death wasn't going to have anything to do with me . . ."

"I should have tackled him on the chalk artefacts thing . . ."

"Why? It was *my* job to tackle him. I just couldn't be bothered. He only did it to embarrass me, to challenge me. No matter what I'd said, he wouldn't have believed me."

It had been toward the end of the interview. Simpson, after the period of silent staring, picked up the photographs of the two ball-shaped chalk artefacts from the earthfall and settled back in his chair, looking hard at the images. He had thrown them on to the desk with an almost contemptuous dismissing motion.

"They're splendid photographs I'm sure, Dr. Whitlock, but they don't illuminate much."

"The patterns are unusual. I didn't notice them for several years. You've seen the first photographs, the balls appear to be perfectly smooth . . ."

"And then, as if by magic, the patterns appear . . ."

Message received by Richard, clearly understood. He said, "I've developed a better chalk wash. It uses a fine oil. In angled light, heavy on the blue, the minutest traces can be seen. These photographs are really just to illustrate the developments in technique. There's much in the museum that should be re-photographed, and I think I'm the man for the job."

He smiled half-heartedly, and Goodman grinned and

nodded supportively, but the room was tense, and he had probably made a tactical error.

Simpson said, "I don't think we'd welcome *too* many patterns emerging suddenly on our exhibits."

Goodman slumped back in his chair. The other interviewers kept watching Richard, but all looked embarrassed.

It was the moment at which he should have attacked. It was an appalling slur on his character.

But the page. The open page . . . that fact. That open, terrible fact!

He answered very coolly, "Until we look carefully we won't know. My camera techniques are the best around. They can reveal more than just decoration, and I hope you'll all welcome the opportunity—with or without me—to re-examine some of your exhibits."

"Absolutely," said Goodman.

But the interview was over. His face was burning. Infuriatingly, Simpson stood, beamed a smile and extended a hand. Infuriatingly, Richard found himself taking that hand and listening to the words from the director's mouth.

"Thank you for giving us this opportunity to consider you, Dr. Whitlock. It's been quite revealing."

They walked through the doors of the pub and hit the steamy, smoky crowd of late lunch-time. There was bench space in a corner and Richard occupied it while Goodman set up the drinks. They squeezed in between two enormous American tourists, who smiled and tried to make conversation, and a group of students who were smoking heavily and talking in the loud, assertive way that was a sure sign of their ignorance and competitiveness.

"We could go somewhere else . . . The Royal George?"

"This is fine. I haven't got long, I have to get back to Ruckinghurst this afternoon."

"Another job?"

"A freelance job. Yes. Ten photographs of a local church for the local council." Richard smiled bitterly.

"Oh, I tell you, Jack, my life is one wild round of excitement and discovery!"

They drank in silence until Richard's frustration had passed.

Goodman said eventually, "I don't know if this is consolation or not, but Simpson will be gone in three or four years. Then the New Wave takes over. You won't be an outsider for long."

Richard chose to ignore the element of patronism in Goodman's attempt to reassure him.

"I made a mistake. I didn't commit a crime by law. But I committed a crime within the hallowed Institute. People like Simpson can't stomach that. Simpson's followers will be groomed in the same school."

"Not necessarily—"

"Oh, come on!" Richard turned sharply toward the younger man. "If you'd thought your job depended on it, would you have sided with Simpson today, if asked?"

"No."

"Yes, you would. I know that much about you, Jack. And that's good. Because that's what I would have done too."

Stung, and looking distinctly irritable, Goodman sipped his lager and said quietly, "And you think that makes it OK?"

"OK? No. Of course not. I didn't mean that. I meant it makes it not necessary for you to bullshit to me. I know exactly where I stand, and how difficult it is to ask for support. And I appreciate yours. But ten years ago I stole from an archaeological site, not for pleasure but for profit. I'm in Limbo for the rest of my career. Freelance work, yes, but never to be invited to the permanence of a job where I could be *really* effective."

"Things will change. You'll see . . ."

"No they won't. Because I walked away from a Neolithic grave site with a flint arrowhead!"

"We've all done it, Richard. There's not an archaeologist I know who could put his hand on his heart and say that he'd never taken a 'souvenir' . . ."

"I don't believe that."

"Believe it. A stone, a handful of soil, a twig: a souvenir. Just a memento? But maybe that twig was part of a doll. Maybe the stone was part of a shrine. Maybe the soil contained bone fragments of a ritual burnt offering. It's all stealing."

"I know. I know . . ."

"And maybe the stone we nick as a souvenir had been used to kill someone. And in that stone, someone like our new psychic archaeologist can hear *vibrations* . . ." He sneered the word, adding, "And it makes me sick. They'll fund a *medium* to investigate stones and statues, but not employ the best bloody photographer in the business!"

For a moment Richard couldn't speak. He watched Goodman, letting the man's words get clear in his head.

"A *psychic* archaeologist?"

"Apparently. It's a part-time position, more of a consultancy, really. It's called ES Past Object Associativity. For ES read Extra Sensory. Do you believe in that sort of crap?"

Richard smiled and sipped his drink. A *psychic*? At the British Museum? It seemed too unreal to be true. And yet, violently stranger things had happened in his own life!

Goodman was puzzled. "What's on your mind? You've gone very solemn."

Feeling the need to change the subject, Richard simply said, "What did you take from a site?"

Goodman stared uncomfortably at the glass in his hand. In a soft, edgy voice he said, "Like you, an arrowhead. Only I didn't get seen doing it."

"Is that all?"

Goodman glanced sharply at the other man. "Yes. Of course. Unless you want to count the mud on my boots at the end of a day." He drained his glass and stood up. "Another drink?"

"Why not. Then you can tell me more about your new vibrator. Psychic vibrator, that is."

The younger man relaxed again, smirking as he eased himself around the silent, eavesdropping Americans. "She's French. Very sharp. She's got the older boys licking the garlic salt from her palms . . ."

"Not you, though . . ."

"Me? Good God, no."

He grinned again and made his way to the bar.

Left alone, Richard felt the full weight of disappointment and panic at not having made it again in an interview descend upon him.

Ten

Michael was sitting on the side of his bed, a battered old book open on his lap, his face propped in his hands as he read the words on the pages and stared at the illustrations of dinosaur skeletons and fossils. His school satchel was open on the floor, spilling its contents of comics, illustrated books, and crayons.

Richard entered the room slowly, hands in his pockets. His son looked up and smiled.

"That's one of Grandad's old books, isn't it? I remember reading it when *I* was a boy."

Michael nodded and closed the red cover to show the faded gold illustration of a Stegosaurus.

"The World in the Past," Richard said, taking the book and turning through the pages. "Where did you get this? I thought we'd given it to jumble."

"Had it in my room for ages."

"I think I'd better get you a more up-to-date book on dinosaurs. These pictures are very old-fashioned. We'll have to go up to London, go to the Natural History Museum. Would you like that?"

Michael's eyes widened and he affirmed his interest vigorously, then took back the book and turned it to the page he'd been reading. Frowning, he said, "But I don't understand what a 'Weald' is."

Sitting next to him, Richard read the passage and explained the nature of the Wealden, the swathe of primordial forest that had covered the Kent and Sussex countryside between the great chalk escarpments of the North and South Downs.

"Weald is just the old name for woodland. It's Anglo-Saxon."

Michael seemed content enough with the explanation.

"Thank you for the present," Richard went on after a moment. He drew the wolf-girl dancer from his pocket, holding it so that it glinted.

Michael stared at the statuette, then looked up at his father. "It was pretty. So I fetched it for you."

"You fetched it?"

"From where it was."

"It's very pretty, Michael. It's made of gold. Did you know that?"

The boy nodded. "It's heavy."

"Very. And very valuable. Will you show me where you found it?"

After a moment, Michael seemed to agree. "In my castle. I fetched it in my castle."

Richard noted the odd word use. He'd *fetched* it *in* his castle. Not found it. Not fetched it *from*.

"Is your castle in the chalk pit? Is that where you make your castle?"

Michael squirmed. He stared studiously at his book, then drew breath and sighed. "My castle's by the *sea*. My *camp* is in the chalk pit."

He's lying, Richard thought. *Or at least, hiding something.*

"Shall we go to your camp and see? There might be another one . . ."

Michael laughed and shook his head, chuckling at some secret thought. "There was only *one*," he said, as if nothing could have been more obvious. But he slipped off the bed and reached for his green anorak jacket.

With Susan leading Carol by the hand, and Richard walking with Michael, they trooped out of the house and through the cornfield. In the evening sun it was rich and peaceful, stirred by breezes that curled up from the marsh, bringing faint, fresh salt smells from the distant skim of the sea. On the other side of the field, they walked slowly through the woodland that rimmed the edge of the quarry, above the sheer, deep chalk walls. They entered the long-disused pit through the narrow entrance to the east, which faced across the distant marshes. There was a safety barrier here, and a danger sign almost lost in the tangle of small trees and bushes, but nothing that could keep out a determined child. Richard saw the signs of Michael's access, a pathway, well trodden down, leading deeply into the quarry's heart.

Michael led them through the quarry, round a beaten track at the base of the sheer, white cliff, where the signs of the vanished machines that had hewn the chalk could still be discerned. This place had not been a favorite childhood haunt of Richard's, but he had come fossil-hunting here on many an occasion with his two cousins, and somewhere in the attic of Eastwell House he still had his collection of ammonites, sea urchins, bivalves and cones, flint shards, and the round and strange chunks of iron called marcasite, which he still romanced were the remains of alien machines. He had shown the fossils to Michael years ago, taking his up to the attic among the stored books and toys of two generations of Whitlocks, but the boy had not seemed very interested. To his uncertain knowledge, Michael still did not collect fossils in the same obsessive and hobbyist way.

The boy had been forbidden to play in the pit, but Richard was aware that he often came here. Chalk marks on clothes and bodies are hard to remove.

Below the steepest part of the cliff was the earthspill that he had tipped here, seven years past, and excavated later, reconstructing the likely shape of the shrine with the help of Jack Goodman. But Michael avoided this rise of ground and led them on to a bushy area of green.

Stooping to enter the space within this dense undergrowth, Richard emerged into Michael's castle.

It was a kid's camp like any other. There were comic books, remains of toys, chocolate wrappers, a bit of old carpet that he used to press down on the hard ground, two wooden crates, white driftwood and beach pebbles; and chunks of chalk positioned around the clearing like a defensive circle.

"Is this the castle?"

Michael nodded. He seemed nervous. He glanced around, then folded his arms across his chest.

Susan ducked through the thorny undergrowth with Carol following her apprehensively.

Richard stooped and brushed at the soil on the ground. He found a piece of intensely colored green marble, broken sharply, a triangular fragment that was surprisingly heavy.

He could also smell something pungent, chemical, like incense.

Susan had picked up the aroma too, fleetingly. "Incense sticks?"

They looked at Michael. "Have you been burning joss stick here?"

He didn't know what a joss stick was.

"Have you been playing with matches? And church incense?"

He shook his head.

"Where did you find the figure?"

Michael hesitated, then pointed ahead of him, into the bushes. "Over there."

Richard led him through the underbrush and into the clearer chalk-spill beyond. Looking around him he said, "Where? Where exactly?"

Michael seemed confused. He turned back the way they had come and said, hesitantly, "Over there."

"Can you show me *where* over there?"

But Michael shook his head. "I just saw it. It was pretty. So I reached for it and fetched it."

Richard dropped to a crouch, getting the boy's attention. "Show me where you were standing when you 'fetched' it. Will you?"

And again they trekked back through the undergrowth, back to the castle, to the first place where Michael had been standing; and again he pointed to the bushes. "I fetched it from there."

Susan whispered, "There's a scatter of sand around. All over the place. Look—in the grass."

Richard had already noticed the sand spread around, like a layer of fine dust. For the moment he was trying to understand Michael's defensive and awkward language.

"Show me *how* you fetched it."

"I can't."

"Why not? Can't you try? Just for me?"

Michael's face was suddenly anguished. He gave every impression of being in a turmoil of indecision. He looked desperately at the bushes, then up at his father. "Chalk Boy isn't here," he said in a hushed, frightened whisper.

"Chalk Boy? Who's he?"

"He's my friend. He plays with me. I have two friends who play with me. Chalk Boy showed me the pretty thing and said did I want it? I said yes, so he gave it to me. I had to fetch it, though."

Richard exchanged a questioning look with Susan. Chalk Boy? Susan shrugged. Michael often played with the younger of Jenny and Geoff Hanson's two children, Tony, and with Bobby Gould, a slightly older lad who lived five houses away and who made adventure films with his friends, using his parents' video camera. Was Bobby's nickname among his friends Chalk Boy?

"Do you mean Bobby Gould?" Richard asked. Michael stared at him, not understanding. "Is Bobby who you mean by Chalk Boy?"

A little shake of the head. A lip nervously bitten. A small body suddenly shaking. "Chalk Boy's just my friend. He lives here. He's my friend. He has a dog that catches birds and squirrels. I like him. We play together a lot."

"Where does he live, Michael? Where exactly?"

Michael shrugged. "Don't know. He lives at the end of a tunnel, next to the sea. I can hear the sea all the time when we're playing. The waves are very loud. There's lots of shadows in the sea, and sometimes they make noises . . ."

"What sort of noises?"

"Like roaring. And crying out."

Susan was smiling. She had picked Carol up and was keeping the slightly restless child quiet by swaying from side to side. "He's talking about an imaginary playmate. Didn't you ever have an invisible friend? I used to play with Marianne Faithfull when I was nine or ten. We sang together, with the Stones of course, went on adventures together, to dark castles and underground cities, even to Mars. For a while she was my best friend. And she still knows nothing about it."

"You had an imaginary friend when you were ten?"

"Shortage of the real thing, dear."

But Richard had no time for Susan's reminiscences. He was intrigued by what Michael had said. "Tell me about the dog? Is he a big dog?"

"Yes."

"Is he like an Alsatian? Like Bonny?" Their next-door neighbor's dog.

"Yes. But bigger."

"What color is he?"

"Gray and brown."

"Are you sure of that?"

"Yes. Gray and brown."

Certainly not Bonny, then.

"What color are his ears?"

"Gray. With white bits."

"When you scratch him behind the ears, how high is he on you? Where does he come up to?"

Michael demonstrated. The dog was huge, far bigger than any Alsatian that Richard knew. Michael went on unprompted: "He smells, but he's nice. He catches birds and squirrels. He has a big collar and Chalk Boy runs with him across the downs and through the woods. They really like each other."

Smiling, Richard said, "But he doesn't really exist, does he? You're just inventing him . . ."

"Not inventing him," Michael said gloomily.

"No. Of course you're not." On impulse, Richard hugged his son, uncomfortable with the way he had to summon the affectionate gesture, and conscious of the boy's stiff, uncertain reaction.

They left the quarry.

As the children ran ahead, back through the corn-field, Susan said, "That's one big dog he plays with."

"Like a hunting hound. Like a dog I've seen be-fore." Richard stopped in the middle of the field. "Do you know which dog I'm talking about?"

"The dog from the earthfall," Susan said softly. She was frowning, clearly disturbed by the thought.

"I made drawings of the dog-shrine—and the dog it-self. Do you remember? I wonder if Michael ever looked at those pictures."

"I don't know. What are you saying? That he's fantasizing about a dog in a drawing you made?"

"It's possible. Either that or the hound's spirit is back among the remains of its last resting place."

Shivering, Susan said, "I don't want to think about it." Then with a pointed glance, she added, "But it's nice to see you take a bit of interest in the boy for a change . . ."

"Don't start on me now. Not now. Please?"

"Your interest in him has cheered him up. He's almost a changed lad."

"It's *him* who usually doesn't talk to *me*."

Susan's laugh was a cutting declaration of her disbe-lief that he could lie so blatantly. "Talking is a two-way process, Rick. The boy misses you!"

She walked on quickly. Richard ambled after her, hands in pockets, wolf-girl in right hand, comforting, one question in his head, nagging.

The gruesome remains of the dog had come from the earth-mass which had tried to kill Michael. That earth-mass had come from *somewhere,* and Michael had been its focus. It had been a part of a haunting that seemed, now, to have disappeared.

The dog had been there, though. Could Michael, as an infant, have been aware of the dead hound?

And even if *that* was true . . .

Who was Chalk Boy?

Eleven

Chalk Boy usually played with him in the pit, but he was in the room now, darting through the darkness and laughing.

Michael laughed too, but the sound was nervous. He felt slightly scared as he sat up toward the top of his bed, and drew his feet below him. He folded his arms and leaned forward, shivering slightly despite his pajamas. The chalk-painted shape danced and ran about the shelves.

"Look at that. Oh, look at that!"

Excited at finding picture books. Flipping the pages rapidly, then stopping in the darkness and gasping with sheer delight. "Oh, look at this. Look at this."

Michael could see the chalk streaks, like slices of moonlight. Through the eerie white, though, the darkness of Chalk Boy was that same scary black, the depthlessness, the void where the boy should have been. It was something that Michael didn't like. He didn't like looking into that emptiness. It made him dizzy. Chalk Boy had no eyes, not that Michael had ever seen. He was just a shadow shape. He watched from the beach where he lived, staring from the tunnel, then playing, and calling for his dog.

He shouldn't be in the bedroom. He should be in the castle by the sea, at the end of the tunnel.

Again, Michael laughed nervously, and watched as Chalk Boy rifled through the drawers of his clothes chest, finding fossils. "Look at this! Oh, look at this!"

Fossils, books, photographs, toys, dolls, colorful

shirts, Chalk Boy found them, marveled at them, discarded them, moving fleetly around the room, sometimes coming close to Michael, stopping, like an elf, like a creature from the sea, coming close, then pausing to look. The stink of sea was strong. Salt stink, seaweedy.

"Look at this! Look at this!" Chalk Boy thrilled. He had found a pile of comics, turning through the pages so fast that they seemed a blur.

Michael eased himself off the bed and went to the door, opening it and peering out into the darkness of the landing. Chalk Boy hovered behind him.

"Look at that! Oh, look at *that*!" Chalk Boy had found the small, red-clay doll that his mother had given him for his second birthday. Hungarian magic, she had said, and protection against night spirits.

"Sssh!" Michael closed the door again, turned and raised a finger to his lips. It was three in the morning according to the clock on the landing. Chalk Boy peered into the house, but then darted back into the room, rifling pages, tossing toys, gasping with his strange pleasure.

The door of his room opened suddenly and the light went on. Michael jumped, coming quickly awake, shocked as he stood in the middle of the chaos in his room staring up at his father. He was still holding a pair of shoes, about to toss them. In a disorienting blur he realized he had only been dreaming of Chalk Boy.

"What on earth are you doing? What's all this yelling?"

Parental eyes surveyed the untidiness. Sleepy gaze focused angrily. "You woke us up."

"It wasn't me."

Michael looked around. There was no sign of Chalk Boy. Comics and books were strewn around, clothes were draped over shelves and the desk, even the lamp by the bed.

"Go to bed, Michael!"

The words were angry. His father watched him until he was below the covers, then turned off the light, adding, "I'll expect this mess to be straightened before you come down to breakfast. Do you understand?"

"Yes," Michael said, confused.

"And no more noise!"

"Chalk Boy?" Michael hissed when he was alone again, in silence. But the room had nothing but shadows now.

The shadows were filled with voices, old voices from another time. They stalked around him, like ghosts, like the apparition of Chalk Boy, come to taunt him, come from tearful years gone by. Michael buried his head below the pillow.

The sounds were muffled in his imagination and after a while he started to listen again, straining to hear them, to remember them, lying there, now staring at the ceiling, aware of the heavy pendulum movement of the clock on the landing, recalling the raised voice, and the crying, from the sitting room below.

He closed his eyes and squeezed back tears. But the voice shadows wouldn't go away, brought on by that flash of anger in his father's face just a few moments ago, that look that had been such a terror to him for so long, from so long ago . . .

"We made a mistake. We have to face it, Sue, we made a big mistake."

"You've been drinking. You're disgusting!"

"Keep your voice down. We don't want the whole world to know."

"We did *not* make a mistake. If you just showed more interest in him. If you just behaved like his father instead of brooding all the time that he doesn't have your *genes* . . ."

"I can't relate to him. Don't you understand that? We're like chalk and cheese. There's nothing there. Nothing in there. Do you understand me? It's a void. His head's a void. Our relationship is a void!"

"Keep your voice *down*. The poor little devil is only upstairs. He'll hear."

"We were so hasty. If we'd just waited, Carol would have come anyway . . . I'm sure of it . . ."

"Sometimes I hate you."

"I know you do. Sometimes I hate myself. But for Christ's sake, what pleasure is there in him? One child, we said. That's all we wanted. One child. A natural child—"

"And it didn't happen. And Michael is part of us now."

"But he's *not*. Maybe he is to you. But to me he's a stranger! He's cold. I can't get close to him. It's the ghost in him, Sue. I'm sure it is. It disturbs me."

"Nothing's happened for ages. The haunting's gone."

"He haunts *me*. He frightens me."

"He just wants affection! You don't bloody well try."

"I *do* try. But he's empty. He's always watching. It was a mistake."

"We can't give him back, Richard."

"Don't patronize me. I know we can't. But what am I to do? He's a stranger in my house. Carol is warm. I can feel her warmth even though she's only little. She giggles, Sue. She sees me and laughs."

"Surprise, surprise."

"You know what I mean. We *feel* for each other . . ."

"What a bastard you are . . ."

"I can't help it. It's like living with a ghost. I never felt right about adopting—"

"You were such a bloody coward. Such a lying coward. If you'd just once expressed your doubts we could have thought about it, perhaps thought it through more clearly . . ."

"You wanted it too much. I didn't know how to say what I felt without causing you pain."

"Terrific."

"I'm sorry."

"Me too. But you have to live with our decision, Richard. You can't just cut the boy out. You have to try. Hard. Harder. Endlessly. He's not a computer game! You can't save the score and turn off the machine in the evening, then come back to it as if nothing had changed."

* * *

Pretty. Pretty . . .

He stared at the ceiling. There was a glimmer in his mind's eye, something gleaming, something pretty. But it slipped away again, and shadows flexed and shifted in the room, the past still urgent to be remembered—shadows: his father's shape looming past him as he sat and drew, years ago . . .

A fine summer's day. The air was still and heavy with the scent of grass. There had been visitors, and from the kitchen came the sound of washing up, glasses clinking, laughter from his parents.

Michael sat at his table below the apple tree, drawing Castle Limbo and the wide beach. Carol was toddling down the lawn toward her tricycle. Michael raised his face and watched her, then glanced down as his father left the kitchen, ran toward the toddling child and swung her high, pretending to toss her, but not quite letting go.

Carol giggled. The two of them walked down to the hedge maze and vanished for a while.

Michael drew.

He was startled by the sudden shadow over his shoulder. He had been so absorbed in the drawing of the castle that he hadn't heard his father come up behind him. He and Carol stood there, dark against the bright sky. Michael felt nervous. He was aware that his drawing was being scrutinized critically.

Carol watched him, one hand tangled in her father's long hair. She wanted to be put down and her father let her go. The man walked away, a broad shape, clad in jeans and a dark shirt. Michael heard him say, "More bloody spirals. Doesn't he ever draw anything else?"

"It's my castle," he whispered.

He drew himself into the picture, a small, yellow-haired figure, and placed his shadow perfectly considering the position of the bright sun at the top corner of the drawing. He drew his mother, standing at the edge of the garden, just outside the zones of his castle. He drew Carol and gave her a big smile, because he always wanted Carol to smile when she felt sad. Then, after a moment's hesitation, he drew his father. He drew a huge open mouth with teeth around the figure of the man.

After a while, after staring at the page for a few minutes, he found a darker crayon.

And with a quick, angry smile, he closed the monster's mouth.

Pretty?

He reached for it, but it slipped away. This was the wrong place. He needed Chalk Boy, he needed the sea. He needed to be able to reach through the tunnel, to fetch the pretty glimmering things that sometimes sparkled in the castle, by the sea shore, by the great chalk sea.

Michael stood by his bedroom window and stared out through the summer night, at the dark woods that huddled round the quarry.

Beyond them, a strange light, an eerie tinge of blue in the darkness, was the ocean, the Channel. It was not the same sea, not the sea that bordered Castle Limbo, but it was a place he could visit, and he hungered for that cold water now, for the pebbles that jarred and jabbed at naked feet, for the rush and swirl, the suck and flow of the ice-cold sea, dragging down into the lost depths of the old land bridge between England and the Continent.

He had read about it all, how below the sea were great mountains of chalk, some of them nearly reaching the surface of the ocean. Millions of years had eroded the chalk hills into these spires and fingers of chalk, part of the downlands. And when land had filled between them, people had walked there, and lived there.

Their bones, their weapons, their spirits still swam in the shallow depths, in the chalk depths.

But it was not the same sea. Not the sea of monsters. Not the sea of screams and cries. Not the sea of shadows that he could touch and smell whenever Chalk Boy came near to him . . .

It was still too dark to leave the house, but he felt

such longing to be in the pit, to smell that ancient ocean.

He wrapped up in his top blanket, curled up on the window sill, staring out through the darkness and over the trees, to the blue glow of the near-dawn.

He sighed.

He listened to the silence in the house.

Twelve

While Susan took Michael to school, Richard went out to the chalk quarry, spade and fork carried over his shoulder. He found the boy's camp, did a superficial survey of the area where he claimed to have found the statuette, then cleared the shrubs and the thin layer of soil. He paid particular attention to the area among and below the tangled, shallow roots of trees.

After an hour he had found nothing. No hoard, no stash, no evidence at all that the gold statuette was part of a concealed haul of stolen good.

So who *was* Chalk Boy? An imaginary playmate? Then he certainly hadn't given Michael anything as tangible as fifteen ounces of very high-quality gold, shaped so exquisitely.

A brief visit to their neighbors, the Goulds, had established that Bobby was at a Cubs meeting during the time that Michael claimed to have been playing with Chalk Boy. And a phone call to Jenny Hanson confirmed the obvious: that her two sons had not been over at Ruckinghurst that afternoon either.

It was pretty. So I fetched it for you . . .

Richard kicked around the camp once more, then walked back to the earthfall, staring down at the low mound. No, it was impossible that he had missed such an object during his sift through. He just *wouldn't* have missed anything so bright, so starkly different to the primitive contents of the shrine.

Later, he called Jack Goodman at the British Museum, arranged a meeting then drove up to London.

Over coffee in his small office, Goodman examined the statuette, making appreciative sounds. "It's a lovely thing. A lovely copy of an Egyptian statuette. Although—I'm almost inclined to think that it's *not* a copy. It's just that is has such a *new* feel . . ." Goodman turned the figure again. Light glanced off the solemn wolf-face of the ecstatic dancer.

"But a copy of what, I wonder?" Richard said. "It's familiar, but I can't place it."

On impulse Goodman rose from his desk and took down four catalog volumes from his shelves. It took him half an hour of turning the pages, thinking, scratching his head, swearing, flipping forward and back through the huge books, but eventually he found what he was after.

"Let's go and see . . ."

Behind the scenes in the museum the rooms were lined with cupboards, drawers and shelves of artefacts, objects and implements not on display. A curator led them to a drawer of gold from the tomb of a minor Egyptian king of the Fourth Dynasty. The goldwork was inferior for the most part, and had been damaged when stones from the tomb's ceiling had fallen at some time soon after the tomb had been sealed. As such the pieces were not displayed.

Among them, though, was a bronze and gold inlaid dancing figure, a human male wearing the mask of a wolf. It was only half the size of the statuette from the chalk pit, and the dancing position was different. But there was something so similar about the two pieces that it caught Richard's breath.

"You say the girl dancer is a copy," he said to Goodman, while the curator listened, "but could it be real? Could it have been stolen from a collection? Even from the museum?"

The curator examined the wolf-girl carefully, shaking his head. "Not from this museum. It's familiar, of course, but I have no knowledge of something this beautiful having been stolen. Besides, it's too new. I agree with Dr. Goodman, it's a superb copy. Where did you say you obtained it?"

"My son says he found it. But if that's true, he certainly found it on the surface of the ground. There's no sign of his digging down to a hoard. I don't know if it's *treasure-trove* or not. So before I go through the normal procedures I want to try and find out exactly what it is."

"I tell you one thing," Goodman said with a smile. "It's worth a few bob. The gold alone, if it's as high quality as it looks, must be worth several thousand."

"It would be a shame to melt such a lovely thing," the curator murmured.

Richard took back the statuette. "I don't intend to. I just need to know where it came from and how it got into my son's possession. You're sure you don't recognize it as stolen goods?"

"Positive. I'd ask at Sotheby's though. They have a department that specializes in detecting the movement of stolen art."

"I'm going there next."

Sotheby's didn't recognize the dancer. The young woman who examined the piece was intrigued and entranced by the statuette, however, and offered to sell it on Whitlock's behalf, just as soon as he could establish his credentials of ownership.

"What would you say it was worth?"

She stared at the wolf-girl for a long time, then looked up abruptly and smiled broadly. "More than the value of its weight in gold," she said. "Beyond that, I have no idea. It's curiously ..." She turned the piece over, shaking her head. "It's curiously old, yet it's new ... if it's a copy, it's so intricate, even to the signature of the craftsman who made it ..."

"What signature?" Richard was surprised. She indicated with the nail of her index finger the tiny head of a bird, marked on the back of the wolf-head. Richard had thought that to be a part of the design.

The woman said, "I have such a strange feeling about this piece. I can't shake it off. It *must* be recent, I suppose. But it has an odd age about it. Where did you say your family acquired it?"

"It was a gift. Out of the blue. Until I'm certain about its origins I'd rather not go into more detail at the moment."

She looked slightly irked. "I can't sell it unless you have established your ownership, and its pedigree, however poor."

"I'm not going to sell it. Not yet. But I do appreciate your time and help."

"My pleasure."

He was held up by traffic on his return to Kent: a Dutch juggernaut had jack-knifed on the narrow section of the A20 close to Charing. A five-mile crawl, taking two and a half hours, meant that he arrived back at Eastwell House after seven.

Susan had made supper, fresh fish and new potatoes. Michael sat at the end of the table, his face a sparkling mask of pleasure and excitement. Weary from the car, frustrated, Richard poured himself a large scotch and listened to his daughter for a few minutes as she conversed about things that didn't *quite* make sense to his adult hearing, but which were presumably important to her. He agreed, supported, questioned, laughed, and cuddled.

Michael watched him, and he smiled at the boy, talking to him through Carol's oddly disorientating conversation.

He talked about traffic. About the museum.

Michael watched him through eyes that blazed, those green eyes, the sparkling eyes of a boy who had a secret to tell.

"Supper's up," Susan announced, and plates of fish were placed upon the table.

Richard sat down and reached for the water jug.

"I have a few things to tell everybody here," he said, and placed the wolf-girl statuette upon the table.

Carol giggled. Michael looked coy. Susan passed the bowl of greens down to her husband.

"Before you tell us what *you've* found out, Michael has a little present for you," she announced in a quiet, steady voice.

Carol said, "Mikey's found something else . . ."

There was silence at the table. Then Michael reached into his pocket and stretched out his hand to his father. "Pretty . . ."

Green eyes watched fervently, hopefully.

Fingers opened.

Richard took the fragment of silver brooch with its massive, embedded emerald and raised it to the light.

"It's for you, Daddy," the boy said. "I fetched it for you."

Susan watched him solemnly. Carol had succeeded in spreading most of her mashed white fish over her face and napkin. She ate and chattered to herself, unaware of the tension behind the silence in the room.

Good God! This must be worth a fortune!

"Thank you," Richard said, trying to control his voice. "It's beautiful. Did Chalk Boy give this to you?"

"He showed me where it was," Michael said, edgily.

"Will you say thank you to him?"

"Yes."

He placed the fragment of jewelry on the table, took a deep breath and looked up to meet Susan's gaze. He smiled and shook his head. She allowed her face to register a restrained delight, then began to eat.

Michael said, "Will you tell me a story?"

Coming back to his senses, Richard said. "A story? Yes. Yes of course. Which story would you like me to tell you?"

"The Fisher King. Will you tell me about the Fisher King?"

Richard stared at the boy, then glanced in panic at Susan, who was watching him with an expression of controlled hilarity. His eyes said it all: I don't know a damn *thing* about the Fisher King. But he said brazenly, "The Fisher King. Old King Fish himself. OK. You're on. The Fisher King. In all his glory. But let's eat supper first, shall we?"

Michael bent down to his plate, delight on his face; he began to fork the fish and potatoes into his mouth with one hand. The other, his left, was clenched into a fist, and Richard noticed that as the boy ate, so the fist beat out a quiet but regular rhythm on the table top.

The camp had been disturbed. Even by the fading light, Richard could see how the screen of blackthorn and elder had been struck by a violent force; branches were broken, cut or cracked. There was a great quantity of crude plaster and shards of stone on the white chalk, and bits and pieces of mahogany (he guessed), a dark wood, a heavy wood, stained, varnished and polished, cracked and crushed now, as if someone had deliberately smashed a piece of furniture.

His impression, as he collected together these artifacts at the base of the chalk wall, was that he was looking at the remains of a dressing-table.

Perhaps the jeweled brooch had been in a drawer in that table?

Chalk Boy's "fetching" was obviously very violent.

Michael bounded up the stairs, tripping on the feet of his pajamas, which were slightly too long. He thundered across the landing, burst into his room and leapt on to the bed, instantly doing a headstand with his feet up against the wall.

In this unlikely posture he greeted his father, who came calmly into the room, switched on the bedside lamp, and sat down on the mattress.

Richard watched the boy, trying not to think of the thousands of questions he longed to ask his son. The boy watched Richard from his bat-like position, then suddenly collapsed down into a heap, sitting up and grinning.

"Headstand," Michael announced.

"I noticed. Are you ready for a story?"

"Fisher King! Fisher King!" Michael chanted.

"I've got a special story for you. One I've made up myself . . ."

Michael subsided, leaning back against the pillow, his freckled face lowering in looks until it registered positive gloom. But he didn't speak. He watched his father through eyes that were suddenly anguished and sad.

Richard said, "Don't you want to hear the special story I've made up for you?"

The "yes" in the boy's voice was so quiet as to be almost inaudible. Michael's gaze shifted to the window. Disappointment clouded him.

"On the other hand," Richard said quietly, glancing at Susan who had appeared in the doorway, "I could always tell you my special story tomorrow, when I get back from work. And tonight . . ."

"Fisher King! Fisher King!" Michael said brightly, and sat upright again.

"Fisher King it is. Shall we get Carol to come and sing in the—"

"NO!"

He had been about to say: to come and sing in the chorus. In the story of the Fisher King—he had just researched it in half an hour flat, finding a children's version that explained a lot—there was a song that could be sung, with a chorus that celebrated the land coming back to life after the Holy Grail had been discovered.

Shocked by the screaming negation from his son, Richard took a moment to recover the initiative. Carol was already in bed, but still awake, the evening having been one of excitement and general good humor. Richard had not expected this violent rejection of the girl, although it was clear to him, instantly in retrospect, that he should have expected such a denial.

Michael wanted his father all to himself, now. It was important.

Richard was shaking slightly. Susan withdrew from the bedroom door, because Carol was calling for attention. Michael's shout had penetrated the house.

"We'll sing the song together, shall we? Just you and me."

"Yes! Just you and me!"

He began the story.

"A long time ago, in a land not so very far away, a Great King lived in a Great Castle . . ."

"The Fisher King," Michael screeched delightedly. "The Fisher King!"

"He had another name, of course."

"What was it? What was his name? What was his name . . .?"

"You'll have to guess his name. Because his story is a tragic and sad one to begin with. Because in all his land there wasn't one field, or one valley that was fertile. He lived in the blighted land—"

"Waiting for the *Grail!*"

"Don't jump ahead of me, young man. If you want the story, wait for the story . . ."

Michael slipped down below his blanket, eyes glowing, face stretched wide with excitement as he listened to his father's careful, slow telling of the story.

Every so often he whispered into the blanket: "When the Grail came everything was all right . . . when the Grail came. . . ."

". . . and one of the fine Knights who came to the castle of the Fisher King was a bold and valiant Knight indeed . . . and do you know what his name was? His name was the same as yours. Sir Michael! He was one of Arthur's favorites. One day King Arthur said to Sir Michael, 'Of all the Knights in my Kingdom, you, Sir, are the bravest. You have the fine ginger hair of the Knights of Old. There are secret messages in the freckles that pepper your handsome features. You are swift on horseback, and a master of the joust. Truly, sirrah, there is no finer Warrior Knight in my Kingdom. And it is to you, Sir Michael, that I entrust the quest to find the castle of the Fisher King. You will find the land barren, a wasteland, empty, mournful, filled with crying, wailing souls, and great empty bogs, and sucking pits, and forests with gray leaves instead of green. There are people there who never laugh, never speak, never cry. . . .'"

I know . . .

" 'And only you can find the true path to the castle doors, young Sir Michael.' "

He saw his father and his mother, and they were ghosts . . .

"So brave Sir Michael—famous for keeping his room tidy—rode on horseback into the barren land of the Fisher King, and at last he came to a great earthworks, the same earthworks that we now call Hawkinge Wood . . . and he crept up those earthen walls and looked over to see the land of the Fisher King beyond—and what he saw there, he would never forget . . ."

No. He won't. He won't. He'll never forget . . .

He had watched from the top of the rise, face down in the leaf mold, fingers digging into the soft turf. The woodland was alive with birds. The breeze, heralding the approach of rain and colder weather, was already causing a sombre, shadowy shifting of light and movement in this favorite picnic place.

Carol was being cradled and cuddled, down there by the picnic fire, down there by the tablecloth, and the wicker hamper, and the cool-box with its sparkling wine.

He watched them as they fussed and loved. He could hear their voices, the songs, the laughter, the hopes and fears for their daughter's future.

What exactly *was* a hole in the heart? They seemed to worry. They seemed to reassure each other.

He heard mention of his grandparents' names. *Gwen* and *Doug.* Poor Doug, his father said. But it had been quick. It had been sudden. He had not been in pain. What had been sudden?

His death, of course. Even as he watched the picnic party from his hiding place of leaf and turf, he knew that they were talking about the death of his grandfather.

Poor old Doug. Poor old horse.

Carol Carol Carol.

How they fussed. How they pampered.

(Where's Michael?)

I'm here. I'm here. Poor old Michael. Poor old horse. I'm here. Call me down to you . . .

(He's playing. He's fine. Leave him alone. If he wants to come and eat he'll come and eat. Sulky little bastard.

(Don't say that. He's not taking it well. He's jealous of Carol, can't you see that? He's having adjustment problems and we need to be sensitive to his feelings.

(Sensitive to his feelings! *What* feelings? He's his mother's son . . .

(We don't know anything about his mother!

(If he wants to be part of us he'll be part of us. If he wants to play silly buggers in the woods that's fine by me. *This* little lady though . . .

(This little lady is wonderful. But Michael's a sensitive child. We *must* pay more attention to him.

(I don't like him, Sue. He gives me the creeps. I don't like him.

(He's your son. He's your adopted son . . . Make an effort, for God's sake . . .

(He gives me the creeps. There's something not right about him. All that shit with the earth. He's haunted, Sue. And that frightens me. I keep wondering . . . I keep wondering—

(What?

(I keep wondering what will happen next.

(Nothing's happened for a long time. It's all passed. He frightens me too, Rick. He gives me the creeps too. Sometimes I can't bear to have him in the same room as me, not alone. That's why it's so good to have Carol. But we have to *try*!

(Where is he now? Keep your voice down. He might be able to hear . . .)

YESYESYESYESYESYES.

I *can* hear!

I *am* here!

Here I *am*!

". . . and so the brave Knight knelt before the pale and ageing King.

" 'Good King, there is only one way for you to save the Kingdom. I must quest far and abroad, I must fight great monsters, and evil Black Knights, and find the

Grail, and bring that Grail to you. And how I do these things, what dangers, hardships, maidens and adventures I shall encounter . . . these stories are for another night, and another tale-telling, because it's nine o'clock, and young Ginger-Haired Knights should be asleep by now.' "

He lay in the darkness, his heart beating fast, more content, now, than he could remember feeling in his life, happier than he had known for years. His father's sudden affection embraced him like a warm and welcome hug. His mind was filled with the story, with the sound of his father's words, the images from the voice that had spoken so softly to him, with such humor and with such affection. It made him chuckle. The laugh came from nowhere he could identify. He just felt like chuckling, staring out through the window to the glow of moonlight on the scudding clouds.

The bad images scattered. The raised, harsh voices faded. Memory shifted and stirred, slipping away into darker regions, and instead he felt the warm glow of sun, the smells of a picnic, and an odd and eerie memory of his mother, bending toward him, making sounds. He dreamed that she was reaching to pick him up. Her words:

Can you hear me, Michael? It's time to go home . . .

He *did* feel at home, now. It was such an *exhilarating* feeling. Yes. He truly felt at home.

Unable to sleep, he climbed out of bed and ran to the window, staring toward the pit where Chalk Boy was resting. Michael wished Chalk Boy could leave the pit, could *really* come and play with him in the bedroom. He had only been dreaming about him the other night, and in his dream he had run around and disturbed things. But Chalk Boy was bound by the ancient sea, trapped by it, or so it seemed. Michael drew tunnels to let him through, but he never came further than the exit. Perhaps he was afraid to leave the rush and swirl of the ocean, and the shifting, scorching sands of the wild shore where he lived, so close to the great creatures whose cries filled the night, and whose movement through the chalk sea cast such giant, frightening shadows.

"Chalk Boy ..." Michael whispered to the night, and at once a shadow seemed to wrap itself around him, startling him. He stepped quickly back from the window. Dull moonlight reflected on the dual imprints of his hands against the glass. His head started to spin. Michael realized he was dripping with fever-sweat. His heart was racing, beginning to hurt inside his chest. He bounded to the bed and buried his face in the pillow, rubbing his skin to dry it. Turning on to his back he lay gasping, feeling the fever-heat surge and flow through his body, but then ebb away, like a wolf slinking slowly back to its woodland cover.

Sitting up in bed he experienced a transient dizziness, but whatever it was, whatever had suddenly surged into him, almost possessing him, had gone. He found his tiny torch and switched it on, using it to locate paper and crayons on his bedroom table.

He drew a circle within a circle, then began to spiral the inner circle tightly, to draw the tunnel close.

"Chalk Boy ...?"

But if Chalk Boy *had* been close to him, he had gone now, and this tunnel was merely a swirl of black crayon, without power. It didn't touch the sea. There was none of the usual sound of waves. There was no heat and stench of seaweed.

The passing shock of a few moments ago had not overly disturbed Michael. He was still too high on the pleasures of the story, and the look of comfort and contentment in his father's ringed and ravaged eyes.

He had looked so tired, like that comedian on the TV, whose face puffed and reddened while he made his jokes. His father looked so crinkled, these days, and he often smelled of sweat and the sharp odor of whisky. But this evening, all of that had softened. His breath had been sweet. His eyes had sparkled, like the golden wolf-girl. The ghost had gone, and the harshness with it.

Something in Michael had known all along that it would just be a matter of time.

He had dreamed hard about it for so many years, determined to make the dream come true, determined to stop his father's distress and anger. And at last he had succeeded.

It gave him a good feeling, and he snuggled down again below the blankets and closed his eyes.

Deeper in the house, in her own room, Carol woke and started to cry; the door of his parents' bedroom opened and there was the sound of someone moving across the landing. A second door opened and closed, and Carol's wailing faded away.

And with it, Michael's consciousness as he slipped into a dream filled with shadows, sea and the thunder of waves.

Thirteen

The day after his eighth birthday, Michael woke suddenly, aware of Chalk Boy's call. It was just before dawn.

There was something new in the pit ... something for him to fetch!

He stumbled through the darkness at the edge of the quarry, entering the gate, feeling for the familiar markers of the pathway that wound inward to the place where he could see into Limbo.

Everything seemed the same, the undergrowth, the bushes, the stones on the path.

But something was wrong!

He ran, then hesitated, crouching between the scrubby trees and thorns. He fumbled for the shaped chalk blocks, the cold iron fragments, the cleverly positioned knots of rag with their twiggy limbs and painted features, the guiding spirits that he had positioned at each invisible gate through each invisible wall of Castle Limbo.

They were all intact. They all allowed him to pass through. He wound his way through the streets of the castle, watching dawn light spread on the high wall of chalk, on the sinister arms of the black trees that surmounted the wall. He pushed through the spiky gorse and brushwood that filled the heart of the pit and approached the place where the tunnel opened.

Here, he stooped and marked out patterns on the dirt-encrusted chalk, using his fingers, shaping the tun-

nels, sketching in the shadows blindly, calling for the
sea and for Chalk Boy.

It came quite suddenly, opening in his conscious
dream, startling him . . .

He felt giddy as the passage stretched away from
him, and the surge and rush of sea deafened his senses.
The salty smell overpowered him. He squinted against
the bright yellow light that flooded from the farther
end of the tunnel, illuminating the patterns on the
round wall.

He stopped tentatively forward, looking for the
bright thing, the gleaming focus that would normally
start to form here, but he saw nothing. He edged further into the cold passage through the rock, his feet
slipping. Spray touched his face, icy, sharp, and he
licked the salt from his lips.

There was a child's laughter, somewhere in the intense yellow light ahead of him.

He tried to call, but his voice rasped hoarsely,
through fear, perhaps, or the strange atmosphere.

A shadow passed through the light. It was utterly
black and fleeting in its movement. Michael beckoned
to it, but all he saw was the surging column of water as
a monstrous wave broke on the beach, somewhere
ahead, crashing against the red cliffs.

Then the shadow again, hovering for a moment,
enticing.

Michael looked around him, sensing the presence of
an object, drawing close to it, but he could focus on
nothing.

So he stepped further down the passage, further than
he had ventured before.

Space opened!

He turned and stepped into the smoky room. Light
streamed from a hole in the roof and children
screamed. The pretty thing was before him, hanging
from a wooden beam, and he reached toward it,
reached for the green glitter of jewels . . .

A dog barked savagely.

His fingers seemed to thicken, to become heavy. A
red face peered into his and shouted. Something hard

passed through him, drawing the wind with it, making the gray smoke from the fire curl and gust . . .

And *closed* on the jeweled figure. *Fetched* it!

Dragged it.

He was suddenly flung back on to the chalk, rolling into a prickly patch of gorse, yelling.

Chalk Boy was laughing! Chalk Boy was amused by something . . .

He covered his face as wood and hot ashes rained down upon him in the half-light. The choking smell of smoke filled his lungs for a moment and he coughed violently.

Then everything became calm and he looked for the doll, which had fallen from his fingers and was now crushed against the chalk wall. He picked it up and grimaced as he smelled the rottenness of whatever existed below the ragged fabric of its clothing. The expression on its face was truly horrible. The eyes were not brilliant and exciting like the green jewel he had found a few days before. They were dull and glassy, protruding from the wooden face, hideously ugly. The body felt soft, unpleasantly pliable, and each time he squeezed it the stench was worse.

Disgusted, and feeling sick, he carried it gingerly around the chalk pit to the gorse scrub that covered the castle's dungeon. Forcing his way through the bushes he found the metal grille that covered the outermost of the deep passages, where so much rusting machinery was still to be found. He reached an arm through, holding the doll by its legs. The smell that wafted from the dungeon was overpowering and he thought of some of the other things he had hidden here, some of the horrors he had fetched instead of the pretty gifts he valued.

A flick of his small wrist and the doll was consigned to its cell. It thudded among the rocks, wood and bone of the hidden place.

It *was* all fantasy, then. An imaginary game.

From the quarry's edge, Richard watched his son in the gray light, listened to the boy crashing through the underbrush, calling for his friend, laughing, then inventing sounds and words, making the crashing sounds of waves. In his pajamas, Michael was just visible below. He was clutching something, a rag doll, maybe, or just a thick twig wrapped with a scarf. In the dull light it was hard indeed to distinguish any detail.

Richard had heard the boy leave the house and had followed after a while, intrigued by the game that Michael played, anxious to know whether or not the boy *did* meet a friend in the quarry.

An imaginary friend, then. Mind games. And there was no sign of the boy digging or excavating for hidden valuables. Only the smell of woodsmoke was an intriguing intrusion into the normality of the quarry.

Michael disappeared for a moment and his father stood, walking round the quarry's edge to see what was happening. The loose soil and exposed roots at the rim of the pit made walking dangerous and he had to step away from the edge for a few paces, before returning to look down into the gloom, leaning on the trunk of a young beech.

In that time Michael had begun to leave his fairy castle, weaving in a strange way, making the noise of gates opening, closing them behind him, calling out to the Watch that "All is well. One more to the Dungeon."

All just games. It had taken Richard a year to feel convinced of this.

So where had the gold figure and the emerald brooch come from? And the more recent "gifts"?

Richard followed his son home across the dark field, and into the house. He entered his study and took out the two treasures, staring at them as he thought about wealth, and a wealth of strange talent.

Later in the morning, after Michael had gone to school, he went back to the quarry and searched the chalk cliff for the raggy doll-thing that he had seen his son carrying a few hours before. He found nothing, and eventually left the pit in some discomfort when he started to smell the unmistakable odor of some dead creature, rotting down among the gorse.

* * *

A week later, clutching her painting book and crayons, Carol walked along the driveway to the front door of her house, chattering on to Jenny, who listened with patient good humor to the stream of dialogue, thoughts, half-jokes and observations that characterized the six-year-old's conversation.

"Doesn't look as if there's anyone home," Jenny said, and Carol shivered slightly.

Her voice grim she said, "Mikey's home."

"But not on his own ... surely ..."

"Sometimes," Carol whispered.

Jenny sighed with irritation. "Well, I'll come in and keep you company until Susan comes back. Shall I?"

Carol nodded, but her apprehension didn't pass away.

In the event, the house was silent. Jenny opened the front door and called out "Anyone home? Michael?"

The two of them went into the kitchen. Jenny made coffee while Carol sat at the table, with lemonade, a sandwich and her paints. At one point there seemed to be movement upstairs, but when Jenny went to inspect the bedroom she found it empty.

She felt irritated that neither Susan nor Richard had told her that they would be late. The arrangement was always that any delay should be communicated to the Hansons.

This was not the first time this irritating abuse of an arrangement had occurred.

The back door opened suddenly and Richard Whitlock stepped inside. His hands were chalky and muddy, and he seemed surprised, then embarrassed, to see the woman. "Oh, Christ. I'm sorry ..." checking his watch. "Jesus, I'm really sorry. I was doing some digging ..."

"That's all right." She drained her coffee, patted Carol on the shoulder, then gathered her coat and bag.

"Jenny, I'm really sorry. I just forget when I get into something ..."

"Leave a note, Richard. OK? Then at least I'll know where to find you ..."

"Yeah. I'll do that."

"Bye Carol."

"Bye . . ."

Richard stooped to kiss his daughter, then washed his hands in the sink. "Where's Michael?"

Carol stopped her drawing and looked up at her grubby father. "I don't suppose he's here."

"Of course he's here. Michael?"

His voice boomed through the house, but if Michael was home he wasn't answering. Richard went upstairs and Carol heard the sound of a bath filling. She left the table and walked into the sitting room, but it was too cold and the heating wasn't on. She went across the hall, through the dark study where her father worked, to get to her mother's studio.

There was a doll on the open door, propped up on the handle, and Carol thought it looked strange and beautiful. She ran over to it but didn't touch it. She stepped past it into the small room and glanced round at the shelves of dolls, puppets and masks.

She loved this room, although she was forbidden to touch anything that wasn't on the small table. Most of the dolls had faces, and the faces always seemed to be watching her, and smiling. Some of the dolls had no faces at all, others . . . approximations: large eyes, or dotted features, or grimacing mouths. Carol didn't like those figures as much as the ordinary dolls, but her mother had told her time and again that they were just "primitive art," and that there was nothing to fear from them.

The doll on the door had a golden face.

Carol prodded at it. It had been fixed to the doorhandle with string. Its arms were stretched out and crooked, and the head hung awkwardly to one side, peering downward through the golden skin. The mouth was wide, grinning, and there was a bit of a tongue showing through the lips. It was dressed in red clothes, a shawl, a blouse, a skirt, and had black cloth shoes on its feet. Carol touched the body through the clothes, and knew that it was made of wood. There was something hard and pointed in its middle, and she lifted the skirt to look at the long twig that grew from the apex of the crossed, broken legs ...

Startled as she was by this strange, disturbing feature, the shout of anger from her brother startled her more. Michael burst out from among the cardboard boxes in his father's study, scattering magazines and books as he leapt with fury on to the desk, yelling, "Don't touch it! It's for Mummy. Don't touch it!"

Carol screamed. Her brother's weight hit her full and hard and sent her flying. Michael straddled her and pressed his hands down on her face. The girl struggled, crying, and Michael leapt up again, as if he was on springs. His face was flushed bright red, and was wet, making him gleam. He was dressed in his school clothes, but his hair was awry, disheveled, and he looked like an animal, panting and wild. Again, he knelt over her.

"Don't touch!" he hissed.

"I was only looking ..."

"Present. Pretty. For Mummy. Don't touch it!"

She began to cry. She was only six years old. She was frightened of her brother, but he had never been so angry before. "Don't hurt me," she managed to say through her tears.

"I'll hurt you! I'll hurt you! I'll hurt you!" he screamed.

"Don't hurt me!" she sobbed.

"I won't. I won't. I won't!" he said with fury. "But Chalk Boy will."

"Please don't let Chalk Boy hurt me."

"He'll send you to the sea where the monsters are. You'll drown in the sea and the monsters will snap at you, big teeth, tearing at you. Eating. Eating. The sea is hot. The monsters are fat and black and full of teeth and screaming at night and you'll never be able to come home from there. The monsters will suck you down and Chalk Boy will dance on the sand by the caves and the tunnels."

"Don't hurt me anymore ..." Carol whimpered, and Michael stood up, still straddling her.

"Don't touch the doll," he said quietly.

His father came running into the room, "What on earth . . . ? Michael? What are you doing?"

"Nothing!"

"Carol. What's the matter?"

Richard helped her to her feet, then brushed at her tear-stained face. "Have you two been fighting?"

Michael was grim, watching his father solemnly, his lips clenched. "Have you been fighting? Michael? I asked you a question."

"Pretty, pretty," Michael whispered. Richard shivered at the sound of the words. The girl stood mournfully before him. "Have you been fighting?"

She shook her head. Michael grinned, but when Richard looked at him the smile quickly vanished.

Now Richard saw the doll on the door. "What's this?"

"For Mummy," the boy said, and suddenly his demeanor was changing. "Pretty. For Mummy."

Richard reached for the doll, undid its fastenings and examined it closely. "Good God. That's a gold mask . . . But what the hell is it?"

"For Mummy," the boy was muttering.

"Is it a surprise for her?"

Michael nodded.

"All right. I'll put it back." He looked down at the lad, but his hand rested lightly on Carol's shoulder. The girl was shaking badly. "Where did you get the doll? Where did you find it?"

Michael said, predictably, "I fetched it."

"When?"

"Yesterday. I heard Chalk Boy calling me."

Richard didn't press the point.

"Do you like it? Do you like it?"

Susan leaned forward in her chair and planted a kiss on Michael's forehead. She held the doll and smiled at him. "I *love* it. Is it a present for me?"

He nodded vigorously. "I can fetch another one, if you want. I've seen another one."

Susan was taken aback. Behind Michael, Richard was giving her a thumbs-up sign. She said, "That would be lovely. Who made the clothes? Did you fetch the clothes as well?"

"I made them in school this morning. Miss Hallam"—his teacher—"showed me how to do it."

"Did she see the doll?"

Michael shook his head. "It was a secret. A secret present for you."

"Well . . . thank you again. I shall put it on my special shelf."

After Michael had gone to bed they stripped the rag clothes from the figure and looked closely at the icon itself. It was fashioned from a gnarled piece of oak. The arms of the figure—a distorted version of Christ on the Cross—were bent awkwardly at the elbow into V-shapes, the second and fourth fingers on each hand were raised in the classic witchcraft sign of the "horned one." The legs, crossed and nailed together, had been sharpened below the knee into a long, flat point, a blade. A grimacing, female face peered from each breast. The phallus was erect and pointed, a stubby, sharpened projection from the midriff. The face of the god was a gruesome, one-eyed, flapping-tongued insult to the idea of Christ. Delicately fashioned from thin gold, it was a removable mask. It covered a carving, in the wood, of a rotting head.

Richard had seen nothing like it, yet it felt old, it felt real. This was no child's invention, no joke, no idly whittled piece of wood. This had been *used*.

He managed to track down Jack Goodman at ten in the evening. Over the phone, from his office, he described the cross in great detail. Goodman was turning the pages of a book at the other end, listening intently.

Eventually he said, "Fantastic."

"You've found something?"

"I don't need to. I recognize the description. It's a Mocking Cross."

"A Mocking Cross?" Richard glanced at Susan who folded her arms over her chest at the sound of the name.

Goodman said, "Your boy has found one of the rarest relics from the time of the Vikings in the Mediterranean. Is it a copy?"

"The wood is very solid, very hard, very new. It hasn't been preserved in any way. I can't believe this has lasted a thousand years. It *has* to be a copy. The gold mask might be old, though."

There was a moment's silence. Goodman said, "I *do* know of wood that has stayed strong for a thousand years or more under ordinary conditions. It depends on the circumstances of keeping. I know of only three Mocking Crosses, a pair from Venice, and the 'Witch-Cross' from Istanbul."

Richard relayed this information to Susan, then asked, "A pair? What do you mean, a pair?"

"The Danes made them in pairs, male and female. They fitted together at the groin. They were sacrificial knives used by one particular marauder we think, a man with a particularly inventive imagination. Most of his output, most Mocking Crosses, were destroyed by the monks whenever they were found, especially in the Middle Ages. They seem peculiar to the Mediterranean, and were made in the ninth century, for some forty years or so. The height of the Viking raids along that coast."

"A Mocking Cross," Richard murmured, turning the carving over in his hand.

"The gold mask with its single eye is obvious," Goodman went on, "the metal used to fashion the pagan calf, plus the image of Odin. The fingers are a way of warding off the evil eye, a superstition that was anathema to the Church. The phallus needs no explanation. Does it?" He laughed. "The faces in the breast are an insult because of the inversion implied, the woman in the man. The female figures have pricks instead of nipples, by the way. Whoever designed them was a visionary: Middle Ages symbolism three hundred years ahead of its time."

"And they were killing knives?"

"That's the likeliest explanation. It would have hurt the very *soul* of a Christian to be blood-eagled by such a cross. The blood eagle was their way of cutting—"

"Yes," Richard said quickly. "I know what the blood eagle was, thanks. Though I doubt a wooden knife would have done the deed."

"True enough," Goodman agreed. "Is there any sign of terracotta clay on it?"

"No. Not that I can see. Why?"

"According to what I'm reading now, which is the report of the discovery of the female cross in Istanbul, in 1924 . . . the cross that was stolen—probably soon after it was buried—was, well, exactly that: *buried*. It was in a terracotta coffin, inside a wooden box, hidden in the catacombs and out of harm's way, I suppose. Someone had smashed the boxes to get the cross. The female was still intact. I was just wondering if this was the match."

"As long-shots go, I think you're stretching credibility."

"Yeah. The wood just couldn't have survived the centuries. Still, I'd like to see the piece . . ."

"Come and visit. And thanks, by the way, for the tip on the jeweler's."

"My pleasure."

Susan had dressed the figure again, and placed the little mask over its grotesque skull. "Michael wouldn't forgive us if we sold it, valuable though it might be," she said quietly.

Richard was thinking hard. When he spoke it was abstracted and frustrated: "If only I could *see* Michael fetching these things. If only I knew how he *did* it . . ." He broke the train of thought as Susan's words penetrated. "I'm not intending to sell it . . . Of course he'd be upset."

"You mentioned a jeweler's."

"Ah. That's different." He reached into his briefcase and drew out a check. "I sold the emerald today. Took it to a place that Goodman recommended. Five thousand pounds and no questions asked . . ."

"Five thousand!"

Susan stood and snatched at the check, her face a combination of shock and delight. "It must have been worth three times that," she added more soberly.

"I'm sure it was. But who's worrying? That's the extension we need on your studio."

"Or the new car . . ."

"Or the holiday we've been talking about?"

Susan sat down again, toying with the Mocking Cross, staring at the check. "Are you thinking what I'm thinking? It's not a good thought . . ."

"Another emerald?"

"If we just knew where he *found* them . . ."

Richard said, "He doesn't find them. Remember? Chalk Boy shows him where they are, and he *fetches* them."

"I don't want to think about it," Susan muttered darkly.

As she left the study she placed the check on a bookshelf, glanced back and said, "The extension?"

"Why not . . ."

She laughed and shook her head. "This is like Christmas!"

First light came at five o'clock. Richard dressed quickly and hurried down to the quarry, bleary and disheveled from a restless, thought-filled night. At the place where Michael had talked about Chalk Boy, in the heart of the boy's imaginary castle, he searched carefully around under the fragments of chalk and the late-summer vegetation.

There was still a trace of the sand he had seen before. But now there was a scatter of dull red terracotta pottery, shards and dust mostly, nothing bigger than a thumbnail. And splinters of dark wood, like cedar, an oily wood, fresh and new.

A terracotta coffin! Maybe Goodman's long-shot wasn't so long after all!

He swept up whatever he could, placed the pieces in ᵗa specimen bag, and returned to the house, eager to talk to Michael.

Fourteen

In the late afternoon, his father started to lead the two visitors down the path toward the cornfield. He was talking loudly.

From his room, where he stood biting a fingernail and watching anxiously, Michael could hear the words "quarry" and "castle." His father was telling the people about him. They were all going to the pit to snoop around.

The thought was less disturbing to Michael than it might have been. He smiled to himself, thinking of the high walls of his castle, the hard gates, the winding path. They'd never find their way in, not to the heart of the place, only into the quarry.

One of the new visitors was a severe-looking man, dressed in black leather trousers and jacket. His eyes were hidden behind dark glasses. He wore a thin, trimmed beard and smoked a thin, trimmed cigar. His expression was sour and solemn and he smirked instead of smiling, always looking round, always peering round, glancing at everything in the garden, staring at the house. It was as if he was searching for clues, but clues to what?

Michael could see that his father was uncomfortable, hands in his pockets, shoulders tightly hunched as he walked and talked with his visitors.

The woman, by contrast, was intriguing and pleasant. She had long red hair and her skin was deeply tanned. She wore a cream-colored man's suit and had an unmistakably French accent. She was also very

aware of Michael. Indeed, as she walked she suddenly
turned and looked up at the house, glimpsing Michael
and smiling, waving at him. Although Michael drew
back quickly, he knew that she had seen him. When he
peered back round the window's edge she was still
looking up, her head cocked slightly to one side, a
smile of amusement, slightly teasing, on her lips.

There had been a very strange incident, minutes
earlier, shortly after the guests had arrived. Michael
had been in the garden, still in his school clothes, looking for suitable plants to draw for the next day's lesson. He heard the car pull noisily into the drive, then
the sound of voices. The two visitors had come round
to the back of the house with his father, making conversation about the garden and the drive from London,
and then had gone indoors. But as they stepped into the
kitchen, the woman cried out, slammed her hands
against the door frame and stood, head bowed for a
moment, moaning in what Michael could only think
was pain. His father and the other man were naturally
very concerned.

"What's the matter?"

"No!" was all the woman said. "Oh, God. No! I
can't go inside. It's too strong!"

"It's all right," Richard said. "We'll stay outside for
a while. Can I get you a drink? Brandy?"

Suddenly the woman relaxed, taking a deep breath
and laughing. She seemed suddenly embarrassed. "I'm
sorry, Dr. Whitlock. I didn't mean to startle you."

"Not at all. What can I do for you?"

"I can't enter the house for a moment. Sometimes
the shock . . ."

Richard was clearly bemused, but he made encouraging sounds and again the three of them strolled
slowly through the small orchard, a man on each side
of the shaken woman. She glanced toward Michael's
hiding place, once, but didn't appear to see him.

Michael took the opportunity to dart indoors, going
up to his room to watch from the window.

He felt nervous of the woman, yet also comforted by
her. It was an odd conflict of emotions that he hardly

understood: a combination of intrigue with her, and
worry that she would see his castle. So he frowned as
they set off down the garden, drew back as she teased
him out with her sudden, startling glance, and when
they had started to cross the field to the quarry he followed at a distance.

Halfway over the field he heard his mother's car,
and Carol's usual excited chatter. But he couldn't help
it if he was seen following the visitors. He wanted to
know what the red-haired woman would find in the
chalk pit.

He raced breathlessly to the wood at the top of the
chalk, wormed his way through the bushes, under
the protecting wire, and lay down where the land cut
sharply away, dropping steeply to the quarry below.

Soon the strangers' voices reached him. He saw
them approach, amused to see them following the
straight path through the quarry, led by his father, and
not the circular, secret route.

The woman, however, was looking, waving her arms
about and making sounds of surprise.

He heard her say, "Dr. Whitlock—"

"Please call me Richard," his father interrupted.

"I'm sorry. Richard ... there *is* something here. I
can't tell what, not yet. But it's very strange. It's almost in the air."

"What does it feel *like*?" asked the other man. He
was carrying a broken stick and used it to strike at the
gorse, damaging the leaves.

Listening from above, Michael grimaced and pushed
himself lower against the grass as he heard her words
in reply: "Like walls. And gates. Yes, like a *castle*.
There are barriers. Your boy has a powerful imagination. The castle he has invented is very strong in the
air ..."

Richard laughed, and something in the laugh disturbed Michael, but the thought faded away as the trio
came closer to the chalk wall and passed into the
camp, the small clearing where Michael could feel the
old sea and the vanished beach most strongly. They
stayed in the camp for a while, kicking around. The

woman crossed her arms and seemed to feel cold. Could she fell the cold sea?

She looked up the cliff, suddenly, frowning. Michael's heart thumped, but he didn't move. His eyes met her gaze, willing her not to see him, and after a moment her focus shifted. She looked around, scanning the chalk wall left to right, then turned away. He heard her say, "There are some good fossils. Do you collect them?"

"Once upon a time."

His father went on, "This is where Michael claims to have found the golden wolf-girl. And I found traces of terracotta here after he brought home the Mocking Cross."

Michael leaned further over the edge, puzzled. The "Mocking Cross"? What was that?

The other man said, "There has to be a cache around here. He must be getting this stuff from somewhere. Dumped from the cliff top maybe?"

Michael jerked back as the man stared up toward him.

"I don't think you'll find a cache," Richard said quietly, hands still in his pockets. "I've searched the place thoroughly. Someone is bringing the stolen objects to him, Jack. Someone a little out of the ordinary."

Jack began to walk away from the others and Michael squirmed forward again to see where he was going. He was ambling toward the dungeon, kicking at the brush, reaching down to pick up stones, chalk blocks and pieces of wood, examining everything. He called back, "This is where you excavated the dog-shrine, isn't it?"

"Just about there. Yes," his father said.

The woman was hunched, shivering, staring back toward the curve in the quarry that led out to the farmland. Michael wondered if she could hear the sea. She seemed to be listening.

"There's a terrible smell here," Jack called suddenly, and again Michael felt anxious. The man was kicking at the gorse cover over the iron-grilled passage where the rags and bones were stored, the things that Michael hadn't wanted to bring home.

Grimly, his teeth biting sharply at the inside of his lip, he watched the man in black leather pull up the gorse and disclose the passage, banging the iron with his broken stick.

"Christ!" came his voice. "There's something dead in here. A dog or something . . . Really *rotten!*"

Richard joined his colleague. The woman stayed where she was, again glancing up the cliff, yet not seeing the boy who watched her from his invisibility.

Jack said loudly, "It's an old tool housing, I think, probably from the quarry days. Covered by an iron grille. Help me with it. Can you?"

The two men tugged at the iron, grunting and straining. The bushes rustled and moved where their stooped bodies struggled.

"Christ!" Again, from the other man. "If it's human we could be in trouble. I hope you realize that. What a *stink.*"

Then came the sound of something giving, metal on flint, or chalk. Disturbed, Michael drew back from the edge, stood up and looked thoughtfully into the distance, toward the sea.

They had found the dungeon. That meant they would find the dead things. He didn't know how his father would react to that. The woman had helped them in their discovery, but he felt sure she would be friendly to him. He was sure she could see the castle, and although she was frightened, or scared of something, she had almost broken the barrier without the map!

But they had found the dungeon, and that meant questions later.

Michael turned and ran home, hiding in his room behind the closed door, but listening hard, listening for the strangers' return.

Jack Goodman backed out of the chalk tunnel and tossed a black object down on to the pile of remains. One hand over his mouth and nose he drew a deep breath, his eyes watering. A few yards away Francoise Jeury stood without expression, her eyes narrowed as she surveyed the growing collection of rotten, rotting objects.

Richard poked and prodded at the artifacts, fascinated and appalled at the same time. The smell was hard to cope with, but pure curiosity had taken over.

"That's about all of it," Goodman said hoarsely. "Christ! I hope you've got a good brandy up at the house. I'm about to die. Tomb robbing isn't my speciality."

"Stop complaining about the smell," Richard said. "Look ... This is human." He had seen a graying, shriveled finger, part of a large, male hand. It had been torn, not cut. The nail was smooth and clean and a slightly lighter coloration at its base suggested that it had once borne a ring.

The main source of the smell of decomposition was a goat's head, with green and red decorative beads tied and tangled in its hair. The head was buzzing with flies even now. It had been cleanly severed at the neck.

"Here's your cache, Richard," Goodman said. "The boy has taken all the best stuff, leaving just the junk. Well, not *quite* just the junk. This is interesting."

He was turning the dulled blade in his fingers. A wide, leaf-shaped knife, the ivory handle inlaid with amber and faïence. The metal was bronze, much tarnished and very pitted. It was possible to see the pattern in the blade still, although its delicacy was much obscured.

The rest of the haul was wood and bone, carved and shaped, dressed and decorated, but without meaning beyond some lost function of ritual. The head of the goat, the human finger and the roughly torn tail of a horse, its hair bound round with bright fabric, were all the obvious organic remains, though Richard found that inside the dress of a crude doll, something that looked Northern, shamanistic, the body consisted of a mummified rat.

Goodman said: "The tunnel goes deeper. There's more animal stuff in there, I think."

Turning the tarnished knife in his finger, Richard murmured, "What sort of a cache—if by 'cache' you mean stolen goods—what sort of cache contains rotting meat as well as gold, emerald and bronze? It makes no sense."

"You're assuming that the gold and bronze was hidden at the same time as the animal remains."

"That goat is newly dead. Days, not hours. But recent."

Like a savaged dog, in a wicker cage . . .

"Maybe someone's trying to discourage kids from nosing around in the hiding place."

Richard shook his head. "I can't believe that."

"Nor can I," Goodman said, rubbing his eyes and replacing his dark glasses. "I need some air . . . let's get away from here."

But Francoise stepped over and reached out a hand. "May I see the knife?"

"Of course."

She cradled the blade, touched it to her mouth, licked it, turned it over and rubbed her slender fingers across its pitted surface. Richard watched her curiously, not yet knowing what to make of her, aware that something strange was happening to Michael, something irrational, but something which might be a part of this woman's experience. He had been skeptical of the supernatural—Hungarian magic and family tradition not excluded—until Michael's haunting had begun. Now he was intrigued by the claim that Francoise Jeury made: that she could tell age, and feeling, in objects that had been associated with powerful events.

She had been employed—albeit surreptitiously, it turned out—by the best archaeological research institute in Britain. If she was a charlatan she was at least convincing. But if she was genuine, a physic, then she was potentially of enormous use to the Whitlocks.

"It's old," she said quietly, her accent less pronounced. "But not very. A few generations. A hundred years. Not thousands. It has no age in it like that. No feeling of real age. And no violence. Just an old knife. A hundred years or so. Maybe more. But not *that* much more."

Goodman was surprised. "That would make it a Victorian copy. But this doesn't look like a copy. I'd place it with the Wessex culture. Two thousand, two thousand and more BC. A *very* old artifact. I've seen them ... This has been ripped off from a museum."

"I've seen them too," Richard said. "They preserve well. And this looks ... Well, it looks right."

"But it has no age," Francoise insisted. Richard saw Goodman's half-smile. She went on, "And a hundred-year-old copy would pit and tarnish just like this, wouldn't it? If not preserved in the heavy earth of a tumulus."

"That's true."

The knife passed between them.

They looked down at the rest of the spoil. Francoise prodded at the oak effigy of a human, armless, legless, the features grimly and sparsely carved in the wood. She picked up a shattered bone, where fresh reds and blues of paint still filled beautifully the carved grooves that formed the shape of a bison. This was probably how ancient bone-carvers had fashioned their charmed long-bones. Colored with ochres and other paints, filled with life, they had been far more vivid and striking than the faint, crumbling remains that were unearthed fifty thousand years after the shamans had used them to sketch their world.

So: another copy. But a good one.

And Francoise, holding the bone, said, "It feels strange, this piece. It has no age to it. No feeling of age. But it has power, like ... like wildness. And wilderness. I have handled bone implements often and I can sometimes feel the time they have been in the earth. But not this. And yet, it is not like handling a modern bone ..."

She shook her head and dropped the fragment. Looking up at Richard wearily, she said, "I am confused and disturbed by all of this. When I arrived at your house something hurt me very badly ... here ..." She placed a hand on her belly, a finger extended, as if being stabbed. "A sharp pain," she confirmed. "Like being opened. Something in your house is terrifying. I think I should touch that terrifying thing. It might help.

If it came from this cache, then perhaps it will tell us more."

"Your son is watching us," she said as they made their way up the path from the field. Richard could smell fresh coffee being percolated. Carol was running down to meet them, her writing pad held under her left arm, her face a wide grin of pleasure.

As he reached the child, and stooped to pick her up, he glanced up at Michael's window, but saw nothing. "Where? Where is he watching us?"

"Up there. He is very anxious."

"I can't see him." Carol's arms were round his neck and she was babbling about the painting of a horse she had done today at school.

"I can," Francoise Jeury murmured, but the window was empty.

"He's in that room, up there. I saw him a moment ago. He is very unhappy, Richard. What have you been doing to him?"

She had expected to feel the same appalling pain on entering the house that had afflicted her earlier. She was surprised and relieved, therefore, to find that she could enter the building without attack. Explaining this to Richard, she said, "Sometimes my senses are attuned very highly to violence or anger . . ."

"Violence or anger *in* an object, you mean? Not just in the air . . . ?"

He was struggling to understand the nature of the woman's reputed power, still unsure of her.

Francoise nodded. "I must tell you some of my encounters. Usually I have to *touch* an object to get the feel of what it is, what it has been. I get visions of the past through objects, especially stone and bones. Not so much metal. But yes—sometimes I feel the power of a totem, or a weapon, without making contact."

"Must make for an uneasy life," Richard said quietly. He was aware that the woman smiled thinly, conscious of his skepticism, but not responding to it.

Susan greeted them. Richard noticed that she was

wary of the other woman and was as stiff as usual with Jack Goodman.

They drank coffee laced with brandy in the sitting room while Carol talked to each of them in turn, showing drawings and demanding attention. Goodman was uncomfortable with the child's attention, but Francoise was enchanted by the girl. "You will have to draw *me*, now. A good portrait for my friend at home."

"What's your friend's name?"

"Lee. He's an American. We search out ghosts together."

Carol seemed less than interested in the idea of ghosts. She sat down on the floor to oblige on the art side, and five minutes later had produced a grotesque caricature of the Frenchwoman, accurate in hair and skin color, but very unflattering in bodily girth.

Francoise accepted the portrait with enormous grace, if slightly startled expression.

On a tour of the studios, she was delighted with Susan Whitlock's collection of dolls. They spent long minutes talking about them, handling prized specimens, laughing. The Mocking Cross doll sat on the shelf and Francoise acknowledged it, but seemed reluctant to touch it. Richard perched on the end of his desk, talking with Jack Goodman, idly examining the wolf-girl statuette. At length, Francoise and Susan came back from the studio. Susan was holding the Mocking Cross. Francoise was quite pale.

She smiled as she saw the golden statue. "This is the girl? It's beautiful."

She held the gold object, pressed it, admired it, and then said the words that were becoming so familiar: "It has no age. It is like the bronze dagger. It has no age at all. This is a copy. Very beautiful, but very new."

Richard asked, "What if the statuette had never been associated with violence? Or with passion, say. What if there was no *emotion* in the piece that had been trapped. Would you still be able to feel something about it?"

She watched him blankly for a moment, her eyes wide and softly green, a disturbing look that made

Richard's skin prickle. Then she nodded. "I am sure of it. I would feel something. Something of the centuries. Even if it was only a sense of confinement, of darkness, of nothingness. No. This is very new."

At last she was ready for the Viking instrument of desecration. As she cradled the wooden figure in her hands she breathed very deeply.

"This is new too. Not the wood. That has a feel to it, but wild. Natural. But this has killed."

Her hands were shaking and she placed the cross down.

"It was used to cut open the belly of a young man. A holy man. It cut deeply through the flesh, killing him agonizingly."

"You can know that from touching the object?"

"As if in a dream," she said. "I live his death. The death is there, and the laughter of the killer. It cut through his belly, cracked his breast. As he died he prayed to Jesus Christ."

Goodman made a sound, like laughter but more derisory. He didn't quite catch himself in time. He seemed to ignore his own rudeness and said, "That would confuse me, you see, Francoise. You say the knife is new. That is has 'no age.' But you also say that it cut out the heart of a young Christian monk. Now if your *talent* is true, then the two things are incompatible. This knife hasn't been used to kill recently. If it was used in the way we think, and which you describe, then that's an event that occurred a thousand years ago—"

"This knife isn't a thousand years old. I am certain of it."

"It has to be. If not, then it has been used for a ritual murder in the last few years—but there's no sign of dried blood on it now, and those chips and snags on the cutting edge are long dried out. Besides, I can't recall accounts of any such murder."

"The man who died was not of this time," the woman said. And now she too seemed confused. "Perhaps my sense *is* awry. Perhaps I can't help." She smiled at Susan, glanced at Richard Whitlock, then shrugged. "I'm sorry. I am a strange tool of archaeology. Sometimes I dig well. Sometimes I don't."

Susan said quickly, "I'd like you to speak to Michael. Would you do that? I'm sure he'll like you."

"He didn't like me at the back door," Francoise said quietly, cryptically, but she nodded. "All right. But outside. Not inside. I want him to take me to his castle."

Fifteen

A hundred yards into the quarry Francoise suddenly caught her breath and stopped. With a smile of delight she said, "This is the outer gate! This is the outer gate of your castle!"

"Yes!"

"I didn't see it before."

Michael was pleased. She was standing right between the chalk markers, where the outer winding path began.

The woman looked up, then raised her hands in a pushing motion. "Cre-e-ak . . ." she went, and laughed. Michael laughed too. She braced her body and mimed the opening of heavy gates, stepping forward (but not along the hidden path). He had been so apprehensive of her, an hour ago. Now he felt she was his friend. He wasn't sure yet whether to tell her about Chalk Boy— Chalk Boy might be angry if he did—but she could imagine the castle, and believed in its walls and gates. She might even be aware of the endless tunnels that riddled the earth below it. He didn't mind if she knew: she couldn't get in, not without help, not even if she could feel them.

They walked on slowly. The dusk deepened and a breeze began to stir the stunted trees.

"Why do you call your castle 'Limbo'? It's a strange name."

As he followed her through the quarry, Michael struggled for the words, trying to remember what the priest had told them at Church. "Limbo is the place between heaven and hell. It's not a bad place. It's not a good place. It's a place where people go when they can't get to heaven, but they're too good to go to hell. It's a place in the middle. People go there when they haven't got a soul. No one can see Limbo. That's what my castle is like. No one can see it." He lowered his voice and glanced away, then on some sudden, confiding impulse said, "That's what I'm like too."

"You? You're like that? I don't understand." Francoise crouched, hitching up her suit trousers. She smelled faintly of soap and coffee. Her eyes were very kind and very strong. Michael felt his body rock back slightly as he watched her, as if she was shaking him with her gaze. The breeze blew her red hair over her face and she brushed at it distractedly. She repeated her question. "I don't understand. Please help me. Why do *you* feel in the middle?"

He whispered, "I was given away when I was born. Nobody wanted me. I don't have a proper soul."

"Of *course* you do, Michael. Everybody does. The soul is just the *person*. There is no heaven, no hell, only conscience. Your priest is very old-fashioned. Of course you have a soul!"

"No I *don't*," Michael insisted, still in a quiet voice. "Chalk B—"

He broke off, biting back the name. The word "adopted" fluttered in his head, but he didn't want to say it. It was a word that hurt him, like a sharp sting. He had wanted to say that Chalk Boy had told him adopted children forfeited their souls. His jaw clenched as he tried to regain control.

Francoise frowned, looking both sad and concerned. Jenny sometimes looked this way when she talked to him. She said, "Chalk? What about chalk?"

Michael shook his head. He shouldn't talk about his friend. Not yet. When Chalk Boy got angry he made Michael fetch disgusting things, and laughed at him. He said, "I only have a *shadow*. Not a proper soul."

"Don't be silly . . ."

"I'm not silly! It's true. That's why my parents can't always see me. They can see Carol because her shadow is inside her, where her soul is. They put the shadow there when she was born. But they can only see me *sometimes,* so they get angry, or think I've run away, or don't talk to me because they don't know I'm there. But when I find the bright things my shadow comes inside me for a while and they can see me properly. Then Daddy laughs and tells me stories."

"How many bright things have you found?"

"Quite a lot, now."

The woman bit her lip. After a moment she reached out and tugged at Michael's hair, gently and affectionately. "Does your father like these bright things?"

Michael nodded.

"Does he tell you stories all the time?"

"He does when he's happy. Do you know about the Fisher King? He ruled over a great wasteland, and all of King Arthur's Knights had to find the Holy Grail to bring the trees and fields back to life. That's my favorite story."

She seemed delighted. "Mine too! Arthur and his Knights. And the grumpy old wizard Merlin. And wily Vivien. And the gorgeous and foolish Lancelot! My father told me the stories when I was young too. I loved them. I still do. If I had children . . ."

She stopped suddenly and tugged Michael's long, ginger hair again.

"Did you find bright things?" he asked. "Did they tell you stories when you found pretty things?"

To his surprise her eyes became tearful, although her face seemed angry. She drew him into a tight embrace. "No. No, my darling," she said quietly. "I didn't have to . . ."

A few minutes later they stood before the empty dungeon. Michael stared hard at the broken gorse bush, his body very tense. Francoise rested a hand on his shoulder. The fragments, organic remains and artefacts were up at the house now, wrapped in polythene, labeled, boxed.

"We found where you'd been hiding the more unpleasant things. It's not healthy to play near to decaying animals. Did you know that?"

"I didn't mean to fetch them," Michael said. "I only like the bright and glittery presents. But sometimes Chalk—"

Again, he bit back the name. But this time he decided not to worry. "Sometimes Chalk Boy shows me things that look pretty, but when I fetch them they're not the same. Sometimes they scream."

Francoise shivered quickly, but was unwilling to press the point just yet. "Chalk Boy? Of course. Your mother mentioned your invisible friend."

Michael felt suddenly cold. Chalk Boy didn't like to be talked about. He looked up at the thoughtful woman and whispered, "He's a secret though. Please don't tell anybody else."

"No. Of course I won't. Can I meet him?"

"He lives by the sea, at the end of the big tunnel. He has a cave there. I can't get to the beach, but sometimes he comes up the tunnel to the castle. He hides in the chalk. Sometimes I dream of him in the house."

"That's some playmate," Francoise said, then confidentially: "Is he around now?"

Michael cocked his head, then sniffed the air hard, like a dog. He was puzzled for a moment, then shrugged. "I don't know. I don't think so. But he hides a lot."

Her hands on his head were gentle, the fingers that touched his skin and his hair were soothing, reassuring. He stood there, watching her, letting her stroke him. She smiled suddenly and drew her hands away. "Mr. Spock could do it. Not me. Only stones and bones."

Michael didn't understand the allusion.

She went on. "I'm staying in the house for a while longer. If Chalk Boy comes back, if he comes out of hiding, will you let me meet him?"

"He doesn't like people to know about him."

"Well, can you put in a good word for me?"

"I'll try."

"Are the pretty things here in the pit? When you fetch them?"

He thought about that for a moment, then said, "Sort of. I see them and reach for them. Sometimes they're hard to fetch and I get thrown out of the tunnel. It hurts a lot sometimes. I get cut and bruised." He pointed almost proudly to the scar over his right eye. "But nothing very serious."

"Tell me something . . . does Chalk Boy ever tell you where he finds the pretty things for you to fetch?"

Michael shook his head. "He can move around the world. He can see everything that's being made, even if it's hidden away for thousands of years. He can see things when they're new. If he wants to be friends with me he brings them straight up the tunnel to the pit. That's why they're so bright. Because they're so new. But that's a *secret*."

His eyes blazed and he realized he was frightened. He had told the secret. Francoise was watching him excitedly. She seemed astonished, half laughing, half thinking. There was moisture on her face now, and her hands on his shoulders were trembling.

He beckoned her to bend lower and whispered the greatest secret of all. "Don't tell anyone . . ." he began, then hesitated.

"Don't tell anyone what?"

"I'm trying to find the Grail. If I can find the Grail it will make Daddy famous."

"My God, yes," Francoise said, suddenly dull, a shadow on her face. "It will do that all right." Then she smiled again. "Is that what your father wants?"

"He doesn't know about it. It's a secret. But if I can fetch it for him he might get his job back. He could write books."

"Have you ever—have you even *seen* the Holy Grail?"

With a quick shrug, Michael admitted, "I don't know what it looks like. But Chalk Boy can find it."

"Chalk Boy . . . Limbo Boy . . ."

A drop of perspiration fell from Francoise's glowing skin on to Michael's hand. She looked uncomfortable and used a handkerchief to wipe her forehead. Michael watched her, slightly puzzled at the fact that she was shaking. Her voice barely audible, she said to him, "You are a powerful young man, Michael. A powerful young man indeed. You have invented a wonderful story, and wonderful friends, to hide a power that is astonishing. No wonder your father tells you stories ... I've never met anyone like you, and I've seen and touched some very strange things in my time, and met some wonderful people."

"What strange things?" Michael asked, intrigued.

"I'll tell you later. Michael: will you promise me that if you hear Chalk Boy come back you'll let me know? I would so much like to be with you when he comes the next time and brings you something."

"I'll ask him," Michael murmured, but he didn't think Chalk Boy would approve at all. More brightly he said, "I'll give you a drawing of the castle, if you like. I'll go and do it now."

"That would be lovely. I'd like that." She took him by the hand. "Let's go back to the house, shall we? I'm starving."

"Me too."

"And while we walk, will you sing me a song?" She held a tape recorder toward him. "Sing me your favorite song."

He laughed, amused by some private thought, and a moment later, without further prompting, broke into a tuneless rendition of the theme from *Ghostbusters*.

The meal was strained. Susan had not gone to a great deal of effort—there hadn't been time—but the food was Italian and good, and consumed appreciatively. The strain came from Francoise who, having been interested and friendly earlier in the evening, was now moody and withdrawn.

Watching her over the supper table, Susan could see that her guest was angry.

The tension from the Frenchwoman seemed directed at Richard. Whatever Richard asked her was shrugged away, or half answered, and the warmth she had shown him earlier was no longer in evidence. She was courteous with Susan, almost as if in compensation for her hostility toward her host. She said frankly that she had felt nothing from Michael, and that the chalk quarry and her conversation with the boy had given her no clues as to where he was finding the treasures.

Richard was less disappointed than Susan would have expected.

She did say that she could sense the barrier that Michael had erected. She had pretended to feel a gate. He *had* erected something to protect the pit, and as such clearly had a defined, positive psychic energy. He left *traces* of his mind wherever he went, and Francoise had detected them. He was defending himself. She had experienced this many times before in pre- and early post-pubescent children.

Jack Goodman wanted to drive back to London, and Francoise would go with him. The meal was not curtailed, but they moved away from the table when they had eaten and Goodman collected his things from the study. As Richard cleared the table, Francoise led Susan to the sitting room, then out into the garden, standing quietly in the darkness, watching night birds over the distant woods.

"Is everything all right, Francoise?"

"No. No, everything is not all right." She turned to Susan, indecisive for a moment, clearly needing to say something. "I am uncomfortable with your husband."

"I noticed. Why, I wonder?"

"Because of your son. Because he is cruel."

"Michael?"

"Your husband. There is a cruelty in him. He is making Michael sing for his supper. I don't like that."

Susan folded her arms, angry, and dropped her gaze. In an icy voice she said, "It's not only Richard. I must take a lot of the blame too, Madame Jeury, if you must know. We both neglected the boy when he was younger. I should have done more ... Richard's needs are very consuming."

"If you start calling me 'Madame' I shall assume you are sulking, and end this conversation. There is no need to be angry."

Choosing to ignore the fact that she had been patronized, Susan smiled her agreement. "This is an edgy family. There are tensions."

Francoise Jeury laughed delightedly. "And how! Oh, my God. It's everywhere. Even in the bathroom. Everywhere."

"You can feel that?"

"I can feel it very strongly." She became serious, picking her words carefully. "At the table, I apologize, but I didn't tell you the truth. About Michael, I mean. Because I want to tell the truth to you and not to your husband. You must decide, of course, what to tell Richard. But I myself do not want to tell him what I know, what I have found out."

Susan watched the other woman, her face hard, a defensive look, an angry one again. Then she started to walk toward the hedges, Francoise following slightly behind. "If you're going to tell me that Michael uses his mind to steal things from museums, we've already guessed that. For a long time I thought it was his natural mother, throwing abuse at us, her own psychic power. There was a lot of earth when he was an infant. He nearly drowned in a massive mud-spill that just *appeared* in the bedroom—"

"His talent was raw. Unfocused. Powerful, but still infantile."

"That's right. Michael himself. Later, he started to 'see' and 'fetch' more clearly. He sees visions of something in someone's house and can steal it. He has invented an imaginary companion to rationalize where the objects come from. He goes down into the quarry, where he feels secure, and 'fetches' things from there, pretending to be in his castle. But he is doing it himself, and he's doing it for affection . . ."

"You must discourage that—"

Furious, Susan turned on the other woman. "Damn it! Don't tell me how to bring up my own child!"

Unbowed, unbattered, Francoise Jeury said grimly, "If you have started to understand, then fine. But that boy is in terror . . ."

"I know."

"He has been excluded. He thinks he has no soul."

"I *know*."

"Then why did you let it happen?"

Susan's eyes filled with tears. "Because he frightens me. Because I can still see the look in his mother's eyes. Because there's something more, something horrible, and it terrifies me to think about it."

"Then perhaps you should talk about it . . ."

Quickly—too quickly—Susan said, "We've *been* talking about it, Francoise. Michael is strange in so many ways. He puts up barriers. From what you say, more barriers than we'd realized."

Francoise Jeury scuffed the damp lawn with her toe. "Is Richard frightened too?"

"Not of Michael. Richard's fears are more internalized, more personal. Michael is just a target for his frustrations. Or rather was. He's better with the boy, now."

The other woman sneered. "Of course. Why not? His son has become Father Christmas."

"That's not fair."

"Of course it's fair! You know your husband better than anyone. You know him! Susan, listen to me. You are almost right but not *quite* right. About Michael, I mean. The power he has is frightening, yes, and perhaps what you fear is the power you aren't aware of. I do not think he has control over what is happening to him because he is too young. I can't be sure, but I feel strongly that he is inventing a world to explain his *own* fears, his *own* talent. And it is a *wonderful* talent. I have experienced it before, but never like this."

"Telekinesis, you mean? That's what he's doing."

"Apportation. It's a much more powerful form of the talent."

"Apportation," Susan repeated, digesting the word and nodding as if this explained everything. Then she frowned. "Which is what, exactly?"

"He *fetches*," Francoise said. "It's as simple as that. He reaches and grasps at precious things, and brings them across space . . . and across time."

In the darkness Susan's eyes glittered with questions and tears. "Across time?"

"These things you have. These objects he has brought to you . . . they don't feel old because they *aren't* old. Because they come from the past when they were new. The wolf-girl dancer was newly made for the tomb of a king. One day, thousands of years later, a young mind saw the new glitter, days after it had been placed in the tomb. No stone, no sand, no wood could stand in the way, no weeks, no years, no thousands of years. He reached into that dark and ancient place and *snatched* the object from the sealed tomb. And when the tomb was opened in the nineteenth century they found everything in place—except that someone had been there in antiquity and broken off a part of the altar ..."

Susan was astonished. "Do you know for certain that that happened?"

Francoise laughed, shaking her head. "No. Of course not. Not for certain. But I can *imagine* it clearly enough to know that *something* like that happened. Then there is the Mocking Cross ... it could so easily be the male part of the pair from Istanbul. Used to abuse a sacrificial victim; then stolen by a priest and buried in the catacombs, golden mask and all. And shortly after it had been concealed, it vanished. A wind came, maybe. And a spectral hand appeared from nowhere and snatched it away, because that was the moment that Michael sent his mind, scouring time, searching the past for something that was *bright* and *pretty*. Do you see? He takes things from time. To me they feel young. But he has covered *centuries* in his quest. Oh, I *must* study him more ..."

"His quest? What quest?"

Francoise's face was a mask of solemn anger. She stared at Susan in disbelief, then snapped out words. "For the story of the Fisher King! What else? For his parents' arms around him! For a kiss good night from your husband! For his *Grail*. He pays for love—"

"That's enough! It's none of your business, *Madame*! Things will change ..."

"Will they?"

"Enough!"

"*Will* they change? That's your business too. But please remember, Susan, that when I have met a remarkable little man like Michael, I can't easily forget about him."

Furious again, Susan pushed past the woman, then stopped, glaring. "Forget about him. He needs love, not his mind probed. There will be no, repeat *no* study of my son. Leave us alone."

After a long moment Francoise expressed her regret that such a tension had developed. "If you ever need to ask me for help, please do," she went on. "I may fail. As I said earlier, I'm a strange piece of archaeological equipment. Sometimes I dig well, sometimes not. But I'm always prepared to try . . ."

"I'm going to tell Richard what you've told me. I don't care if you feel angry about that. I can't have secrets from my husband."

Francoise laughed. "I'm not angry. I think he already knows. He just hasn't told you. You tell him what you want. Too many secrets," she added with a sideways glance and a smile that sent cold fingers down Susan's spine. "Too many secrets, kept for years, can be unbearable. You're right. Don't add more."

"I don't know what you mean by that."

"Of course you know what I mean by that."

"Don't call me a liar! Don't *dare* call me a liar."

"I *do* dare. Why not. It's your life. It's your lie. But Susan, I have seen that lie—oh, I don't know what it is, of course, and frankly I don't want to. But I have seen it. And more to the point, I can see it poisoning you."

And with that, Francoise turned quickly and led the way grimly back to the car, where Jack Goodman was in deep conversation with Richard. A moment before they arrived she whispered, "You wear your darkness like a veil, Susan. I hope you can lift that veil soon."

Susan was in a cold sweat, her perception heightened through shock and emotion. "I really don't know what you mean," she muttered, but she knew that her face betrayed her.

At the car, Richard passed Francoise a scroll of paper. "From Michael, for you," he said with a slight bow.

"Ah. The Castle Keep."

She unfurled the paper and looked at the confusion of broken circles and diagonal lines. She was reminded of a maze, or some sort of puzzle. In the center of the picture was the representation of a sea with mountains behind it. On the area of the beach a small figure had been drawn, standing below a bright sun. Its shadow stretched away from it like a thin cross. Placed outside the circles, standing on a low hill, was a representation of Madame Francoise Jeury every bit as indulgent as Carol's earlier effort, all bust and auburn hair. She had been outlined in heavy black pen to make her stand out.

"I am not flattered," she said with a laugh, "but I'm grateful for the gift. Will you tell him that I'm pleased?"

"I will," said Richard. Goodman and Francoise Jeury took their leave.

Watching from the landing window, Michael raised a hand, waved silently as the car pulled out of the drive and on to the London road. Then he went back to his room and sat in the corner, thinking about the woman and the map of the castle that he had given her.

He smiled, then chuckled. He reached under the bed and pulled out the white sheet on which he had drawn his castle earlier. He ran a finger through the tunnels and in the secret spaces between the walls. He had given Francoise an incomplete map; but she would always be able to find him at the heart, if she ever came back. Michael felt an intuitive trust of the woman, and if she *did* come back, and he was hiding, she could come to him.

He grinned and touched the place where heavier doors hid the tunnels.

He wondered in which of them Chalk Boy was sleeping tonight.

Jack Goodman's telephone call a week later was short and to the point. "I'm in a rush, Richard. A meeting. But I thought you'd be interested to hear that our metallurgist has examined the blade from the quarry—"

"The bronze dagger?"

"The bronze dagger. I'll spare you the technical details, if you don't mind. You know how bad I am at chemistry. I'll send you a copy of the report, if you're interested. Essentially: it's authentic. Southern German manufacture, cast about 900 BC, perhaps a little later. they used a casting process that riddled the metal with a particular impurity. No Victorian copyist—no *any-time* copyist—would have known how to duplicate that. It's genuine."

Richard sat down and stared into space for a few moments, smiling as he let Goodman's words sink in. "Your colleague, the psychic, said it was only a hundred or so years old."

"I know. But you know my doubts about that particular lady. The casting, the way it was made, dates it precisely. It's nearly three thousand years old. I imagine our forensic laboratory will confirm that in time. I've already sent the specimen over. The bone, by the way, the painted bone? It's recent. Radiocarbon dating is quicker than the laborious process of dating metals. It's from this generation. Even had human skin scales on it."

Richard said nothing for a few moments, then smiled. "Well. Thanks for calling, Jack. I appreciate the information."

"Before you go: if you want to sell the blade to the collector's market ... I think it will fetch a moderate price."

"Do it for me, will you? I'd appreciate it."

"Happy to. Anything else arrived on the scene?"

Richard transferred the phone to his study and stirred his fingers carefully through the box of remains that was still on his desk, letting the sound travel to the other man.

"Glass?"

"Glass. Glass singular, I think, some sort of drinking vessel. It's completely shattered. My impression is that it was Roman, one of those exquisite glass-within-glass pieces they produced, like the 'Lycergus' cup in your own museum. Michael's very upset that the cup was destroyed. I'm not sure why."

"Now that *is* a shame. That it's smashed, I mean. Roman glass is a *real* collector's item."

"There'll be other times," Richard said. "In the meantime ... a reconstruction job? A private commission?"

"Let me think about that," Goodman said. "I don't know who could do such work without drawing attention to the object. That may be a no-go for a while. Let me think about it."

The hesitation at the other end of the phone was tangible and Richard was unable to end the conversation. Eventually Goodman said, "Do you think there's another cache? Is that where the glass came from?"

"Michael has access to another cache," Richard agreed quietly.

Again, after a pause, "Do you know where it is?"

"Yes. But I can't get to it myself. And nor would you be able to."

"That doesn't make sense, Richard. You know it doesn't."

Almost instantly Richard said, "Just sell the blade for me, Jack. Will you do that?"

"Of course."

"And don't throw away that shaman's stick. New or not, I think it may have more value than we realize."

"You're very mysterious, Richard. I never did like guessing games."

"Just keep the bone-charm. And look carefully at what's carved and painted on it. Get a good record."

"Then I'll hear from you again, will I? Soon?"

"That all depends on Michael. Good night, Jack. Thanks for your work."

PART THREE

Quest for the Grail

Sixteen

In the late summer, nearly a year later, Richard was offered photographic work in west Scotland, near a place called Torinturk in Argyll. A lake dwelling, two and a half thousand years old and in a remarkable state of preservation, was being removed from the peat that marked where the lake had once existed. Whether or not to take the job was a difficult decision to make. He was unhappy about leaving the South and his family, especially Michael. As Michael fetched his trickle of precious artifacts, so Richard grew more protective toward the boy. His reluctance to go away for any period of time was founded on a deep sense of distrust, although distrust toward whom or over what he found hard to identify. He just wanted to be *there* when Michael came running in, grinning, and holding a time-torn object of worth.

But a photo-opportunity like the *crannog* was not to be dismissed lightly, especially after Jack Goodman had set it up for him. He *had* to keep Goodman happy. Jack, after all, was his passport to wealth in two very different ways. Besides, the money offer in Scotland was surprisingly good; and, since it was a major excavation, to be much publicized, including a TV documentary series, his photographs would be seen widely.

The project would be good for his profile if not for his health: he loathed the climate of west Scotland, which in his experience consisted of gales, dull days and a landscape often so silent that it chilled him.

The extension to the house was also under way, a

two-story development that would give Susan more studio space, create a better darkroom facility for himself, and give the children a playroom/studio which they could fill to their hearts' content.

The financial situation was uncomfortably tight, however. After a year of splendid, if historically uninteresting gifts, over the last two months all Michael had "fetched" was a battered bronze beaker and an iron decoration with ivory inlay, probably a Carpathian horse trapping. They had not sold for much, and Goodman was taking 25 percent of everything that he disposed of on the Whitlock's behalf. The shaman stick had been sold as Art to an eccentric Swedish businessman, and had fetched two thousand pounds. The extension to the house was costed at ten times that, and there would be an uncomfortable shortfall in funds unless Michael tapped his time-cache of treasures for something more worthwhile.

The lad was happy, though. He played more naturally than Richard could remember, and was better friends with his sister, now. Every night there was a story and after a few weeks Michael's possessiveness had passed and Carol was allowed to sit in on the telling too.

During the second summer since the discovery of Michael's gift, each day the boy visited the chalk quarry while Richard paced restlessly among the trees above, behind the plywood walls of a castle he had built for Michael for fun. But so often Michael just played, without result. Richard had tried to remind his son that once, years ago, he had fetched a spear fragment in the woods, near Hawkinge. Didn't Michael feel that he could see things in other places than just the chalk pit?

The boy had shaken his head, an almost nervous gesture.

"Chalk Boy lives there. I have to stay in the castle . . . Otherwise he won't come."

"Where was Chalk Boy in the woods that time when you were a toddler? Was he with you then?"

Michael shrugged. "Can't remember."

The conclusion was inescapable: Francoise Jeury was correct when she theorized that the chalky, imaginary playmate was Michael's rationalization of a talent that scared him. He had created an imaginary structure around himself, and was effectively locked into that "castle" as if he were in a prison. Only on this "safe" ground would his mind unlock to time.

Irritated that the treasures were now so slow in coming, Richard renegotiated the building arrangements with the company, and settled for the outer walls and roof being completed. Inner structures would wait for a later deal. Susan expressed concern that they had realized so little money from Goodman's sale of their prizes, and questioned Goodman's honesty. Richard, too, had given thought to the other man's integrity. He explained to Susan that they were selling treasure-trove illegally, and so they were only earning a fraction of any artifact's true worth. She was irritable, but accepted this.

Eventually Richard decided to accept the Argyll job and spent a day in London preparing for it. At the beginning of October he drove north into the Scottish gloom, and was pleasantly surprised to find blue skies and warm breezes. The site was vast and filthy, and over the days he learned to forget the constant stain of peat on his face and hands. It was practically impossible to get clean, though he managed, naturally, to keep his cameras in pristine condition.

At half-term Susan drove north to meet him, the children a trial of noise and nausea in the back seat. The journey to Haltwhistle, near Hadrian's Wall, was seven hours, and too long for two children who hated car travel. Once there, however, Michael's mood transformed into one of intense delight. They stayed at a farm within sight of the ancient frontier, and went on Roman marches, attacked imaginary Picts, the painted men who had harrowed from the Borders in Roman times, and explored the museums and reconstructions at the nearby fortresses.

Michael adored the museum models. Carol loved the walking. They walked for miles in the crisp wind, feeling remote and isolated from the world, sucking in the silence of the vast, empty land to the north, and the stark shadows of the earthworks and hills to the south.

"Did you bring Chalk Boy with you?" Richard asked Michael on the third day, as they stood, high on the Wall at Crag Lough, staring through the trees here at the dark sprawl of the conifer forest, a mile away on the land below.

Michael shivered. "He's in the pit," he whispered, his face shadowing. "I told you. He stays there."

"Perhaps if you called to him he'd travel from Castle Limbo to find you ... Maybe he can find the right tunnel."

Michael squirmed, frowning, brushing irritably at his ginger hair, blown by the wind on this exposed promontory. "I don't think so."

Susan was photographing Carol as she stood on the crumbled wall of the Milecastle, a guard's station in a good state of preservation. Richard watched her, but his mind was on the boy. If only he could unlock Michael's mind here ... what sights might the boy see, what might he be able to reach for?

At last Richard had inspiration. He said, "A Roman guard once walked here, you know. A very famous one. His name was Parnesius. Have I ever told you the story?"

Michael looked up and shook his head, suddenly interested.

"It's from Puck of Pook's Hill. By Rudyard Kipling. Would you like to hear the story?"

It was a silly question. Michael drank stories like water. He thrived on them.

"Come on then. Back to Housesteads Fort, and I'll tell you on the way."

But at the end of the day, with Kipling mangled hopelessly, often hilariously (it was years since Richard had read the book), Michael remained as closed to the past as he had been on the Wall.

Or so it seemed at first.

* * *

The sound of someone breathing close to his ear woke Richard abruptly from a deep, heavy sleep. When the children had gone to bed, he and Susan had dined on steak and red wine: too much red wine by far and he felt wretched now, his mouth dry, his scalp tight. But he almost jumped out of his skin as he saw the small figure by him, its eyes wide, reflecting stray light from the porch lamp that shone all night outside.

The room smelled strongly and familiarly of earth.

"I've seen him," a small voice whispered.

"Michael?"

"I've seen Parnesius. I think I've done something bad . . ."

Susan stirred next to him but didn't wake. The clock showed five in the morning. It would soon be day.

"Where have you been?" Richard asked quietly. He climbed out of bed, pulled on trousers and shirt and led the boy to the bathroom.

Michael was caked in mud from head to foot. His shirt—his brand-new shirt, bought only yesterday—was torn down the front, and one sleeve hung ragged on him. His new trainers were torn and filthy.

He had blood on his face, a splash that had mingled with the dry earth, but which was unmistakable.

Richard's heart began to race with excitement. He knew, now, what such marks, such filth meant, but first he searched for the cut.

"I'm not hurt, Daddy."

"Aren't you?" Richard said grimly. He couldn't find a cut, which was first puzzling, then alarming. He sat back on the toilet seat and stared at the trembling boy. "Where have you been?"

"Outside. I had a dream. It was really exciting. I dreamed I saw Parnesius. I *did*."

"The Soldier on the Wall?"

"He spoke to me."

"What did he say?"

Frowning slightly, Michael said, "I didn't understand him. I tried. But he was speaking a funny language."

"Can you remember any of the words? Any at all?"

Michael thought for a moment, then said, "*Spaycter.*
He kept saying *spaycter.*"

Another missed beat of the heart. Spaycter: spectre?

Richard tried to remember which legions had been
on the middle section of the Wall, near to the farm. He
had a memory that Spanish and Belgian auxiliaries had
been here at one time. *Spaycter* sounded more
Germanic.

"You haven't been up to the Wall itself, have you?"

"I told you. I was dreaming. When I woke up I was
outside the farmhouse, in the porch. But in my dream
I walked up to the little castle and went inside. The
Roman gave me this . . ."

With a triumphant grin Michael held out his hand.
Silver gleamed there, with a dark, twisted leather cord
looped through it. Richard reached for the amulet and
turned it over. It was crude, the silver of low grade, the
workmanship coarse. It showed the face of a bearded
man, with a crescent behind him. It was a protective
charm, unmistakable.

It had been offered to a "spectre" in propitiation.

"He gave it to you?"

"I had to fetch it," Michael said quietly, and bit his
lower lip, averting his eyes.

"Show me where. Show me where you fetched it.
Take me to the castle."

"It was in a dream." Michael repeated nervously, but
Richard rubbed a finger down the boy's face and
showed him the dirt.

"This isn't a dream, Michael. This is very *solid* filth.
This is *mud*. Show me where you went."

Outside, the first gray light was hinting at the trees on
the eastern horizon. It was bitterly cold. They put on
their anoraks and walked up the steep hill to the main
road running between Carlisle and Newcastle.

Across that road, clearly visible on the line of the
Wall, were the square remains of a Milecastle, the guard
house and shelter for perhaps forty men who had pa-
trolled the Wall eighteen hundred years before. Even
from the distance of half a mile, Richard could see that
something about this tiny ruin was different now.

"Did you cross the road?" he asked his son.

Michael nodded. "But only in my dream."

"Didn't we tell you when we first came here that you weren't to cross this road? It's a dangerous road, Michael. You can't see the traffic because of the hollows. Didn't we tell you that?"

"But it was only in my dream," Michael protested feebly. His father's hand on his shoulder seemed to reassure him. The road was empty at the moment and they crossed it quickly, into the field where thistles grew thickly on the grassy slope leading up to the ruin.

Michael had fetched the amulet from here, there could be no doubt about it. The Milecastle, one of the best preserved on the Wall, looked as if it had been vandalized. The small stones from a ten-foot section had been scattered in a wide arc into the field. There was a deep gouge in the earth, and the turf was scattered in a similar pattern to the building stone. The "fetching" of the amulet had been as explosive as ever; perhaps more so.

But Michael was unharmed. There were no obvious cuts on his begrimed features, and he complained of no bruises.

"You *were* here, Michael. Weren't you?"

The boy ran round the Milecastle wall. "Only in my dream," he said again, and then smiled. "This was the door. I went in through the door." He walked through the narrow gap in the stones where once a wooden gate had protected the interior. Richard followed him into the square space and stood on the low mound where once the barrack building had been constructed. Michael turned toward him, stepped up on to the mound and glowed with excitement as he said, "It's cold now, but there was a fire here. And two Romans. One of them was very smelly. The other one was drinking. He's the one who gave me the present. They both seemed frightened by me, but I told them I was just dreaming and looking for Parnesius. Then the thin one put on his helmet. He looked angry. When he gave me the amulet I reached for it . . ."

There was a sudden hesitation, a guilty glance

behind him, then Michael stared up at his father, his eyes tearful in the harsh dawn light. The wind was brisk.

"What happened, Michael?"

Sadly, the boy said, "I fetched it, but I fetched the helmet too ... I didn't mean to. But it *was* only a dream."

And yet, he could see well enough that it hadn't been a dream. He seemed sad now, his excitement dulled.

"Where's the helmet, Michael?"

Again, the boy looked round, then pointed across the interior of the Milecastle. Richard saw the brown object, leaning against the gray stone. It looked like a smooth cowpat, blending almost totally with the natural browns and greens of the grass that overgrew this place. It was a helmet, though, in traditional Roman style, a leather cap over metal, with a neck fringe and cheek guards.

It was not complete. It had been cut across, as if by a sword, so that it consisted only of crown and left cheek-guard.

Richard stooped and picked it up, and something wet and bloody slipped from inside, landing heavily on the ground. The piece of skull was covered with short-cropped auburn hair. The ear was scarred and deformed. Mercifully, the eye was closed.

"What is it?" Michael asked nervously from the wall of the Milecastle. Richard turned quickly.

"Go into the field and wait for me. *Don't* cross the road. Is that clear?"

Silently, Michael departed, glancing furtively back. He knew what he had done. He was expecting to be punished.

When the boy was out of sight Richard scooped the skull fragment back into the cold helmet and carried it through the north gate of the wall. Here the land dropped smoothly to fields and a copse of wind-wrecked trees surrounding a shallow, muddy pond. His hand shook as he held the human remains by the ear, trying not to gag. He reached out over the pond and pressed the cut bone into the mud, skin side down, burying it deeply.

"What did you see, I wonder?" he murmured to the water grave. "What was it like to see the ghost? What did your companion make of your sudden death?"

It was a strange and disturbing thought. He wondered if the rest of the body of Michael's "Parnesius" was buried anywhere in the area. He wondered whether an account of the attack had been written up in dispatches. Perhaps somewhere in the archives the tale of the murder could be read.

"One of them was smelly?"

Susan shuddered violently and sat down on the bed, staring distantly through the window. Richard paced up and down, then reached for the lucky charm, dangling it in his fingers.

"Astonishing, isn't it? Just a few hours ago this was slung round the neck of a Roman auxiliary. If we took it to a forensic laboratory they'd probably find his skin scales, bits of hair, even his blood type. There's sweat on the leather—" He rubbed the thin thong between thumb and forefinger. "Roman sweat, *circa* 300 AD. And Michael smelled it. Yes. He smelled the odor."

"All his senses engage with the past," Susan murmured. "I wonder if they see *him*?"

"Of course they see him. They called him 'ghost.' They offered a gift to him to get rid of him. They saw something that wasn't solid, but was real enough to frighten the living daylights out of them."

He smiled grimly at a sudden thought. *Daddy, I found Kipling's Parnesius, but I killed him* . . .

Susan stood and went to the window. She was feeling sick, she had said, and she certainly looked it. "No Chalk Boy this time, Rick. He did it all on his own."

Wearily, Richard agreed. "I think Francoise may have been right. Chalk Boy was his own game, his way of rationalizing the power. There was no Chalk Boy in Hawkinge Wood, that time. Nor when he was raw power just fetching dirt by the barrel and room-full . . ."

Susan turned and smiled grimly, then reached for the

cold charm. "This feels uncomfortable," she said, passing it back. "Sell it. As soon as possible."

"I intend to. Won't get much for it, mind you. In the meantime, I hope Michael can see something a little bigger, a little brighter ..."

"I'm worried he'll get hurt. Sometimes the fetching is so devastating."

Richard also worried about that, but the fact was, Michael had never suffered more than a cut or a bruise. He said, "The worst he's done is the earthfall. And he wasn't in control."

"He was cut very badly by the Egyptian dancing girl ..."

"His talent was new. But he does control it more now. He's more focused ..."

He spoke the partial lie with is mind's eye firmly fixed on half a head, falling from a shattered helmet. He spoke it with a mind's view of the damaged wall. But Michael had not been hurt, only dirtied. He had somehow been missed by the explosion he had summoned: he had stood, safely, at the center of the storm.

"The older he gets," Richard murmured, "the more he'll be able to handle it."

"How do you know? How can you be sure?"

"Gut feeling," Richard said feebly. "But look, this is the first time he's focused away from the chalk pit. The first time he's 'done it alone,' if you like. I think he's learning to manipulate the ability more. Which can only be good for all concerned. And he seems happy to fetch things. And as long as he's happy ... we should encourage him."

Susan looked disturbed. "I don't know. Oh God, Rick, I don't know. Who is he? What caused it? What did his mother do to him? I still dream of her, watching. I still see her face, watching. It was not a good birth."

"Nonsense. It was a perfectly good birth. Wasn't it ... ?"

He noticed that she looked round sharply, her eyes dark, but he didn't pursue it. He had long forgotten how distressed Susan had been by the circumstances of the adoption, and to be reminded of it was now unwelcome.

"Michael's fine," he said. "He has a talent. We've got used to it. Just about. We had a stroke of luck. We love him, we'll cherish him, he'll always be happy." He glanced at his watch. "Listen, we have to go. It's a long drive for us both. I'll be home next weekend if I can, otherwise, two weeks' time."

They packed up their walking clothes and left the farm.

Seventeen

There was another letter from Francoise Jeury waiting for them when they arrived home and Susan opened it wearily and warily. The memory of the terse and pointed exchange between them, a year ago, still smarted. Susan had felt threatened, attacked by the simple awareness that Madame Jeury had demonstrated. She also hated to be called a liar . . . especially when she knew that being a liar was the truth of the matter. But Francoise had not let go, writing regularly, asking to visit Michael. Susan had always refused. Now Francoise was inviting the whole family to London.

Michael was agitated. He had liked the woman and was keen to visit her. Francoise had invited him and Carol to see the British Museum, and to visit her own research building and see "psychic archeology" at work.

Eventually, Susan agreed. She had had another thought, a visit that she herself needed to make. And what harm could Francoise Jeury do? She knew about Michael's talent, had been discreet about it—Jack Goodman, as far as she knew, was unaware of Michael's gift. Perhaps it was time to allow Francoise access to Michael.

She got permission from their school to take the children into the city on Tuesday, and they caught an early train to Charing Cross. As arranged, Francoise Jeury met them there, ready to take the children with her to her research rooms in the Ennean Institute for

Paranormal Studies. There was a strained smile, a cautious exchange of pleasantries, and an arrangement to meet later in Russell Square.

Susan made her way immediately to the clinic near Harley Street, and sat for nearly two hours waiting for the consultant who had treated her infertility in the late 1970s.

Dr. Wilson eventually bustled through into reception, flushed and apologetic, his white coat opened in a casual way to reveal the sharp gray suit beneath.

"My dear Mrs. Whitlock, Susan, I can't apologize enough for keeping you waiting. Come this way, won't you? Have you been offered tea?"

He never explained *why* he had kept her waiting so long. His room was heavy with the smell of a chemical, mixed nauseatingly with the reek of a cigar. As if aware of her discomfiture he opened a window, then sat down behind his wide, gleaming desk. He looked very much older than when she had seen him last, deeply lined, his eyelids sagging at the edges, giving him a sad and weary look. The whole room, in fact, seemed sad and weary. Only the desk and his clothing were immaculate. The paint on the walls was faded, as was the carpet. His shelves of books were untidy. The glass bottles and containers, filled with the pale and gray specimens of things that Susan preferred not to think about, were a dusty jumble now, rather than the neat display she remembered avoiding years ago.

"How is young Michael? Doing well? What seems to be his interest? A doctor perhaps? Mathematician?"

Cutting through this small talk, Susan said, "In one way Michael is fine. He's fit and he's healthy." Her voice was quiet, and she stared at the man very firmly. "Dr. Wilson, did you tell me everything?"

Dr. Wilson frowned. "Everything? Everything about what?"

"Years ago. When I was your patient. There was a problem with Michael's birth. We couldn't have him for a while. You can't have forgotten, surely?"

She hadn't intended to put the edge in her voice, but it appeared there, probably the result of her impatience in the waiting room. Wilson flushed, then licked his lips. He glanced around, then stood and walked behind Susan, an infuriating thing to do. She twisted in her chair so that she could keep watching him, denying him the authority he was seeking.

"No," he said quietly. "I haven't forgotten. Why do you bring this up now? I asked you to keep what was done completely to yourself . . ."

"Which I have done. Faithfully. Absolutely. Not even my husband Richard knows. I've honored our agreement. What I want to know is: did you tell me *everything*?"

"What did I tell you, exactly? It's been a long time. Memory dulls."

Susan felt her hands shaking. She was anxious, she realized, although mentally felt quite calm. Repressing her impatience she said, "Michael's birth-mother changed her mind after twenty-four weeks and insisted that you abort her child. She tried to do herself damage, which you managed to prevent. You were very shocked by her distress and started to inject her with what you called a chemical cocktail that would have done the job of killing Michael in the womb. But then she changed her mind again. You said it was as if she'd suddenly seen a clear light and realized the consequences, not just for her, but for me too, the prospective mother. She stopped you in time, but you were afraid that some damage might have been done to Michael. What you were doing was illegal, as was our private deal, so I've kept silent about it. As I said, even from Richard."

"Times changed quite fast," Wilson said with a weary sigh, returning to sit behind his desk. "Within two years of that dreadful day the law was changed . . ."

"Never mind that. You told me that you were sure no damage had been done to the embryo. To Michael."

"I'm sure of it. No damage to Michael at all. Why do you ask? Now? So many years later."

"Because there's something very strange about my son . . ."

"A physical strangeness? Susceptibility to disease? What, exactly?"

"He has a talent." What should she say? What *could* she say? "It's what you might call a psychic ability. He has a quite incredible degree of extrasensory perception."

Wilson's quick smile was infuriating. Susan leaned forward on the polished desk and almost shouted at the man. "It's terrifying, Dr Wilson. The boy is frightened. I'm frightened. We're *all* frightened. It's a part of our lives, now, but what's going to happen in later years? Perhaps you can't imagine it, but this sort of—this sort of *ability* affects a family at its core! The mood of the family, the plans of the family, the happiness in the family, everything has to adjust itself to one focus, one frightening, uncontrolled, unbelievable focus! Is it possible that you did something, something that other clinics have since reported, something that can affect the mind? *Did* that chemical cocktail as you called it get into the fluid around Michael? What was in the cocktail?"

"I swear to you that it didn't," Wilson said in a half-whisper. "I have tried to forget that incident, Mrs. Whitlock. I can't begin to tell you how ashamed I feel about what happened."

"But *nothing* happened . . . According to you, *nothing* happened."

You're lying. You're hiding something . . .

When Wilson remained silent she repeated again, more calmly, "Nothing happened, you said. His mother tried to inflict self-damage. But she didn't. You tried to inflict damage. But you didn't go through with it."

She leaned back, shuddering. She felt cold, despite the heat of her words.

Wilson nodded. "Everything you say is true."

"Then it *has* to come from his mother." She straightened again, met Wilson's gaze as calmly as possible. "You *must* let me speak to the mother. Please. You refused me before. But I must speak to her. Please!"

"She didn't want to have anything to do with you or to know who you were. She made that very clear to me, and I'm sorry, Mrs. Whitlock, but I have to respect those wishes."

Susan slapped her hand on the table, a gesture of frustration. "That was nine years ago. Perhaps she's mellowed. Perhaps things would be different now. Dr. Wilson, I'm not doing this for myself. I'm not asking this out of some selfish need for one mother to face the other. This is for my family, and for Michael himself! There's something terribly wrong with him, except that . . ."

Wilson prompted her to continue.

"Except that in one way it's very right. In one way it's wonderful. But it *can't* be right, and deep down I feel this. If I could just speak to the woman. On the phone even. Couldn't you arrange that?"

Quite abruptly, Wilson stood, remaining behind his desk, clearly signaling that the interview was over. His florid face had paled around the eyes, and Susan noticed that a touch of sweat gleamed along his hairline. "I made some decisions in the seventies which I would not make now, and about which I feel no pride, nor satisfaction, but only guilt . . ."

Private abortions for ridiculous fees, private exchanges of unwanted babies for ridiculously high fees, yes Doctor, I know all about that . . .

"I want very much to forget about those years."

"But I'm not going to let you," Susan said defiantly. She stood and smiled, then reached out a hand which Wilson slowly met, shaking the tips of her fingers as he watched her calm face.

"What do you mean?"

"I mean I'm going to nag you to despair until you agree to at least tell Michael's birth-mother that I urgently need to speak to her."

Relishing the alarm in Dr. Wilson's face, Susan waited a moment before adding, "Don't worry. I made a promise to you which I intend to keep. But I can be very persistent, Dr. Wilson. Just try for me. That's all I ask. Just try."

The man sat down, equally defiantly, it seemed to

Susan. He stared at her with an expression that dissolved from panic to supercilious contempt.

"You paid a great deal of money for Michael . . ."

"Yes. Money that I didn't really have. A fee that has affected our lives ever since. Except that—" she smiled at the thought, "Michael seems to be doing his best to pay us back."

When she refused to elaborate, Wilson drew breath and scribbled a note on his pad. "Very well, Mrs. Whitlock, I'll see what I can do."

Eighteen

"Now let's see what you can do. Are you ready?"
"Ready!"
"Are you steady?"
"Steady!"
"Then ... Go!"

On the screen in front of Michael the pin-points of light began to run, to move and zigzag, avoiding his cross-hairs brilliantly. The chair in which he sat rocked and twisted, giving a tremendous sensation of speed and movement as he chased the aliens. His fingers gripped the control sticks and he fired, but missed, then fired again, missing sometimes by only a whisker. The helmet he wore was not comfortable. It began to tug at his ears, rubbing the skin, but the game became so fascinating that he forgot about the chafing. As he concentrated on the chase and the kill, so he focused harder. He quickly learned to concentrate on just one of the small, spiraling spots. He went after it for all he was worth.

He missed again, then again he overshot, but as the chair went with him, and his cries of delight filled the room, so the target spot seemed to glow more brightly.

Get into the center. Get closer!

He concentrated, as Francoise had told him to, on slowing the spot down. He willed it to get into the cross-hairs. He held it steady in his mind, holding it, slowing it, making it reluctant to move, chaining it like an animal so that it could only struggle, not escape.

After five minutes of exhilaration, the "alien" came into the cross-hairs.

He fired, screaming as his thumb pressed the trigger.

The spot exploded in a sequence of concentric circles and the word AAARGH appeared flashing on the screen.

Carol was clapping her hands with delight.

"I *did* it," Michael exalted. "I *did* it!" He removed the helmet and passed it to Francoise, who was watching him and smiling.

"Well done," she said. "That's one spot that will never live to fight another day."

"But what did I *do*?" the boy asked. He knew this was a test of his power. Francoise showed him round to the back of the game unit, where strips and ribbons of black material told him that cable connections were in profusion.

"The idea of the test is to see if you can manipulate the electron stream that creates the white spot on the screen. By concentrating very hard and letting the natural power—which we call telekinesis—take over, some people can bring the spot into the cross-hairs very fast. They can override the program that governs the movement of the stream. Do you see?"

"And I did that? I did that?"

Francoise's hand on his shoulder was reassuring. He saw her glance away at a technician, and almost at once intuited that perhaps he had been a bit slow in manipulating the stream. But at least he had done it!

Carol had a go next—at her own insistence—and he watched her struggle with the attack game. She was hopeless, although eight minutes later she too suddenly and unexpectedly shot the target. He was glad she had been slower than him!

"I suppose that means we've both got this teleskin . . . telekis . . ."

"Telekinesis," Francoise corrected carefully. "Well, whether you have or haven't doesn't really matter. You have a much stronger power, Michael. And I'd like to hear you talk about it. Where's Carol gone now?"

Carol was peering into a dark chamber where

gerbils, in a re-creation of the night desert, were scampering around, burrowing and feeding. She had adored this particular experiment when shown it earlier, but not for any reason to do with the attempts to demonstrate inter-rodent ESP (a project that had been running for years, Francoise had said tiredly), but simply because of the gorgeous little creatures themselves. Later she would be given a gift, a mating pair of gerbils, and Susan would groan at the thought of what that meant in terms of feeding, cleaning, and looking after them. With the exception of her painting, Carol was a girl of brief enthusiasms. The story of her guinea pig was still too painful to recall.

For the moment, though, Francoise arranged for Carol to be shown more of the animal experiments . . . those at least that dealt with *fauna intacta*.

She took Michael back to her office and sat him down in the reclining chair, letting him play with the controls for a while as she busied herself with some paperwork.

There was something very comforting in this room, Michael felt. Its walls were nothing but shelves, and on those shelves were statues, weapons, bits of glass and metal, stone heads and wooden masks . . . many books too. It was a feeling with which he was quite familiar from his father's studio, and his mother's workroom, where the books and dolls were constantly breathing their history and their mystery.

He had asked a thousand questions about the objects in Francoise Jeury's collection. He had pressed her for facts and hints about the Holy Grail. What did she think it looked like? She reminded him that he'd asked her about this before.

Was it still to be a surprise for his father when he found it? Yes. And how desperately he wanted to find it!

"Sometimes, when I'm searching for it, I think it's made of glass," he said.

Francoise seemed surprised. "Glass? The Grail made of glass?"

"Beautiful glass, with the face of Our Lord and a

swimming fish painted on its outside. That's the Fisher King. I can see it faintly, sometimes, but I never manage to reach it. To fetch it. I always get something wrong. It's . . ." he thought hard to remember the word he had read. "It's *elusive*."

"Tell me how that feels. Fetching. When you get it wrong?"

Michael was confused. It was something he hadn't thought about sufficiently to articulate.

"It's like reaching into water for a pebble, but you see your hand going to a different pebble. Wherever you try to go, you go somewhere else, and you can't control it."

Francoise laughed. "There used to be a game in my seaside town in France. There was a crane in a case and you had to try to pick up chocolate bars. But if you tried to make the crane go to the right, it would go to the left. Everything was in reverse. It took a very skillfull child to get it to work properly."

"I've seen them," Michael said politely. "In Brighton. Places like that."

"It's a strange sensation."

"Yes."

"And you feel something physical like that when you try and fetch? You are almost on target, but sometimes are forced away?"

"Yes. Like pushing through a blanket. And the object changes sometimes, so that it isn't the object at all. I've reached to somewhere else, somewhere that wasn't in the dream. It's like a speeded-up film of clouds and seasons. Like in *The Time Machine*."

"The Time Machine?"

"It's a film. Daddy loves it. We've got it on video. Years pass over this man's head as he sits in a time machine in his laboratory, looking outside."

Michael realized that he was sounding excited and grinned and lowered the pitch of his voice. He noticed that Francoise was watching him intently. "It happens to me sometimes. I reach toward something, but I get shifted into other places and the seasons change. Sometimes it's very hot, but mostly it's cold and wet."

"But you always fetch something?"

"Not always," Michael said uneasily.

"Why do you think you miss the target? What makes you miss?"

Michael shrugged. It seemed obvious to him. "Chalk Boy, I suppose. I can't see anything at all without Chalk Boy."

"Why would Chalk Boy make you miss the target?"

Michael seemed to have no answer. Eventually an idea occurred to him. "Perhaps he's like the Time Traveler, moving so fast through time that he can't focus on any one thing. Not all the time. Sometimes he does. Did you see the wolf-girl? That was the first thing I fetched. It was like *flying*."

"Was Chalk Boy there?"

"He was hiding. He always hides. But he was watching. I could hear him laughing."

"Can you remember how it was to fly? Can you remember in detail?"

Michael couldn't. It was like a dream now, fragmented, colorful, but partial. He remembered the faces vaguely. He remembered reaching for the wolf-girl. He remembered the smells of the place, such a cold place, a stone place, the odd light . . .

Francoise was saying, "Can I talk to you in a special way, Michael? Would you mind? I shouldn't do this, of course." She leaned forward, meeting his gaze steadily. "I have to tell you very truthfully: without speaking to your mother or father, I shouldn't do this. But I don't think they'd say yes. So if you want to say no . . ."

"What special way?"

"I want to relax you. When you're relaxed I'll talk to a part of you that's hidden."

"You mean hypnotize me?"

"Not exactly. Something very new. A new technique. Something far more interesting. A way of talking to you that can hear voices in your head that even you didn't know were there. There is no harm. We've developed the technique for talking in this way over the last three years. And I'll make a record for you."

"What sort of record?"

"A record of your inner voices. You'll hear the voices you speak in your dreams. You can take it home and play it, if you want. As soon as I've confessed to your parents. It will sound just like you, but it's you when you were dreaming, not when you were awake. Can I talk to you? Will you let me?"

Michael felt frightened. He liked this woman. She exuded nice, comforting smells, and much security. But Chalk Boy was shifting and restless. Chalk Boy liked to hide. Chalk Boy didn't like to be seen, or heard. And anyway, if Francoise went into his dreams, then she might see that Michael was just a shadow, just a not-quite-boy. And he had felt so *full* talking to her. He felt real. He didn't want her to see the hollow inside his head, the Limbo land, the sea and its monsters, the shadow that was all that was left of his soul.

He shook his head, instantly aware that the woman looked disappointed, failing to hide the emotion before she smiled and shrugged.

"I just wanted to ask you what you saw when you fetched the wolf-girl."

Hesitantly, Michael said, "That would be all right. But you mustn't ask to speak to Chalk Boy."

"Oh, I wouldn't. I won't. I promise. What else mustn't I do?"

"Don't go down to the beach. Don't go near the sea. It's dangerous."

"Then I promise I won't go down to the sea. I just want you to tell me what you saw when the wolf-girl was 'fetched.' Nothing more."

"All right."

With obvious relief, she said, "Thank you, Michael. Now then: lean back and half close your eyes, and watch my mouth. The first thing I'm going to do is sing to you."

"Sing to me! Why?"

"I'm afraid I'm not up to Tina Turner standard—"

"I don't like Tina Turner."

"You don't? I think she's wonderful. But my little

song is a key to your mind. It's a program. And you'll like it, I'm sure ..."

Susan came to the research center in time for a late lunch. She was on edge, perhaps disturbed by whatever had happened at her own meeting that morning. Francoise therefore excused herself after just a few minutes, leaving the Whitlocks to eat on their own. Later, she would take them round the British Museum, if that was still of interest, but for the moment she returned to her room and sat quietly, listening to the whispered voice of Michael's journeying shadow, and its disappointingly fragmentary report.

It had been hard to gain access—even though she rejected the comparisons between mind and computer, she still found herself thinking in crude and basic computer jargon—to Michael's dream mind, the harmonic memory plane where he would be storing the dream structures of the actual psychic event associated with each apportation. Unlike ordinary memory storage, these packages were mainly impulse-noise and transient-RNA, cyclical and shifting little whirlpools that were very hard to phase into.

She had sung the cadences that she believed would trigger the cortic-aural access, but he had simply smiled and shifted, obviously comfortable with the sound, but not responding. As she sang she watched the vocal signal of his own song, recorded on tape the time of her visit to his house. She could see the points of access, the stress points where her own vocalization would need to establish a monotonal contrast, but she couldn't maneuver her own voice into quite the right position.

She felt like a child, targeting a pin-point of light to shoot it. The comparison made her smile.

Her song flexed. She struggled to combine the signals, the living signal of her voice, and the static signal of Michael's voice-profile. All the time the feedback from the chair showed red.

Then—strike!—the feedback lines flushed green and Michael went strangely stiff.

And she managed to enter him. With questions, of course, not with her mind.

She listened to the voice, to the memory of a journey:

The beach is a scary place. The Fish Lizards hide in the waves and strike suddenly on the shore. Their jaws have a formidable array of fang-like teeth. The Sea Dragons are as long as their contemporaries, but rather broader. The beach is very dangerous, but I can run across it and call from the quarry.

Where is this beach? Tell me more about the beach.

It's where the Wealden disappeared. Very quietly and gradually the forest and plains, the tall trees and hideous reptiles of the Wealden passed away—

Who has told you this? These aren't your own words.

—the slow sinking of the whole area caused deeper and deeper water to appear in the creeks and river channels. The lakes that ended the Chalk Age had an immense duration in time and space—they were vast meres, bordered by extensive marshes—they are Limbo, and the Fish Lizards prey upon the Limbo souls—

If the beach is so dangerous, why do you go there before you "fetch"?

Have to go through it to hold on to Michael—

Who is talking to me now?

Michael's shadow.

Chalk Boy?

No. Chalk Boy is hiding. I'm Michael's shadow. I come into Michael to make him visible. Then he can breathe real air. But when he's breathed properly I guide him through Limbo to other times.

Tell me how you guided him to the golden wolf-girl . . .

(But Michael twisted uncomfortably in his chair, head shaking, flecks of spittle at the corners of his mouth. His tongue licked out and his eyes half opened, like those of a corpse. Before Francoise could interrupt proceedings, however, he had calmed.)

My shadow is sinking into ice. I am moving at great

speed. Now I can breathe again and everything is still.
It's so cold. Deep snow has piled against the lodge. I
am by the huge pile of Mammoth bones, touching their
icy surfaces. The old man has been here with his two
drums and selected five of the long-bones to repair the
Moon Lodge where the women go, which blew down
in the storm. I move over the snow like a shadow. Only
the dogs can see me, and they snap and miss. I flow
into the Drum Lodge and reach for what the old man
is working on. He is unaware of me. The lodge smells
badly of fresh skins, blood and fat. The fire in the center is dull, but there is drifting ash in the air and a haze
covers the bright animals and grinning faces drawn on
the skins. Two women watch me, they can see me now,
but they cover their faces with crossed pieces of bone
and I can't see them. The old man holds out his pipe
to me. The paint is fresh on the white bone. His eyes
are narrow and he is smiling. He follows me with his
eyes as my shadow passes round the smoky room, always holding out the pipe. His words are like hisses,
but I can hear that he is asking a question. I don't want
the bright bone pipe. I want brighter things for Daddy,
but they are not here. I have come to the wrong place.
I move slowly, like wading in deep water. When I
reach for the pipe my hand misses and touches the
spikes of hair on his head, making them bend. They are
sticky with fat. The rest of his hair is hanging in
bunches and decorated with painted shells and stones.
His head rattles as he turns to follow me. The women
are visible again and they are crawling through the low
tunnel, between the doorframe of white bones, and
making funny sounds. So I fetch the pipe and the loge
collapses, the first is scattered, and the old man
screams and curls into a ball, holding his arm. The
pipe is broken, but I run with part of it through the
snow and the shadow leaves me on the beach and I am
back in my castle . . . But Chalk Boy is laughing . . . he
is mocking me, mocking me . . .

Michael! Sing to me. Sing to me, Michael.

(Michael started to cry.)

Mocking Boy ... Mocking Boy ...

Michael! Sing. Sing "Ghostbusters"!

(The boy's lips moved and, in the faintest of voices, he emitted the hesitant words of the song ... If there's something strange ... in the neighborhood ... Who do you call? ... Ghost *busters* ...

(And came back from his journey.)

Nineteen

The work in Scotland finished midway through the second week and Richard found himself unexpectedly released from the project. He was delighted. He gathered his belongings, ran through the driving rain to the main hut and said his good-byes. Everyone was thoroughly miserable and morale was so low that the Project Director was calling a halt until the spring. The site would be covered. Photographs were now not needed.

Rain lashed the car as far south as Barnard's Castle in County Durham, but then clearer weather made the drive easier and faster. By four in the afternoon Richard was at the service station at Watford Gap, calling home.

Susan sounded thrilled, and not just because her husband was coming home a week early. There was something waiting for him at home ... she wouldn't say what ... no, it was a surprise ... but just assume that Santa has visited early this year.

Michael's fetched something new? From the pit?

Wait and see.

How *is* Michael?

Excited, happy ... longing for the story of the lake village you've been digging up.

There *is* no story about the lake village. It's just a *crannog,* there's no legend associated with it.

Susan laughed. Lover, she said, you've got about four hours' driving to come up with one. And make sure it involves the Grail. And preferably two of Ar-

thur's Knights. Any two will do. Michael is longing to
hear it. He says . . . he says he's already dreamed about
the lake village.

He's dreamed about it? What has he dreamed?

He says there's something bright there, something to
be found, something buried beneath the house with the
wooden "watching-man." Does that mean anything to
you?

Wooden watching-man? No. At least, not yet. I'm on
my way.

There were presents for everybody. Michael had
wrapped them in Christmas paper—long since on sale
in the shops—and placed them, labeled, on the dining
table. There was an orange-crate of other things on the
floor, at the side of the room, but these were all broken
or ugly, and he knew that his father would probably
want to sell them to his friend in London.

He thought he had seen the Grail, but he had been
wrong. Nevertheless, the crushed metal vessel—like a
miniature witch's cauldron—that had crashed through
the pit a week ago, as he had fetched it, had been full
of glittering things, some of them very pretty.

The night after that he had dreamed of the wooden
watching-man, its face just two eyes and a grim mouth,
its arm stretched out, its legs stuck into the mud with
the bright shield between them. On the shield was the
face of an animal, surrounded by swirls and lines. It
was a funny-shaped shield, in the dream, kinked in the
middle, not round or square like a Roman shield. One
day he'd like to fetch it, if he could.

Where *was* Daddy? It was getting dark. And he
could hear Chalk Boy calling him from the pit. There
was a funny breeze in the pit, a freezing wind that just
went round and round, between the bushes; near where
the earth was so hot, the earth-spill that Michael knew
was from the house, from when he had been born. The
funny wind had been there for a day, and although he
hadn't heard from Chalk Boy for weeks now, he could
hear the boy's voice in the distance. Chalk Boy
sounded as if he was in pain. It was quite frightening

for Michael, and he felt uncomfortable in his castle. But it was there that he had seen the treasure cauldron. And he had fetched it *without* Chalk Boy.

Downstairs, Carol shouted loudly, there was running, a door opening, and outside the sound of the car on the gravel.

Smiling, Michael settled back into the corner of his room, his heart racing as he imagined what his father would feel when he saw the gifts.

"This one's for you . . ."

Richard reached for the small, paper-wrapped object. It was heavy and he almost dropped it as he accepted it from Michael's shaking grip. The boy watched him eagerly. The family were sitting round the table, while the smell of roast chicken came from the kitchen.

"Hurry up. Hurry up . . ." Michael urged. Richard caught Susan's eye and she raised an eyebrow.

"Do you know what's in here?" he asked with a smile, and she shook her head.

"It's a surprise to us all," she murmured, but her look told Richard that she'd already seen all the objects that Michael had fetched. This was Michael's game. She'd been sworn to secrecy.

He unwrapped an egg, slightly larger than a hen's egg. It was of gold, of course. It was covered with designs. His breath caught, for a moment, in total shock.

Then he said, with a laugh, "Where's the goose?" and looked under the table.

Michael said earnestly, "It's not a goose's egg. It's a Grail treasure."

"Don't you remember the story of the goose that laid the golden egg?" Richard smiled as he spoke.

Michael's face darkened. "It's a *treasure*. It's not a goose egg." He became agitated.

Momentarily taken aback by the vehemence in Michael's voice, Richard quickly regained the initiative.

"No. Of course it's not, Michael. It's beautiful. By God, it's beautiful. It's the best Grail treasure yet!"

Susan had seemed alarmed, but relaxed as the moment of missed-point and anguish passed.

"What funny—what lovely pictures. They seem to tell a story ..."

He turned the lump of gold around. It reminded him of the Phaistos disc, a terracotta disc discovered on Crete and dating from late Minoan times. This egg had a descending spiral channel scored into its skin, a channel that was divided into compartments, or cartouches. In each cartouche was a set of designs: faces, ships, houses, ears of wheat, bronze ingots, signals familiar to him, and others besides that were indecipherable. Each group of glyphs would represent a word. This was writing that pre-dated Linear A.

"This is *wonderful*. It's a wonderful present. Thank you. I shall treasure it."

"Don't sell it," the boy said hoarsely and with great meaning.

"Of course not. I shall treasure it."

Susan leaned forward. "Can we open ours now?"

Michael was staring hard at his father, his face open, his eyes filled with a longing that Richard had no idea how to fill. He kept repeating how beautiful the story-egg was. And then he remembered his duty and mentioned that he had a great story for Michael that night, all about the lake-village—he referred to it by the common name of *crannog,* but appended the word "castle" ... Castle Crannog—and the story of a Lost Shield.

Michael's face dissolved into knowingness and pleasure. He anticipated the story, but also being able to talk about his dream.

Susan unwrapped her present. It was the arm and part of the torso of a silver figure, female, originally about twelve inches high, Richard guessed. It had been broken raggedly, and there were the marks, on the broken edge, of a blade used violently. A figurine hacked to pieces for booty, perhaps. Michael had thought it part of a doll, and so it was an obvious present for his mother.

Carol was visibly nervous as she unwrapped the paper on the flattened object that was Michael's gift to her. It was a shell, a brilliant piece of mother-of-pearl, carved delicately to show two horsemen of proud bearing against a high mountain behind. It had been bored round the edge to make twenty tiny holes. Not a necklet, then, but something that had been tied in a frame. Carol thought it was very pretty. Michael said, "You can paint it. Or draw it." He was still occasionally cautious in his approach to his younger sibling, perhaps remembering the fights of past years, in particular his assault on her when she had tampered with the Mocking Cross.

Carol thanked him, staring at the shell in a confusion of pleasure and puzzlement. When he deemed it appropriate, Richard examined the piece of art carefully. He noticed that the riders were wrapped against the cold. The mountains were not the familiar high hills of Chinese geography, more the mountains of Central Europe. Indeed, the details of the weapons and objects, even the dress of the two horsemen shown, suggested that this shell was something that had been carved four or five thousand years ago.

He could hardly be sure. He just felt that he was holding a preciously saved piece of proto-Indo-European art.

This was from the first period of real migration history. The riders could have been going west toward Greece and the Danube, or east toward the Ganges and a rendezvous with the Orient that would develop into the earliest of the great myths of India.

If it was real, this shell, and if his interpretation was right, this simple piece of carving was more valuable than anything that had yet come through Michael into the present.

"I think I'd like to paint in the colors," Carol said.

It was a moment of agony for the archaeologist in Richard Whitlock.

"Don't you think it's very pretty just the way it is?"

Carol stared at the shell, her brow furrowing. Then she said, "The horses are very small. They don't look like real horses."

"That's true. They don't. Why don't you paint them on a piece of paper? *Imagine* what color they were. See if it looks right."

"That's what real artists do," Susan said helpfully, and this simple statement was enough to resolve the doubt in the girl's mind. She seemed delighted with the suggestion. Richard was relieved.

The children went to bed, suppered, scrubbed, cleaned, happy. Richard was tired and Michael was given a teaser for the big story the next day, and he seemed to accept this, understanding that his father was tired and that guests were coming. For the boy, the simple pleasure of Richard's delight had been enough to send him scampering to the sheets, to dream of shields and wooden watching-men.

Jenny and Geoff Hanson were coming round for a meal, by prior arrangement, and Richard was certainly now in the mood to celebrate, so they had decided not to cancel the evening.

As Michael washed and dressed for bed, prior to his brief good night story, Richard searched through the rest of the contents of the cauldron.

The cauldron itself was iron, very old, much used, and patterned with a simple design. It had been crushed from one side, and the handle was missing. The crushing looked new—a probable consequence of its fetching—but the loss of the handle seemed to be a part of its history.

It was a votive-offering collection vessel. It had probably been carried during a migration, or perhaps kept in a shrine. The shell would have been something inherited, if it was as old as he suspected, since the iron cauldron couldn't have dated from much before the first millennium BC.

The Minoan egg and the silver statue fragment would have been the accumulated wealth of a clan accustomed to raiding to the south of their tribal lands.

Much of what was in the cauldron was fragmentary: gold, silver, faïence, amber, some jade (which was beautiful), much bronze, more shell, very broken, and an astonishing little carving in jet of a hare on the run.

The total worth of the haul was hard to estimate: but

many thousands, if Goodman's contacts were as effective as they had been up to now.

Richard quickly drove to the local off-license and bought two bottles of cheap champagne. By the time Jenny and Geoff arrived, their hosts were practically dancing on the table and the chicken had begun to burn.

At the beginning of the spring, Richard was requested to travel north again, to the site of the Iron Age crannog. The excavation had been re-started three weeks before, and almost immediately—prompted by Richard's earlier communication—a satellite hut had been found. This building had been constructed apart from the main village platform but still within the lakes, and was probably reached by a bridge. It was a shrine hut, and as such was both rare and the signifier that this particular village was a tribal center, perhaps the settlement of a king.

Richard's job was again to photograph the confusion of objects and building materials that were emerging from the peat.

Among them were the fragmentary remains of a large oak statue, male, a deity. It was broken in many places, and much was lost. All the signs suggested that it had been shattered in antiquity by an act of appalling violence. Parts of the effigy appeared to be scattered over several yards. As if—as one student remarked— as if someone had set a bomb off below its sprawling legs.

Had a shield been discovered among the litter of this destructive act? Richard asked.

A shield? No. Why should there be a shield?

Richard walked over to the deep cut in the peat and stood on the planking, thinking about a lake and a small enclosure in the middle of the silent water, reached by a walkway, or perhaps isolated from the main village, its concealed god accessible only by canoe. Had Michael been there in his dreams? Had he snatched that shield into a time still in his own future?

It was a strange and thrilling sensation, imagining that event. But how had Michael dreamed of the place?

Had he focused his mind through his father's own senses? Had he followed his father to the North, demonstrating a greater attachment than even Richard had been aware of?

There were too many questions, too many confusions, and he returned to the Portakabin where he kept his camera equipment.

PART FOUR

The
Wasteland

Twenty

The flight from Orly airport was delayed by fog and didn't set down in Gatwick until after midnight. Francoise Jeury, tired, restless and distracted, was furious with the hold-up, made a fuss at the flight desk and insisted on the airline paying for a taxi to take her to London. The visit to her home, in Brittany, had been distressing; memories of her first husband were always strongest at this time of the year, when autumn was freezing rapidly into winter.

She sat in silence for the hour's drive to her flat in Clapham, fending off the attempts at conversation by the driver, and not complaining at all when he set the radio to play midnight jazz. She hardly noticed the journey, the streaming lights of the motorway, the darkness of the land beyond.

At two o'clock she found Lee curled on the sofa in his dressing-gown, reading. The flat was freezing.

"I thought you'd be in bed."

The man looked tired, unshaven and slightly irritated. "A friend of yours has been calling."

"A friend? Which one?"

"They'll call again." Lee Kline stood, kissed Francoise, then shivered. "Electric fire, I think."

"Electric fire, I *know*," she said. "How can you sit in this cold?"

"Saving money."

"We don't need to save money."

"There's a recession looming. Didn't you know?"

"There's always a recession looming in this wretched country. Which friend? I'm not in the mood to talk."

"Nor is he. Not to me, anyway."

"Aha!" she laughed and pinched Lee through his robe. "Now I understand. The man is jealous because it's my other lover calling me to whisper sweet nothings to me."

"Since when did you start dating children?"

She frowned. "A child?"

"A child who whispers down the phone."

"A child who whispers down the phone . . . ?"

"A child who calls you 'Frances.' "

"A child who calls me *Frances*?"

"Who tap dances."

"Who *tap dances* . . . !?" she broke off, frowning. "Is this a joke?"

Lee was laughing.

"Don't joke. I'm tired. I'm not feeling well."

"I'll get some tea. Then bed. We could always take the phone off the hook."

As if to counter that, the phone rang, unnervingly loudly in the still, cold night. Francoise carried it to the fire, sat down on the floor and lifted the receiver.

"Who is this?" she asked.

There was the sound of sea, like rushing waves. Then the sound died away and a voice hissed, "It's Chalk Boy. Are you Frances?"

"Francoise. Is that you, Michael?"

"Michael's sleeping," whispered the eerie voice. "This is Chalk Boy. I want to see you."

Francoise was confused, the tiredness in her head not fully evaporating as she tried to work out what was going on. Why was Michael playing this funny game? And so late at night! It was a year or more since she had seen him in London. Again, Susan had put a barrier between her son and the other woman.

"It *is* you, isn't it, Michael?"

"Michael's sleeping. I told you. Come to me now. I want to talk to you."

"Michael—Chalk Boy, I mean: it's very late, and I'm very tired."

It was as if fury possessed the figure at the other end. The sea surged, the waves crashed, Francoise could hear pebbles, or . . . the boy making sounds *like* the sea. He was very good. As the sea-sounds stopped, so the voice hissed again, "You said you wanted to talk to me. You told Michael you wanted to talk to me."

"I haven't forgotten. But Michael never called me when you were around."

"Daddy . . ."

"Daddy? What about Daddy?"

"Michael's Daddy," said the voice, "didn't think he should. But you must come and talk to me. Come to the castle."

"I'll come tomorrow," she said wearily. "Have you got something to show me?"

"Come *now*. Come *now*."

"It's a long way to drive, Chalk Boy. It will take me two hours."

"Come anyway. Come to the castle. I'll wait for you at the castle."

"And Michael?"

"I told you. Michael is sleeping. This is Chalk Boy. You said you wanted to see me. Now you can."

"All right. Two hours."

"In the castle."

"In the castle."

The line went dead.

Lee tried to be firm with her, but failed. "You'll crash. You're in no state to drive."

She shrugged him off. Her mind was full of images: of Michael Whitlock, of his father, of their house, of the chalk pit, of a gold mask on a wooden knife. Something in the boy's tone—and she was in no doubt at all that it was Michael who had called, even if he was playing the pretend game—something in his tone had communicated genuine urgency, genuine need. He had rung six times during the late evening and early morning, whispering from the hallway of his house, a boy terrified, freezing, alone in his mind, alone in his castle. Francoise felt for him. He was in trouble. She *had* to respond to his call.

She was so damned tired!

"Will you drive me?"

Lee Kline shook his head, picking up a sheet of paper and holding it out to the woman. She had forgotten that he was due in York at noon the next day. It would be an early start for him too.

"Go in the morning," he said. "Three hours won't make any difference."

"Maybe not. But if they did, what would I do then? He sounded desperate, Lee. I don't know if I can help him, but I know he thinks I can. I have to go. I'll get a taxi."

"It'll cost you a fortune at this time of the morning."

"Perhaps I'll get a valuable present from Chalk Boy," she muttered darkly. With that idea came thoughts of Richard Whitlock, and an anger that she remembered feeling two years or more ago, when she had been at the house in Kent.

It made up her mind for her. She called a taxi, and gasped at the quoted fare, but accepted it. Then she searched her records for the Whitlocks' address before quickly changing her clothes and making a thermos flask of hot, strong coffee.

It was still dark when the taxi reached Ruckinghurst village where the Whitlocks lived. Francoise asked to be driven slowly through the silent street until she identified the dark shape that was Eastwell House. There were three cars in the drive and a long extension to the side of the property. The Whitlocks were doing well. A hundred yards or so up the road was a narrow lane leading out on to the open farmland. The taxi parked here and Francoise shared her coffee with the driver.

They talked quietly and tiredly about the supernatural, French politics and tennis. Eventually a gleam of light in the distance told of the dawn. For a few minutes Francoise watched the pink become shimmering gray-red as the sun lit up the English Channel, visible over the black ridge of the Downs. Then she settled the account with the taxi driver, wished him a safe journey home, and stepped out of the car into the icy November morning.

Her breath frosting, she huddled into her coat. There was a layer of frozen dew on the field and she walked slowly, not liking the sound that her weight made as she trod down the crisp grass. Why she wanted to stay silent she couldn't imagine. Perhaps it was that she felt like an intruder in this virgin, silent dawn.

Someone had crossed the field before her, a line of small footprints quite visible on the wettening grass. They came from the Whitlocks' house and led straight to the quarry.

Francoise followed them.

The light increased and the movement of birds in the winter trees became a distraction. Nevertheless, she was certain she could hear a different sort of movement, farther into the quarry.

She entered Michael's castle through the old access, and tried to remember how he had drawn the circular passages and high gates that marked each level of defense until the Castle Keep was reached. She couldn't recall the drawing at all, and smiled to herself, but even so she couldn't resist the sound effects of pushing back the great wooden gates, and hauling up the drawbridge single-handedly.

She moved steathily through the scrub, aware that the open paths were lined purposefully with chalk and flint blocks, and fragments of dulled iron (what was it called? Marcasite, she thought: iron deposits that formed in chalk under pressure, but were often thought to be the remains of past civilizations, or old weapons from life-forms long extinct). These were Michael's markers and she walked carefully between them, reaching down to touch the iron in several places, feeling for any sign or sense of use by human hand: The iron was cold and dead, however, giving her no ghost-echo at all.

When she emerged and faced the rising wall of chalk she felt uncomfortable. There was something there but not there, a disturbance on the quarry wall that was tickling her senses but not her perception.

She called out for Michael, then corrected herself and tried to summon Chalk Boy.

Daylight, crisp and sharp, crept over the wall and cast stark shadows in the pit. There was a strange line on the sheer rise of chalk, a curving edge, soft and smooth, a ripple like the shadow of a corpse, deepening, lengthening. It seemed to shake, to tremble. Francoise glimpsed it, turned away, glanced up at the azure of the sky, saw birds in dark, dawn flight, felt the tremble of wind in the dying foliage, the flutter of life, the whisper of drying leaves, the movements of life returning from the chill night.

She looked back at the cliff and the shadow had moved. Now it deepened suddenly and abruptly, becoming human-shaped, a tall, slender, elfin shadow that stretched away across the white rock, flowing as it traversed the jagged, uneven surface.

The boy stepped toward her, his eyes opened now, his tall body trembling as the cold ate through his chalk clothes.

White as the chalk, white as the dead, totally white, totally naked, only his eyes a darker shade, but a pale shade, watching and blinking at the woman who stood there, shocked and shivering.

"I've been waiting for you," the figure hissed.

"Aren't you cold?"

"Freezing. It's always cold in Limbo."

"Michael?"

"Michael's sleeping. I've already told you that. Michael sleeps. Chalk Boy is awake. Chalk Boy is here with you. Chalk Boy will show you things. Welcome to Castle Limbo, Frances."

"Francoise. My name is Francoise. I'm French. Glad to meet you."

"I am Chalk Boy. I am angry. I am from a time before human time. My world is cold. Monsters scream in my world. The chalk is new in my world. Where you stand is a beach. Where I stand is a cave. Where the trees grow is the sea. In that sea there are creatures that will eat people who hurt me."

"Who is trying to hurt you, Michael? I mean, Chalk Boy."

The boy was silent. He was still shaking with the cold and Francoise felt concerned for him, but also very confused as to what to do. Remove her coat and offer it to Michael? But he seemed to want to enact something, a ritual, perhaps, or a dream, or part of his imaginary life. He was a boy with talent, with power, and Francoise wanted to know what part of that power was being demonstrated here.

She said, "You look *very* cold. Why don't you take my coat?"

"No."

Below the paint, or chalk, or whatever it was with which he had daubed his body, the goosebumps on his skin stood proud and odd. Francoise thought he looked like a plucked chicken. He also seemed unusually un-embarrassed about his total nudity. He turned and led the way severely round the wall, walking stiffly. The chalk cracked below his buttocks and behind his knees, revealing pink skin.

"Where are we going? Where are you taking me?"

"You are in Limbo," Michael/Chalk Boy growled. "I want to show you the Limbo Creatures."

He had stooped to crawl through the sharp gorse that covered the metal grill, where a hundred years ago quarrymen had scoured into the chalk wall to make a shed for their tools. Francoise could sense fear in the air; perhaps it was Michael's sweat, or his manner, but she could sense it through all her channels, a tangible feeling of terror in the boy.

He emerged from the coarse brush and held out a bundle of sacking. The chalk was beginning to smear on his face. Lines ran through to the flesh below where the sharp thorns had gouged him, scraped him. She could see the ginger of his hair emerging from the calcite.

"What have you got there?"

"Gifts. Things I fetched. Things from Limbo. Chalk Boy's things. *My* things," he corrected quickly.

"Let me see them."

He dropped the sack and opened it. Francoise felt her stomach turn as she surveyed the graying, blackened bodies that were revealed. She counted six even before she approached to look more closely. Chalk Boy had backed off, again pressing himself against the quarry wall.

They were mummified creatures: a cat and a rabbit seemed obvious; a rat or large mouse; a bat seemed obvious when she looked more closely and saw the crushed wings. The fifth creature was unrecognizable, although its jaw was gaping, revealing tiny white teeth. All these creatures were hairless, tiny, contorted, and if she was to take a guess she would have said: unborn. They were fetal creatures, preserved, mummified after being taken from the womb.

The sixth was the fetus of a human, its eye sockets empty, its arms slightly stretched, it mouth open, its belly oddly protuberant. A stiffened length of umbilical cord thrust from the tiny shape.

She reached down and closed the sack over the grotesque shapes, then looked up at Michael.

"Why did you show me these?"

"The Grail," he whispered. "I wanted to find the Grail."

"The Holy Grail?"

"The crystal glass cup of the Last Supper. I thought I saw it. I kept trying to fetch it. But all I fetched was these . . . all of them . . . one at a time."

He was shaking more violently, not with cold now, but with distress. Tears had smudged the chalk below his eyes. Birds were noisy above the quarry, flapping in the winter trees.

Michael's voice dropped from its whisper to a lower sound, a confidential murmur. He seemed terrified. "I'm not really Chalk Boy," he mouthed, the words almost too faint to hear. He leaned closer and repeated what he had said.

"Are you Michael then?"

"Yes," he breathed, then put a finger to his lips.

"Why did you tell me you were Chalk Boy?"

"He *is* here," Michael said desperately, his eyes

wide. "He's hiding. But he wants to see you. I know he does."

"How do you know he does?"

"Because he started to talk about you. But I don't know where he is now."

"So was it Chalk Boy who called me on the telephone? Or you?"

"Me," Michael whispered. "I didn't think you would come to see me unless you thought Chalk Boy would talk to you."

No. I'm sure you didn't. You poor little man. You poor, desperate little man.

"I think that was clever of you. But you should know, Michael, that I *would* have come down, even if you had not pretended. But you did the right thing."

What had gone wrong? The boy was still trembling, looking nervously about. Something terrible had happened to him.

"When you were looking for the Grail, did you see it? Clearly?"

"I thought so. But I think I was being tricked. I think Chalk Boy is angry. Now he's hiding. Sometimes I dream bright things, but when I fetch them, they're all dead. I think he's laughing. He's hiding in the caves on the beach, but he's angry with me."

"Why is he angry?"

Michael's white face creased and his head shook almost imperceptibly. "I don't know. But I can't *find* anything anymore."

Francoise understood. "You mean pretty things. Valuable things. Presents for Daddy and Mummy."

He nodded grimly. "I can't find anything to fetch."

Francoise felt totally at a loss. She reached out a hand for Michael's and squeezed the cold fingers in a gesture of futile reassurance. "But what can I do, Michael? How can I help you?"

"Come with me."

"Come with you? Where?"

"Into the tunnel. Where I fetch things. Perhaps Chalk Boy will come out again if you're there too."

"But how, Michael? How do I do that? You fetch

things from here . . ." She tapped his head and smiled faintly. "I can't get in there with you."

He took off one of the marcasite necklets and passed it to the woman. "I've been wearing these for weeks. I remembered what you said about being able to see and hear things in precious objects. Maybe you can use this to come with me into Limbo."

Nervously, Francoise drew the necklace over her head. She had already gauged that the crystalline metal gave her nothing. It was empty of ghost-echo, despite the boy's best intentions.

The white chalk gleamed in the early morning winter sun. Michael's face became shadowy, his eyes distant. His tug on Francoise's hand was almost urgent, a compulsive grip that relaxed then tightened.

Suddenly the grip loosened and Michael's body went limp. He was still standing, but his jaw had slackened and his eyes dimmed. It frightened Francoise, and she placed her hands on the boy's crown, but felt only the faint vibration of his body, a high-pitched shudder, as if he was in deep shock.

"Chalk Boy?" she called quietly. "If you're there, come out and say hello to me . . ."

For a few moments nothing changed, then the body stopped shaking, stiffened completely, a muscular rigor that alarmed Francoise deeply.

The trees in the pit began to move in a sudden, circulating wind, a freezing wind that flew dead leaves and chalk dust in an increasingly violent spiral about the motionless figures by the quarry wall.

"Michael . . . ?" the woman whispered. Michael's body shuddered. He drew in air suddenly, sucking it in like a drowning man, almost gasping. A strange sound came from him, a keening that shifted into a second drawn breath, then was expressed again in a distant, agonized cry . . .

"Come back, Michael!" Francoise whispered urgently.

But the boy was too far gone. The storm increased. His right arm reached out, the fingers flexing, grasping for some unseen object. His eyes were wide, his mouth stretched into a mask.

The sound still came, desperate breathing, an attempt to cry out resulting in nothing more than a whine.

The explosion was so sudden that Francoise screamed with the shock of it, ducking down and covering her head as the air was filled with stone shrapnel and stinking mud. The blast toppled her. She felt a bruise and a cut on her face. Two of her fingers were in agony, though not broken. A slab of concrete had struck her forcibly.

In the middle of this mayhem Michael was a huddled shape, collapsed, one arm still reaching out, but holding something now, something that glistened, something that flexed, five legs, curling in ...

He threw it away and sobbed. He was clutching the back of his neck, rubbing vigorously where he had been struck, or hurt in some way.

As quickly as the explosion had come, so there was peace. Francoise sat up and brushed dirt and dust from her jeans. The stone fragments were not concrete, but white stone from heavy blocks. There was a lot of gold-inlaid wood, shards only. Some red cloth, and duck feathers. The air smelled of incense and candles.

The living hand had ceased to twitch now, but blood still glistened and seeped from the torn wrist.

Michael was howling, hiding his face. When Francoise went over to him he refused to stand, so she crouched and put her arms around him.

"I'm here. It's all right, Michael."

"He tricked me again! He tricked me again!"

Francoise couldn't stop looking with horror at the hand, its pigmented skin, its smooth fingers: a man's hand, large, undecorated.

Michael sobbed. "I thought I saw it. I reached through stone and there was a man sitting on a chair, watching me. He was dying. I think he was guarding a king in a coffin. There was a candle. He shouted at me. I think he was frightened. When I went to fetch the cup, he tried to stop me and all I got was his hand ..."

Again tears, and the reaction of a terrified boy, a huddling, a rocking down, a crushing of his body into as tight a ball as possible.

She placed her jacket round his shoulders, reached round to button it. "You'll catch you death. Chalk isn't very warm."

"Thank you."

They sat for half an hour or more and the quarry became very still. All sound seemed to have evaporated. On the cold air Francoise could smell the sea. The sky above the pit was an intense and brilliant blue and she lay back on the cold ground, watching that vacancy, that splendid emptiness. Like Michael himself, she was feeling a sudden, powerful peace.

Michael became conscious that he was naked but for a jacket. He seemed embarrassed.

"I ought to go home," he whispered. "I have to get up for school."

He rubbed vigorously at the chalk on his face. When he stood, Francoise's jacket covered him to above the knee. He was getting very tall. He was a thin figure, ten years old and vulnerable, swathed in denim, the sleeves just longer than his hands. He seemed very sad.

"What's the matter?" Francoise asked.

"He's gone."

"Chalk Boy?"

Michael nodded. He seemed very forlorn as he looked at the high wall of the quarry, then closed his eyes, as if listening. Francoise waited quietly. Tears filled Michael's eyes as he turned and walked awkwardly along the cleared path through the trees, Francoise following in silence. Michael said, "He's closed all the gates. He's blocked off the passage. I can't see him or hear him. He's shut me out."

How often had she heard this! This sudden feeling of being shut out, shut off from a world that had been familiar, so real.

She felt sad and sick at heart, distressed for the boy, but she knew exactly what was going on.

Michael's talent was dying. It was as simple, and in

a way as tragic, as that. Perhaps this fetching would prove to have been his last. Chalk Boy had been Michael's way of externalizing the gift that had developed in him, the strange power. His imaginary friend, in an imaginary Limbo world, guiding him to the past, the imagined vehicle of his apportive power. Now that talent was fading as Michael grew older. And he rationalized the death of talent by the closing of gates, by the loss of his friend.

I'm so sorry, Michael. But when it goes it goes forever. I know so many people like you ...

She glanced back at the quarry as they left to walk over the field to the house.

The place was dead.

Susan was in the kitchen in her housecoat, making coffee and toast. The arrival of Francoise Jeury and her albino companion startled her. If Francoise had expected maternal anger at Michael's camouflage, she was surprised. Susan said tiredly, "Get washed and ready for school. Hurry up."

The boy shrugged off Francoise's denim jacket and padded up the stairs.

Susan looked bone weary, not just the sleepy dishevelment of early morning. Her eyes had that haunted, hunted look associated with depression, fear or too much television.

"What are you doing here?" she asked quietly. "What have you been doing? More singing? More adventures in Michael's dreams?"

"Michael called me. He asked me to come and see him."

As she poured coffee into two mugs, Susan glanced suspiciously at the other woman. "When did he call you?"

"At two o'clock this morning. I'd just come home from my family. In France."

"You came here at two o'clock?"

"I was here for sunrise. I met him in his castle."

Susan gave Francoise a mug of coffee, then walked

past her into the crisp, cold dawn, sipping her breakfast and thinking hard.

"Why did he call you, I wonder?"

Francoise leaned against the doorframe, aware of the concern and fear emanating from the woman before her.

"His talent is gone. It's all over for him."

Susan turned sharply. "No. It can't be."

"I'm afraid so. These things, these gifts—I mean, the gift of having the power—they never last very long. It might transform, of course. Mine did. But there is something very empty in Michael now. I think he has lost the gift completely."

The silence with which Susan greeted this opinion was disturbing in its tangible selfish concern. After a moment she sighed. "He hasn't brought us anything for months. Nothing useful. Nothing pretty . . . We try to encourage him. But it just upsets him."

Patiently, Francoise explained what she understood would be now driving Michael's behavior. "Of course. He's frightened. He's been frightened for weeks. You should try to remember something: to Michael, Chalk Boy, for all his teasing and malicious behavior, was very real. He has been losing a friend. He has been losing a shadow that was very comforting to him."

Susan smiled thinly, then gave an almost perceptible nod. "We depended on him too much. Richard has gone away for a while, some sort of business. He's an edgy and irritable man these days. He's frustrated."

"You're very candid. That reminds me of me. Therefore I like it. But I don't envy you what you have to do for the sake of your family now."

She drained her mug and stepped back into the house. "Perhaps I should have been firmer before. I should have told you that in my world we learn very fast to depend on nothing beyond the five senses that we all share in common."

Susan had followed Francoise into the kitchen. "What did you mean by *transformed*? You said your talent had transformed."

"When I was a girl I had a very strange power. Very frightening. Forgive me if I say no more than that. But when I was ten, it changed into what I can do now; listen to stones. Listen to bones. I have had some good encounters, though."

"And Michael might do something similar?"

With a sympathetic smile, Francoise shrugged. "Who knows? It is a rare event. You must start to get used to the fact. Michael is an ordinary boy now. Love him for what he is, not what he brings."

"You have a way of getting my back up, Francoise," Susan said sharply.

"Good."

Twenty-one

O n the last day of the Christmas term the heating in
Michael's school failed and classes ended half an
hour early. The children gathered in the main hall, a
restless, noisy mob, excited at the prospect of holidays
and the impending snow.

Michael stood apart from the other children, peering
out into the lamplit darkness of the frosty afternoon.
Many parents were already in the school grounds, collecting their charges, but there was no sign of his
mother, and that meant he would have to wait ... The
thought made him apprehensive. If he waited around
too long, Tony Hanson would almost certainly start to
pick on him.

A teacher came past, called to him, "Are you all
right, Michael? Is someone collecting you?"

Michael stared up at Mr. Hallam and nodded. "I
think so. Mummy usually comes in the car."

"Would you like me to make a phone call?"

The main hall was beginning to chill. He had a scarf
round his neck, and mittens on, but as the heat dissipated rapidly so his breath began to frost.

"Yes, please," he said. Mr. Hallam walked away,
stopping briefly with some of the other children, before disappearing into the corridor to the staff room.

"Roman coin! Roman coin!"

The voice chanted derisorily from across the hall.
Several children laughed, several grouped tightly together, as Tony Hanson ran across to where Michael
was standing. The boy's eyes were wide and wild. He

pushed Michael hard against the cooling radiator by the window.

"You said you were going to get me another coin. Where is it?"

"I couldn't fine one," Michael said, and gasped as the other boy pushed him in the chest again. The assembly hall was emptying fast. Two other boys came over and stood behind Tony as he bullied Michael. They were breathing hard.

Michael had brought a Roman coin to school, late in the summer term, as part of a project where every pupil talked about an object or a book that interested them. After the class, set upon by Tony and his friends, he had given the coin to the older boy to save himself from being beaten. He lied about where he had found the *sestertius,* pretending that he knew where there was a secret Roman stash. That, naturally, had been the wrong thing to do, and a form of blackmail had begun. He had been able to buy his way out of a fight in early September using a tiny, jade-green cat, but then Chalk Boy had started to play games with him, hiding from him, laughing at him, taunting him, and sending him to fetch only mummified corpses.

At school, and at home, a terrible tension had begun to develop.

Mr. Hallam called across the hall. "Michael? Your mother's on her way. Tony, leave Michael alone. If I see you push him again you'll be for the high jump. Do you hear me?"

"Yes, Mr. Hallam," Tony called with a sour smile, and with a final vicious shove at Michael, he walked away.

Michael went quickly out into the schoolyard, shivering and shaking, his eyes watering with the cold and with anguish.

He was almost the last child to leave the school. An oppressive silence had enveloped the playground yard, relieved only by the spill of light from the main hall and some of the classrooms where cleaners were at work. When his mother's car pulled up at the curb outside the school gates, Michael ran for it gratefully. He

climbed into the front seat and looked quickly away
from the hard face of the woman who sat there.

"Why are you off so early?" she asked, pulling out
on the road.

"Heating broke down. It was freezing in the
classrooms."

"Put your seat belt on."

He twisted to obey, then settled back in the seat.
The drive home was conducted in silence.

He ate tea with Carol, who, full of cold, was sneezing
loudly. She had been off school for this last week. Susan busied herself with work. The phone rang a few
times and Michael listened to his mother's voice, the
edge in it, the strain.

"Daddy's home already," Carol said, squeezing her
nose with a tissue. Her eyes, watery, could not conceal
their discomfort at the thought of what she had just announced. Michael looked down at his plate of beans,
apprehension clawing at his chest.

When he had finished eating he put on his coat again
and walked down the garden, to the chalk pit. The
wooden walls of the fun castle were broken now, but
the rope ladder was still strong enough to bear his
weight. As he crunched through the crisp undergrowth
in the winter copse, approaching the hardboard walls
of the defense, he heard a sound from the quarry
below.

Cautiously he peered over the edge, and drew back
sharply as he saw the torch shape of his father. The
man was sweeping through the bushes, searching. Michael could hear the angry muttering in his voice. The
mound where the dog was buried had been dug over,
fresh chalk and earth showing together. Peering over
the edge again, Michael saw his father creep into the
tool-housing and clatter about inside the deep passage.

"There must be *something*," came the man's voice.
"Damn!"

His father came out holding his head and looking at
his hand for signs of blood. "Damn and *blast*!"

He moved away from the wall into the heart of the

quarry, searching under bushes, kicking around at the
bases of the trees. At one point he stopped and looked
sharply up at the mock turrets where Michael
crouched. Michael drew back quickly and waited a full
two minutes before he dared peer down again into the
torch-illuminated darkness.

His father had disappeared, although the darting
beam of light told of his movement toward the
entrance.

Michael had wanted to go down into the cold castle
and call again for Chalk Boy, but now he felt too
frightened. He returned to the house, running, saw his
mother in the window of her extended studio, and crept
in and up to his bedroom, closing the door behind him.

Later, his father entered the house. Michael huddled
in a corner and listened to the sounds downstairs. After
a while the phone went and he crept to the door to listen. There was an angry conversation.

His father was saying, "Damn it, Jack. There's nothing I can do about it . . ."

A silence, and then, "Yes, I know. I *know* they need
the money . . . but what can I do? He's dried up.
Christmas is over before it's even begun. There's nothing for me to give you . . ."

Again, a tension in the silence, with his mother, now
in the kitchen, talking softly to Carol.

"Jack, for God's sake. Put them off. I *told* you the
supply would be unpredictable. It's your damn fault if
you made too many promises . . .

"I *can't*, Jack, I just can't . . .

"You shouldn't have promised . . .

"What am I supposed to do?

"The boy's supply has dried. It's a bugger, I know.
But there's been nothing for months, now.

"Let me think about it. If that's the only solution,
then we'll just have to do it. I know. I accept that. But
as a last resort!"

And then, with a last angry shout, "Get off my back,
Jack! They'll just have to wait for their cash! I don't
have it now, and I don't know when I'll get it. But I'm

damned if I'll be blackmailed by them. Or by you, for that matter!"

The phone was slammed down. Michael heard the sound of a table being kicked, and a door banged shut.

Carol started to cry, and his mother's voice soothed her.

There had been a time when the sound of his father's steps on the stairs, moving toward his room, had thrilled Michael. He would huddle under the blankets, waiting for the knock, for the smiling face that would peer round the door, for the pillow fight, the mug of chocolate, the story, the long, complicated story before the kiss good night—and then the dreams. It was such a simple pleasure, and he missed it desperately. For those few years he had felt that his soul was back inside his body. But now he remembered again how his shadow stalked the world outside, only occasionally slipping back into his head and his heart. He was a boy without a soul. And now that Chalk Boy had left him, his father and mother couldn't see him properly anymore.

What they saw was a "wrong Michael," a false-boy, and that was why they were so angry with him all the time. They wanted the pretty things, but they couldn't understand that without his *shadow* he was a *false-boy*. He couldn't touch the places where the pretty things were hidden.

And now his father was angry all the time. Michael felt terrified every time the door opened and the pale face of the man looked in, and the thin lips parted to speak words that Michael often tried not to hear.

He was coming up the stairs now.

Michael closed his eyes.

In his dreams he could still smell the sea, and hear the booming cries of the creatures that swam there; he could sense the heat of the sand on the red beach, and imagine the colors of the strange trees and rocks that grew out of the shore. But he couldn't touch that place anymore, and Chalk Boy, if he was still there in Limbo, would not reveal himself to Michael.

The footfall seemed to make the house shudder. The

air in his room drained away so that Michael's chest became tight and he gasped for breath.

The door opened and the pale man stood there, eyes like wet hollows in a tree, somehow sightless, depthless. The door closed and the man swelled in view, towering over the boy. Michael watched the shadow move toward him, crushed himself further into his corner. The smells came, then: of sweat, and chalk, and whisky.

"What are you doing?"

The sudden words in the silence startled Michael. They struck his head like explosive whispers. Although he heard them, he couldn't comprehend them. He peered up at the dark shadow with its white face. There was such anger there. Eyes like water. Hair like the wild rushes on the bank of the canal. No smile on the mouth that gaped open, loose, expressionless.

"What are you *doing*?" the shadow repeated, and air filled Michael's lungs.

"Nothing," he whispered.

"Why are you huddling in the corner? What's the matter with you? Are you ill?"

"No."

"Then get up. I want to talk to you . . ."

Michael stood slowly and followed his father as he prowled around the room. He watched as the man ran his fingers over the pictures of statues, chalices, dishes and golden masks, the decorations on the wall, the enclosing, comforting representations of the sort of bright and precious treasures that Michael had been able to see in his dreams. His father picked up the wooden horseman that Michael had fetched two years ago, its eyes and armor beaten out of thin bronze, its trappings of fine leather and flax still flexible and perfect. It was a favorite piece of Michael's. He had glimpsed it in a darkly cavernous place. In his fetching dream he had smelled charred flesh and bone and sensed rats scurrying through the rotting mass of clothing that covered the tumble of metal and wooden objects. He had been, in that dream, in a stone place. He remembered his father talking to him of the Bronze Age, and passage tombs, and mortuary houses. But all he had wanted was the story, the story of Knights, the stories of the wasteland, the King, and the search for the source of peace and wisdom: the Grail.

His head reeled with versions of the Grail legend, with the stories that he had listened to, night after night. If Michael was aware of his father's strain in telling the tales, it was a minor thing, an insignificant blemish on the backdrop of comfort and joy that had been the tale-telling itself. Contradictions in detail didn't matter. Michael was well aware that different stories told the same legend in different ways. It was to do with time, and how people took aspects and details and enlarged or changed them to suit their purposes. What was important was the *telling*. In the telling of the story, the story came close. Each time they talked of the Grail, the Grail had come closer, closer to release from its prison in time and memory.

It was like a mystery. Tracing through the stories for the vision that was not *false*. For the True Sight.

The truth, bright and shining, like the crystal cup that Arthur had sought for so many years of his life.

The horse was placed down. The brooding man moved round the room, then turned, sat down on the small bed, pale and watery eyes watching the boy.

"Have you heard anything from Chalk Boy?"

Michael shook his head, watching the way his father's mouth moved, a pursed, pinched shape, being bitten from the inside.

"Michael . . ."

A hand on his shoulder, a squeeze of fingers. Hesitation. The moist fumes of alcohol mixed with the burnt-grass smell of cigarettes. Michael tried to pull away, but the man maintained his grip and made the boy stand still.

"Michael, do you remember two years ago when we had that lovely holiday on the big Wall? Hadrian's Wall?"

Michael nodded, squirming slightly and trying not to breathe.

"Do you remember the funny Roman you saw in your dream? And the lucky charm he gave you?"

"Yes."

"There was no Chalk Boy then. Was there? Do you remember? Chalk Boy was still in the pit. You were in the North, you couldn't hear him, but you could still . . ."

The man's eyes drifted, his right hand fluttered in the air. "You could still fly . . . like a bird . . . through time and space . . . like a bird, swooping and flying and seeing ghostly Romans, and cold places, and fires, and bright things . . . there was no Chalk Boy then. On the Wall. Was there?"

Michael shook his head.

"So why does Chalk Boy matter? What has happened, Mikey? Why can't you . . . fly . . . why can't you fly anymore? Aren't there any bright things in your dreams?"

"I can't see any," Michael whispered.

"Do you try? Do you look? Are you *trying*?"

Michael felt the fingers on his shoulder clench. His father's face was ashen. There was an odd intensity in the gaze and Michael's fear increased. He was suddenly aware that the man's face was covered by stubble, a dark, ragged growth of beard against the white skin that made him look menacing.

"I can't dream anymore, now that Chalk Boy is hiding."

"But you don't *need* Chalk Boy. You know you don't."

"I do!"

"You *don't*! Michael, you *don't* need him. You can do it on your own. Try. Just try for me. Try for Daddy. Try dreaming, try flying. There must be some wonderful things to see . . . The shield in the lake. Remember the shield? You haven't fetched it yet, Mikey. So you *can* still do it. Can't you try? Please? For Daddy?"

The grip hurt. Michael touched a hand to the heavy, pressing fingers, and eased them off his shirt.

"*Please,* Michael. Try for Daddy?" came the voice.

"No, I can't. Chalk Boy is angry with me."

Michael was flung back by the violent motion of the

man rising to his feet. The air around him felt lashed
with his father's furious obscenity, a word uttered like
a whip-crack. He watched the man's tension wither.
His father turned then, softer. He crouched again,
breathed out once more and smiled.

"I'm sorry, Michael. It's been very hard for us these
last months. Your mummy and me . . . we're very tired,
very upset."

"Why is Mummy upset?"

"Because her boy isn't helping. Because you're not
helping, Mikey. Because she's worried how we're going to get through the next years. We'd come to depend
on you. You helped us so much. And Uncle Jack needs
you too. Uncle Jack is very upset."

Uncle Jack! Uncle Jack!

Michael looked away, feeling a moment's anger. He
hated Uncle Jack. He wasn't a true uncle, anyway. He
just liked to examine the treasures that Michael fetched.
He was not a nice man. And Francoise didn't like him.

Uncle Jack!

His father was saying, "Uncle Jack is very important
to me. I don't know if you know how important, but he
got me a very good job. That's why we have the lovely
holidays. That's why we can go and stay in nice hotels
all over France and Germany and Scotland, because
Uncle Jack spoke to important people about me, and
I've got a wonderful job, looking at ancient things, and
photographing them . . . and without Uncle Jack, none
of this would have been possible."

Michael said nothing. He didn't know what to say.
His father seemed almost sad at one moment, then
bristling, as if he were going to shout.

"I promised Uncle Jack to show him treasures and
funny things, and you said . . . do you remember?
When we were telling each other stories? You said you
would always give me things to show to Uncle Jack."

"I remember," Michael said.

"But I haven't been able to show anything to Uncle
Jack for a long time. And he's not very happy.
Couldn't we try and help him out?"

Gritting his teeth, speaking in an almost inaudible

and angry tone, Michael murmured, "Don't give him the golden egg."

His father straightened up, then looked sad.

"That would be a shame. But you see . . . if I haven't got anything else to give him, I may well have to give him the egg—"

"NO!" Michael screamed. His vision had reddened. The egg was a special present. It was precious. It was for his father. Uncle Jack *mustn't* have the egg.

"NO!"

Angrily, his father said, "Don't shout at me, Michael. If you can't give me something else, then the egg must go. If you want the egg to stay, then find something else! Now! Do you hear?"

"I can't without Chalk—"

"*Bugger* Chalk Boy. Just *look* and *reach* and *fetch*. You can do it, you little . . . ! You can do it, Mikey. You know you can. If you don't, then everything else will have to go. *Everything*."

"NO!"

"Everything. The egg. Carol's shell. Mummy's cross—"

Michael felt sick. He howled and screamed. He was aware that he was fighting his father and that his father's fists were holding his own.

"NO!"

The door opened. Michael fell, sobbing. He crawled under the bed and let the screaming and shouting drift around him. He didn't want to hear the words. He didn't want to hear the fighting between his parents. He didn't want to hear Carol's hysterical screaming. He just wanted to go away, to be in the tunnels, to be by the sea with the swimming giants . . . anywhere . . .

Anywhere but here!

Twenty-two

Two hours later Susan returned from Jenny's house, where she had fled to recuperate from the fierce and frightening argument with her husband, and walked quickly into Richard's office. Richard was slumped at his desk, pictures of artifacts spread before him, the inscribed Minoan egg perched on its end and propped up with music cassettes.

The man looked shattered. His thinning hair was awry and his eyes dark-hooded. The room had a sweet and sickly smell about it, and Susan realized that he had been sick in the waste-paper bin.

He looked up as she entered the lamplit room, closing the door behind her.

"Well, well. She's back."

"Yes. I'm back. Don't ever hit that child again, Richard. I mean it. Don't ever hit that boy again!"

Grimly, she leaned back against the door. She was shaking, partly with cold, partly with apprehension. Richard grinned awfully, his face like a mask splitting open at the lips. He shook his head.

"I *didn't* hit him—*darling*. He hit *me*. He went for me like a creature wild, all tooth and claw and voice of night."

"Very poetic. But the bruise on his face wasn't self-inflicted."

"Self-defense, lover."

"You hit him."

"Accidentally."

She sneered and looked away, then took a deep,

calming breath. "It was no accident. You were in a rage. You were drunk. I don't care *how* angry you are, or frustrated . . ." She turned and tried to fix him with a hard and powerful gaze, but she knew she was too frightened of the force in the man, of his self-interest, to make it effective. "I don't care what trouble we're in, you and I, or as a family, or with the bank. Just don't you *ever* hit that boy again. I'll use that cross on you if you do! I swear it. I'll use the Mocking Cross!"

"How very moral: I hit him, you kill me. All square."

"Bastard," she murmured.

Richard stood at the desk, then slowly sat again, sighing. She smelled the drink from across the room. The more she looked at him the more she loathed him. In the last few moments his pale skin seemed to have become stippled with stubble, an effect of the light. He looked shocking. He looked ill and haunted, a man not in control.

"You have to stop drinking Scotch, Richard. It makes you violent."

"Tell me about it."

"I'm telling you about it. You get out of control. We're in trouble, I know. But you'll not help matters by blanking your reason with malt whisky."

"You don't know the half of it. You don't know how *much* trouble." He slumped, then twisted in his chair, not meeting Susan's gaze. "That little bastard! That little *bastard*! Why did it stop? Why the fuck did it stop? We had everything going—it would have been—*shit*!"

After a moment, Susan said quietly, "It happens." She thought of mentioning Francoise Jeury's visit a few weeks ago, but decided better of it. "What do you mean?" she went on carefully. "What do you mean: I don't know the half of it?"

Richard seemed to sag further, then cradled his head in his hands. "We're very broke, Susan. Very broke indeed."

"How can we be broke? We have thousands in savings. You have a good job, now. Thanks to the supernatural, we've set ourselves up for years, if not for life.

I don't understand how you can feel so upset by the passing of the gift."

"The passing of the gift," Richard echoed. "Is that what's happened? The talent has gone? The boy has grown out of it?"

"That's what's happened, Richard, and you'd damn well better get used to the idea."

"And you'd better get used to the idea that if the talent has gone, then we're bankrupt."

Susan folded her arms. She knew she'd gone pale. She felt icy cold as she watched the shambling wreck of the man she loved. He thumped a fist against the leather-bound books on his shelf, turned and flicked through the photographs of Michael's "fetchings." He smiled ruefully.

Susan said, "I'm waiting, Richard. What have you done?"

His answer was quiet. He didn't meet her eyes. He was defensive. "Invested. Made promises. Made guarantees . . ."

Her heart began to drum out her growing fear. Everything in the room became oddly clear, starkly outlined. "Invested in what?" she asked.

"A company. They're building a tourist complex in Essex. A sort of historical experience center, plus all the fun of the fruit machines, and the roulette wheel. It's a huge project. The chance to be a partner was too good to miss."

She was silent for a moment, letting the full force of the statement, and the betrayal it represented, sink into her clear and terrified consciousness. "A partner. A project. Historical experiences . . . Tell me, Rick: when did this happen?"

"That I signed on? About a year ago."

"A year ago!" she said, her voice a strangled, painful gasp, her eyes briefly closed. Then she smiled and shook her head.

Richard went on, "The profits will be phenomenal. They're even planning to have chariot racing. In the Roman style, of course. You can indulge in any period of history. You can wager on gladiators, chariots,

games of bowls played by Francis Drake lookalikes . . .
it's a big project, Susan. I was very taken by their enthusiasm and ideas."

"Thank you for letting me in on your little secret,"
she said dully. "If I can be of any help, please don't
hesitate etcetera, etcetera. And what were you to be,
Rick? Consultant?"

"That was the idea. Consultant and partner. And
when Jack Goodman—"

Susan laughed sourly. "I thought *his* name would
start cropping up."

"Jack's involved too. He knew the company. He
knew they were looking for finance. He suggested me,
and we did the deal, and Jack has made promises on
my behalf."

"Promises? Money promises?"

Richard nodded. "As I said, they invited me to be a
partner. I accepted. We're talking big money."

"You're talking big bullshit, Richard. I never trusted
Goodman, and you were a fool to trust him yourself."

"What was to trust? I could see the plans for the
complex. I met the company."

"The company!" she sneered. "The company. You
keep saying the *company*. I don't suppose they wore
black suits, black glasses and drove black Mercedes,
did they? No chance that their names might have
rhymed with Kray? You idiot!"

"Why idiot? This is a major tourist complex. It's a
guarantee of finance for life. All I do is act as consultant in the building and design, and then take my
quarter-share of the profits as a partner. Why idiot?
This is an investment, Susan. This is for life!"

"But your little investment source has dried up. And
you've sunk all our money into it, so we've nil in the
bank, and we start over. You *fool*, Richard."

Something in his glance, a shudder in his body,
and Susan felt the blood in her face drain away again.
She had been heated with anger, now she was chilled
with fear.

"How much do you owe them?" she asked quietly.
"How much have you promised?"

"Quite a lot," he said, sitting down on the edge of the desk and again not meeting her eyes. "They knew it wouldn't come in one lump, but they expect it within the year. Goodman made a guarantee to them. I made a guarantee to Goodman. I really thought . . ." He shook his head suddenly, sinking into himself. "Oh, dear God . . ."

"How *much*, Richard?"

"I really thought the 'fetchings' would continue. Why not? Eight pieces of ancient gold last year, not to mention the glass, the silver, the carved bone. A small fortune, a real gift. A true gift from the gods."

"How much?"

He looked up. After a moment he laughed and shook his head, "I've guaranteed them half a million."

Susan screamed, slapped hands to her mouth and felt her knees buckle. "Half a million! Oh, my God. Oh, dear God!"

She felt her legs give way. Richard went over to her quickly and supported her, but she turned on him, sobbing, a hand raking out to slap at his face. She walked to the door to her studio and flung it open, collapsing heavily into her leather chair, crying with full voice. After a minute or so she leaned forward on to her work-bench and tried to stop herself being sick.

"My God, my God," she wailed, and around her everything dissolved into blackness.

Michael sat with Carol on the stairs. They both wore their pajamas and dressing-gowns against the cold. The central heating had turned itself off about an hour ago and the temperature in the house was dropping. Carol held her horseman shell and a doll dressed in Hungarian national costume. She was shaking badly, and Michael had his arm around her shoulder.

"Katherine's Mummy and Daddy don't live together anymore," Carol said. "She cries a lot. She says it's like living nowhere. She has to go and see her Daddy every fortnight for one day. And the rest of the time her Mummy just talks to people on the phone and not to her. I don't want Mummy and Daddy to live in different houses."

"I do," Michael said grimly.

Carol started to cry and Michael clenched his jaw, then stood and tugged his sister to her feet. He felt confused and sad for the girl. He knew (although it was a drifting thought) that he shouldn't be so hard with her. "You'd better go back to bed. I think the shouting's finished."

Carol sniffed violently, and used her shirt-tail to blow her nose. She walked upstairs, a forlorn shape, mousy hair hanging lankly around her shoulders. Michael listened until he heard her run along the landing to her small room, then he stepped down to the hall, pushed open the study door and peered at the distant light, where his mother sat alone at the work-bench, her whole body limp, like a tailor's dummy. Occasionally a dark shape passed back and forth across the light framed by the door: his father, pacing restlessly.

Richard was saying, "I don't know what the house will fetch. But not less than a hundred thousand."

"That's right. Take my home. Take the children's home away from them . . ."

"We have no choice, Susan. These people mean business. I've got a year. I told you. They knew the money would come in dribs and drabs . . ."

"Each drib and drab being fifty thousand pounds. That's some dribbing and drabbing."

"We sell the house. The Minoan egg is worth forty thousand for its gold alone. Goodman will get us twice that . . ."

"And take his 25 percent—"

"He'll have to take less, damn him! This is a crisis. Then there's the Mocking Cross—"

Michael's heart stammered and his face flushed with fury. He almost ran into the room, but his mother's voice sounded sharp, angry:

"That was Michael's special gift to me. That cross stays. I'd never sell it."

"It's worth forty thousand, Goodman says."

"Goodman can take a flying fuck."

"I don't like that sort of language from you, Susan. It demeans you."

"Dear God, listen to the fool. Who the fuck do you think you are, Rick? You're an *alcoholic*! You're a wasted, gambling, selfish, child-hitting *monster*. I live with you because—because I don't know where else to go. Don't tell *me* about my language. The temptation to laugh is too strong. The fact that I don't laugh is mainly because I want to cry: at my own stupidity for not watching you. At not realizing what a sod you are."

Ignoring the abuse, his father went on: "Carol's shell is valuable. It's priceless in archaeological terms, but valuable enough on the art market. We can sell the cars. We'll have a shortfall of no more than two hundred and fifty thousand."

"Is that all? Well, what are we worried about? We can have a *boot* sale. Soon make up the difference."

"We'll re-mortgage the house. Get a bank loan. I'll do some private work . . . Things will be fine. Things *will* be fine."

There was a long, terrible silence.

Then Michael heard his mother crying softly.

Every time the telephone rang now, a sudden chill flooded through the house. Voices murmured, sometimes shouted. Michael came to dread the sound of the bell. He couldn't look at his mother's face when the telephone sounded. She looked so frightened. Sometimes when the caller turned out to be a friend, she cried with relief.

Christmas was a miserable affair. Susan's mother came to stay with them, and after a few hours of false jollity she too settled into the routine of gloomy, chilling silence. It snowed on Boxing Day, but there was no walk, no play in the garden with the adults. Michael's father sat and read a paper, magazines, then a book. The TV was grazed constantly. Susan worked on a doll in her studio, and the children played Scrabble and Monopoly.

Although there had been presents, generosity was conspicuous by its absence. The year before the house had rocked and whined with models, trains, robots and gadgets. This year there had been books, paints and a family game.

They ate goose for Christmas Day, and Michael hated the greasy taste. Carol spat hers back on to the plate and was told off, as much as her mother ever told her off.

Now, again, Michael spent most of his time in his room. When he tentatively asked for a story he was ignored. His father was too busy. Too busy to play, too busy to read to him, too busy to go for walks. But in the evenings, as the new term began, he would sit with Carol on his knee and watch her work out her homework, encouraging here, correcting there, testing, talking, laughing with the girl.

Michael did his homework in his room. The winter was mild, after the snow flurry of Christmas, but still the chalk quarry was a cold, dead place. He went there often, but the walls of the castle were gone, the sense of a structure there, of tunnels and passages, of the route down to the ancient sea, all this had dissipated.

Then the winter began to turn.

On a Saturday in early March, Michael left the house after breakfast, depressed and lonely, and trudged across the ploughed, frozen field toward the winter woods. Behind him, Carol called to him. She was wrapped up against the chill, and was wearing her new glasses. She didn't like wearing them, and had been teased at school, but Michael had been staunch in his defense of his sister, and had received a bloody lip from Tony Hanson in a fight on the last day of the week.

Carol had stayed very close to her brother all the way home, and that night insisted on Michael sharing her story before she went to sleep. When he refused to come from his room, she and Susan came to his chamber of wall treasures, and Carol climbed into bed next to him. Susan, reading from a book of Grimm's fairy tales, was probably aware of her son's irritation, but Michael soon relaxed.

It was only with the greatest reluctance that Carol

returned to her own room. But in the morning, when Michael wandered off, silent and surly, she chased after him.

"I want to see your castle," she said. Her spectacles slipped on her nose and she grumbled, "They're too loose."

Michael took the frames and looked at them.

"Don't break them!" Carol said anxiously as Michael twisted the ends of the arms slightly.

When she placed the glasses back on her face they held more firmly. She looked like an owl, he told her, and Carol was amused.

So he took her to the castle. They dropped down the tree rope, Michael getting rope burn as he tried to show off to his sister. At the bottom he led the way to the storage tunnel. He had a pen-light and turned this on as he stooped to crawl into the deep, gloomy tunnel.

"I'm scared," Carol said, hovering at the entrance.

"There's nothing here," Michael murmured, adding, "except dead things from the past . . ."

As far as he knew, Carol had no idea what he had been hiding in this passage, and she hesitated then grinned, not believing her brother. She crawled forward into the thin ray of light. "It smells."

"Dead things always do."

"There aren't any dead things . . ."

His hand reached for the mummified body of a cat, still wrapped in shreds of cloth. The wooden container was around somewhere, broken during its transition through his mind. He felt the stiff, animal body, and the way it started to crumble beneath his touch. He flung it away, deciding not to shock his sister.

"Do you want to go deeper?"

Carol said that she didn't.

"Coward."

"I'm *not* a coward. It's cold. And smelly."

"Then why did you come? You said you wanted to see my castle."

"I had a funny dream," she whispered.

"What dream?"

"You were all covered with chalk and running with

a big dog over some hills. You were frightened. You hid in a cave in the chalk, but the men found you and dragged you away."

Michael shuddered and crawled back further into the passage. His sister's eyes gleamed with tears in the thin beam of light. "What did they do to me?" he asked in a whisper.

"They put a spear into you. Then they put you in a hut. They locked the door with a tree branch. They stood around and watched the hut and it rained hard, and everything was muddy."

He had had that dream too! It had been vivid and frightening, only it hadn't been *him* in the hut, it had been Chalk Boy.

Something moved through the passage, a gentle, cool wind, stirring his hair, making Carol blink. Michael turned sharply and flashed the pen-light into the cramped gloom. The rags on the mummified cat were crisp. When Michael crawled forward his hand descended on the creature's remains and crushed them to dust.

"Where are you going?" Carol hissed.

"Deeper," Michael said.

There was a place at the far end of the tunnel where the chalk entrance was narrow and hidden behind some pieces of wood. His father hadn't seen this entrance to the deepest of the caves, where Michael had kept Chalk Boy's unpleasant surprises of last summer.

The wind was stronger. Carol was talking behind him, but her words washed over him.

Chalk Boy . . . ?

He felt the hair on his neck prickle and rise. Then there was the feeling of pressure, as of hands gripping his shoulders, crushing down on his back and neck.

"I can see the sea . . ." Carol said, her voice muffled by the rock.

Michael was gasping for breath. He was half through the narrow slot that widened into the deeper cave. His arm before him, he flashed the light around the wood and stone that was discarded here. He could hear the

sound of a third person's breathing, and for a second—
just a second—there was the smell of the ocean.

"I can see the *seaside*!" Carol said, more loudly, and
then laughed, almost delightedly.

The pressure went from Michael's back, the hands
withdrew, the moment's touch of Chalk Boy faded.
Again Michael felt deserted by the ghost that had been
his friend for so long.

His shadow was outside of him again. He felt empty
inside, and eased his way back to his sister.

Carol sat in the darkness, her pale face aglow with
pleasure. She was holding a small doll. It was made of
china and dressed in red clothes, with a red bonnet
over golden hair. It was very small, and two fingers
from its left hand were broken.

"Where did that come from?" Michael asked quietly.

"I found it. It was just here after the ceiling opened
to the beach."

She was staring up at the ragged roof of filthy chalk.
Michael stared after her. Carol put out her arm and
pointed. "Just there, through there. I saw the beach at
the end of a tunnel. There was a little boy and he gave
something to me. I think it was the doll. It's pretty.
Look at it . . ."

Grimly, Michael took the figurine and stared at it.

What was Chalk Boy playing at now?

Twenty-three

The house was empty, as usual. Michael let himself in through the back door and took off his heavy school coat. It was the end of March. The weather was still cold, but he could smell the new season on the air and it was good to be home before the evening set in. There would be time to visit the pit, time to explore the garden, time to walk to the shop in the village and buy a bar of chocolate.

The house felt very hollow. The noisy heating was just coming on. The oven made creaking noises as the evening meal began to cook, ignited under its own instruction. There was no note, no plate of sandwiches for his tea. Just an empty, silent building, surrounded by rain clouds.

He went up to his room and idled for a while with his comics, his models and his thoughts. From his window he could see the cornfield beginning to mist over. The quarry was in gathering gloom. Somewhere in the house there was a sudden movement.

Puzzled, he peered into Carol's tiny, tidy chamber, but it was quite empty. He checked the bathroom and toilet, then the guest room with its stale smell of old blankets and furniture. Finally he opened the door to his parents' bedroom, scuffed through the deep pile carpet, ran his hands over the velvet curtains on the window, opened the closet.

It was so strange to be here, a room where he had not been welcomed, nor taken, for years. His mother's clothes had a heavy feel and smell about them. She wore a lot of corduroy. Belts hung from hangers, and silk scarves too. On shelves below the dresses were black and brown leather boots, sports shoes, and packs of unopened tights.

He opened the drawers to her dressing-table and looked at the scatter of objects, from hairbrushes, curlers, tubes of "guck," cotton buds, elastic bands, empty photograph holders, bunches of real hair (from all the family) for doll-making, shards of china, wooden and porcelain limbs, knitting patterns. He ran his fingers through these, his mother's private things.

Closing the drawer he felt a thrill—it was like being a spy entering the house of a suspect.

Again: the sound of movement somewhere close by.

"Who's there?" he called out.

The response was the sudden sound of footsteps on the stairs. He raced to the bedroom door, stood panting excitedly on the landing. But again silence had descended.

"Chalk Boy?"

He peered over the banister at the hall below.

"Chalk Boy?"

The house creaked as heating flowed and the oven settled down to its cooking.

Downstairs: the sitting room was in darkness now, a cold place, full of shadows spilling from the hall. He entered his father's study and ran his left hand across the cold, leather books; through further to the long studio where his mother's dolls lined the walls. There was a sharp smell here, like candle wax. He crossed the room, opened the door to the extension and stepped into the place where he and Carol had once played games, where boxes of toys stood by the walls, where pictures were pinned, the crude pictures painted by them. The family's bicycles were here, too, his own still with its thick tires flat after he had punctured them the previous summer.

A box was moved above him, something thumped gently on the floor.

The upstairs part of this silent extension was reached by spiral, metal stairs at the far end. There was nothing in the dark room, save for a few jars of preserves, boxes of magazines, some empty shelving, and a pine table that his father was renovating.

Michael stood in this heavy stillness staring through the window at the slim moon over the trees. Then a figure moved furtively through the shadows in the cold room, and quickly he switched on the light.

Carol yelled, and cowered back, drawing her school anorak tightly around her.

"I didn't want to give it to him!" she said loudly, and her face creased into tears.

"Give what? What's the matter?"

Standing at the top of the stairwell, gripping the cold rail, Michael was alarmed at the fear and anguish spilling from his sister.

"The shell," the girl said in a small voice. "The horse shell. But Daddy took it. He said we all had to make sacrifices. He said it was valuable and would have to be given away."

For a moment Michael didn't know what she was talking about, then he remembered the shell with its carvings, the present he had given his sister two years ago. It didn't upset him. He had just thought she would find the shell pretty.

"It doesn't matter," he said quietly. "I'll find you a fossil in the pit."

But then a thought occurred to him, and his vision reddened. He raced down the stairs, crossed the playroom and flung open the door to his mother's studio. Anxiously he scanned the shelves of dolls, the smiled with relief.

The Mocking Cross doll, his special present for his mother, was still there, in pride of place above her work-bench.

An hour later he heard his parents come home. He was at his desk doing his homework, and there he stayed, uneasy with the feeling of the welcome silence broken by sudden activity. There was movement on the landing, doors opened and shut, food smells surfaced, voices chattered, sounding strained. The telephone rang, then rang again.

After a while he was called to supper. He ate quietly, conscious that his father was in a grim mood and his mother was pale and tired. He kept trying to get her to look at him, but she wouldn't. From frequent experiences he knew this probably meant trouble was brewing.

After they'd eaten he went into the sitting room and watched television. His parents went to their separate studios to work, but after a while he heard raised voices and he blocked his ears against the argument. He turned the TV up loudly, sitting grimly watching a comedy, until the door opened and his father shouted, "Turn that bloody thing down!"

Immediately after that, the front door was slammed shut and his father's new car skidded on the gravel drive as it was driven furiously on to the village road.

Carol was called to bed, and the girl went reluctantly. She was still upset about the shell. Michael had given her a fossil sea-urchin from his small collection, but the new gift had not pacified her.

Standing at the bottom of the stairs Michael heard his mother's murmuring voice, reading to Carol from one of the story books. He went back to the TV and turned the volume up again, then kicked fiercely at the armchair where his father usually sat, jumping on the cushions and aiming his blows at where the man's head would usually have been.

The sudden jarring ring of the telephone made him jump, catching him in mid-savagery. He stepped down from the armchair and picked up the receiver. He felt like shouting, something along the lines of "Leave us alone!" Instead he just held the receiver to his ear and listened above the laughter on the TV.

"Hello? Dr. Whitlock?"

"It's Michael, Daddy isn't home."

"Hello, Michael. Is your mother there?"

Michael thought about this for a moment, then shook his head.

"Hello? Michael?"

"She's not home either. She's out at a dance. In Maidstone." He smiled and bit his lip, the lie seeming funny and scary at the same time.

"That sounds nice. Is someone shouting there, Michael? It's hard to hear you."

Michael used the remote control to turn down the television. The man said, "That's better. Now, Michael, can I trust you to leave a message for Dr.—for your father?"

"OK."

"I'd like to speak to him as soon as possible about the Mocking Cross."

Michael felt a sudden, intense shock. "What Mocking Cross?" he said.

Upstairs, Carol laughed loudly and there was a sound of walking about. Michael stared at the ceiling, his face burning.

"It's the lovely wooden cross with the gold mask that your father sold. I'm the man who bought it and I need to know some details about it. I'm sure he can spare the time. After all, I made him quite a rich man a week ago. Michael?"

Michael let the telephone receiver fall and dangle. He could hear the man's voice rising in pitch as he tried to call attention down the line, but all Michael could think of was the Mocking Cross, his gift to his mother, the precious gift of doll and mask that his mother so adored.

She had promised him she would never sell it. She had *promised* him.

It was still in her studio. He had seen it there a few hours ago. It was still in the studio . . . what was the man on the telephone talking about?

He walked swiftly into the room where the dolls were shelved and stared up at the glinting gold of the mask.

Then he looked more closely.

"No!"

His scream was uncontrollable. His head filled with noise, his eyes with tears. Rage tightened his muscles until he felt he would burst, break, tear open with the pressure of it.

His howl brought his mother running down the stairs. He was aware of her sobbing cry, "Oh, Michael! Oh no, Michael . . . !"

But he was already clambering up to the shelf, snatching at the doll. The papier-mâché crumbled in his hands. The cardboard with its gold paint buckled as he crushed it in his fist. The clothes came away, the same clothes he had used before. But they covered nothing, just a copy.

She had sold the doll!

She had made Daddy very rich!

She had betrayed him!

He ran past her, still screaming abuse. He flung the crushed thing at the tearful woman who reached for him. He felt her hand clutch his arm, trying to pull him to her, and turned and sank his teeth into the fingers, drawing blood, eliciting a howl of pain and anger. She let him go and he ran from the room, from the house. Outside, in the night, he stood and stared at the black sky. He was shaking violently. His mother's blood tasted strong and sharp in his mouth and he let the taste linger.

Betrayed!

But after a while the hot anger became cold and dead. He sat down among the hedges that created the maze in the garden, drawing his body into a tight ball, curling up, crying softly as the night's cold edged and seeped through his clothing and his mother called for him, and called, and cried, and called . . .

Twenty-four

Michael's outrage passed in time, but he woke each
morning now with a deep and abiding sense of
sadness and anger. His dreams were no more than tormented visions of being alone, of being abandoned, of
always looking up at dark figures moving by, shapes
that never stopped. And search though he might for a
stronger sense of Chalk Boy and the great sea at the
end of the Limbo tunnel, he could only glimpse him in
the distance, and then only by shadow and echo, not by
clear sight.

The spring term passed. Easter was a miserable affair. His eleventh birthday passed almost without ceremony. His father was away in the North again, working
eighteen hours a day to earn money, and his mother
maintained a silent, angry distance from him. She
spent hours in her studio, writing notes for lessons and
making dolls to sell. She had sold the most valuable
items in her collection, although the shelves were still
crowded with bland, watching faces and the darker designs of masks and puppets.

One day, Carol gave her mother the small china doll
that she had found in the pit. Michael watched from
across his father's study as the girl parted with the
lovely object. He saw how quickly Susan reacted, how
the life came back into her.

"Where did you get this? Did Michael get this for
you? Where did you get it?"

As her voice rose with excitement, Michael clenched
his jaw with anger. His mother's sudden hope was an

irritation to him. If she was so keen to have more gifts, why didn't she ask *him*? He couldn't supply them, but she could call him in and ask *him*.

Carol said, "He gave it to me years ago. I forgot about it. It was under my bed."

Michael was astonished, so much so that he withdrew from his watching place and went into the hall.

Carol hated lying, but she had lied to her mother. He wondered why? Why had she protected him?

Later, his sister took him by the hand and tugged him outdoors. Shushing him with a finger to her mouth, she ran ahead of him to the quarry and crouched down behind the battered wooden walls of the fun-castle.

"If we can get Mummy some more dolls, she'll be happier. I dreamed about dolls after the last time we were here."

Another dream! Why was *she* dreaming now, and not him? Michael stared at his sister, then nodded. They slid down the rope ladder and crouched in the dead pit. They waited an hour or so, but nothing happened, and it started to get cold again.

Carol was disappointed, of course, but she had a sturdy and optimistic constitution and returned to the house more determined than resigned. And indeed, a few weeks later, things changed.

Sitting again in the cramped tunnel, holding hands and chanting a mumbo-jumbo they had invented, a spell of summoning to try to induce the return of Chalk Boy, Carol suddenly said, "I can smell the sea!"

Instantly, her nose wrinkled and she made a sound of disgust. "It *stinks*!"

"You can smell the sea? Can you hear it too?"

Frantically, Michael closed his eyes, trying to remember the sound of the sea-shore, to feel the heat, to sense the deep caves in the rock face where Chalk Boy lurked. He heard laughter, and felt a shadow-wind in his mind, something passing him by again, always passing him by.

Carol's laugh made him look up. Her own eyes were

huge, sparkling, and her lips were parted in an expression of childish wonder.

"What is it?" he hissed. Her fingers tightened on his own. He felt strange, as if blood was moving between their bodies, through the fingertips and the palms of their hands. He tried to detach his grip from hers, but she squeezed more tightly, and laughed again, a sound of delight. She was focusing into nowhere, a million miles away, a million years away.

"Carol!"

He began to feel weak. In his head there was the noise of wind, stormy, gusting, and now he too could smell the wild, wretched sea. It flowed into him and through him, and—his eyes wide open—he glimpsed a shadow running lightly across bright sands, following the wind, reaching for the girl.

He grunted and tugged at his sister's hands, trying to disengage, but she screeched suddenly, "No! Keep hold!"

"Carol, let me go!"

"NO!"

Her yell was angry; her voice sounded odd, rasping, not like the girl at all, despite its childish pitch. Her gaze had focused more on her brother, but her eyes were suddenly narrow. She looked ugly, hard. Her mouth, still gaping, seemed set over a jaw that jutted forward, as if she was clenching her muscles, holding her mouth open so that she could breathe. She looked determined, but feral and frightening.

The flow from Michael to this savage incarnation of his sister increased, and Michael kicked quickly, his foot shoving against the girl's stomach.

At once she released her grip on him, but her hands reached out, as if to catch something. The tunnel thudded, a sound like dull thunder. The wind went from Michael's body, he felt punched, and he was flung to one side. When he sat up and looked at his sister, by the dim light coming from the quarry, he saw her cradling a child in her arms.

"A present for Mummy," Carol said quietly. "It's like a little wrinkled baby."

Michael nervously reached for the doll. Carol wouldn't let it go, but she let him touch the face. It was made of wood, hard and black. It had funny eyes and a funny mouth. The arms were loose and movable below the coarse, dyed clothes, a red and yellow dress made out of an old sack, by its feel. The hair was black and quite long and felt very like real hair. When Carol shook it, the doll rattled. They investigated under the garment and realized that the body was hollow. There was something hard inside it.

Carol scampered off, back to the house, but Michael remained in the quarry, and in his mind's eye he started to reconstruct the walls of his castle.

He had believed that Chalk Boy had gone forever, but he was just hiding. What Michael couldn't understand was why he had given Carol a present, and what that strange feeling of flowing had been. What was Chalk Boy trying to do?

The quarry was dead again, the brief opening of the tunnel to Limbo was closed. Try as he might, there was no contact, and the evening was drawing in. Carol had been back at the house for twenty minutes, and tea would soon be ready.

But before Michael could leave the pit, he heard someone running toward him, through the scrub. Carol's voice was distant. She sounded upset. Michael reached for the rope ladder up the chalk face, but a moment later he heard his mother call to him sharply.

He turned to face her. She was sweating and red in the face, her hair wild, her eyes wild. She ran up to him and he yelled, backing away as she reached for him. He had thought she was angry, but she simply screamed at him.

"Where did it come from? Where did it come from? Michael. Michael! Where did you get it?"

She shook him by the shoulders, her fingers digging painfully into his flesh. He struggled in her grip, but she didn't let him go. Tears were flowing from her eyes, her mouth was wet. She kept repeating, "Where did it come from? Michael! Help us! Help us please!"

"Let me go . . ."

"Michael! Tell me. Tell me!"

He was shocked by the vehemence in the woman's voice, then cried out as a hand slapped across his face. Again he was shaken violently, his body hitting against the chalk.

"Get us something. For God's sake, get us something pretty! We're going to have to sell the house. There'll be nothing left for us. Michael! Michael!"

"I can't!" he wailed through the distress and despair that flowed over him. Above him, Carol was sobbing. She was trying to get a grip on the rope ladder and shouting at her mother to leave Michael alone.

Michael was vaguely aware that the woman who was fighting him was in hysterics. Whereas once he had bitten her hand, now he just stood still and let the flow of words, her screams and her anguish, pass over him, not touching him. His shadow came out of his body, crawling over the graying chalk, emptying him, making him invisible. The grip upon his shoulders ceased to hurt.

"There are no pretty things. There is no gold. There's nothing there," he said dully, and was half aware that no sound had come from his mouth.

A scream, then, and the violence stopped. A shocked face, suddenly ashen, turned up to the sky.

Carol had slipped. Half holding the rope she tumbled down the chalk pit and struck her mother. The two bodies fell heavily, and Carol cried loudly, holding out a hand skinned red and raw with rope burn. One of the fingers was bent awkwardly and gently her mother put the joint back into place, weeping quietly and kissing the girl's hand.

"I'm sorry, love. I'm so sorry . . ."

She picked her up and carried her, weeping. "I'm so sorry—I thought he could help us—"

Crying, hugging, needing, leaving . . .

"Oh darling. I'm so sorry . . ."

Abandoned again, Michael climbed the rope to the woods and watched as his mother led Carol gently back to the house. He followed across the field, stood in the kitchen staring at the sandwiches ready for tea, listening to the soothing voice in the front room.

Later, Carol came to his room. Her hand was bandaged and in a small sling. Unexpectedly, and firmly, she gave Michael a kiss (he rubbed it off at once, frowning) and offered to play Scrabble with him, but he wasn't in the mood.

"Then I'll read you a story," she said.

He shook his head, staring at her darkly.

She blinked at him through her glasses, her mouth working as she tried to think. "I know. I'll paint you a picture. I can still paint with my other hand."

He nodded. "Paint me a picture of what you saw in the pit."

She looked blank for a moment, then frowned. "I can't," she said.

"Why not?"

"It was just a shadow by the sea. There wasn't anything there."

"What about the chalk boy? The white boy?"

"I just saw sea. And a shadow. And felt someone holding on to me round the neck and crying."

"Crying?"

"It sounded like you. Crying."

"I *don't* cry!"

"Yes, you do. I've heard you. It makes me sad."

"I *don't cry!*"

"Yes, you *do*. Anyway, that's what it sounded like. And it felt like someone trying to hold on to me. But I can't paint that."

"Never mind," Michael said grimly. "Has Mummy found out what's inside the doll?"

Carol looked uncomfortable. "It's a human bone with a tooth in it. She said it was the spirit of the doll, and probably wasn't meant to be played with by a girl at all. It was probably used by an old man, a witch doctor, or an old woman. She said it's African. It's probably magic."

Michael said nothing, but turned away from the girl and stepped up to the window, looking out over the night fields to the moongleam on the sea.

After a few minutes he said, "Chalk Boy is dangerous. Don't go back to the quarry."

"But I want to give Mummy some more magic dolls."

Michael turned and went over to his sister, leaned down to her and with all the seriousness of a big brother said sternly, "Chalk Boy is not your friend. He's not my friend either. He's dangerous . . ."

"Mummy said there isn't such a person as Chalk Boy . . . Mummy said it's all you. Your talent. She said you're just inventing Chalk Boy to disguise your cyclic talent."

"Psychic talent," Michael corrected.

After a moment Carol whispered, "Can't we just get one more doll for her?"

"Not even one."

"But Mummy says we'll have to move into a caravan unless we get some money."

"I know exactly what Mummy and Daddy say about money. But they don't believe in Chalk Boy. And I do."

"He's your imaginary friend."

"He's a very real ghost. He lives in Limbo. He's trying to escape from Limbo, but I'm not going to let him. And he's trying to hurt you. And I'm not going to let him do that. And I'm not going to let *them* hurt you either. Or me."

Carol looked suddenly terrified, her eyes widening and moistening. "Are you going to run away from home?" she asked anxiously.

Michael watched his sister control her tears for a moment, then shook his head. "No. Not from home." He straightened up and smiled. He looked around the room, at the pictures and photographs, the golds and silvers of precious antiques, the horses and glasses and swords and shields that lined the walls on paper. And in the middle of them: the golden chalice, with its studded reds and greens of precious jewels. He went over to the Grail and placed his hand against its picture, then quickly tore down the poster and crushed the paper in his hands. "Doesn't look like that *anyway!*"

He turned and kicked the ball of paper against the

window. Carol watched him impassively, her legs dangling over the side of his bed.

"No, I'm not going to run away," he said. "I'm going to rebuild my castle. I'm going to hide in my castle. No one will be able to find me, only Chalk Boy. And you, if you want. When I'm there, you can come and visit me, and bring me food. I won't let you into the castle itself. It's too dangerous. But I shall depend on you. But only you, no one else. Do you understand?" She nodded nervously, gaze fixed on his.

"Good," he said, and added with a sudden laugh, "No one will ever get into my castle again . . . They'll look for a hundred years, but they'll never get in! *Never.* They'll only see the shadow, only the shadow. Nothing but the shadow. They'll be in Limbo, and I'll be watching them. And laughing!"

PART FIVE

The Totem
Field

Twenty-five

In the early evening, with the light going, the boy moved away from the white wall of the chalk quarry, slipping slowly into the green shadows of the scrub wood that filled the center of this ancient pit. Above him, the rim of the quarry was a dark, broken line of trees, stark against the deepening sky. He could hear a voice up there, his mother coming toward that edge to find him. He knew he had to hide.

He slipped deeper into the bushes, crawling between tall, tangling blackthorn and crowding gorse, merging with the green, his chalk-covered body swallowed by the leaves and bark, so that he was lost within the undergrowth, creeping along the twisting tracks he had marked out over the years.

His name was called again. His mother was very close to the deep quarry. She sounded agitated, her voice distant but clear in the calm evening air.

He froze and watched the spiky line of the pit-edge wood against the sky. Then he moved on, touching the heart-shaped fossils he had carefully laid down on the trails. He picked up a chalk block and used it to whiten his body further, rubbing hard against his skin, his face, then crumbling the skin of the chalk and smearing it through his hair.

His name . . . the voice quite anxious now.

The breeze from the silent farmland beyond the quarry curled in through the "gate" to this place, his castle, the open end where men had once approached to work the chalk. It stirred the gnarled branches of the alders and thorns, whipped the bright gorse, eddied in the pit.

A new shadow appeared above him, against the sky, a figure that peered down and crouched low.

He froze and closed his eyes, knowing that the gleam of light would reveal him.

He sensed the shadow move. Earth and chalk rattled from the edge, tumbling down, to crash and spread within the quarry.

"Michael?"

It's coming back. I saw it again. Leave me alone. It's coming back . . .

He turned his head, denying the name. The figure prowled above him, searching the greenery below, scanning the white chalk of the pit.

"Come on, Michael. It's time for supper. Come *on* . . ."

He tried to draw more deeply into the white shells that covered him, into the ancient sea, into the dry dust of the creatures that had formed this place; *hide me, hide me. It's so close again. I saw it. Hide me.*

He imagined the sounds of earth movements, the dull, deep echoes that would have passed through the heaving chalk waters. The feeling soothed him. The shadow called again.

"It's time for supper, Michael. Come on. Come home, now."

The sea in his mind caught him. The trees in the pit shifted in the current. He floated through the chalk sea, grasped the branches of the gorse and thorn that waved in the gentle evening light.

It was coming closer. He couldn't go home now. He had to wait. The shadow on the rim of the pit would have to wait. It was coming back. And that was what she wanted, wasn't it?

And from above, his mother's voice, harsh and angry:

"Can you hear me, Michael? Michael! It's time to go home!"

The words struck him like a hand.

Old memory surfaced to hurt him. He stood up from his hiding place and listened to the sudden shout of outrage, the woman's voice, shocked by his appearance: "What have you *done* to yourself?"

With a sad glance backward, Michael began to walk out of the pit . . .

He was on the hot, stinking beach! The waters of the vast sea drew back then parted spectacularly. The dark body of the creature thrust up and out of the ocean, towering high above him as he screamed and ran back, stumbling on the dry, coarse sand. The monster came down on to the shore, water streaming from the gray-green weeds that draped its head and heaving body.

Another creature followed, rising like a dark cloud from the sea's edge, blocking sun, blocking light, groaning as it fell, shaking the earth. The stench of rotting weed was overpowering.

Around him, the shadow of Chalk Boy moved with lightning speed. It was before him, then behind him, and Michael felt the sharp nip of teeth on the back of his neck as the not-here shape struggled to hide. He ran, then, with the shadow of Chalk Boy like a trailing cloak around him.

He saw the whirling pool of darkness that was a tunnel home and raced for it, as the shoreline shook, and the screaming shapes rose higher above him, shedding water from the wrack that encased them. In the tunnel he saw the glitter and gleam of crystal, and as he stumbled through the twisting space, and sensed the chalk pit and his mother's voice, he saw the vessel ahead of him, the face of the Fisher King watching him, etched on the glass, arms raised as if in welcome . . .

The Grail! It was there, so close!

But Chalk Boy laughed, and dropped away, and as Michael felt the world of Limbo slip back into the past, he saw the shadow on the sand, passing between the heaving, feeding masses of the giant creatures, fleeing into his hole up on the hill of the sandstone caves.

The vision of the Grail faded, but Michael was triumphant . . .

He looked up at the silhouette of his mother. He watched her grimly, ignoring her angry shouting. The smell of sea-wrack was like an old friend. His body still shook with the encounter.

It was coming back! It was coming back!

He ran from the quarry, reaching home before his mother and locking himself in the bathroom, here to draw out the long spikes of blackthorn which had bled so profusely over the chalk skin that had for so long been his hiding place.

Twenty-six

The note was passed to Michael at the beginning of the class with Mr. Hallam. Mr. Hallam was a brusque if genial man with a heavy Scots accent. He always reeked of tobacco and wore a brown, lab-technician's coat. He tolerated a great deal of disturbance when he was writing on the blackboard, or the overhead projector, but could be spectacularly angry with no prior notice.

Michael was not alone in being slightly afraid of him, but particularly enjoyed the sense that Mr. Hallam was interested in him, especially in his stories.

The class today was a discussion session, centered around stories, or objects, or facts, the pupils had found out during the week.

Today, Michael wanted to talk about the Grail. Mr. Hallam had approved, and there had been laughing and teasing from one side of the room, where the younger Hanson boy sat.

The note that reached Michael five minutes after Mr. Hallam had started to talk about King Arthur, read simply, "They're going to get you after school. They want a Roman coin in payment. Run for it."

The note was anonymous, but he recognized the crudely disguised handwriting. Graham Peake sat dumb and downcast, staring at his notebook, his cheeks slightly flushed. He wanted to be Michael's friend, but Michael had no friends, and resisted all attempts at contact.

Still, he was glad of Graham's warning.

Mr. Hallam eventually asked Michael to come to the front and talk about the Grail. Steven Hanson and his friends went very quiet, watching Michael, then signalling aggressively with their fingers.

Michael had drawn the image of the Grail on a sheet of perspex. He sat at the projector and positioned the drawing, and Hanson laughed out loud.

"Looks like a fish with fingers. Fish fingers!"

A ripple of laughter, a crusty response from Mr. Hallam, and a stern minute's instruction to everybody to take these things more seriously. "After all," he said in his growling accent, "they're a part of our heritage. Folklore and myths are the source of all human behavior, so why don't we give the wee lad a chance, let him show us his ideas. We can disagree with him afterward if we feel the need, but in the proper fashion of debate, with courtesy, and interest and fairness of thinking."

Mr. Hallam had a way with words, and a way of smothering resistance. He turned back to Michael and pointed a finger. "The floor is yours again, laddie. Let's see what you have for us."

Michael's enthusiasm, based on the vision of the Grail, was in the form of a re-depiction of the vessel which had been present at Christ's Last Supper. He declared that he believed the cup to have been made of glass, that it was more like a vase than a chalice, held between the hands and passed around the table; not a golden cup at all. Mixing and mingling his misunderstood mythology, he showed how the face of the Fisher King had been inscribed into the crystal.

"This is all very interesting, of course," Mr. Hallam interjected irrelevantly from the side of the room where he was watching the talk. "We should remember that an early symbol of Christianity was the fish. Not that I'm a great expert on these things, of course, but perhaps the wee lad has something here ..."

The wee lad waited for his moment again. He talked about the Wasteland, and the Quest for the Grail—

"Laddie, why exactly *was* he called the Fisher King?"

The question from Mr. Hallam interrupted Michael's

thoughts and he frowned. Mr. Hallam seemed genuinely interested. "I'm confused, son. Educate me. But
I'm most interested in what you have to say."

The class laughed, and Hanson was a disruptive influence, this time ignored by the teacher.

"Fishers of Men," Michael said in a low voice. It
was all he could think of. His image of the Fisher King
was a man, tired, sad and alone in his Fortress, waiting
for the blight to rise from the land. He had no idea why
he had been called Fisher King. All he could think of
was the Church lesson that so often referred to Christ
saying, "Henceforth you shall all be fishers of men."

Mr. Hallam seemed duly impressed and content with
the answer.

"But he doesn't look like a king. Not the way
you've drawn him there. This is no criticism, you understand, merely a search for greater understanding.
But the lad drawn there looks like a Prince. He has a
young face. Even if a fishy one."

"He's the king," Michael said hoarsely. "Jesus
looked on him when he drank the wine. The face of the
fish and the king in the glass."

Mr. Hallam seemed amused. "I don't remember
reading that in my Matthew, Mark, Luke and John. But
I'm sure you're right." He quickly calmed the restive
and giggling class, then added, "So tell us, young Michael. D'you know where this Grail was taken by the
bold knight who found it?"

"Into the past," Michael said, and the classroom erupted with laughter. "Long into the past," he said defiantly.
"Millions of years. Thousands of millions of years, down
to a beach by an ocean, into caves in rock that's made of
red sand. It's guarded by hideous beasts . . ."

He got no further. Mr. Hallam raised his voice to
calm the hilarity that had suddenly interrupted the proceedings. Steven Hanson was making frantic and
meaningful threatening gestures with his forearm, grinning, the spark of violence in his eyes.

"Be quiet, you lot! Maybe you'd all like to write out
a poem by Robbie Burns—forty times before leaving
school for the day?"

The class—shocked by memories of this punishment—fell instantly silent.

The lesson continued, with another pupil talking about what she'd seen through a microscope in the local tap water.

Michael was aware of the tall man in the brown leather Windcheater, standing across the road from the school, and some sixth sense made him respond with the thought; he's waiting for me.

The schoolyard was hysterical with children, departing on this fine summer's evening, rushing home to play. Cars pulled out of the park, buses slowed and gorged themselves on the young, and somewhere an alarm bell rang, a persistent and nagging tone that was ignored by everyone.

Michael, aware that Tony Hanson and his brother were after him, left through the gymnasium, and ran quickly along the path behind the scout hut. From here he was able to scramble up an earth bank, through scrub and bush, and get down on to the railway line. He followed the tracks until he came to the signal box, where children had gouged out an access from the nearby estate across the lines to the ponds and woodlands beyond.

Michael followed this path into the red-brick estate, then hauled himself up on to a high wooden fence, staring at the distant school.

He had hoped to see the Hansons and their friends lurking somewhere between, waiting for him, but to his slight concern he saw no sign of them.

He also noticed that the brown-jacketed man had disappeared. For some reason that frightened him more. The man had been standing by the bus stop that Michael normally used. He could see a bus now, coming toward the school. He could catch it if he ran through the estate. If he missed it, there wouldn't be another for about half an hour.

He started to think white. He covered himself with chalk, painted his figure out from view. He closed his

*eyes, willed the chalk sea to wash around him, dry on
him, make him white, make him invisible.*

He started to run.

*Glitter of gold. The swirl of dark that was the
shadow cast by Chalk Boy. Glitter of gold, coming
closer, the sharp, salty smell of the sea in the air . . .
running . . . round the houses . . .*

He didn't see what hit him, and was too stunned to
think about it. His face had struck the ground and was
singing that tuneless, buzzing whine that accompanies
a sudden, painful blow. Everything was red and
blurred. He was dizzy. He felt pressure on his back,
and a pummelling sensation on his shoulders. His hair
was wrenched and a stinking, pickled egg was being
forced into his mouth. He spat and twisted, but the
hand was too hard, and the sulphurous mass passed his
teeth and made him gag.

*Flexing! Huge! Rising from the sea, the shadow of
the boy fleeing before it in delight . . .*

There was a chant in the air; gold coin, gold coin!

It was Hanson, of course, trying to get more booty
from the younger boy.

"Gold coin. Gold coin!"

Michael struggled, but arms held him down. He
managed to spit the disgusting, vinegary egg from his
mouth, twisting to stare up into the fat face of Tony
Hanson.

"Where's the treasure?" the bully taunted. "Tell us
where the treasure is, or we'll feed you my father's
fishing bait . . ."

Michael stared in horror at the small glass jar with
its contents of long, black, flexing lugworms. The
other boys laughed.

Flexing . . . building . . . moving toward him . . .

"Leave me alone!"

Laughter.

"What you gonna do, Mikey? What you gonna do?"

Laughter.

"CHALK BOY!"

Laughter.

"Chalky chalky chalky. Poor little Mikey, only got one friend, Chalky Boy, Chalky Boy. But no Chalky Boy here now, *Mikey!*"

"CHALK BOY, HELP ME."

Laughter.

"HELP ME."

Laughter. "Chalky chalky chalky. Bring us some gold. Bring us some gold."

Laughter!

"Get the scissors. Cut his hair!"

A hand jabbed at Michael's stomach and he yelled as the pain took his breath away and sent a renewed surge of nausea through his body. He felt his head wrenched back and heard the sound of scissors closing sharply. Golden hair drifted in front of his eyes, blown by laughter, blown by hands waved in delight as the humiliation occurred ...

The shadow came. It punched through from the beach, bringing the sharp scent of sea air. It swirled up the main tunnel, a glimpse of light and dark, a shape that couldn't be seen, only sensed, and yet which seemed powerfully present in the corner of his eye, screaming just outside of hearing ...

And came through Michael's arms, and *struck* like a punch.

The housing estate shuddered. The very ground shook. Windows rattled.

The five boys were blown apart.

The shockwave, the dull thud, the moment of explosion, had been muffled, but had punched into this world like a thousand tons of hard, coarse iron.

The five boys were blown apart.

They struck houses, fences, lamp-posts, letter boxes. They were stunned. Slowly they picked themselves up, staggering, holding cut faces, bruised arms. How they managed to walk was astonishing. Michael sat up and looked around him. The whole area was silent. The shapes in their sneakers, colorful Windcheaters and jeans limped away in different directions, like shadows, fleshy shadows, creeping off to lick their wounds.

Michael realized that he was deaf.

Slowly his hearing returned, and he heard the sobbing. He heard defiance from Tony Hanson, but only despair and confusion from the other boys. His head sang, a single tone, high-pitched. The smell of the sea was strong.

Always that sea.

Always the same sea.

"Chalk Boy?"

A shadow fluttered around him, vanished into the evening sky like a bat, a passing moment of grayness, turning back, dropping and dipping, then flowing into nowhere.

Michael spat again, the last taste of the rotten egg. He climbed to his feel and picked up his satchel, sucking the deep cut on his index finger. Two or three adults had come out of their houses to see what the sudden disturbance had been. They didn't seem to link the vibration of the ground with the scruffy, dishevelled boy who stood in the street, battered and bleeding.

And then Michael saw it. It glittered at him. It screamed its gold at him. It almost rolled toward him!

He ran quickly to the hedge and grabbed the ice-cold artifact. It was the object he had glimpsed during the torment, a disc of gold, heavily inscribed with the oddest of patterns and marks. It was heavy. He felt it tug at his shoulder as he hid it in his satchel and started to walk from the estate.

It had come back! His talent had returned!

Almost too excited to think, and still hurting, he ran across the road, aware that a bus was approaching.

He drew up suddenly against the man in the brown leather jacket, stepping back quickly, frightened and confused. The man looked down at him, then reached out a hand and took him by the shoulder.

"Michael? You *are* Michael, aren't you?" He smiled and squeezed, the fingers getting a good purchase on the boy's jacket.

"No."

"Michael Whitlock? Yes. I think you are. I'd know

that ginger hair anywhere. Why are you squirming, sonny? Don't be afraid. There's nothing to be afraid of. What's this? Hurt yourself? Let's have a look ..."

Michael couldn't fight against the man. He was too strong. His arm was lifted, the cut on his finger examined. "That's all right, Michael. Soon heal. I've seen worse cuts than that. I've seen whole fingers cut off. Nasty. Very nasty. It *is* Michael, isn't it? I know your dad. Father. Dr. Whitlock."

"How?"

"He's a friend of mine. I worked with him. Talked a lot with him. Know him well."

Michael was released. The man dropped to a crouch. His eyes were like a fish's, pale and watery, round and dead. His mouth smiled and there were deep furrows in his face. He smelled of aftershave and had three thin gold chains round his neck. The leather jacket parted slightly over his chest and a smell of sweat made Michael recoil.

"Your daddy told me that you have a quite remarkable ability for finding treasure. That true?"

"Found a coin once," Michael said, and tried hard not to touch or pat or shrug the satchel as it tugged at his shoulder, heavy with gold. He could hear the bus pulling in. It belched diesel, applied brakes, and droned to a halt at the stop.

"That's my bus."

The man looked up, then back, smiling. "I'll give you a lift home. Ever been driven in a Jag? Smooth ride. Like riding on air. Come on ..."

There was meaning in the man's words. Michael nodded, ignored the extended hand, and started to walk with the stranger, away from the bus.

At the last possible moment he turned (slipped! The satchel was so heavy!) and ran for the bus, holding out his arm. The bus driver let the door open again and Michael scrambled on to the step. The man in the brown jacket had turned and grinned, standing where he was. The bus driver said, "You all right? Is that man bothering you?"

"Offered me a lift," Michael said, and the driver swore.

As the bus pulled past the stranger, the driver extended his left arm and flourished a V sign. On the pavement the man watched Michael, grinning and slowly wagging his finger.

Twenty-seven

As if waking from a dream ...

Richard swung his legs from the hard hotel bed and sat for a moment watching the gray summer rain sleet against the window. A dull dawn light made the room seem austere and cold. His foot knocked the half bottle of Glen Morangie as he stood, and he caught it in time to prevent its remaining contents draining on to the carpet. The smell of the spirit made him feel sick. He straightened up, stretched, rubbed a hand across eyes that were sore and tired, then collapsed wearily back on to the bed, sinking forward.

"What the hell am I doing?"

It was truly like emerging from a dream. He looked around with horror at the scatter of his clothes, at his camera equipment spread on the dressing-table, on a chair, even in the small bathroom. Rolls of film were unlabeled and unsealed. Lenses lay gathering dust. Filters were lying around like parts of a board game. He swore loudly, then reached to pick them up, breathing on them almost by instinct, polishing them.

"Dear God. What a mess ..."

In the bathroom he looked with horror at the ashen, unshaven, dark-eyed man who stared back, tramplike and hungover, from the cruel reflectivity of the silvered mirror.

"I don't know you," he whispered. He felt like crying, but managed to hold back the unwelcome emotion. He stared at Richard Whitlock, faced him for the first time in months. And he saw a shadow in the face there, the shadow of a yellow-haired boy. His son. A boy who no longer smiled, just stared at him like a mask, eyes moving, but without expression. A dead face.

The tramp blinked at him, breath misting on the glass.

"I don't know you. I refuse to know you. I'm going to send you away . . ."

He banged the edge of the sink angrily and bruised his hand. The pain was its own catharsis and he laughed, then cried for a moment, cradling the aching flesh, turning from honesty to reality. "Jesus. What a mess. What a fucking mess."

The phone trilled. He lurched into the bedroom and snatched the receiver from its cradle, hoping to hear Susan's voice, but it was Mandy from the site. She sounded subdued.

"What's up? I'm not supposed to be working at the dig today. Day off."

"There's someone here to see you. He's a friend. Dr. Goodman?"

Jack? Jack here? What was going on?

"Send him over to the hotel, will you? I've got some equipment repair to do, and some developing." He glanced guiltily at the rolls of exposed film. If he cleared his head enough he would be able to remember the sequencing. There was no real difficulty save for his own laziness.

He bathed and shaved, and drank black coffee with wholemeal toast in the cramped breakfast room of the small hotel. The owner, a charming Ulsterwoman in her sixties, chatted to him with new enthusiasm, having treated him with the utmost wariness during the preceding days. Perhaps she thought he was an eccentric photographer. Richard ate, smiled, talked, and gave her every reason to believe that he was a man of deep and changeable mood, and great artistic sensibility.

Goodman arrived soon after breakfast, but not before Richard had telephoned Susan in Ruckinghurst. Susan also was subdued, almost frightened, he thought, and sounded anything but enthusiastic when he said that he'd be driving home.

"My work's not finished, but I can't help that. I've got to leave. I've been a fool, Susan. We both have, perhaps. But me particularly."

"A fool? What about? What have you been a fool about, Rick?"

"Everything. Michael. Everything. And what else is there?"

"Carol!" the woman snapped furiously. "There's Carol. And me. Remember me?"

"Of course. Of *course,* Susan. I *know* that. I meant our family. Of course. I've been a fool about our family, and what Michael does, and what we've done to him . . ."

"What *you've* done to him. Don't you start wrapping me up in your web of deceit and hatred. God! What a bastard . . ."

Her voice, so dead, so tired, so full of repressed pain, became a barrier to conversation. There was so much he wanted to say to her, but the words became insults as he shaped them. They wouldn't pass some internal censor that whispered to him: You'll make things worse. Just shut up and leave her to think. Just shut up and go home.

"Look. We have a lot of talking to do. I know that. I'm prepared for it. And I accept that you're angry . . ."

"You sound like some kid who's just learned his first lesson in 'dealing with people.' You sound patronizing."

"I don't mean to. I'm not feeling very well, and I have a lot of thinking to do."

"Good. Think hard. You have a long drive ahead of you, plenty of time to think *hard*. So do it. And think clearly."

"How's Michael?"

"Hiding, of course."

"What does that mean?"

"He's hiding. We don't see him anymore."

"Where's he hiding? What do you mean? In the pit?"

"He's always hidden in the pit. But this is worse.

He's hiding inside himself. I can't see him anymore, Richard. I just see the body. I can't see the boy."

He shook and felt sick for some moments after the call, but he had a worse shock when Goodman rang the bell at reception. Richard went to the small sitting room and found Goodman leafing through a magazine. The younger man was wearing dark glasses and seemed tense and cold.

"Jack?"

"We're in trouble," Goodman said. And sagged, suddenly sitting down heavily into one of the armchairs in the room. He leaned back and took off his dark glasses and Richard looked away quickly. The man's eyes were yellow and black with bruising. He watched Richard through slits in lids that were puffed with fluid. Without speaking he unbuttoned his raincoat and tugged his shirt from the trouser band, revealing a midriff of blue and purple abuse that made Richard feel queasy.

All Goodman said was, "As you can see, they're a little impatient."

Richard was devastated. "Christ, Jack. I'm sorry. Have you contacted the police?"

"The police?" Goodman laughed sourly, then added, "I like my legs exactly where they are, Richard. Attached to my hips. I find that a useful arrangement."

"There's no money, Jack. There's nothing I can do. Michael's talent faded and what has been 'fetched' has been 'fetched,' and there's no way back. The boy is dry. I woke up this morning and realized what a bastard I've been. My head is clear for the first time in years. Something happened to me, Jack, something very bad, something from the animal world. A sort of mindless, instinctive hoarding behavior. I used my son like a machine. I never thought about him at all. And I'm ashamed . . ."

"Very touching," Goodman broke in. "Very touching I'm sure. We all made mistakes, Richard, not just you. I made mistakes too. Have you ever tried vomiting when your stomach muscles don't work, by the way? Difficult. Especially when three crew-cut eighteen-year-olds in army boots are standing over you urinating. So I'm very touched. But we need to make some decisions here . . ."

"There is no more money. There is no more treasure-trove . . ."

"Then that's very sad," Goodman said dully. "Because it means that soon there'll be no more Michael."

Richard's shock was fleeting, but he was across the room and wrenching Goodman to his feet in a second. Goodman delivered a precise and painful blow to Richard's chest, knocking the breath from him. Piglike eyes in bruises blinked and a wet mouth twisted into anger. "Not from you. Not you. I've taken enough because of you. You keep your distance, Dr. Whitlock. I'm ready to do some damage myself, and I'm not feeling particularly well disposed toward you at the moment."

"*What* about Michael?" Richard hissed, holding his chest where the blow had landed. "What did you mean about Michael?"

Goodman picked up his shades and covered his battered eyes. "They're paying him a visit. They want to encourage him to open up a little more."

"Tell them the treasure is all gone. It was a limited find."

"Can't do that. Sorry. When six very large black boots are conversing with your groin, truth does have its funny little way of coming out."

Shocked, Richard stared at the bitter man for a moment, scarcely daring to believe what he had heard. "You told them? About apportation?"

"I held out, Richard. I held out for a long time. Three, maybe four seconds. It suddenly seemed like a good idea to start being honest. They didn't believe me at first, of course. But the idea of apportation was sufficiently interesting—or perhaps baffling, I think I saw a brow or two crease—that they thought they'd better tell their employers. So Michael will be getting a visit. And I suggest that you get home as fast as possible, and if possible, tell the boy to start dreaming, and dreaming hard. Of gold not stainless steel, and emeralds in preference to moonstones."

Richard's awareness of the other man expanded and he realized how shocked, how utterly defeated Goodman suddenly was.

"I'm sorry, Jack. I'm really sorry."

"Me too."

"Thanks for coming. You could have called me by phone. Susan has the number here."

"I thought this would help convince you," Goodman said wearily, tapping his glasses. "Besides. This is my last stop in Britain. I fly out of Edinburgh tomorrow, and I shan't be coming back for a while. Sorry to leave you to it, Richard. But I wouldn't be any use to you. I'm too frightened."

"What about Francoise Jeury? Do they know that she knows? About Michael? Is she in danger?"

"I imagine. I don't know. I just want to get away, to recover my pride, to mend my wounds . . ."

"I might need to talk to you."

"I'm not abandoning you in that way. I'll call you often. I understand that you might need to know what else I've said, what else is happening."

Goodman buttoned his coat and walked stiffly from the hotel. Richard watched him limp to his car, then went upstairs and packed his bags in a hurry. He called Susan, unable to make the decision between panicking her or leaving her in ignorance. It seemed better just to warn her.

"Don't ask questions. Just get Michael away. Take him to your mother's. Take him to the Hansons'. But get him out of the house."

"He's at school."

"Then meet him. I'll be home in eight or nine hours. Just trust me, Susan, for God's sake! And get that boy into a safe house until I get there."

Twenty-eight

The telephone call shocked Susan. Richard's voice had sounded ... anguished. There was no other word for it. He had also sounded like the old Richard, all violence gone, the self-pitying, paranoid whine vanished. So she had been disturbed at first, but the simple implication of menace to the family had frightened her. She had been shocked.

She rang Jenny at once, and received a second blow. Jenny sounded strained and unhappy about the idea of Michael and Carol lodging with them.

"Why? They've been there before."

The edge in Jenny's voice was transparent. "They've been dumped on us before, you mean."

"What?"

"Oh God. I'm sorry, Susan. I'm sorry. That was uncalled for ..."

"You *called* it, though. What do you mean? Dumped."

Jenny drew breath at the end of the phone and then—being Jenny—laid it on the line. She and Geoff felt they were being used, used as a depository for the Whitlock children, used as messengers, childminders, catch-alls, and—while they were always prepared to do favors for friends—for heaven's sake: most of the time Carol was being left with them as a convenience to distracted parents. There was little or no thanks. Carol was unhappy about spending nights away from home. And there was such a degree of thoughtlessness in the way Susan treated her kids that perhaps it would be better ... well, better to *not* put them out at night for a while.

And anyway ...

"Anyway? Anyway? What other little lessons, Jenny?"

"Were you aware that my boys beat up—to use an Americanism—beat *up* on your son?"

Susan felt her head reel. "No. No, I wasn't."

"Good God, Sue. Don't you ever listen to what anybody tells you? My sons *hate* your son. I'm sorry, love. I'm just a 'Mother.' I can't do anything about the bullying at the heart of these young animals. Tony and Michael fight all the time. When Michael stays here he's mostly in a state of apprehension. I try, with Tony. I tell him to behave. But after dark ... well, what they get up to is nobody's business. I know I should have said something to you before, but you're so ... inaccessible, Sue. Doesn't Michael ever talk to you about this?"

Susan shook her head, then said aloud, "No. No, he never does. I thought they were all friends. I thought they all got on."

"One day they will. When they're men. But not at the moment. Listen, Sue, it really wouldn't be a good idea to have Michael here. And for God's sake, Sue—be a little more aware of your kids!"

"Christ!"

She slammed down the phone. It rang again, but she ignored it. She felt threatened. It was bright and sunny outside, although the rain that was lashing Scotland was moving south.

"Michael ..."

She didn't know what to do.

The phone rang again, and this time Susan answered it. Jenny was concerned but unapologetic. Susan said, forget it. I'm sorry. I'll not burden you. I've got a problem. No, you can't help. Forget it.

She locked the doors and windows. She put up the metal grills that Richard had installed years ago, when mud appeared in Michael's room, mud from Michael's birth-mother, they had thought ... It made her smile to remember their confusion. How little they had realized what wealth, followed by what anguish, that mud-flinging would herald.

She rang the school and insisted that neither Michael nor Carol be allowed out of class before she herself came to pick them up. This was agreed, and she felt more relaxed. Then, overwhelmed by a sense of unreality, of having let time pass without focusing, of just having *drifted* for so long, she went upstairs, picked the lock on Michael's door (really just using her own key, since Michael insisted that his room was his sanctuary) and sat down on the bed, sobbing quietly for a while, staring at the ripped fragments of poster and picture on the walls.

Michael's room was an empty place, now. It was slept in, yes, but where once it had been lived in, now it was barren. It was shredded, shattered, partial. Fragments of a childhood were here, and shards of a life that had begun to grow but had been disturbed by the hardening of a power, a power that had made this room the source of riches. In tears, Susan picked the unread books from the shelves, leafed through them. There were crayons and pencils, papers and designs, but nothing ever changed ... nothing had changed for a year. It was as if Michael came into this place and just died. No life possessed the room, just the sleeping body of a boy. To bed, to sleep, rising, leaving. In the interim, just a frozen body, staring into space.

There was one change, she saw: a drawing by Carol, pinned on the wall above his bed where he might stare at it before switching off his lamp. It showed a small, thatched hut, surrounded by stones, with white chalk balls and a tethered dog. Funny, she had never noticed this before, but then, this was only the first time in ages that she had entered the sanctuary to feel for the *boy,* and not to search for artifacts.

The drawing reminded Susan of the way Richard had described the dog-shrine, the remnants of the tomb that had been fetched in that almost devastating earth-fall, years before. The drawing was unmistakably Carol's. Peering more closely she could see that the odd shading by the hut—or shrine—was the shadow of a man. The shadow had no origin, it was just that: a touch of shade.

She felt intrusive, then, and left the room, locking the door behind her and tapping a fist against her chest three times in the traditional pre-Christian manner of warding-off evil after having behaved in a way that might summon it. But later she returned to Michael's room and searched the drawers, the cupboard, the secret places of the sanctuary, looking for a doll, or a piece of the past, something that might signal Michael's continuing relationship with his waning but still cherished power.

Although she found nothing in the room, the smell of tomato-stalk, emanating from the creased ball of handkerchief, made her think about the garden, and the greenhouses that had been in Richard's family for so many years. She unlocked the back door and walked slowly across to the humid environment. Nothing was growing here save for the tomatoes themselves. Trays of seedlings had been unattended and had wilted. The tomatoes were self-sustaining because of their connection with a steady water drip.

There was dirt on the wooden slats by one of the plants, and the cane supports were at an angle. Puzzled, Susan peered more closely and realized that the pot had been disturbed. She tugged the whole plant from its container, and the glint of gold at its bottom made her heart miss a beat.

When she lifted the disc she nearly died.

Golden. Heavy. Beautiful. She recognized it at once as Babylonian, the shallow cuneiform being unmistakable. It had other symbols on it too, and radiating lines, like sun.

Mind whirling, she replaced the gold, burying it again below the plant that secured it. Guiltily she swept the potting compost from the table and the floor. When she left the greenhouse she stopped for a moment to breathe deeply, eyes closed. Her whole body was shaking. She was close to tears.

"Oh Michael! Michael . . . Oh no . . ."

She hardly dared think what this might mean in terms of a return of Michael's true power. And she felt a confusion of emotion: wealth might still be promised, which would buy off the "businessmen" and their enterprise in Essex. But Richard had clearly stated that trouble was already on its way, and she was frightened by that. Too much control might be passing from the family to the outsiders. And what would Michael do if that was to happen?

"Don't come back . . . Dear God, don't come back, not now. Not ever. Just leave him alone."

She went back to the house where the phone was ringing. Thinking it might be Richard she ran into the sitting room, breathless, but it was the French psychic, Francoise Jeury, asking if she could come and visit. Susan put her off, then poured herself a large Southern Comfort.

Twenty-nine

The first thing she noticed was the cooling of the air in the room, a phenomenon so common that it no longer alarmed her. It was an atmospheric change that invariably accompanied a psychic event, and Francoise Jeury had a well-established routine whenever her extra senses, or one of the five ordinary senses, detected an unexpected change in the environment.

She switched on a small tape-recorder, activated the corner video camera, put loops of coarse iron around her neck, wrists and ankles, then rang down to the main lobby of the Institute.

"Room 4b. I have an AC positive, getting stronger."

That was all she needed to do. All the corridors in the Institute were monitored on a routine basis for the passage of "hard located" or "moving" presence—that state of alertness would now be increased to critical. A medical team would be on standby, and a psychologist ready to access Francoise's unconscious mind, or dreams, if a phenomenon occurred and was transferred too deeply during the encounter.

She quickly rang Lee, then, and was relieved when he answered. He had been intending to visit a new Roman site being excavated on the Thames embankment, near Fleet.

"Do you want me there?"

"Please!" She spoke urgently, uneasy for reasons she couldn't fathom. There was a sense of approach, of something coming closer, and it was making her pulse race. "As soon as you can."

"Get out of there if you think it's going to be dangerous . . ."

"Just come!"

"Shall I bring a shield?"

"Yes."

A shield was a simple defense against psychic attack, not always effective, but an enhancement to confidence. The Institute did not possess the sort of high-tech weaponry and monitoring equipment that had been romanced in a recent film. "Ghostbusting" was still in the realm of fantasy, but she smiled to herself as she remembered occasions, not long past, when she could have done with a little more control of the psychic event that was occurring around her.

The Atmosphere Cooling passed, but the hair on her neck—an invaluable sensor—was sharp and itching. (I have a positive on spine tingling . . .)

She got on with her work, typing slowly, distracted now. Around her, on the shelves, the artifacts and natural materials that she had accumulated over the years were quiet, innocent.

A minute later the temperature dropped dramatically, a shock of cold, and the air thickened around her. She pushed back from the desk, and tried to stand, but her legs felt suddenly sluggish. She forced herself up, rising as if through a soupy liquid—

A nagging memory of a conversation . . . too distracted to remember clearly . . .

There was something in the room with her. It filled the space by the door, then seeped away, but pulsed back a moment later. She could smell the sea! A sharp, salty tang, with the sweeter stench of rotting weed. It made her gag for a second, and she sat down again, eyes wide and alert, mind open but sensing nothing except this false ocean . . .

The sea! The ocean! Michael Whitlock!

Shimmering, then: a shimmering shape materializing before her, arms outstretched. It was taller than the room. She could see the vague outline of legs and arms, the head halfway through the ceiling. Then it stooped. Great fish eyes, dead and watery, glittered for a moment, then faded. Fingers flexed, stroking the air of the room, reaching toward the shelves.

The dead face took on a momentary feature, and she saw Michael's face, eyes closed, ginger hair flaring. Then again the dead thing, the drowned thing, then just the fingers of the left arm, swelling, flexing, becoming impossibly jointed, curling round a stone on the shelf, a spherical piece of black obsidian the size of a cricket ball.

"Michael . . ." Francoise shouted. "Michael, can you hear me?"

The room pulsed, seemed to shrink, then expand again, and Francoise felt the air snatched from her lungs. She gasped and struggled for breath, but the air came back, and the round, dead face was close to hers. The fish eyes slowly closed, but the toothless mouth opened in a faint and echoing scream, that dissolved into weird, distant laughter.

The shelf that held the stone was suddenly shattered. Fragments flew across the room and Francoise, acting on instinct only, flung herself to one side as the blast of air and pottery exploded toward her.

And at once the room was silent, very still, settling. The presence had gone.

Francoise picked herself up, brushed at her clothes. She surveyed the mayhem. Her desk was overturned, one corner broken off completely. The telephone was wrapped around the ceiling light, its cord trailing.

Searching through the scattered objects on the floor she established that the heavy stone had gone. She remembered the video. It was running, but . . .

"Damn!"

It was pointing along the wall. It had been dislodged. It had a wide-angle lens, but at some point it had been thrown out of line. Hands shaking she removed the camera and ran the tape back, reviewing the film through the finder.

There was a flash of shape, a clear visual image of the presence in the room, then the field of view shifted alarmingly, finally being flung to face the wall.

The sound of the scream and laughter was on the tape recorder.

Two technicians arrived in the room, flushed and breathless from running. First reports suggested that no other room had witnessed the phenomenon, nor had the monitors in the corridors. This didn't surprise Francoise, although she said nothing for the moment. She was too shaken, and too excited.

A minute later Lee Kline stepped cautiously into the room, smiled at Francoise, then looked around at the mayhem and the busy technicians. "Spring cleaning, I see."

His smile was thin, his concern showing. Francoise shrugged then held out her hands. Lee walked over to her, unbuttoning his leather jacket. He took her hands in his and asked two questions, which she answered. He pulled her close and kissed her on her open mouth, staring into her eyes, looking hard. All the time his fingers felt the deeper pulses in her wrists. Her taste flowed. Her response to the kiss would have been clear to him after the years of practice. Finally, she did the thing with her tongue that they'd agreed would signal at least the continued presence of Francoise's memory, even though she might have been "inhabited" after the encounter.

As Lee pulled away, he pecked Francoise affectionately on the cheek.

"You're clear. At least, as far as I can tell."

She touched a finger disappointedly to the area of flesh and shook her head. "The romantic American— more passion in the 'test' kiss than in the greeting."

Lee grinned, scratching his dark hair as he looked around at the scattered artefacts. "I notice you've had garlic for lunch."

"No entities would dare try to possess me."

"Well, there's trying and trying . . ."

She noticed Lee's teasing laugh but ignored it, save for a smile, then described the apparition and outlined her idea as to its source.

It *had* been Michael, disguised somehow, dressed in his Fisher King guise, or perhaps as the boy who haunted the primeval sea, his alter ego, his chalky imaginary friend. Perhaps he had reached through space and "fetched" a tribal artefact from the culture of the Aztecs, a stone imbued with echoes of the lives it had taken as it had been used to smash the skulls of its victims.

But something about the image of the ghost disturbed her . . . it was familiar to her . . . a familiar appearance . . . Had Michael drawn it for her? She couldn't remember.

She drank a cup of coffee and relaxed, but still struggled to recall the source of the ghostly image. After a while she abandoned the mental quest and phoned Susan Whitlock. The woman at the other end sounded subdued, quite defensive.

"Susan? Is Michael there?"

Susan's voice was strained. "No. He's at school. Why?"

At school! Not in the pit, then. Francoise said, "I was wondering . . . has he fetched anything in the last little while? Has there been any sign of his talent returning?"

"None at all," the other woman said stiffly, and Francoise had the very human sense that Susan Whitlock was not telling the truth.

"I was thinking not of valuable things, but rocks, or earth, stones . . . wood . . . that sort of thing."

"Nothing," said Susan. "No stone or wood that I'm aware of."

Francoise hesitated, then prompted, "Something very simple, like a black ball of stone, chipped and shaped to be sharp on one side . . .?"

"I've seen nothing like that."

"I see. Well, thank you." She hesitated, made uneasy by the hostility pouring down the phone line. Lee's presence beside her was reassuring, his hand resting gently on her shoulder as he listened. "Susan . . .?"

"Yes?"

"May I come and visit Michael? Perhaps later this evening? I'd like very much to talk to him, to ask him some questions."

There was a sigh of irritation, or perhaps frustration. Then came the answer, curt and to the point: that the Whitlock family had some sorting out of its own to do. Perhaps Madame Jeury wouldn't mind waiting a few days. Then, yes ... by all means come and visit. But not today.

"Thank you."

Staring at the mess around her, the evidence of an explosion caused by a boy reaching through time and space, Francoise came to the odd and exhilarating conclusion: Michael was fetching from the future. He had reached back from some future time to this moment in 1989 in London.

The event—the presentation of a black stone trophy to his parents—was still to occur in the life of the Whitlocks.

Francoise couldn't know when exactly the event would occur, but as she discussed the idea with Lee she made the assumption that it was still some months off.

Thirty

At the end of the class, at the end of the day, Michael was called to the teacher and told to wait behind with Carol. Then they were taken through the school to the car park and personally delivered into their mother's care. Susan hugged him and opened the door for him, and at once he felt cold. He pulled away from her, his arms rigid by his sides. The chatter and laughter of the pupils faded and that buzzing returned, the angry buzzing that blanked all his senses, except for the sea and the beach, and the red sandstone caves.

He watched his mother suspiciously. As she drove from the gates he looked for the man in the brown jacket, but didn't see him.

Daddy's friend had not returned, then, to try and tease more treasures from him.

At home he was again surprised and suspicious when he was taken straight to the house and told to stay inside. Carol seemed content enough, despite the day being still bright and hot. Michael wanted to go to his castle, but his mother locked the back door and started to make tea.

"I'd like to go and play outside," he said grimly from the kitchen doorway.

"Not until your father gets home. I want you to stay indoors." She looked round at him as she stirred the saucepan, and smiled. "Why didn't you tell me that Tony Hanson was a bully? Why didn't you tell me you and he aren't friends?"

The thought of Hanson made Michael's blood run

cold. The memory of nights at Aunt Jenny's made him shiver, remembering the creaking of floorboards as the Hanson boys would come into the room and try to steal his clothes; or the kicks beneath the table during supper; and the simple, increasing sense of menace whenever he stayed there.

He had never said a word. He had always hoped that he would become invisible, that the boys would cease to see him, aware only of his shadow as it passed fleetingly across the floor or the garden.

"Well?" prompted Susan. "Are you deadly enemies?"

"I don't like them. They're rough."

Jenny's boys *rough.* And Jenny and Geoff so reasonable, so liberal . . . Susan's mind couldn't cope with the contradiction.

"Well, you won't have to go back. I won't send you to stay there any more. All right?"

"Thank you. May I play outside now?"

"No. Not until your father comes home. Don't you have homework to do?"

Grimly, Michael nodded and went up to his room.

They had tea. The sun was still warm and the quarry, and its access to the ancient shore, beckoned and called to Michael.

From his room, as soon as he had eaten, he shinned down the wall outside and ran, head low, down the garden to the greenhouses.

Inside, he checked the tomato plant where he had hidden the heavy gold disc. It was undisturbed, and when he tried to lift the large pot it was as heavy as yesterday. The treasure was still inside.

He straightened the canes a little, and made a tighter tie of the long, fruit-laden stems of the plant. Perhaps he had been wrong. Perhaps his mother hadn't, after all, found his secret.

But the nagging anger wouldn't go away. Her smiles, her warmth, the way she had looked at him. She was up to something. She *knew* something and was keeping it quiet. There was a change in the wind, and Michael experienced apprehension in anticipation of what that change might be.

When he got to the quarry he saw at once that some-one had been here. The bushes were bent and broken in places. Someone had used a trowel to dig into the earthfall at the base of the chalk wall. Michael, trained to see signs of interference from outside, could see the footprints of a man wearing large shoes. They led through and round the pit, approached the concealed tunnel, but hadn't entered the cave.

Brown Leather Jacket had been here, then. Daddy's friend, snooping and searching, trying to find some-thing that Daddy had missed. More gold for Daddy. More pretty things for the art market. More money for Daddy.

Heart racing, his face flushed, Michael scanned the dark edge of the quarry, making certain that no one was up there watching him. Then he shed his clothes and found the chalk paste with which he painted his body. Pressed against the chalk wall, he summoned the gates and walls, then moved, invisible, through his pri-vate world, checking the iron, wooden and stone mark-ers that guided the path through the defenses.

Chalk Boy's call delighted him. Michael turned to the wall and the whiteness dissolved into the long, shining passage. Sea spray wafted from the distant ocean, and he could hear wind, loud, strong, swirling. He ran along the tunnel, passing the middle place where normally he would be stopped, there to peer in frustration at the glimpsed world beyond. But now he walked on, the sound of the surf louder, the howling wind louder. Above these sounds of atmosphere and ocean came the stark, disjointed cries of the creatures that flourished in this world.

For the second time, but more controlled, Michael stepped into the past, his lungs filling with the fetid at-mosphere, his face wet with the dashing spray that came from the billowing waves. The sand was soaking. The caves in the red sandstone glistened and gleamed and he saw much movement there, the shadows of souls, the limbo creatures among whom lived Chalk Boy. Great black clouds whirlpooled above his head, and distantly the air was alive with purple light, flickering and discharging energy.

The shore was thick with flexing green and orange weed. The bones of some decaying animal, vast in length and girth, were scattered whitely among this restless sea-wrack.

Chalk Boy's shadow flowed through the soaking air, disturbing the weed and the sodden sand, surrounding Michael and blinding him for a moment. Michael felt the grip on his neck, but less ferocious this time, and he turned from the storm shore back into the tunnel.

Rain sleeted across a silent, grassy land. He saw a distant wood, dark beneath glowering clouds. The shrine, with its low, turf roof, was beginning to sag, its walls leaning heavily, its wicker doors already broken and scattered. The tall figures in wood, the guardians, were featureless now, with time, rain and rot. The iron chair that had tethered his dog was rusted, but still hung, moving slightly in the rain, from the sagging beam that ran across the door. The mud was heavy on his feet and he moved in slow motion toward the empty, silent shrine. A fire had burned here once, a great fire, kept alive by men, kept burning for the sake of hope. Now the land was barren, the men gone, the women gone, even the animals fled to the great wood, where they had returned to their wild ways.

He dragged his feet through the mire, slipping on the mud, tripping on the coarse tufts of grass. The rain was icy and miserable, a drenching, driving downpour that saturated him to the very bone. But he stooped to enter the shrine, and the Grail gleamed and glistened there, its crystal face bright, the face of the Fish aware of him through its closed eyes, the fins with their fingers spread in welcome, drawing him to the Glory, to the memory of the life that had been sacrificed for the sake of a greater life.

Fisher King. Michael reached for the vessel, struggled to hold it, stretched his arm to fetch the shining vessel, but could not approach close enough to it. His fingers spread wide like the fingers of the King etched in the glass. His mouth opened in a cry of pain like the mouth of the Fisher King, opened and calling, calling for release from the Wasteland that was his realm.

The Grail was so beautiful. It scintillated. It was so welcoming, so urgent, so serene in its simple shape. The Grail of Jesus, the cup of an earlier age that had been used to symbolize Jesus's own sacrifice . . .

He fetched. He fetched with all the will and strength in his tormented muscles, but his hand reached into another place and touched living wood . . . He gripped the wood . . .

He fetched it back . . .

Earth exploded around him, and he was flung across the pit, bleeding from the mouth, holding the flexing, whirring figure, which blinked at him and grinned.

He picked himself up from the ground, and spat mud and blood from his mouth.

So close. He had been so close!

The figure was a clockwork puppet, its mechanism in full, noisy function. Its head turned, its legs worked, its eyes opened and closed, and below its green trousers something rose and fell. It smelled of tobacco. In a part of his memory Michael could hear men's laughter, and smell the fire, and sense the small, candlelit room and the wide table and the shadows of the men sitting there, suddenly disturbed and terrified when a hand had reached among them. Wherever he had "fetched" had been away from the depressing rain of the shrine, where the Grail had been shown to him. He tossed the dying clockwork doll into the deep tunnel in the chalk, then tugged his clothes on, covering the chalk on his skin.

The rope ladder had broken a few days before and he left the quarry through the old entrance. It was getting gray as dusk approached and he watched the house, across the field and the low mound of the barrow, with nothing but a cold, dead feeling in his heart. He'd be in trouble, of course. He'd disobeyed his mother. She would be angry, then she'd withdraw as always, and fuss over Carol, or over her lessons, and later in the evening she would cry, and no matter what he said, he would get the sharp edge of her tongue.

At the garden gate he began to feel desperate. The pounding in his head grew louder, and the sudden, unexpected gentleness from his mother began to nag at him again. He started to feel angry. It was such a hard thing to understand. His jaw was clenched, and so were his fists, and he spent a long minute staring at the path through a red and blurred gaze with which he had become too familiar, listening to the thunder in his skull, and remembering the taunting cries of Chalk Boy whenever he had felt sad with his parents' behavior.

He looked up toward the house and frowned. He could see his father in the sitting room (so he had come back from Scotland!). Carol was sitting at a table, in the light by the open French windows. His father picked her up and swung her round. Carol seemed delighted, her arms waving with pleasure. He saw his father put her down and ruffle her hair, then stand, for a while, staring over her shoulder at her painting.

Michael looked down again. The red rage wouldn't recede.

Now he was mocked again. Carol. Always Carol. Swung in the air, pampered, loved.

It wasn't Carol's fault! It wasn't Carol's fault. Don't be unfair to Carol.

But the rage remained, and his head thundered, a sea pulse, a wave pulse on a distant shore. He felt sick.

Then he heard his mother's voice, raised, he thought, angrily. And then the deeper tones of his father. He walked along the path, looking for them, and realized with a surge of fury that they were now in the greenhouse. He ran toward the glass windows and could see their shapes standing there, blurred, dark outlines through the dirty panes.

Gold glinted. It flashed in the dying sun more brightly than a torch.

They had found his disc!

His father laughed, an almost hysterical sound, the sound of delight. Inside the plant house, the shapes of his parents hugged, then drew apart. He heard his father say, "It doesn't matter. Not for the moment. As of now I'm going to be the best Daddy in the world to young Michael. I'm *really* going to tell him stories. He deserves it."

The words filled Michael's ears and made him howl silently, his whole body shaking with rage.

I'm really going to tell him stories . . .

You never loved me! All you care about is Carol. You can't even see me. All you see is the treasure!

As of now . . . best Daddy in the world . . .

You think that's all I did this for! And you sent your friend to bully me. You just *want* . . . you just *want* . . . you just *take* . . .

Michael's silent scream almost erupted into the world, but it was a shadow scream, adding to the cries of the creatures that prowled the sea's edge in the million-year-old past. His body shook and shuddered, a sort of *rigor mortis* in his muscles so that nothing functioned save for the nerves themselves, which made him a trembling, grimacing statue in the garden, a point of rage that was soundless but slowly splitting.

He saw a gleaming stone, a polished stone, black and smoothed, a heavy piece of ancient rock, smoothed by skilled hands, used in brutal ways . . . and he reached for it, reached through the sluggish air, fought against the thick barrier, fingers flexing and grabbing to fetch the stone.

His hand touched it with such ease. He closed his grip and fetched with all his strength! He could hear his name being called distantly . . . but he ignored the sound.

He yanked it back, stumbling as it came to him, keeping his grip upon the heavy object and waiting for a moment as the pulse and thud of air and detritus from the past dissipated, leaving him stunned, but clear in mind.

Without even thinking, acting only on impulse, he twisted his whole body back. Like a discus thrower he flung the stone with all his strength toward the greenhouse, not even waiting for it to find its mark before he had turned and fled the garden. He heard the crash of rock through glass. Still he ran, drawing the evening air around him, sucking the tunnel in his mind closer to him, drawing in the sea and the sand and the ancient storm, dragging all of this behind him like a cloak, a looming, billowing cloak, which slowly folded to cover him, falling across the silent pit like the blackest of nights, settling upon the chalk and the brushwood, and sinking in upon itself, taking everything away from the world except the past.

The past danced around him in a blur of brightness and shape. He laughed at the splendor and exhilaration of this sudden vision. He reached out and touched here, fetched there, brushed his hands through rooms, tombs, through woods, across faces, across surfaces and over the warm grasslands of lost times. Where he reached he touched: and his eyes *saw,* and his ears *heard,* the fears and screams of those who felt this spectral caress, reaching to them from beyond the thinness of the air itself.

Michael's castle was complete.

Thirty-one

Richard had called Susan from St. Albans to confirm that he would be arriving later than anticipated, at about seven in the evening, as he had a visit to make. He would say nothing more. Susan was waiting for him by the gate as the car turned into the drive. She was apprehensive and physically cold and the sight of her husband induced in her an emotion of confusion and fear. They looked at each other like strangers for a long while, then hugged with cautious detachment. But the embrace grew tighter, and perhaps there was a real need on both sides. They didn't kiss, but neither seemed willing to release the other. After a moment Susan drew back and stared at the partial wreck of a man that her husband had become, flicked at his lapels and shook her head, then started to cry.

"You look terrible," she said through the tears.

"A good bath, a shave, a change of clothes, a good talk ... I'll be my old self. I know it sounds pat to say that, but we really *do* have to talk. And I really *am* back to normal. It's just ..."

She looked at him moistly, then shook her head. "Richard—you're *not* back to normal. I don't suppose you ever will be."

He looked shocked, but then dissolved into acceptance. "I'll try, love."

"I know you will. But let's have no illusions, shall we? Neither of us is 'back to normal.' I can't see us ever getting 'normality' back. Not ever. No lies, Richard. No more lies."

"No. No more lies."

"For Michael's sake, if no one else's. He's in trouble? Is he in real trouble?"

"Possibly. But I'll get us out of the situation. Even if we have to get the police involved, I'll get us clear of this mess."

He thought how pale Susan looked, and found himself touching her cheeks with trembling fingers. She had lost weight, and her eyes were tired gray hollows. Her hair smelled of sweat, and he guessed that she, too, was letting herself go a little.

Susan and he would deal with their own relationship later, however, and at great length. It would be a long process of healing. For the moment, Michael was on his mind.

He asked after both his children.

"Oh, Carol's fine, of course. Drawing and painting as usual. And yes: more enthusiasm than talent. But who needs Picasso in the family? Michael's locked in his room."

"Locked in his room? Why?"

"He locked the door himself. He does that now. He'll come out when he's ready. And besides, I told him to stay inside today. What *is* going on, Richard?"

"Someone may try and get to Michael. They think he's found buried treasure, and that we're keeping it from them. They may even know what he can truly do. Goodman had some difficulties with them, gave the game away, but had the decency to warn me. Let's get inside."

He hesitated, then smiled and reached into his jacket pocket. He unwrapped the fabric from around the Mocking Cross. Evening light glanced from the grimacing features of the golden mask. Susan said nothing, just reached to touch the precious object, her fingers gliding down the gnarled wood of the blade. "Was this your errand?"

"He took some convincing. He didn't want to let it go—"

"But he gave it back to you?"

Richard smiled weakly. "What do you think? That

the man is God's gift to the family? No. It's a loan.
I've promised him to try and find its partner. He has a
document from me saying that I've taken temporary
ownership. I can't screw him around. But if I can buy
it back I *will*. I thought it might help to convince Michael that things are different now."

Susan was uncertain, but she was glad to see the
carving, despite its hideous appearance. "It meant a lot
to Michael, this cross. It was the one thing we
shouldn't have sold. It broke him completely. The fury
came through. I think he'll be impressed."

But Michael didn't answer the door to his room. Listening at the wood, Richard couldn't hear a thing, and
assumed the boy was maintaining his usual sullen silence. When he spoke, Richard was gentle in tone, the
beginning of a rehabilitation with his son. He felt helpless and cheap, especially as he announced the return
of the Mocking Cross, but if there was to be a new life
it had to start now. There was no point in delaying. Michael would not respond, however, and Richard was
unwilling to open the door uninvited. He went
downstairs.

Carol was in the sitting room. She looked pale and
alarmed as her father entered, but Richard walked over
to her and swung her into his arms.

"How's my favorite girl? I've missed you so much.
It's so cold and wet in Scotland I could have done with
some cheerful, chirpy company."

Carol struggled in the grip, uncomfortable and close
to tears.

With a forced smile, Richard let her down, then
fussed over her painting. She ignored him, glanced into
the garden and shivered. The dusk was coming down,
but the garden was bright with flowers and bushes, un-
tended but mostly able to look after themselves.

"We're going to have such fun from now on. I
promise you, Carol. Such fun."

"I'm painting," the girl said softly, and Richard
fluffed her hair and stepped away from her, following
Susan back to the kitchen.

It was going to take time. He had no illusions about

that. The last two years had been a living nightmare. He felt as if he was emerging from Limbo, picking up pieces here and there, picking up the smiles of his family again.

He desperately wished Michael would open the door to his room.

"Is Michael in danger? Answer me truthfully."

"Truthfully: I don't know. Jack Goodman had a rough time with some hired thugs. They want the money promised to them. Jack can't deliver unless I deliver. Under boot pressure he told them about Michael. So I imagine they're going to come and try to get Michael to 'perform' for them. What we have to do is plan a strategy to deny them. We have to protect Michael, ourselves, and our lives. If that means getting police protection, then we'll have to do it."

Susan was shaking. Arms folded, she stared at Richard through weary, faded eyes. "We've dealt in treasure-trove. We've earned money and not declared it to the Revenue. We're criminals, Richard. We've committed crimes. We've screwed up our children's lives. And what have we got to show for it? Three cars, an extension to the house, and a boy who won't speak to us."

She straightened up and beckoned to Richard. "I have something to show you, while Michael is out of the way. Something that might be old. Something that might be new. But something that doesn't, absolutely *doesn't* mean the beginning of a new period of growth in the tourist industry! Do you understand me?"

Richard nodded. The tone of Susan's voice was enough to sober him. He followed her through the warm evening to the greenhouse. She lifted a tomato plant from its earthenware pot, dragging the whole compacted bole of compost out in one go.

"Reach in," she said softly, and he did so. He drew out the gold disc, brushed the dirt from it, and closed his eyes.

"Good God. It's Babylonian. See? The symbols are cuneiform. It's a Sun Disc . . ."

"I'd realized that."

"And pure gold. Good God. This might date from 3000 BC."

Susan was bitter. "So that's all right, then. We'll flog it through Goodman and pay off some of the debt. Maybe we'll find more little treasures in the seedling trays, or in the potato ridges ..."

Richard stopped her with a gentle finger to her mouth. He waved the golden disc—with difficulty, it was very heavy—and said, "This is Michael's. This doesn't matter. It doesn't matter anymore. We're taking nothing more from the boy. Nothing at all. What he brings, what he does, is up to him. We have to live for him, Sue. You know that."

"I know it. I never had any real trouble knowing it. I failed him, sure. But I was *failing*. Period. I just couldn't cope with anything."

"Then just give me time to show that I'm back. Please. Just give me time to show that I'm back, and real again. I'm out of Limbo, back in the real world. Back on Earth."

She stared at him, then softened and smiled. "If there's one thing that Michael could do well to fetch now, it would be Cleopatra's bath of asses' milk. You really are a smelly man at the moment. Time for a good soak!"

Richard roared with laughter. It was a feeble joke, in its way, but it marked closeness again, and he found her humor to be cathartic. He hugged Susan, lifting her off her feet.

"It doesn't matter. Not for the moment. As of now I'm going to be the best Daddy in the world to young Michael ..."

"Not before time," Susan said wryly and softly.

"I'm *really* going to tell him stories. He deserves it."

My God, he thought. How much he deserves it. Poor little lad. All he ever wanted was love, affection, and a thrilling tale of Arthur and his Knights. Or this odd character, the Fisher King.

Again, he hugged Susan. "I've been a fool, Sue. I've

been frightened, blinded, greedy, and frightened again. Even Carol rejects me . . ."

"She'll come round. She always asks about you. I often see her looking through your photograph books, sitting in your chair in the study."

"I have so much to do. There's so much to do. And we have to be careful, now. I really think that Goodman's warning is right. We might be getting some unwelcome visitors."

They stood for just a moment, watching each other in sadness and despair. Then Susan said, "Put the disc back. I don't want Michael to know we've found it. It's his to reveal when he wants, if at all. If you're serious, Richard, then this might be the key to winning back his trust in us."

Richard sighed as he agreed. "Let me photograph it, though. Those symbols are fascinating."

"Later . . ."

He started to place the heavy gold object back into its hiding place.

The earth shook slightly, and dust, or spray of some sort, splattered against the greenhouse windows. Both Richard and Susan glanced up in alarm, and through the smeared and filthy glass saw a silhouetted, shadowy shape flexing, twisting.

"What's going on?"

The glass above them shattered. It exploded inward, and a great stone, a black rock, polished smooth and reflecting the last sun's rays, curved through into the plant house, striking Susan a glancing blow to the face. She screamed and fell. Glass shards covered Richard, and one splinter went into his left eye, so that he froze for a moment, tugging down the lid to stop the glass penetrating his cornea.

"Oh, my God!"

Susan stumbled to her feet, moaning softly. Blood stained her face, but she pulled herself upright, leaning heavily on the shelf which supported the tomatoes.

"Don't move," she mumbled.

"Glass . . . in my eye . . . glass . . ."

"I know . . . Don't move."

Her legs buckled, and she wiped a hand across her face. All the energy and life had gone from her features. She was slack, loose, her eyes half closed, blood flowing freely from the gash.

She reached toward Richard, and slumped down to her knees. As he watched her, frozen into immobility by the pressure-pain of the shard in his eye, so he felt the fragment move, loosen. He tentatively reached two fingers down into the sensitive area of his lid, felt the hard, sharp sliver and eased it out. His eye was sore. The shard was thick and coarse. It would probably have done little harm.

Distantly he heard a vibrating explosion, and a strange darkness passed fleetingly over the field at the bottom of the garden.

"Quickly. Get up, Sue. We've got to get back to the house . . ."

"Michael . . ." she moaned.

"I know. I know. We've got to make sure he's all right. Whoever threw that stone is still out there. Come on. Get up."

They staggered from the greenhouse, limped up the path to where Carol was waiting for them in the back door, her face blank, a frightened mask.

"Get inside. Get Michael out of his room. We have to talk. All four of us. Hurry, Carol."

Carol just stared at him.

"Darling. Hurry!"

"Michael's not in his room."

Oh God. Where was he, then? Richard looked frantically around, wondering where the man was who had thrown this stone, the vicious opening move of his declaration of intent: to get Michael's treasure.

"Where is he, Carol? Did you see where he went?"

She pointed to the distant chalk quarry. "He went there."

I'll have to get him.

"Carol, Mummy's been hurt by a stone. A bad man threw a stone and hurt Mummy. Will you get some cold water and plasters and help her to bathe the wound? Will you do that?"

Carol started to cry.

She said, quite simply, "But *Michael* threw the stone. *Michael* threw the stone. I saw him . . ."

Richard felt his world slip again. He eased Susan down, to sit on the steps of the back door, and looked towards the trees that surrounded the quarry. There was a darkness over the trees, and a swirl of birds, circling the thin wood, streaming down at times, into the wide space where the chalk had once been dug. He could hear no sound.

But he knew that Michael was watching him.

Thirty-two

Michael's room was empty, of course. Susan leaned out of the window overlooking their garden, and called briefly for her son, knowing that he was in the quarry and that her voice would never carry. She spent a moment letting her hurt, her pain, control her, the feeling of resentment from Michael, his rejection, his act of violence, and the pain on her brow, where the glancing blow from the stone had left a cut and a bruise. Her left eye was closing slightly, and she was beginning to get a headache. Then, quite aggressively, she closed the window and locked it.

Richard had unloaded his traveling case and camera bags from the car and had checked around the house, nervous about the threat passed on by Jack Goodman. He checked the locks, the cellar, and peered into the loft space. Now he was buttoning on an anorak. His legs, through his cord trousers, seemed chunky. He had pushed newspapers down as protection.

"Why?"

He looked at Susan, then smiled thinly. "I get the feeling that Michael is angry. Do you get that feeling?"

"Only for the last six years."

"When he *fetches* he causes mayhem. I don't want any more damage than is necessary. But I've got to find him. I owe it to him."

Carol stood by the back door, her face twisted with concern. She watched her father as he went to leave the house. "Michael said no one would ever go to his castle again but me. I'm supposed to bring him food."

Dropping to a crouch, Richard put his hands on the girl's shoulders. "I need to find Michael. I need to explain things to him. I can get into the quarry and talk to him—"

"No, you can't. You won't be able."

"Somehow I think I'll be able," he said with a half-smile. "But if he needs food, I'll tell him that you'll be bringing it. Food for the prisoner in the castle. All right?"

Carol's eyes showed the concern she felt. "He's *not* a prisoner."

"Isn't he?"

"No. *We're* the prisoners. He's in his castle. He's hidden."

"I have to bring him home, love. I have to get him to safety. I know he's angry, but I can't let my son be alone at the moment. It's a dangerous time for us, Carol. I want you to talk to Mummy about it."

Susan turned away, her sigh one of despair. Richard said again, "You have to know all about it, Carol. So go and talk to Mummy."

"I have to take food to Michael," the girl pleaded. "He told me to."

"Later. We'll do that later, if need be."

He went to the top of the quarry, stepping carefully through the wire and wood remains of the fun-castle walls that had once been erected here. Holding on to the leaning elm, he peered down the sheer wall of chalk, searching the dense green shrubbery below, peering as far up the defile as he could, before the quarry wall obscured his sight of the entrance to the pit.

He called for Michael, but his cry disturbed nothing. Not even birds in the trees, and that sense of avian silence drew attention to itself. He looked up and around, shouted again, then listened.

He heard utter silence only. There was no bird life here at all.

On the air he could smell sea; and he could also smell frost.

He walked round the quarry's edge, and slid and

skidded down the grassy slope to the bottom of the
scarp. As so often before, he walked between the
carved gates of the quarry, stepping cautiously into
the confining walls, and following the uneven ground
towards the main excavation area. But before he could
even turn into the deep pit, he felt that frost again, an
icy wind that stung his eyes and ears.

Above him, the summer sky was lowering towards
dusk; the clouds, fleecy and still, had orange rims, and
the sky was iridescent blue.

But in the pit there was the smell of winter by the sea.

He called for his son again. From the corner of his
eye he thought he saw movement amongst the trees
that grew here, but he could focus on nothing. When
he took a few steps forward he felt a cold so intense
that it stopped him.

His voice, when he shouted, echoed strangely. He
had the feeling that he was in a mine-shaft, or some
deep, barren amphitheater, not this bush-filled chalk
working. In the distance he could see the high, white
wall where Michael stored the rubbish of his
apportation, but as Richard walked toward it, so the
wall seemed to shift in position.

Richard began to feel afraid. He was aware of the
broken nodules of gleaming marcasite that were scattered around, and the fossilized urchins and shells, all
placed in a pattern, he remembered Michael telling
him, although the nature of the pattern was not
discernible . . .

Again: "Michael! Come home, son. Come back to
the house. It's for your own good!"

Why would he believe me? What reason does he
have to trust me? Shit! Just give me a couple of hours.
Two hours to let him breathe air that is clean again.
Come back to me, Mikey—give me two hours to take
the first step with you again . . .

"Michael!"

The silence suddenly engendered a real fear in Richard, but not, now, for the boy's sake. The whole quarry
seemed to watch him. There was no movement here,
yet there was movement in his mind. He was walking

through space that flowed about his body, not thin air and the smell of dusk. He was being dragged toward a sea whose sharp odor flushed through the space around him in regular waves, like the crashing of surf on a beach.

Time to go home, I think! This boy is just too angry!

The cold had started to seep through to his bones. He turned and ran. The quarry was frozen, cold like the spirit of his son. The quarry *was* his son. The understanding was almost natural. This was Michael's castle. The place was the shadow and soul of the adopted boy. As Richard ran so these thoughts shouted at him, nagged at him like a pestering bird and he fled back to the open farmland, scrambling up the scarp to the cornfield and sight of his house in the distance.

On impulse he returned along the quarry's edge, back to the trunk of the leaning elm. He peered into the pit for the second time, and again felt the frost and the raw *anger* that emanated from below. In the tree next to him a bird fluttered, startling him so that he nearly slipped. He straightened up and glanced round, and saw the black, feathered shape on a low branch. But it was no bird.

He grimaced as he noticed the stitched bones, the black rags and feathers weaved between them, and the grim little human skull, its lower jaw missing, that watched from a hood of black cloth. He tried to open his mouth to shout to Michael, but his jaw wouldn't work. Panicking he wrenched his hands at his cheeks, but his mouth wouldn't open.

The empty eyes of the tiny skull watched him, and from the pit below came a distant, gentle laughter. Even the sounds Richard tried to make seemed to throttle somewhere in his lungs.

He grabbed a broken stick and struck the dummy from the tree. It shattered and scattered and his jaw— aching and twisted—opened. He gasped for air, swore softly, then walked stiffly and with growing terror back to the house.

* * *

Carol's distress took an hour to deal with. She was anxious for her brother, whom she believed had locked himself into his imaginary castle and would now need food. She felt she would be letting him down if she didn't take supplies to him.

Richard reassured her as best he could, and at the girl's insistence promised to return to the quarry and lower down a carrier-bag of sandwiches and milk later that evening. The promise was solemnly made, but the eight-year-old watched her father with such a look of suspicion and disbelief that Richard felt like crying.

With the girl tucked up in bed, he returned to the front room and joined Susan, staring out into the dark night. There was a glow over the quarry, but that was just moonlight reflecting on the distant English Channel.

"There's been a change," he said after a while. Susan looked round at him, her face a sad reflection of pain and fatigue.

"What sort of change?"

"I think he's focusing better. He brought a fetish, some sort of bone doll, brought it out of God knows where but actually *sent* it into the woods. It was on a branch, watching me. It locked my jaw and my vocal cords. It was a tease. A violent tease, but Christ, it was effective!"

"A fetish?" Susan's tone told Richard that despair was again creeping into her heart.

"It was almost alive. It had a soul of its own. Something . . . magic. Something powerful in the object itself. It blocked me for a moment. It frightened the life out of me. I thought I was going to choke to death."

Susan was silent for a minute, watching the night. "Why is he so angry *now*? What happened to make him *do* this? Your coming home?"

The thought occurred to them simultaneously. "The gold disc! He must have seen us looking at the disc. He must have thought . . ." Susan covered her mouth for a moment, eyes closed in shock. "Perhaps he thought we were going to use him again."

She remembered Francoise's phone call then. The

woman had rung to ask if Michael had fetched anything recently, and Susan had been cautious in her response. It only occurred to her now that she had asked about stones and wood. In particular, a black stone, shaped at one side.

"Where's the rock that struck me? What did you do with it?"

"It's still in the greenhouse. Why?"

Susan shivered, glanced at the garden again. "Francoise knew. She *knew*. She rang me this morning . . . hours before it happened . . ."

How had she known? Perhaps, with her own talents, she had sensed that Michael was changing the direction of his focus, that he was reaching for different artifacts now, for objects imbued with power of their own.

But how had she known about the stone?

"Fetch it for me. From the greenhouse. Please? I'm going to ring Francoise . . ."

She went to phone and punched in a number. Richard found a torch, then opened the French windows carefully and stepped into the night. Behind him he heard Susan swear, and put the receiver down.

"She's not answering. What's that smell?"

He looked apprehensively down the garden. Sea spray touched his face, a cold caress.

On impulse he called, "Come home, Michael. Come and talk."

Something was moving across the field, coming towards the house, away from the quarry. It was hard to see . . .

He ran to the dark greenhouse, flashing the beam of the torch nervously around. The tomato plant where the gold was hidden was leaning awkwardly. It was clear it had been interfered with, and he felt a nagging regret that he and Susan had touched the hiding place.

The heavy, black rock was under a trellis table. He picked it up and shone the torch across it. Part of the ball had been shaped deliberately to make an angled surface, just right for pounding, or crushing.

Again his mind switched to the pot of gold. Should

he take the disc into the house for safety? Again, his better reason dictated that he should not. But as he stared hungrily at the hidden treasure, he glimpsed movement across the lawn, a fleeting shape seen dimly through the dirty windows and the darkening night.

"Michael?"

He started to run from the greenhouse, but an instinct made him duck, just as glass shattered spectacularly above him. He flung himself down, arms raised protectively as whitewashed shards scattered across the plants and ledges. A heavy object fell with metallic clangor a foot or so away from where he crouched. He flashed the torch across the mass of curved, rusting iron that had descended through the glass, flung from a distance. The compacted metal was wet and stinking with river mud. He leaned closer, then drew back as pain lanced through his arms and chest, a slashing, cutting pain. He gasped for breath, and waved an arm protectively across his body, as if warding off a sword blow. For a second he had felt himself being whipped by an icy wind, then imagined himself drowning in a fast flowing flood. The flash of conscious dream was stunning in its power. His heart rate had leapt with shock, and his whole body had panicked as water seemed to be pouring into his lungs.

Staggering to his feet he looked again at the iron mass, and confirmed what he had already suspected. The iron shapes were swords, bent, broken, fused together by time and corrosion. He had seen such "votive offerings" from river and peat bog sites all over Europe. The Thames at Battersea had given them up, and at Flag Fen, in Cambridgeshire, this sort of broken, ritual offering was commonplace.

Only now, though, did he realize that the swords had been sacrificial weapons.

Their power had been retained. He had glimpsed the pain in the old blades, the remembered agony. Michael was reaching with very different and definite purpose now!

Holding the heavy stone, Richard stepped round the sword-mass. As he fled back across the garden he heard, rather than saw, movement among the trees. Beyond the gate, close to the flattened tumulus, a tall, motionless shape had appeared. It had the night attributes of a scarecrow, but was taller and thinner, although it was swathed in ragged clothes, which were blowing in a breeze that Richard couldn't feel.

Above him there was a wing beat, and at the house the sound of a window banging shut. Susan's voice was a sudden scream, quickly controlled. Then his name was called with increasing urgency. Glass shattered at the front of the house and as Richard started to run again, so he heard doors banging and Carol's frightened voice calling urgently from her room.

The lights in the sitting room went off suddenly. He stopped on the lawn for a moment, shocked, then felt movement beside him that startled him. A second later he was flung to one side by a pulse of air that seemed to make the world go dead. He was deafened, blinded, lungless and powerless, struck hard in the solar plexus, struggling for breath. Then he was conscious again and breathing for his life!

The smell of dust and decay . . .

A small, shrouded figure lay sprawled beside him, arms cracked and twisted, legs drawn up at the knee, like someone sunbathing. The stink that came from the corpse was overpowering. The rags moved and flexed, animated from within. Richard heard the sounds of small creatures, but there was a life in this dead thing that seemed unnatural. He stepped heavily through its rotten chest as he stumbled to the doors, then kicked off the tainted shoe, flinging it out into the garden.

Susan was still calling for him, almost hysterically. He found her in the hallway, huddled and shaken, her face pale, tears streaming.

"What's happening? Oh Christ, Richard . . . what's happening to us?"

"I don't know. What *has* happened?"

"In my studio. In my *studio* . . ."

He looked at her blankly and she screamed angrily, "Don't just stand there! Go and get rid of it!"

He walked quickly through his office and into the

long workroom with its shelves of dolls. Before he
even turned the light on he could see the moon-white
face inside the window.

Approaching slowly through the darkness he met the
dead gaze, chilled and sick to his stomach.

It was a mask, the face the soft, dead features of a
corpse, the mouth gaping, but it was fringed with thin
shards of bone, not human bone, he thought, more like
the slender bones of a large bird. Everything gleamed
white. It was fixed to the window by ice, and even as
he watched, the ice was spreading in a jack-frost pattern, holding the object more firmly to the glass.

The door to the playroom slammed shut! He heard
someone clambering up the metal staircase.

"Carol?" he called, puzzled for a second, then
alarmed. He crossed to the door and opened it—

And recoiled with a gasp at the sickening stench that
flooded from the playroom.

A boy laughed, distantly. Richard dragged the door
closed again, trying not to see the grinning stone statue
that blocked his way, its face dripping with red, its
eyes bulging, ram's horns curling from its temples. It
was a crouched shape, a Lucifer Stone, and it mocked
him as it blocked him.

"Susan!" he screamed. "He's in the house! Get
Carol! He's back in the house!"

The ceiling was pounded as someone ran across the
landing. Richard raced back to the hall to find Susan
leaning against the wall, covering her face, except for
her eyes, which watched him through tears.

"Don't just stand there!" he shouted.

She pointed to the front door.

Through the glass he could see a dark shape, motionless, pressed close and watching. He swore, then
reached for reassurance to Susan's arm. The woman
nearly jumped out of her skin.

"What's happening?" she whispered again, and began to collapse into Richard's arms.

Upstairs, Carol screamed. Somewhere, Michael
laughed, his voice a strangely echoing sound, not really like Michael at all.

"Oh, Christ!"

A window smashed in the sitting room. A bird screeched, and came winging into the hall, beating round Susan's head as she ran, her voice a series of punctuated screams. The bird had a broken wing— *broken when it was fetched*!—and trailed colored ribbons from its neck and legs as if fell heavily to the floor. It was enormous: an eagle, wing-tips white, neck feathers green, its beak a brilliant yellow, now opening and closing as it gasped for life. Its dying eyes blinked and watched Richard as he stood frozen on the stairs.

Susan came back into the hall with a mallet. Sobbing, she smashed the creature's skull before running up the stairs, pushing past Richard to get to her daughter's room.

The girl was in bed, the covers drawn over her head. Hanging against the window was a bird in slow flight, but like the tiny doll in the wood by the quarry, this was no more than stitched-together wings and legs, an obscenity of bleeding, ragged tissues, bones and feathers, the heads of three rooks, beaks torn open wide, slung crudely in the middle of the rotting mass.

It was not flying. It was suspended from the curtain rail by a thin length of gut, swaying like a pendulum at the end of its life.

To Richard it seemed unthreatening, and he opened the window on impulse, tearing the gut rope and depositing the cruel tease on the lawn below.

That is for show. Not power. He doesn't want to attack Carol. Good . . .

Susan sat with the girl, hugging her, fulfilling many needs. Richard went downstairs again and peered more closely through the front door at the monstrous wooden effigy that now stood there.

With the lights off he could define its shape more clearly, a tall, manlike structure, a wooden figure, built from thin branches, its legs wide, its arms stretched horizontal. The tiny head was carved with no features at all, save for the horizontal slash of a mouth. Where its breath would have touched the glass, had it been possessed of such life, ice was forming, spreading rapidly in a pattern of frost that began to obscure vision.

On impulse, Richard tried to open the door, determined to break whatever seal Michael had established. But as his hand reached for the latch his fingers began to freeze, curling painfully into his palms. The eyeless, gaping face seemed to mock him.

Michael's odd laugh sounded from his study. Without hesitation, but terrified, Richard returned to the darkened room. An uncanny and heavy silence greeted him and he turned on the light. The door to Susan's studio was just closing. He ran to the workroom, peered in, aware of frantic movement and the gleam of the white death-mask on the window.

The shelves had been stripped bare. The air was full of dolls, flung and flying as if storm-tossed, as a pale shadow span and screamed in the center of the room, arms outstretched, hair flying.

For a moment Richard saw the vague outline of his son in a swirling tumult of dolls; a second later a deer's head was flung against him, the antlers catching on the frame of the door. A great spray of hot blood caked his face and chest. The creature's face worked, the tongue licking hideously between stretched jaws. It stank of fur, heat and sweat, a heavy animal stench. Its eyes rolled in the sockets, but then the lids closed. Richard cried out in horror, scratching at the stickiness on his face, aware of the bright decoration on the antlers; the ribbons, the leather, the feathers, the painted patterns on the face, around its eyes—and the glittering of glassy stones, strung between the inner tines of each antler.

A present for Daddy ... Pretty ... Pretty ...

He couldn't get past the monstrous sacrifice. He took the head by its horn, dragged it to the hall, but couldn't approach the front door. He pulled it to the entrance to the cellar and flung it down the steps, slamming the door closed.

A trail of fresh blood gleamed on the polished wood of the hallway.

"Susan! He's upstairs again!"

Richard could hear the sudden movement of the boy above him. Carol shouted something, and a door was banged closed. Then laughter. Mocking Boy's laughter.

Is it Michael? It just doesn't sound like him . . .

To Richard's astonishment, the door of his study was flung wide. It stopped his heart for a second, but he launched himself into the room, switching on the light, staring through the swirl of frost-laden mist at the cluttered bookshelves.

Above him came the sound of someone running heavily on the spot, a dance, an exercise . . .

The ceiling seemed to shake, the light fixtures trembling. The temperature dropped further, and the chill began to numb Richard's skin.

The ceiling exploded downwards!

He flung himself away from the huge column of painted wood that crashed through the plaster and paint, descending into the room. It slid down heavily at an angle, crushing his desk chair and denting the floorboards but not breaking them. Dust swirled around the monstrous effigy, and woodsmoke filled the air . . .

And the echo of a cry! Such a strange sensation, that echo! Like voices raised in fear, but only glimpsed, a faint reflection of a moment of horror in another time.

And woodsmoke, sweet and heavy, like cedar!

The totem-tree settled. Its grinning, staring faces, painted in garish reds, greens and blues, seemed to die a little. Richard picked himself up and met the eyes of otters, eagles, owls, deers, wolves and men. The wood was old, scored and cracked, parting along its flaws. The faces were twisted, riddled with the pecking holes of birds and the scouring trails of beetles. Fungal growth filled the crevices.

And yet everything about the monolith was fresh! It was new! It had been recently used.

It sang at him, driving him from the room as it settled to a time when the fires were cold and the dancers were dead, its memories new, but fading with the sounds and scents of the world from which Michael had wrenched its massive bulk.

A face peered in through the study window, a white

face: grinning. It waved a mass of rattling, raggy objects, round-faced, rouged lips, false hair, pressed them
against the window, then fled. Richard was vaguely
aware of the figure shrieking with delight, triumphal,
passing away into the darkness, dragging his haul behind him.

He stepped round the totem and went into Susan's
studio, staring at the empty shelves, the dolls pur-
loined, taken hostage. A few shards of doll-corpse
were scattered here and there, half a head, an arm, a
foot, a tear of cloth. The blood from the severed head
of the stag had spread everywhere. It had spattered the
walls, the work-bench, the pictures, even the window
and the pale mask that watched him from the ice that
still held it to the glass.

He had taken Susan's dolls! But why?

He couldn't leave the house. Each door was denied
him, turning him back either with fear, or cold, or
some intangible barrier that made his legs go weak,
then stop functioning.

But he could look. He could still see out into the
night, although frost and ice were creeping over every
window.

From the sitting room, from the French windows, he
surveyed the night and the garden, with its new crop of
totems, poles and statues of all sizes, some quite vertical, others leaning or collapsed, a forest of animal and
woodland energy, formed like an orchard around the
house, silent, sensuous, sinister guardians.

The last thing he saw, before ice covered the glass
completely, was the white shape of a naked boy, moving quickly through the night, down towards the gate
and the cornfield. The pale figure merged with the
hedges, then reappeared. After a moment there was a
dull pulse of air, an implosion, and an immense tree
appeared, standing by the gate, beginning to lean, its
lower branches lopped away, the upper limbs bare of
leaves and shaped into the profiles of wolves and
birds. Fire licked up the dark trunk, bringing momentary sight of faces and bodies cut into the bark. The

white shadow of the boy ran round the burning totem, illuminated eerily for a second or two, yellow fire on white skin. Then the flames died and the shadowy movement passed away, back across the field, back to the chalk pit and the strange summer night.

They were trapped in the house. They froze if they tried to open the door at the front. At the back, nausea overwhelmed them, emanating from the squatting idol that grinned from grass. Behind it, a massive totem tree cast a faint moon-shadow across the kitchen floor. It was old, this tree, blackened and cracked, carved with crude eyes and sinuous, snake-like shapes. It had been burned in antiquity, but someone had daubed ochres on to the charred features, giving sinister life to the black guardian.

In the cellar, two wicker shapes guarded the exit to the garden. They were stitched and rough, slumping scarecrows, the hair made spiky, the faces white, the bodies stuffed with some black material. They screamed at Richard when he tried to enter the cellar, driving him back in pain. Susan, at the top of the stairs, heard nothing, but when she also tried to enter the cramped space, the eerie shrieks terrified her too.

In Susan's studio, the goose-bone mask stared blindly from the window. To approach it, now, was to feel a constriction in the throat, a terrible strangulation that stifled breath and movement. Beyond, in the playroom, a ragged dress made of skin had been crudely nailed to the outer door. This was decorated with stick figures and half-skulls dripping with dull beads, slashed by knives, ragged and torn at its hem, and Richard recognized something similar to a ghost-dance cloak. To approach it was to feel drowned in cold, muddy water, head pressed by hands, lungs filling . . .

It was the worst defense. It was the most powerful.

Upstairs, the windows grinned with dolls. There was no way out of them. Richard had a fear of falling from heights, and the sensation of plummeting when he reached for the window handles was sickening. Susan was less vertiginous, but even so she couldn't open the panes. Her body went weak with the sense of falling miles down a vertical cliff.

Michael had imprisoned them as effectively as if he had closed and locked the bars of a cage.

At two in the morning the house began to freeze. The family dressed in overcoats and scarves as the temperature dropped rapidly. The central heating pumped hard but the flames in the boiler didn't seem to heat the water in the radiators. Nor did the oven work. They found two electric fan heaters but the air that was emitted was icy, even when set for high temperature.

Quickly, Richard laid a fire, but this too was frustrated: As he struck the paper alight a stinking breeze blew down the chimney and extinguished the flames. The smell was sulphurous and acrid. When he shone a torch up the chimney shaft he could see a bulging, ebony face and dangling ribbons, something wedged across the airway, staring downwards.

Carol was awake again now, and warmly wrapped. She was very quiet as she sat, huddled in blankets, on the sofa. Breath frosting she sang a song to herself, staring all the time through the French windows to where the outline of the totem could just be seen.

Susan tried phoning Francoise again, but there was no reply. She called Jenny but the number was permanently engaged, the phone off the hook perhaps, or Michael interfering with the line. When she tried a neighbor she found the same problem. She dialed numbers at random, working through her address book.

Only the number for Francoise Jeury's home worked.

"He's cut us off. Except for Francoise. He's freezing us out. Except for his friend. But she's not there . . ."

Carol sang her song, a simple nursery rhyme tune. After a while Susan listened a little more attentively to the barely audible words that emerged from the huddled, frozen child.

"Watching-man comes out of the ground, watching-man comes out of the wood, watching-man can see me here, but can't harm me if I watch him good . . ."

"Are you making that up?" Susan asked as she cuddled closer to her daughter.

"It's Michael's song," Carol whispered. "He said he wouldn't hurt me and he wouldn't let Chalk Boy hurt me. He taught me the song in case Chalk Boy tried to trap me."

Richard was by the window, staring through the frost into the winter's night. He smiled as he listened to Carol talk, then said, "I think we'd all better learn to sing the song of the watching-man . . ."

At dawn the ice began to melt and the house warmed up. As the frost faded from the glass, the pale sun cast the long shadows of totems across the sitting-room floor. The kitchen was similarly darkened by shadow, and the family moved tentatively upstairs to Carol's room, the only space where they felt unwatched and unthreatened.

Thirty-three

Michael was in the room again. Carol sat up slowly, drawing the blankets round her shoulders. A gray dawn light made the room look cold. Over by the wardrobe was an area of darkness, and Michael was lurking there.

The room was warm. It also smelled sweetly of summer flowers. Carol watched the patch of darkness, aware that the whole house was murmuring around her.

"Michael?"

The darkness shifted.

Something scurried across the floor, too fast for her to see it, and the curtains closed over the window, blocking out the encroaching day. In total darkness, she felt the small, bony hand on her shoulder. The bed shifted as a weight moved on to the mattress. Her hair was ruffled, the lobe of her ear tweaked.

"Michael . . . don't tease . . ."

"Not Michael."

The voice was the winter voice. It was cold air on her ears, and frost to her nose. The words were rasped from the invisible thing, and again the lobe of her ear was tugged between tiny, bony fingers.

"I know who you are. You're pretending to be Chalk Boy. But you're Michael."

"Not Michael!"

Her ear was pinched, and she stifled the yell, but slapped at the tiny tormentor. "Watcher-man, off you go, or out of the window your wood I'll throw!"

Laughter from the fetch. It dropped off the bed and

lurked again in darkness. She could hear its movement, sense its single, open eye (the other was quite blind. She had established that the night before by shining a torch at it.)

Hissing: "Not the watching-man. Can't frighten me."

"You can't frighten me either. You're Michael. You want food. I'll bring it when I can . . ."

"Food now. Food now."

"When I can. Now go away."

"NOW!" breathed the fetch.

Carol picked up a book from her bedside table and threw it at the elemental.

"When are you going to let Mummy and Daddy out of the house? It's time you stopped being angry."

"Food!" said the wooden thing.

"I'll bring it when I can. How do I get out of the house? You've blocked us in. And there isn't much food anyway. We're eating it all. There's not much for you. *Or* Chalk Boy. Why don't you eat chalk?"

She giggled. "You could have urchin stew. Sea urchin stew."

The fetch scurried around for a moment, and Carol savored the mixed smells of winter and summer as cold air and the scent of rose-hip drifted through her room. Then she heard the voice start to sing in its tiny, reedy voice, "Watching-man, watching-man, sing to him and run if you can . . ."

"I'll try," Carol said. "But if you make me frightened I won't come to the quarry. Now go away. I've got to get dressed."

The entity returned to darkness. Carol got out of bed and opened the door to the landing, feeling the fetch's icy breath on her legs as it scurried into the house. With the door closed she opened the curtains again, then dressed in jeans and a jumper. She made her bed, carried her hot-water bottle to the bathroom, and emptied it into the basin. Her bladder was full, and she eyed the closed toilet with some apprehension, but then lifted the lid and poured in some Ajax liquid. Staring into the toilet she satisfied herself that there were no *things* down there (yesterday's encounter had been terrifying!) then sat down for a minute or so, although all the time she was relieving herself she peered between her legs into the dully reflecting liquid below.

Flushing the toilet she thumbed her nose at the swirling waters ("Drown, drown, all spooks down!"), then closed the lid.

Her parents were sleeping in the sitting room, huddled together in blankets on the sofa. Carol thought that the sound of the toilet flushing would wake them, but they remained in pale, agitated slumber in the cold room.

After peering in at the body masses of her parents, Carol went into the kitchen, aware of the shadow of the totem outside the back door now being cast across the floor by the first stray light of dawn. She raided the fridge for cheese and ham, then cut several slices of bread from a farmhouse cob. Michael liked sweetcorn pickle, so she packed a jar of the relish into the same carrier bag that she now filled with these simple supplies. What would he want to drink? There was no milk. She found a can of Coca-Cola and a half-finished bottle of ginger beer.

She tied the top of the bag, then unlocked the back door—

"What are you *doing*? Come back. Come back at once!"

Her mother was in the doorway. Sleepy, disheveled, holding her housecoat closed around her body.

"Come *back*. Do you hear me?"

Behind Carol, the totem vibrated, and its cold power reached into the kitchen. For a moment Susan's eyes widened and her resolve lessened. She was distracted by the power of the barrier, the totem or fetch that guarded the back entrance. But then, like the mother she was, her fears for her daughter overwhelmed the fear of the outside force.

Her voice angry, her focus sharp, she came running for Carol. "Get back here! Don't go out. Don't go!"

Carol ran from the house. The totem swathed her in its fear. She struggled against the cold, against the feeling of being throttled, then called, "Watching-man, let me go . . ."

The force faded. She heard laughter from across the field, from away in the distance. Looking up at the totem she kicked it. The wood shuddered, leaned a little more towards the house.

Her mother was screaming. Carol ran.

A chalk shape now guarded the entrance to the quarry. It was as high as a tree, a stooped figure, arms tucked into its sides, hair, chipped and scoured from the chalk, depicted as hanging lank. The face was hidden. The creature seemed to be asleep on its legs, but there was something in the coarse, rain-roughened effigy that suggested it was ready to stand erect and pursue.

Carol stood before this monstrous statue, clutching the plastic bag of food and calling for Michael. She heard his laughter distantly, but was still too frightened to move.

"Don't let it hurt me!" she cried defiantly, then again remembered the fetch/Michael's instructions for safety.

"Watching-man, go away. Chalk Man stay."

Had the statue shifted?

Her hair pricked and her heart raced, but it was just cloud shadow across the gleaming chalk. The effigy was quite still. Quite dead.

"I'm going past," she shouted at it. "I'm bringing him food. So stay asleep!"

She stalked down the right-hand path, but as she passed the chalk giant she broke into a run, not looking back as she fled through the bushes, tripping and skidding on the scatter of perfect fossilized heart-urchins and iron marcasite balls that made this castle approach so hazardous.

Suddenly confused, she stopped, clutching at the bag nervously. She had been walking toward the far wall, where she could see the remains of the rope ladder dangling from the leaning elm, but now found herself facing back the way she had come. There was that continual and unwelcome smell of sea and rotting weed, but the quarry had become breezy now, a chill wind that stirred the gorse and bushes.

"Michael?"

She turned again and started to walk deeper into the pit. The chill seeped quickly into her bones and she started to tremble, shaking quite violently. She stepped back a few paces and the tension in her body faded.

Skirting this odd place, she became entangled in bushes, protecting her face with her arm as she edged cautiously deeper.

Something crunched beneath her foot. Looking down she gasped as she saw the china face of one of her mother's dolls, now cracked into little bits.

"Michael ..." she whispered; shocked. The doll's arms were further up the track. She found the plastic body of another, stripped of its clothes, discarded, then the luxurious red hair of the Victorian doll that Susan had found in London, years ago, and which had perhaps belonged to a Royal princess.

So intent was she on searching for the scattered remnants of these toys, that she came into the graveyard clearing without realizing it. When she looked up she gasped with horror.

A single thorn tree grew there, thick-trunked, twisted, its branches reaching across the space. From its branches dangled the corpses of dolls; dark, shrouded effigies, hung by necks and arms, some with grinning faces, others with small, peering eyes, some colorful in Red Indian dress, others in furs and moccasins, but mostly swathed in torn, spectral rags. They dangled there like the shriveled corpses of squirrels which could sometimes be found in Hawkinge Wood after the squirrel man had completed his autumn murder.

Around the tree were the discarded bodies of her mother's precious collection. They had all been stripped. The clothes had been tied into a single, long braid, which dangled from the highest branch of the thorn, moving in the breeze.

Carol felt sick. The dead dolls on the branch seemed to watch her as they fluttered and swung. Old sounds from old years ebbed and flowed through her mind. Old winds, old fires, ancient songs, the last spirits of the spirit dolls. She turned to leave this mortuary place.

He was in front of her before she was aware of his approach. One moment she had been edging through the underbrush, back to the chalk effigy, the next he was there, white-painted and naked, grinning at her. His ginger hair was spiky. He had rubbed chalk into it and made it stiff.

"You look funny," she said to him.

"So do you," he retorted sharply, then reached for the carrier bag. "I'm starving."

"It's all I could find. There isn't much food left. Why did you kill Mummy's dolls?"

He ignored her question, peering at the contents of the bag and looking angry. "Bread and cheese. And ginger beer. Ah. Pickle!"

He led her out of the tangled wood, then opened the jar of sweetcorn pickle and scooped the contents out with his fingers, licking his whitened lips as the sweet sludge was swallowed. "Love chutney."

"I'll try and find some more. Why do you cover yourself with chalk?"

"Secret."

"Aren't you cold?"

"Michael's cold. Not me. I'm Chalk Boy." He laughed and threw the empty pickle jar into the bushes, then licked his fingers again. "You thought I was Michael, didn't you! Didn't you!"

"You *are* Michael."

He tapped a finger to her nose. His breath smelled of relish, but was also unpleasant. "Wrong. Michael's hiding. I've banished him."

"To the wooden doll?"

For a moment Michael looked puzzled, then he understood his sister's meaning. "Clever, eh? It's a living doll, a little wooden puppet that runs on fragments of people's soul. I just hitch-hiked a ride on it, into the house. It was funny watching Mummy and Daddy from the shelf as they looked for me."

Michael emptied the rest of the bag's contents on to

the ground and picked up the bread, tearing it into chunks and swallowing the morsels whole.

"You're just showing off." Carol said irritably. "You want to pretend you're wild. But you're just my brother."

"Michael's your brother. But not *really*," he emphasized.

"I'm going home now. I'll try and find some more pickle."

She turned and started to run, but a body slammed into her from behind, knocking her down. She struggled and screamed, but the hands on her arms were too strong. Distantly, from a million miles away it seemed, she could hear her father's voice, raised in alarm, screaming her name.

She twisted on the ground and fought at Chalk Boy, raking her nails through the white on his face and grazing his skin beneath. Angrily, roaring with a childish fury, he jumped up, then hauled his sister to her feet.

"I'm not finished with you! I don't want you to go yet."

"I'm *frightened*," she howled, and let the tears come. Again she turned, but took only a step or two away from the quarry before she saw the arched, sinister back of the chalk giant.

Her father's voice was a distressed cry, again from a long way off.

The hand that touched her shoulder was more gentle, now, and she turned to look at her brother, seeing tears in the bloodshot eyes that stared from the flaking, scratched mask of white.

"Got something for you," he whispered. "Want you to bring it out of Limbo."

"What? What is it?"

"Got to come and see. Got to follow me. Won't frighten you again."

"Why are you talking like that?"

"Carol . . . please come with me. I want you to fetch home the Grail. I've found the Grail. Please come with me. Fetch it home . . ."

She hesitated for just a moment, conscious of the

closer sound of her father, of his distress as he approached the pit, but aware too of a strange, almost radiant power coming from Michael. He seemed serene, all of a sudden, and his smile was genuine. His eyes sparkled. He had reached a hand towards her and she took it, now, and squeezed his fingers.

"You've really found the Grail?"

"I really have. And now everything will be all right. But I need you to carry it home. Are you coming?"

"Don't hurt them anymore. Please? Mikey?"

A shadow passed over the face of the chalked boy, but then he smiled again. "I'll see what Michael has to say. But I won't hurt *you*. I promise. Come on." He tugged at the girl, and Carol, after a moment's resistance, let herself be led by the hand, along the winding path, deeper into the quarry.

A moment later, a great and terrifying sea was breaking on to the shore before her, and the spray from the giant waves had drenched her as she stood and stared in shock! Something raised a vast head across the ocean and bellowed, sending creatures scurrying up among the caves. Purple light flickered and flared and a dull roll of thunder made the ground shake—

Carol saw little of this. She had screamed, turned and run, Michael chasing close behind, angrily calling to her.

He caught her when she was weaving hysterically between the inner bushes of the quarry. She was unaware of the transition from beach to pit. There had been no disorientation at all.

"Come back!" Michael growled, and tugged at her long hair, jerking her head. The sudden pain made her furious and she turned and kicked her brother's naked shin. He hopped back, holding his leg, then shouted, "Please! Just come to the shrine and take the Grail for me. I *need* you to. The beach is just where Chalk Boy lives. It's his dream. Nothing can hurt *you*. It isn't really there. It's Limbo . . ."

"That's why I'm *wet*. And it *smells*." Water still dripped from her hair and clothes, rank smelling and sharply tangy.

"You've *got* to help me—" Michael growled, and he was suddenly menacing. Carol was about to run again, when a voice called down into the quarry.

At once Michael was alarmed. He stepped closer to his sister and tugged her down, looking hard at the top of the chalk cliff. After a moment the man in the brown leather jacket appeared, leaning on the elm, peering down.

"Michael? Michael? Where are you, Michael? Daddy wants to talk to you."

There was laughter. A second man stepped to the edge. He wore a long, black coat and dark glasses and was smoking. At the entrance to the quarry Michael heard movement. A third man was approaching, striking at the undergrowth with a stick.

On the cliff, Brown Leather Jacket taunted him. "Come out and play, Mikey. Come and play with Daddy's friends."

The silent smoker flicked the butt of his cigarette into the quarry and walked past the elm, leading the way round to the gate.

"Go!" Michael whispered with urgency. "Go home. Quickly."

"You come too."

"Uh-uh. It's me they want. And I can hide!"

His name was called again, a long, drawn-out cry, mocking and menacing.

"Go *on*. Go round that way, it's bushier."

Carol crept off, her head low. When she looked back a second later, there was no sign of Michael, nor could she hear him.

He had vanished into the chalk.

Thirty-four

As he saw Carol running back across the field, Richard tried to break out through the totem ring, but was driven back by the power in the wood. He clutched his stomach, breathless, nauseous, but yelled for Susan, then pressed himself against the window, watching his daughter, watching her run . . .

"She's safe. Thank God! Carol! Run, love . . ."

The girl stopped at the gate and kicked viciously at the wooden effigy that leaned there. She was furious, he realized, her face red. She was drenched, her hair hanging limp. Again she kicked the effigy, and the house shook slightly, or perhaps that was imagination.

Susan had come into the room, and now she too stood against the cold glass, calling for Carol. The tall image-trees stared at them, and it was impossible to avoid their mocking, sneering gazes. And yet: they were only carvings. How could wood have power? How could a tribal totem carry energy and influence, so much energy, so powerful an influence that it could affect the awareness of modern human beings?

It was impossible. Richard stepped boldly through the French windows.

A hand twisted inside him, drawing him empty, clutching at his heart and squeezing so that he shrieked with pain . . . The face of a wolf lapped at his lips, bringing up his gorge, sucking at the food in his stomach . . .

He staggered back, weak and sweating, clutching at his chest.

"Don't keep trying," Susan said, holding him. "Don't keep trying. You'll kill yourself."

"There *has* to be a way through . . ."

Carol walked cautiously through the totem field, then arrived suddenly and breathlessly in the sitting room. She stank of the sea.

"Men are getting Michael," she gasped. "Three men. I think they're going to—*abduct* him." She pronounced the word carefully, unfamiliar with it, conscious that she had heard it used in reference to her brother. "But he's all right. He's managed to hide from them."

Richard hugged the girl, crying with relief. Susan stroked her saturated hair.

"Don't do that again, darling. Do you promise me? Don't leave the house again. You nearly killed us with worry."

"I have to take Michael food," the girl said grimly, obstinately. She stared at her mother, a defiant challenge. "He needs food. He trusts me." Then she lowered her voice, looked away. "He says he's found the Grail. He wants me to fetch it back for him . . ."

"You'll do no such thing. Do you hear? You're to stay with us until we can get you to safety. It's not safe in the pit. We have to get Michael back too. Those men are not nice men."

"He knows that. But he's hiding from them. He's hiding in the chalk."

Susan took the girl by the hand and led her up to the bathroom. "How did you get so wet?"

"He lives by a beach. It frightened me, so I came home. But I think I have to go back. He really needs me . . ."

Richard listened to the girl's voice as she ascended to the washing-place. Susan said, "But we need you too, love. And it's dangerous in the pit. Something very evil is happening to us, all around us. It's going to take a long time to understand it, but we're trapped here . . ."

"The watching-men don't want me," the girl said. "Only you."

"Yes. They don't seem to affect you. Aren't you frightened, Carol?"

"A little. But they're only Michael's dreams. When Mikey dreams he can make things seem real. You don't have to be scared."

"Oh, but we are. And we're scared for you. That's why we don't want you to leave the house again. You mustn't go back to the quarry."

"But the grail's there. Michael can't touch it. He needs me to bring it home for him. That's what he said. I can't let him down, and he's hungry. Can we let him have some of our food?"

"We'll have to think about how to feed Michael. But of course we can. Perhaps we can throw some jars of pickle into the garden and he can come and fetch them. It's too risky to let you go across the field again." And after a pause, "What beach? Where did you see a beach?"

Carol said, "When you step into the chalk it's right there. But it's only a dream. The Fish Lizard was really scary, though. But Michael said it wouldn't hurt me. It's only a dream. It's where Chalk Boy lives."

"This water is no dream. Nor the odor."

"It's a very smelly sea," Carol agreed. "I don't want to swim in it."

As Carol bathed, Susan stood behind her husband, arms around him, sharing his desperate search of the distant quarry.

"He'll hide. He'll be all right. The bushes are very deep, they won't find him. Dear God, I had enough trouble spotting him yesterday, and I'm used to him being covered in chalk. *And* he was bleeding from the thorns, and I still couldn't see him."

Richard's hands touched hers, holding them into him. Susan realized that the man was crying. With his face pressed against the glass, the tears ran down the panes. She lay her face against his broad back, fighting down the waves of pain she felt herself, partly generated from within, perhaps partly the effect of the looming, leering rows of totems.

"He'll understand in time," she whispered.

"He's got to. I want him back. I want him back, Sue. I need him."

"Good. That's a fine start." She couldn't help laughing. "Do you realize that a middle-class couple, one archaeologist, one dolls' expert, can't move from their house because ancient spirits are blocking them in? It's a reasonable sort of day's experience, isn't it?"

He turned and shook his head, unable to summon a smile, the tears glistening on his cheeks. "I don't feel odd about it. You're right. It's strange. I just accept it. Next door they're watching Oprah Winfrey. Or maybe listening to Derek Jameson. They do that, you know. They play him at top volume."

"Tell me about it . . ." she muttered darkly.

Hugging closely, they grew more secure.

"Michael will be fine. Other children must have this talent. It can't be a one-off thing. Can it?"

"Francoise didn't know of any others."

Richard's body stiffened with anger. "But I don't believe her. She works for an Institute that in one room is trying to get a kid to move a spot of electricity a centimeter across a screen; in another they're reading minds left, right and center. There's a lot of deceit, a deal of covering-up going on in London. They know more than they're telling us . . ."

"Paranoia strikes . . ."

"It's not paranoia. They don't dare share what they know. Anyway, these talents die."

"And get reborn."

"But die again. Michael's gift won't last beyond adolescence."

"Nothing would make me happier."

"Me neither. I love him, Sue."

"Good."

"And I love you."

"I never doubted it. You just stopped knowing who you were. I didn't know how to handle that. I hated you, the false-you, the shadow you. But I never stopped loving Richard Whitlock."

"Does that mean you still love me? Now?"

"Of course. I'll always love you. Why do you ever doubt it? But right now our son is out there, hiding, perhaps frightened, and we're . . . we're in some sort of limbo state. Look around you, Rick. Just think what's happening to us. It's a fantasy. But it's real. It's crazy. But it's happening. Someone did something to Michael, years ago, and we're living in ghost land. Look at it!"

"I've accepted it . . ."

"Yes. Yes, I can see you have. And it's odd . . . it's odd, but I have faith in Michael. He's strong. I feel it. Is it possible for me to have a mother's intuition? He never grew inside me. He and I never grew together. He never took food from me. He isn't my child. But I have the strangest feeling . . ."

She pulled away, suddenly frightened again. Her body went chill. The field, the woods, the quarry, all seemed so quiet. Yet Michael was there, being approached by men who had sinister intentions.

And yet . . .

She felt calm. She felt at peace.

She turned to Richard and couldn't help laughing. "I don't know why . . . I don't know why I think this . . . but . . ."

"But what?"

She shook her head, looked back at the quarry.

"I think Michael's sent them away . . . and I don't mean with a flea in their ear . . . I think he's sent them away permanently. I think he's safe."

In the late afternoon Richard saw his son at the edge of the woods. The boy glistened white, though his face was a black mask, now. He was holding a tall pole, and ribbons fluttered from its length. Through binoculars Richard thought the ribbons were bits of tiny clothing. Michael moved restlessly along the edge of the copse, then held the pole above his head, as if signaling. Pressed against the upstairs window, fighting the vertigo, Richard beckoned to the boy, but Michael ignored him. And yet the lad wanted something, that much was clear.

And Richard knew it was Carol.

The girl sat on her bed, her face set, her body a testimony to the betrayal she was feeling. She kept whispering, "I must go. He needs me . . . I must go . . ."

Richard was quite determined that she wouldn't. He made a large parcel of food and dropped it from the window. He talked to his daughter, hugged her: "It's too dangerous . . ."

"He needs me."

"If he needs you that much he'll come to the house."

"You don't understand. He's got the Grail. He wants to give it to you. It's a gift. He wants me to fetch it home for him . . ."

"He can bring it himself. When he comes to the house, all this evil will vanish. These totems will just be wood and masks and bits of stone."

Carol shivered, and Richard felt the prickle of power, the watching, listening, breathing essences of the past that crowded in upon Eastwell House.

Then downstairs the phone began to ring.

"Stay here!"

He was in the sitting room in moments, but Susan had already reached the phone and was listening to the sounds that issued from the earpiece.

"Who is this? Who is this please?"

She suddenly slammed the receiver down. The line had gone dead, but her face was a furious red, and her eyes blazed.

"Who was it?"

"Michael's mother. I'm sure of it . . ."

It had been her! She had finally called. The voice was so soft. It was so sad, and yet so angry.

"Why did you interfere? Tell him to go away. Tell him to leave me alone . . . I don't want him here. You shouldn't have done that to the doctor. You shouldn't have found out. Tell him to leave me alone!"

That was all she had said. But the voice . . . it was the birth-mother. Susan knew it. She knew it in her heart. She had finally called.

"Tell him to leave me alone. Tell him to go away."
What was happening?

* * *

On impulse Susan rang Francoise Jeury's number. She didn't know why. She just felt a need for the woman at this moment. All hostilities were ended in her mind. She needed Francoise.

The phone was answered and a tired, American voice muttered, "Lee Kline speaking. How can I help you?"

"Could I speak to Francoise, please?"

"Francoise? She's in Kent, visiting a client. Is it important?"

"Very."

"Then I'll give you the number. I guess it'll be OK."

"Please. I'd appreciate it."

There was a moment's pause, the rustle of paper, then the man read out the Whitlocks' own telephone number.

"But she *isn't* here!"

"You're the Whitlocks? Michael's parents. She's supposed to be there. Been calling you on and off for a day now. All she was getting were gremlins on the line. She's taken a chance on your hospitality. Look around outside. Maybe she's lost. She went down this morning. I thought she'd be with you long since—"

Susan slammed the phone down and went up to the landing, then into her own bedroom, skirting round the top of the tree that still rose above the hole in the floor. There was energy here, but no evil, not until the window, where a rag fetish dangled disgustingly, blocking access to the world outside. From here, though, she could see across the drive, on to the road outside.

There was no sign of the Frenchwoman. No sign of anyone. She noticed that the gates were closed, something that Michael had done.

It was Carol who found their visitor. Francoise had climbed over the gate earlier that morning, unable to raise the family on their phone, and had at once been drawn into the pattern of anger and violence emanating from the totem field and the scattered fetishes that had resulted from Michael's rage the day before. She had

started to run, trying to escape the influence and the
screams that began to fill her head. Sickened, exhausted in seconds, she had been unable to escape the
field, and had finally staggered into the greenhouse
and collapsed.

When she had regained consciousness she had
crawled under one of the trellised potting ledges,
pressing into the corner among the cobwebs and curling up into a ball. She had tried to scream, but couldn't
utter a sound. Later, when she had cried in pain and
fear, Carol had heard the distant sounds of her distress.

The girl came into the greenhouse and took
Francoise by the hand. "Come on. Come home with
me. You'll be all right. Come with me to the house."

Through her tears the woman had smiled, then
hugged the girl. "Did Michael do this?"

"He was very angry," Carol said, tugging at the
woman to help her up. Francoise eased herself upright,
shaking. The presence of the girl had had a remarkable
effect on the ghostly field around her. Carol was like a
path through the fire. An astonishing radiance of calm
and peace flowed around the child, driving back the
darkness. They walked hand in hand through the totem
field and into Eastwell House, where the shattered,
ravaged faces of the Whitlocks stretched like skulls
into welcoming, fear-stained smiles.

When she had recovered, when she had finished a pot
of black coffee, Francoise listened to what had happened to the Whitlocks. Carol stayed close to her. If
the girl moved away, the power in the house was intol-
erable to the psychic. Carol was her shield. All three
adults clustered around the girl, in fact, drawing their
peace from the slender, bespectacled child. For the moment, Carol's anxiety about her brother had been replaced by concern for the visitor.

"The reason I rang you the other day was because
Michael came to visit me in London."

The Whitlocks were astonished. "That's not possible.
He hasn't been to London for months, now."

"He came into my office two days ago. He stole

something from one of my shelves. That's why I called you. He fetched something from my office—"

"The stone! Of course!" Susan walked quickly across the room and picked up the black stone from the corner. Francoise smiled, accepted the object and turned it in her fingers.

"It belongs to me. It's from Mexico, a magic stone. Is this what caused the damage?" She looked meaningfully at Susan's face.

"Yes."

"It was a strange sensation when your son came to me. He looked something like Michael, and something ... odd ... like a fish. It was a huge apparition, taller than the room, though I noticed he bent to see. I don't understand that part of it. When he reached for the stone his fingers were unreal. But he touched and grabbed the object before everything exploded. So I have seen the fetching technique of your son, in his guise as Fisher King."

Richard added, "And now he's found the Grail. He has it in his castle."

"The Holy Grail? He's found it finally?"

"He says he has."

Carol shifted uncomfortably. "But he can't bring it out himself," she said sharply. "He needs me to do it. But Mummy won't let me go ..."

Her feet kicked irritably against the chair. Susan watched her daughter squarely, the plaster over her left eye reddening slightly as blood seeped from the raw wound below.

"Anyway ..." the girl went on. "It's too frightening where he lives, so I suppose I won't have to go anyway. I don't like the beach."

Francoise queried this with a raised eyebrow. Susan said, "It's a part of Michael's Limbo. There's a beach and caves, and monsters. We think he has access to a past time, and goes there to hide. I don't understand it, how it works, but if he's reaching for objects, maybe he can hide in the past too."

"I know about the beach," Francoise said thoughtfully. "I was just surprised that Carol had been there. What did it feel like, Carol? Can you tell me?"

"The Fish Lizards are dangerous," Carol said, and at once Francoise was excited, leaning forward, remembering.

"The Fish Lizards? Did you *see* the Fish Lizards?"

"That's what Mikey said it was . . . It was huge, but it didn't attack me."

"What about the Sea Dragons? Did you see those too?"

Carol frowned. "He didn't mention the Sea Dragons. And I wasn't looking. I was running."

"What about the forests of the Wealden?"

"Didn't say anything about the forests."

Now Richard too was intrigued. He stared into the dead fire, struggling to recollect something that Michael had read to him. "Those words: they're familiar. Did Michael use them?"

"Yes," Francoise said. "To begin any fetching he has to cross the beach. When I asked him about the beach . . . well, hear for yourself. I taped our little conversation. Do you remember? That time you brought Michael to London?"

She placed the small recorder on the coffee table and switched it on. They listened to Francoise and Michael singing, then Michael's voice, a dreamy, sleepy voice, almost a whisper:

". . . the Fish Lizards hide in the waves and strike suddenly on to the shore. Their jaws have a formidable array of fang-like teeth. The Sea Dragons are as long as their contemporaries . . . Very quietly and gradually the forest and plains, the tall trees and hideous reptiles of the Wealden passed away—"

Richard remembered suddenly. "The book! Grandad's old book about dinosaurs . . . of course!" He went up to Michael's room, hating the cold feel, the sense of endless space that inhabited the room, as if this was a passage to infinity, without soul or presence. But he found the book, the old leather-bound volume called *The World in the Past*. It had been published by Frederick Warne & Co. in 1926, and time and reading

had reduced it to a tattered collection of sheets and illustrations, still loosely held inside the red cover with
its faded golden image of a Stegosaurus. He knew
nothing of the author, B. Webster Smith, but remembered being entranced by the language and the enthusiasm of the writing, the sense of pure wonder that the
descriptions of coral, and urchins, and ancient seas,
and ancient geology had evoked in him as a child.

And there they were, the words that Michael had
spoken, descriptions of Icthyosaurs (the Fish Lizards)
and Plesiosaurs (the Sea Dragons), accounts of the
Wealden forest, the chalk downs, the sandstone cliffs.
All of it was here. Francoise read the passages with delight. The volume sat between them, opened, like a
gate into another world: Chalk Boy's world. Richard
understood at once.

"Then his beach is a construct. Images from this
book, shaped into the hinterland, the perilous place to
be crossed before the Grail is reached."

"We call it Received Image Reconstruction."

"Do you remember those drawings he used to make,
Sue? The monstrous mouths? The cliffs? He must
have first seen and read this book when he was a toddler. I wondered how it had come to be on his
shelves."

"So that's where he hides," Susan whispered, her
face pale as she looked at the bleak photograph of a
red sandstone cliff in Utah.

"It's very wet and stinky," Carol added.

"It's a real place," murmured Francoise. "I've met
this talent before. The beach *exists*. Like the walls in
the castle, like the sounds of anger from these wooden
idols in your garden, it's a real place. And like you, I
believe it is remote from us in time. We must be very
careful."

Thirty-five

Francoise woke suddenly, her body racking with pain. She reached for Carol but her hand closed on empty air, and she twisted from the sofa, gagging and struggling for breath. She managed to articulate the beginning of the girl's name, but that was all. She was vaguely aware that a stark light was beginning to brighten the room. It was dawn. She had slept for hours.

"Carol!" she managed again, but then the pressure of winds and screams and pain and chanting and mocking laughter drove her back into a curled ball, her legs working like an hysterical child's, her hands over her ears.

Suddenly she was calm.

"Wake up! Wake up!"

The girl was with her, a small, cold hand on her face, eyes wide and anxious behind the gleaming lenses. The glasses were askew, one frame higher than the other and Carol fiddled with them for a moment.

"I've got food for Michael. He needs me—"

"Don't leave me. Please. Don't leave me!"

Francoise was suddenly aware of desperation. She swallowed hard, sat up and ran hands through disheveled hair. Her mouth tasted foul and she licked self-consciously over her teeth. The girl was watching her in a fever of indecision and concern.

"I'll be all right," Francoise said. "You're my shield. I didn't mean to sound angry."

Carol leaned forward and whispered something.

Francoise, not ready for the instruction, made her start again, listening more carefully. The girl sang: "Watching-man comes out of the ground, watching-man comes out of the wood, watching-man can see me here, but can't harm me if I watch him good . . ."

"That's a funny song. Is it a charm?"

"Sing it. It'll keep you safe. Probably," she added, with a nervous glance.

"Thank you."

"I have to go."

Francoise tugged at her. "You mustn't. Michael will be fine. We have to break the totem field first. Michael will be fine. Please don't go!"

Carol looked desperate. The shadow of a totem was across her pale face. She struggled physically and in her mind, clearly torn. "Men are hunting him. I *have* to go. The Grail is there and I have to fetch it back for him. He's asked me to. I *must* go."

Astonished, Francoise fought for clarity of thinking. "Have you seen the Grail? Have you really seen it?"

"Only Mikey's drawings. But he's found it now. He says it's beautiful. It will make everything right again if I can bring it back. Everything will be lovely. The anger will go away, all the anger. Everyone will be free at last. I have to help him. He's my big brother." The girl became even more conspiratorial. "He frightens me and hurts me, but I think that's the other side of him. It's not Michael at all. It's Chalk Boy. Chalk Boy lives in a cave near the beach and if I can get the Grail for Mikey, Chalk Boy will never get off the beach again. He'll be stuck there. That's what I think anyway. Chalk Boy was killed in a shrine. Thousands of years ago. Men chased him and killed him, his dog too. Then they hid the Grail in the shrine. I had a dream about it in the pit. Michael has found the Grail in the shrine, and I have to get it. He can't touch it because Chalk Boy is hanging on to him, strangling him, making him unhappy. Chalk Boy is very bad. *Very* bad. Michael isn't really as angry as he seems . . ."

"Too much," Francoise said, dizzy with the breathless flow of the girl's words. "Too much to take in.

Too early. I need you to say all this to me again. But I need coffee. Is there coffee?"

"I have to go."

"No!"

"I *have* to. Sing the song and the watching-man won't hurt you."

"Please don't leave me. It hurts, Carol—"

But the girl shook her head, hiding her eyes from the woman. She picked up her plastic bag and ran from the room.

Mikey's drawings. Mikey's drawings of the Grail ...

Pain! Screaming! Francoise curled up on the sofa again, face twisting with agony, mind trying to hold on to the thought of Michael's drawings, Michael's drawing of the Holy Grail ...

Watching-man comes from the ground, watching-man comes from the wood ...

Release. A sense of calm ...

Mikey's drawings of the Grail ... Chalk Boy is hanging on to him, strangling him, making him unhappy.

Determinedly, if shakily, she went upstairs and sang vigorously at each of the fetishes, marking a clear space through the house, a corridor of psychic cease-fire. In the boy's room she found the desk, opened the lid, leafed through the sheets of white paper. She found images of the Grail, and they reminded her of the simple drawing of a simple child, naive, rough and ready, every feature either exaggerated or reduced. From her bag she took out the drawing of his castle, the picture he had given to her years before, the circles and walls, the gates and the bizarre and unflattering figures—herself especially! She smoothed the drawing out and sat at the desk, letting Michael's imagination, his creativity, start to seep into the turmoil of feelings and images that comprised her own mind at the moment ...

Terrified, Carol walked through the quarry. She was suddenly cold. She clutched the bag of food to her chest, ducking through the thorns, gritting her teeth as she edged through the gorse. The pit was eerily silent.

When she entered the place where a rise in the ground marked the site of the disposal of the earthfall from years ago, she felt like crying out, but managed to stay silent as she stared at the sad, hunched shape of the body that crouched there. The man seemed to be bowing to the East. He was kneeling with his head tucked down, squashed up as if hiding, face to the chalk wall. His head was very bloody. There was a spatter of blood on the chalk.

It was Brown Leather Jacket, as Michael called him. By the body lay the shield that had killed him, the shield that once Michael had described to her, tall and thin, painted green, with the silvered shape of two hares drawn on the face. It was part of the armor of a king, and had been kept beside the watching-man where Daddy had been digging, up in the North, up in a peat wasteland in Scotland.

The shield had been summoned at last. Carol edged past it, seeing how sharp it was, how bloody it was down the side where its edge had sliced through the evil man.

Michael was suddenly behind her and she dropped the bag of food in shock. She bent down to pick it up then looked anxiously at her naked, white-skinned brother. He had painted himself with chalk again, except for his eyes which were black. And now, too, round his neck he wore three small, shriveled creatures on a piece of leather.

"What have you got for me?" he asked suddenly.

Carol clutched the bag harder. She could smell something nasty in the air, and half realized that it was coming from the dead man behind her.

"Did you kill him?" she whispered.

"Sort of. The others ran away like rabbits."

"Did you kill him with the shield?"

Michael grinned, then did a little dance. "Fetched it. Fetched shield. It came like a discus. Sliced head. I didn't even touch it. Daddy will be proud of me.

Daddy went to where I fetched it. Daddy dug. Daddy knew."

Again, the hungry look, then in his normal voice, "What have you got? I'm starving."

"There wasn't any pickle left," she said nervously.

Michael looked angry. "So what have you got for me?"

"Some cornflakes. A tin of tomatoes. I've got the can opener too. And some ginger biscuits, but they're a bit soft."

He watched her furiously. She shook in her trainers, holding the bag to her chest harder, not liking the anger she could sense in the starving body of her white-skinned brother. "It's all they had . . ." she said, close to tears. "There's no food left. Everything's rotten in the freezer . . . everything else has been eaten."

He snatched the bag from her hands and peered inside. "Brown sauce? No brown sauce?"

"All gone. We made soup with it last night."

He threw the bag away. "Wasn't hungry anyway."

Still shuddering with tears, Carol said, "Francoise is in the house. She's very frightened. Can't you tell . . . please tell Michael to forgive them . . . Please let them out."

He hesitated, then reached up and clutched her face, drawing her close. She resisted slightly, but was too overpowered by the presence of her brother, by his anger, to struggle. She thought: *Don't hurt me . . .* but the words stayed inside.

He said, "Listen to me. Are you listening?"

"I'm listening."

"Will you take the Grail home for me?"

"Yes," she said in a slight voice. "But I'm frightened of the Fish Lizards."

"Listen to me. Do what I say. When you follow me, close your eyes! Trust me. When you smell the sea, run. If you trust me, nothing can harm you. If you trust me, you can bring me home. You can carry me home. You can take me back to where I belong."

After a brief, frightened moment, Carol nodded. Using her blouse to clean her glasses, she looked appre-

hensively at the wall of chalk through which, in a
moment, Michael would lead her. She had hardly returned the frames to her eyes when Michael grabbed
her and her world dissolved.

*Sea spray, stinking of weed, and the eerie cries of
monsters, black shapes that thrashed hugely in the
surf, close to the beach, preying on the shadows that
lived there* . . .

Suddenly, breathlessly, she was in open country,
looking up a hill through driving, miserable rain at the
sagging shape of a crude hut. There were poles outside
the hut, with bits of limp rag hanging from them. The
roof seemed to be made of grass. Mud streamed in the
drumming rain from where the door had been churned
up by people walking in and out.

She was cold. The rain saturated her, running down
her face, through her clothes, down her legs. Michael's
chalk began to smear, and as the white ran from his
face so the black paint was revealed beneath. His gray-
green eyes raged at her, urgent.

"Go and get the Grail. It's inside. Please. Go and
fetch it."

"Where are we? Where are we, Michael? I'm
scared."

"This is where our house used to be. Over there. It's
all different now. Go into the shrine. Go!"

He danced a wild dance, a dance of frustration, a
wet boy shifting urgently from side to side, running in
front of her, bullying, pleading, rain dripping from
nose and ears, running down his body and carrying
away his skin.

Saturated and frightened, Carol stooped below the
wooden lintel and entered the stinking hut. Light came
in through two narrow windows. Rags hung everywhere. There was a smell of animal dung and damp.
Water was dripping through the sagging roof on to two
balls of chalk that she vaguely recognized from her father's study.

"Hurry! Hurry!" screamed Chalk Boy from outside.
She glanced back through the door and saw him stooping to peer at her, then he was running again, left and

right, ducking and weaving in his impatience. "Hurry!
He's coming. At any moment! Get me out! Get me
out!"

She didn't understand his words, but was disturbed
by them. As she stepped through the twin bands of
light, through the cold drip from the roof, she saw the
Grail.

"Is it there? Can you see it?"

His voice was distant, soaked up by the drum of
rain.

"It's glass."

"That's it! That's it! Get it, Carol. He'll be here at
any moment!"

"Who will?" she shouted.

"Michael! Bring it out now!"

She could see the face watching her. The Grail was
not a chalice, more like a glass container, with a lid. It
was full of liquid. She stepped closer and realized that
the face was not carved, not inscribed. The face of the
fish was inside.

With a jolt of shock she recognized the thing that
floated there, and started to cry uncontrollably, running
back into the rain, banging her head on the lintel as she
struggled, sobbing, from the collapsing shrine.

"Where is it? Where is it?" Michael screamed, furious and raging, dancing in the rain, pink now, washed
clean, exposed.

Through tears, through her racking grief, she said,
"It's a little baby. It's just a little baby. It's all dead and
drowned. It's a little baby."

He was in front of her in a second, lifting her by her
clothes. Heat came from him, pouring from below the
black stain with which he had covered his face.

His voice was a snake's hiss, not Michael's voice at
all as it spat at the girl: "Then get the little baby for
little baby's brother! Get him NOW!"

He flung her back into the shrine. She emerged a
moment later, clutching the specimen jar, still weeping.
The fetus turned and twisted with the motion, its dead
eyes bulging, its outstretched hands raised almost in a
gesture of submission. Michael watched the face, his

own eyes huge. He backed away from the girl, beckoning. "Come on. Come on. He's coming toward us. I can feel him. He'll be here at any moment. Come to little baby's brother. Bring him to me ..."

Carol walked stiffly, sadly forward, her tears lost in the rain, only the wretched grimace of grief on her face telling, in the relentless downpour, that she was crying.

Behind her the shrine exploded, a great burst of muddy earth, turf and wood, rising in uncanny slow motion into the air, then vanishing, sucked into nowhere, releasing a blast of air that knocked Carol forward.

She clutched the Grail, not dropping it. Michael stared up at the earth that fell around them, then at the excavation in the Downs, into the deep pit where the temple had stood a moment ago. Most of it was scattered about them, but he knew that a central part had gone to the castle, and he laughed as he thought of his father struggling through that mud, searching for a baby boy.

"I did that!" he cried. "That's me. I did that!"

And he had the Grail!

His brother was safely in his sister's arms!

"Come to Mikey," he whispered.

"You're not Mikey," she said quietly, yet still she walked toward him, out of the rain, back toward the beach, and the pit and the world she knew best ...

He had drawn glass, he had drawn the face on the glass. The fish ... so like the fishy thing that had appeared in her room, the Fisher King, pulsing in and out of the features that belonged to Michael Whitlock, the handsome boy with his sad expression.

It wasn't a fish!

Realization came with horror. And with realization came understanding, and a recognition of Michael's terrible danger. It had been there, so obvious, so clear, transparent like the glass itself. And like the revelation of the meaning of a crossword-clue—so impenetrable when you struggled with it, so obvious when you knew it—she understood that Carol had to be stopped.

Her cry woke the house.

Her fear shattered the totem field. Richard, when he saw her, when he heard the primal shriek of comprehension, when he was aroused and affected by Francoise Jeury's insight, became a man possessed. He screamed for his daughter. He grasped the Mocking Cross and broke through the back door. He passed the great totem. The earth shuddered for a moment, then was still, but Richard was already running towards the bluff, to the grassy slope that led to the entrance to the quarry.

From the landing window Susan watched him go. She had heard the sudden chaos, woken from a deep sleep in which her dream had been of walking on a high hill on a cold day, and come into Michael's room in time to hear a part of Francoise's garbled, almost incoherent desperation. She followed the other woman into the sitting room and watched as Francoise dressed more completely, murmuring the words "watching-man . . ." all the time.

Dazed and confused, Susan said, "Are you going to tell me too?"

Francoise showed her the drawing that had finally resolved itself under her lingering, careful gaze. "Michael's drawings of the Fisher King were of a fetus. When his spirit appeared in my office it was shape-shifting between Michael and this face, the face of a dead, unborn child."

"Chalk Boy?"

Francoise stared at her, her face puzzled, then shook her head. "You might try ringing your Dr. Wilson. I think Chalk Boy is Michael's brother. Michael may have been his mother's second attempt. The spirit of the dead boy has been adrift in time, in its strange Limbo, but has been *haunting* Michael. Carol said it this morning: Chalk Boy is hanging on to him, strangling him, making him unhappy. I think Chalk Boy is trying to get full possession of Michael's body—"

"Oh, Christ! How?"

"Translocation of spirit. If the fetal remains can be brought out of Limbo—Carol carrying them, I imagine

Michael's body can't—the link with time will have been broken and there might well be an instantaneous flow of spirit between the two bodies. Only Michael is hardly in control at all now. He's almost buried and helpless in his own body. He'll be banished into the fetus and die at once. Chalk Boy will have Michael's body all to himself. Susan, I think Chalk Boy has been trying to achieve this for years, a desperate effort to return from Limbo. He has clung and clung to life by clinging to his living brother and *using* him. But I don't understand how he managed to make the link. Unless . . ."

She gazed hard at Susan, then seemed shocked.

"What is it?"

"Why don't you try calling Dr. Wilson? I think he's probably expecting you. I think he might have an answer for you. And for me too. Or perhaps Michael's mother does. Try calling him now . . ."

The phone line was working again. Susan dialed the number for Dr. Wilson. When he answered, after a few seconds, she almost sighed with relief. Without preliminaries, she said, "Michael's mother rang us. But she hung up. You *must* let me speak to her. You *must* tell me her number."

The voice at the other end of the line was quiet, tense and charged with anger.

"Is this Mrs. Whitlock?"

"Of course it is!"

There was silence for a moment, then a breath was drawn. Wilson spoke in a furious whisper: "Do you know what she did? Did you know she came here? Destroyed everything! Did you know that? Are you aware of that? *Are you?*"

Shocked by the sudden fury, Susan couldn't think. She went ahead blindly: "What do you mean? What do you mean she was there?"

He was shouting now. "She stole the body of her other son. She came here and *stole* it. She destroyed my office in order to get the specimen. How dare she. How dare *you!*"

Ice cold, eyes closed, harsh realization making her

smile, Susan said, "*That's* what you were hiding! What a bastard you are, Dr. Wilson. What a bastard. I sat in your office, begging you to help me, and Michael's dead brother was there, right by me, watching me from the glass jar. I couldn't bear to look at those specimens. You knew that. Did that amuse you? Did you wink at the dead child when you walked behind me? You're a sick man, Dr. Wilson."

"Don't be a fool. You only asked me about Michael, remember? Michael wasn't harmed. I culled the twin—"

"*Culled* the twin? *Culled* it?"

"His *mother* insisted on it. And I told you truthfully: Michael wasn't touched. I didn't lie to you about that. There was and is nothing wrong with Michael. The injection was administered only through the amnion of the smaller child."

Almost too shocked, too sick to speak, Susan said, "Why did you keep the corpse?"

"The chemicals had an odd effect. For a few hours after its death it transformed slightly, a form of structural regression. It was of interest to me."

"It was of interest to you . . ."

"Yes. It was of *interest* to me. It had become a specimen. I don't throw specimens away. It was worth preserving. The thing was dead. Why fuss about it now? I didn't label the jar. No one but I would have known. *Why do you interfere?*"

"Because *Michael* knew. Because *Chalk Boy* knew. The shade of the dead boy *knew*. That's why he got Michael to fetch it. Eventually."

"What *are* you talking about?"

"The mother knew too. Michael's mother. She must have been in agony. All these years. Poor woman. Poor lonely woman. But it was of *interest* to you. So glad. I'm so glad. Science has been served!"

"She shouldn't have taken it."

She didn't take it. Chalk Boy took it."

"Who the hell is Chalk Boy?"

"The product of your *culling,* Dr. Wilson. My son's shadow. A little boy who clung to life after Dr. Wilson's needle had thrust through the *amnion* and penetrated his heart, changing him from child to *specimen*. Perhaps if you hadn't 'preserved the specimen' . . . who knows . . . who knows what peace there might have been."

She drifted, gaze taking in the totems outside the window, skin registering the deathly cold. She put the receiver down, ignoring the bluster still coming down the line. She looked again at the sketch of the Fisher King that Michael had made and there were tears in her eyes as she focused on the wound, clearly shown not in the "thigh," as in the story, but in the breast, above the heart.

Where the cocktail had been administered . . .

The death of the prince.

"What a bastard you are to be sure, Dr. Wilson. Dear God, strike the man down . . . strike him down now!"

Richard stopped suddenly before the great chalk giant that partly blocked the entrance to the quarry, startled and terrified by the sight of the monstrous effigy. Cloud movement made the statue's muscles flex. It seemed to be rising. He didn't want to see the face that might be revealed. He tried to edge past it but his legs began to shake. Heart racing, he stood for a long while, indecisive.

Then Francoise Jeury ran past him and passed the statue without hesitation. She glanced round and shouted sharply to him, "Come on! This is dead. It's a joke. It has no power. It's just Michael's joke."

Her confidence broke the spell—he had been paralysed by his own apprehension, not by magic. He ran after the woman.

Deeper in the pit, Francoise was more tense.

She could feel the walls of the castle. She could feel the pain coming from the sacrificed dolls, torn out of time and slung on the blackthorn. They found the body of a man, and Richard went cold, imagining the inquest, and the years of difficulty that this particular act of murder would probably entail.

Francoise was more interested in the castle itself. She had no time to worry about dead men. She had to stop Carol bringing back the corpse of Michael's brother.

"I can feel the walls. I can feel the way he has designed the place. But I can't feel the entrance to his Limbo beach."

She unfolded the drawing Michael had given her years before, when she had first visited. There had been a smile on his face when he had waved good-bye from his window. She had realized, quickly, that he had given her the plan of the route that led to the deeper tunnels. She smiled at the irony. She had thought it had been part of the game he played with her, a little tease. In fact he had been showing her almost everything she needed to know. Desperately she tried to penetrate the images of the drawing, scanning the circles and spirals, following the paths. But she kept focusing on the picture of herself, outlined in heavy black pen, a bloated, red-haired figure ... all bust and bustle.

Richard was shouting for both his children. His voice was loud and echoing in the quarry, and he thrashed about aimlessly, moving quickly to the place where Michael had had his camp.

Francoise called him to her and quietened him.

"Maybe he can hear us," the man said.

"I'm sure he can. But I can't hear myself think when you are bellowing in that way." Her hand on his face was brief, gentle and reassuring. She flicked at the tearstains on his cheeks.

"You understand my concern? That somehow, by bringing back the little body, which is certainly what is in the Grail, the spirit of the dead boy will become Michael himself. The life that is Michael will remain behind, trapped in Limbo, trapped in the dead child."

"I don't really understand at all," Richard whispered. "I just believe that you're right about the Grail. And I know that it mustn't come back to this world."

"Chalk Boy was very real. It was a terrible mistake of mine to think otherwise. We have been romancing with shadows, even the *shadows* of shadows, all of them aspects of a dead boy who has been hovering between here and the otherworld, clinging to his brother. But now the poor little clinging boy is ready to return, and his brother will pay the price."

Richard remembered a time in the woods, when Michael had run amok, holding the back of his neck as if stung. There was a birthmark there. It was small, but it was real, and it was one of two such marks upon him. It was Chalk Boy's mark, and the place where the dead boy had clung to Michael, desperate for life. Half in the world, half in hell, he was caught in Limbo, grabbing for time and space, reaching desperately, holding on, holding on . . .

In his despair, in his need for his children, Richard turned to the cliff wall and began to strike at it. The new sun cast his shadow shallowly and distortedly around him on the curving wall of chalk.

Dark outline!

Francoise looked again at Michael's drawing, at the black outline around her figure. It was shown quite *even*.

"Richard—move round the wall. Slowly . . ."

The man did as he was told, stepping close to the chalk. The wide shadow to his right narrowed, that to his left came into view. In seconds, as Francoise watched him from the mound of the earthfall, he was blinking at her, staring against the bright sun to see what she was doing. She was watching him, observing the gray penumbra that outlined him against the white.

He said, suddenly, "I can smell the sea!"

"That's it! That's the beginning place. Come with me. Follow me!"

Francoise stood with Richard and sensed the walls of Michael's castle. Then, following the routes on the map, she ran away from the cliff, crawling through the underbrush, doubling back, curving in and out of the scrub wood as she traced the path of the spirals.

"The entrance shifts with the rising sun, shifts around the curve of the wall, but he *had* shown me the way to find the start. Come on. Come *on!*"

They came back to the chalk.

"Here! Can you hear it? The sea?"

She pushed violently past Richard, smashing against the cliff, then spreading her arms and straining, as if struggling to see. Her body doubled slightly, she groaned, she rubbed against the chalk ...

"I can't get through," she shouted. "I can't pass through. But I can *see*. They're coming back. They're walking over the beach. Carol!" she screamed suddenly. "Put down the Grail! Put it *down*!"

The girl stopped, tugging back as the naked boy dragged her across the beach. Waves surged. The girl was shrieking, but holding tightly to the glass jar ...

Francoise yelled again. Shadows fled like cloud patterns across the red cliffs. The naked boy looked furious through his blackened face. The waves crashed again, and flooded around their legs, surging, then sucking back into the shallow waters.

The boy tugged at his sister, but Francoise's voice had stunned the girl.

Furious, the boy leapt across the soaking beach, came towards the woman who shouted. Anger was like a cloak around him, and he leapt to face her, ran up along the tunnel and leapt right out of the rock. Behind him the girl began to panic.

Black-faced, naked, his eyes wild and angry, Michael stood before his father, screaming. Richard had stepped back, disorientated by the sudden appearance of his son from the sun-glare of the chalk cliff. He had heard the boy running, he had heard his cry of fury, but the moment of apparition had been dizzying—as if Michael had been there all the time and had suddenly and aggressively stepped away from the white wall.

Francoise had been knocked aside. She was slowly standing, shaking her head, holding her right shoulder.

"Get away!" Michael screamed. "Let her come through. It's the *Grail*. She's bringing home the Grail. Daddy ... don't interfere ... *please*!"

"It's not Michael," Francoise gasped, as she struggled for breath after the winding collision with the boy. "Call Michael. He's still there!"

Richard watched the fiery eyes of the boy before him. He could smell sea, mingled with wet earth, a confusing, wafting aroma that was quite wrong for the pit.

"Michael—I've brought something back for you."

And he held up the Mocking Cross, its brilliant golden mask turned towards the boy.

"I fetched it back from the man who bought it from me. It was wrong of me to sell it, Mikey. It was wrong of Mummy. But we love you too much to give away something so precious, so we've got it back for you. The Cross is ours again, and we'll always look after it."

Michael was silent, but his black-dyed face writhed, his whole body shook as if an electric current was passing through the muscles. He began to reach for the Cross, drawn back to life by this evil mockery of Christianity.

Watching the turmoil in the boy, sensing the huge struggle that was occurring within the pitiful, ravaged body of his son, Richard was aware of the irony of what was happening. Michael was being tugged not by the Cross's religious symbolism, its magic, but by its simple meaning, its family meaning. The "True Cross," which was so often used to banish evil, had been warped into something, in its mocking form, that would banish good—but this Mocking Cross was summoning back the *good* in the boy! Human concerns had overwhelmed the dark religion of the carving, rendering mysticism impotent.

To reach for the Mocking Cross was to reach for life again, and family, and comfort.

But Chalk Boy was too strong. The shadow-face grimaced, a mocking smile.

"I'm coming home," the boy whispered, and laughed—

"Daddy . . ." the boy breathed, the face melting for a second into an odd mask of confusion, the voice sad. Then:

"I'm coming *home*! I want stories, Daddy. I want all the stories. I want to hear them all . . ."

"Michael—come back. We love you. We need you, Mikey. We'll never use you again."

"Mikey's *dead*. Tell *me* the stories now."

But the hand of the boy rose, stretched, reached to the Cross, struggled for his father.

Richard stepped closer. "Mikey ... forgive me ..."

Michael's eyes widened suddenly, and he turned and ran at the chalk, blurring, dissolving, decaying into white light, his terrified scream of "Don't open it!" echoing and resonating in the quarry, deafening his father, shattering the dawn.

He was gone.

Only Francoise's sudden grip upon his arm stopped Richard smashing his own body against the hard chalk, and from damaging himself as he struggled to enter a place that was forbidden to him.

He cried out for his son and for Carol. Francoise touched a firm finger to his mouth, then cocked her head, eyes half closed.

"Let me listen. Let me listen ..."

But Richard would not be silenced.

Carol stood alone on the strand. It was a cold and wet place, and each time the sea surged toward her the waves soaked her legs, splashing her dress and her face. As the waves pulled back she felt them tug at her, but although the sand sucked and drained around her feet she stood quite still, holding the jar and its silent, staring creature.

Lightning made her blink. The earth shook with thunder. A long way out across the sea a tall neck rose, its head snapping. The body that followed was broad and black, and it collapsed back into the waters like a whale dancing. A moment later the air was deadened with its cry, an eerie shriek that dissolved into a series of grunting calls.

Michael had left her here. She was afraid. She was angry with him. He had *abandoned* her. The sea surged and pulled at her, but she held her ground, nostrils filled with the sea stench, eyes blinded suddenly by a splashing spray that drenched her spectacles.

The baby in the jar looked like a fish again, and she cradled it.

And heard her father's voice calling to her—

"Let the baby go. Leave him there, Carol!"

He sounded like he was panicking. He sounded more frightened than even she was.

She opened the jar, grimacing at the funny smell of chemicals that wafted from the liquid.

Then she heard Michael shout. She turned to where the tunnel opened and saw his black-masked, pink body running toward her, arms outstretched. He was terrified. He was running towards her, heels kicking up sand, shadow flowing beside him.

Her father called again, his voice like the voice of a creature in the sea, booming and echoing, oddly comforting, thrilling, demanding of her . . .

"My little fish," she said to the blind thing in the jar. "Go and swim in the sea, my little baby fish . . . Go down into deep waters."

"NO!"

She ignored Michael's scream.

She tipped the little fish into the sea, and it was sucked out into the deep tide, swirled down into the gray waters, lost, staring, drowning, dragged down to where the Fish Lizards waited for the shadows on the shore.

Michael had collapsed suddenly. There was whiteness on his mouth and he lay, rigid yet trembling, caught in a fit that suddenly relaxed into limpness. Carol dropped the Grail jar and tugged at her brother's arms, dragging him towards the tunnel. Even as she reached the place, and with a last glance at the silent, watching shadows in the caves, she knew that there would never be a Limbo again. With a final haul (which hurt something in her back) she heaved her brother into the chalk quarry, and struggled for a moment when strong arms grabbed her, hugged her, lifted her.

She relaxed as she felt her father's tears and kisses on her face.

Take of English earth as much
As either hand may rightly clutch.
In the taking of it breathe
Prayer for all who lie beneath—
Not for the great nor well-bespoke,
But the mere uncounted folk
Of whose life and death is none
Report or lamentation.

from "A Charm"
Rudyard Kipling

Thirty-six

That evening the phone rang and as Susan picked up the receiver she knew at once that it was Michael's mother. The woman breathed quietly for a while, saying nothing. Susan waited, then said, "This is Susan Whitlock ..."

"Something has happened," came the gentle voice. "What has happened?"

"The other boy is at peace. Now Michael is at peace."

"I am too. It happened this afternoon. I slept for a while. When I woke up the haunting had gone. I've been haunted for years. It was such a terrible thing to do. I didn't really want to do it. But I was so afraid ..."

"That's why he stayed, perhaps. The other boy. That's why he clung on to life—a sort of life ..."

There was silence, a sad, lonely silence. The call seemed to be long distance, slightly echoing, perhaps coming through a satellite. Then: "And is Michael well?"

"Michael's sleeping. We think he'll be fine when he wakes."

"Thank you. Thank you for peace."

"Tell me something," Susan waited for a response, but there was only silence. "Hello?"

"I'm listening," came the quiet voice.

"Who was Michael's father? Will you tell me something about him?"

After a brief pause Susan heard the other woman breathe out slowly. But all she said was, "I think I'd

better not. Not now. Not after all this time. He's
been—out of my life—for a long time now. I think I
must keep my memories to myself. I'm sorry ..."

"So am I. But I understand."

"Again ... Thank you for peace."

The connection went dead.

Michael slept for twenty-four hours, finally waking
into a vague, silent state in which he sat and stared
blankly, rubbing his neck and breathing shallowly. It
would be a week before he was fully recovered.

Francoise sat with him while he slept, watching him,
stroking his hair and thinking about the wonderful talent that had been his for a while, and the gift, however
weak, however transformed, that might still remain.

And she tried desperately to understand what might
have happened to Michael during the time of his incu-
bation in the womb, and after.

"Perhaps Michael will have some answers for us,"
Susan suggested over coffee, late that night.

"That doesn't follow. I don't know how much Michael was aware of what was happening to him. But
with your permission I can try and find out."

Susan shrugged. She was completely disheveled and
hollow-eyed. "You'll have to come to us to do so.
We're planning to move to the remoter parts of Argyll,
well away from the friends of the dead man."

Francoise ran a hand gently over the sleeping boy's
head, smoothing the brilliant shock of ginger hair. Michael murmured in his deep slumber, curled more
deeply under the blanket.

Susan said, "Do you think everything he did was
just a reflection of his brother trying to come alive
again?"

"I think so. But how can we be sure? His brother's
soul hung on to him during birth. That I can understand. But why did it get loose in time? For that to
happen the gateway to time must already have been
open. So: one of the boys already had the talent for
apportation. But which one? Once born, the spirit
locked into what might have felt like a source of local

power, the shrine, once built close to your house. From there it moved between Limbo and your son, looking always for a way to return."

"Yes. You said that yesterday: Chalk Boy had been trying for years to get back."

"I suspect," Francoise said, "that much of the gift-bringing had been to create the right emotional environment for the passage back. At first he tried pleasure, making Michael happy. Then he tried to work through Carol, helping her see dolls, but that failed. Then he withdrew the gifts and tried anguish. It was only when Michael cracked, when he became uncontrollably furious, that the way truly started to open. And of course, the spirit knew that its preserved corpse was still available. It was a touch of inspiration to create the idea of the Grail in Michael's mind, to make him focus obsessively on the glass jar."

Susan finished her coffee and rubbed tired eyes. She could hear Richard outside, dragging one of the totems down the garden to where he kept his stones and pillars, and where, now, a large museum of wood was being formed. They had all wanted the staring, blank-eyed, grinning fetish-faces away from the house.

It was late and Susan went to bed, not at all at peace. She woke, the next morning, to the feel of being gently shaken. She opened her eyes and started with shock, but Richard's face resolved through her sleepy gaze. He was cold and his breath was unfresh.

"What is it?"

"The body's gone. The body in the quarry. Someone's taken it away."

There was nothing she could say. It was immediately obvious who had removed the corpse. She turned to ice, wondering what would happen now. Richard went on, "I saw tire tracks just outside the pit, a large car. They've fetched their own. Maybe they won't make trouble for us. Maybe they won't want to tamper with things they don't understand."

"You've been reading those children's stories again. The bit where it says 'happy ever after.' I think we get the police, and get them now."

As she stretched and rose from the bed she became aware of the sound of singing. For a second she was puzzled, then realized it was Francoise, downstairs. The psychic had spent the night in an armchair, close to the boy.

Richard was on the phone. Bright light showed up the layers of dust and filth on the windows. Susan tugged on her tracksuit, listening to the odd, reedy voice of the woman.

Francoise suddenly shouted!

She was standing by the sleeping boy when Susan raced into the room downstairs and stared at her. The woman's hands were over her mouth and she was shaking. But it was a sort of laughter . . . a surprised, shocked laughter. Richard was there too, leaning down, brushing at the boy, brushing at the blanket.

"Oh God. It's like when he was an infant . . ."

Dry red earth stained Richard's fingers. Michael shifted restlessly and the small earthfall poured off the blanket on to the carpet.

Outside, the biggest of the totems, which had been leaning dramatically since it had appeared at Michael's command, began to move, its shadow sweeping through the room as it crashed heavily and dully to the lawn, then lay still.